Acclaim for Joseph Epstein and

"Known mostly for his polished familiar essays, Joseph Epstein has quietly cultivated a double literary life as a writer of short fiction . . . His stories . . . have an old-fashioned fullness."
— *Washington Post Book World*

"Joseph Epstein has brought to fiction his trademark learning, wit, and, yes, elegance." — *Weekly Standard*

"A substantial and affecting collection . . . Simply fabulous."
— *Atlanta Journal-Constitution*

"The stories contain the same charm and humor . . . that make Epstein's essay collections . . . Epstein's literary voice is distinctive: intelligent but not difficult, serious but not solemn, funny but never trivial." — *Tampa Tribune & Times*

"Wonderful . . . A welcome treat." — *Oregonian*

"Falling into an Epstein book is like falling into a heaven where all the angels are quick with a story and ready with a punch line."
— *Buffalo News*

"It's wonderful to read a writer who can repeatedly make you smile . . . [These stories] are immediately hospitable to everyone — Jew or non-Jew — with quick wit and just a touch of reverence for life."
— *Hudson Review*

"Solid, subtle, endearing, and refreshingly without gimmick."
— *Minneapolis Star Tribune*

"The stories themselves — with their thunder-and-lightning-free angst and quiet drama — call to mind early Philip Roth, vintage Bernard Malamud, and even the pacing and turnabouts that O. Henry relished. Still, Joseph Epstein's storytelling is very much his own."
— *Houston Chronicle*

BOOKS BY JOSEPH EPSTEIN

Envy

Fabulous Small Jews

Snobbery

Narcissus Leaves the Pool

Life Sentences

With My Trousers Rolled

Pertinent Players

The Goldin Boys

A Line Out for a Walk

Partial Payments

Once More Around the Block

Plausible Prejudices

The Middle of My Tether

Familiar Territory

Ambition

Divorced in America

Joseph Epstein

FABULOUS SMALL JEWS

❖

A MARINER BOOK
Houghton Mifflin Company
BOSTON • NEW YORK

To Neal Kozodoy

the best in the business

❖

First Mariner Books edition 2004

Visit our Web site: www.houghtonmifflinbooks.com.

ISBN-10: 0-395-94402-3 ISBN-13: 978-0-395-94402-8
ISBN-10: 0-618-44658-3 (pbk.) ISBN-13: 978-0-618-44658-2 (pbk.)

Library of Congress Cataloging-in-Publication Data
Epstein, Joseph, 1937–
Fabulous small Jews : stories / Joseph Epstein.
p. cm.
ISBN 0-395-94402-3
ISBN 0-618-44658-3 (pbk.)
1. United States—Social life and customs—Fiction.
2. Jews—United States—Fiction. I. Title.
PS3555.P6527 F33 2003
813'.54—dc21   2002027621

Printed in the United States of America

Book design by Robert Overholtzer

QUM 10 9 8 7 6 5 4 3 2 1

Grateful acknowledgment is made to *Commentary*
and the *Hudson Review,* where many of these
stories first appeared.

Contents

This is the Oxford of all sicknesses.
Kings have lain here and fabulous small Jews
And actresses whose legs were always news.

—KARL SHAPIRO, "Hospital"

FABULOUS
SMALL
JEWS

❖

Felix Emeritus

ELIX ARNSTEIN was dismantling his library. It would, he decided, have to be reduced by at least three-fourths, possibly more. At the Northwood Apartments, the old-age home (no euphemisms for Felix, thank you all the same) into which, after much thought, he had resignedly decided he must now move, there was scarcely room to accommodate even a fourth of his books. Felix could have done nicely without the Northwood Apartments altogether, but the standard symptoms of old age had begun to show up in him with too great insistency. Clearly, there was now nothing for it but to make the move.

Still, Felix might have fought off this move if his various illnesses hadn't conspired to cause him to require so much medical attention. Along with his angina attacks, Felix had colitis, and now, in his late seventies, diabetes had shown up. If his mind seemed to be closing down on him at a considerably slow pace, his body was closing in much more relentlessly. These days he seemed to spend more time in doctors' offices and in hospitals than out of them. At the Northwood Apartments there was a physician on the premises and nursing care when needed. He would get, in addition, all his meals, maid service, his laundry done, haircuts, a bedroom, bath, and small sitting room — all this for $1,700 a month. Between his income from his pension from the university, his Social Security checks, and the small royalties that his books still brought in, he could afford it easily.

The last time Felix had given a little dinner party, he had begun to run water to wash the dinner dishes in the kitchen sink while serving the dessert, napoleons bought at the Tag Bakery on Central Street. Half an hour or so later, a phone call from the occupants of the apartment downstairs informed him that water was coming through their kitchen ceiling. The leaking water, of course, was caused by Felix's neglecting to turn off his kitchen faucet. This was the third time it had happened.

Constanze, Felix's sister, worrying about his having further angina attacks, insisted that he buy a cellular telephone, so that should he have another attack or even fall in his apartment, he would have the phone ready at all times to call her or at least to dial 911. This all sounded reasonable enough, except that Felix kept misplacing the new phone; being portable, it was also misplaceable. Then there was the morning he woke to find that all the electricity had gone off in the apartment, only to discover, on calling Commonwealth Edison, that he had neglected to pay his electric bill for the past four months.

No, Felix had to admit that, approaching eighty, he was losing — if not, thank God, his taste for and interest in things of the mind — his ability to concentrate on the quotidian details of life. These had never, true enough, been his strong suit. Until now, though, they had never threatened to sink him. He was able to get by, to make do, but, little as he liked to own up to it, apparently no longer. Who was it said that a man is likely to hang himself on the loose threads of his life? Felix couldn't remember.

Felix decided that he must give up his volumes of Fontane. He would retain his Karl Kraus, his Thomas Mann, his Robert Musil. The 143 volumes of his great Weimar edition of Goethe would have to go, of course. Also the many volumes of von Hofmannsthal; a lovely man, Hugo von Hofmannsthal, but, truth to tell, not a writer of the first class. Werfel and Zweig, out; so, too, his volumes of Zuckmayer, though he would retain the autobiography, a lovely, cleanly written book. His Ernst Jünger volumes, out also; a Nazi, Jünger, but a real writer nevertheless. Ah, the mysterious contradictions of art. Out, too, the books of Joseph Roth.

A bachelor, Felix had tried to keep himself free of too many possessions. He enjoyed travel, spent many of his summers in Tuscany. On three different occasions he had lived for an entire academic year at other universities — at Harvard, at Oxford, at Stanford — residing in other people's houses and apartments. He thought of himself as traveling light through life, unencumbered, disentangled, a free man. Yet he now saw that he had nonetheless managed to accumulate a great deal. He must have nearly two thousand books in this small apartment. Then there was the furniture: simple Scandinavian things mostly, bought in the 1950s, meant more for utility than for comfort — how different from the richly ornate furniture he had grown up with as a boy and young man in Vienna — but now pretty well worn out. Most of this would not go with him. He would take his reading chair to the Northwood Apartments and his desk and a small couch and chest of drawers. The rest would be dealt with by the Salvation Army people, called in by his sister.

Dear Connie was helping him with this move. She, his only surviving relative, and her husband, Moritz, who worked as a chemist at Abbott Laboratories, were all that remained of Felix's family. The rest had been murdered by the Nazis. Felix, Connie, and Moritz had been in America for more than forty years, yet all three retained their Viennese accents, their old-world ways. Felix could remember to this day the terror that he felt, departing the ship upon his arrival in London in 1946, when he realized that he would have to wrestle with and conquer the English language. Conquer it he had never quite succeeded in doing, at least not as a speaker. But all his books had been written in English, and over the years more than one reviewer remarked on his mastery of English prose style — a source of pride to Felix. He was nearly thirty when he had left Vienna, and while he had left it for good — having returned only once, and then with the most complicated of feelings — its accent had never left him, and also, in many respects, its way of looking at things.

Felix's fate had been that of permanent exile. Much about America he loved. The country had been good to him. By all accounts his had been a successful, even distinguished career. He had published six books of criticism, was the Haverling Distinguished Professor of European Literature at his university, had been a major contributor on his subject to the *Times Literary Supplement* in London — he was highly regarded in England, which, as a bit of an Anglophile, much pleased him. Yale had offered him a professorship and so, too, had the University of California at Berkeley, but he could not bear to move far from his sister and her husband, who gave his life such ballast as it had.

For Felix was in reality a double exile, or so he had long thought himself. Along with his living away from the country of his birth — Arnsteins had lived in Vienna since early in the eighteenth century — Felix's secondary exile had to do with his homosexuality. It was something with which he had long ago learned to live. But well before that he recognized that it had put him outside what he thought of as regular life. A card that life had dealt him, such was how he had taken his homosexuality when he first recognized it in his late adolescence, and he had since come to learn that the pack of life was full of such jokers. His homosexuality gave him freedom from certain kinds of responsibility — from women, from children — but it also cut him off, sometimes he felt in fundamental ways, from the simple everyday pleasures of life. It made him realize that he had, in a way that men with children had not, only one life to lead.

His age and his bad health had in any case caused Felix for some years to be beyond sexual activity. He alternated in his view of homosexuality as a mixed blessing, rather like the bow of Philoctetes in the Greek myth, and as an all but unbearable complication. Although Felix had his arguments with Freud, and especially with the Freudians' peculiar way of twisting literature to make their master's points, he nonetheless believed Freud when of homosexuality he wrote that it could not be changed by therapy because, essentially, you could not persuade anyone to give up something that gave him intense pleasure. Felix was what he was — though, he reflected, his illnesses long ago having rendered him sexually *hors de combat,* he was perhaps no longer even quite that. He was, he supposed, if an exact category were wanted, a former homosexual.

Bitterest of bitter ironies, the one time in his life that Felix did not feel in exile was during the three years he spent at Buchenwald. Hateful dark years, monstrous in every way, and yet now, in retrospect, Felix sometimes viewed them as a period when he lived without the weight of introspection, lived chiefly with survival on his mind, lived truly in a community, however degraded and humiliated a community the one shared with his fellow captives might have been. It was not something he had ever spoken about, not even to Connie or Moritz, both of whom were able to elude the Nazis in their successful flight to America. Nor did he ever advertise himself as a survivor of the Nazi camps; he even avoided short-sleeve shirts lest the still unfaded tattooed number on his forearm show. He did not want his years at Buchenwald to define his life, thus giving Hitler, or so he thought, the ultimate victory over him.

Felix had met many people who did, who thought and spoke of little else but the camps, for whom the subject swallowed up their entire lives. It was not difficult to understand why. At least once a month, sometimes more, Felix himself would dream about those dreadful days at Buchenwald; these dreams were of course nightmarish, as the days there had been. But, hideous though they were, at Buchenwald Felix, for the only time in his life, did not feel himself somehow separate and alone, an exile. Many were the oddities of life — many more, he had come to realize, than he would have time to contemplate.

All this was fine with Felix, who, after being freed, had determined as best he could to enjoy and be amused by life. This seemed to him more sensible than to be perpetually tragic and endlessly shocked by it. Men were capable of enormous beastliness; he had been witness to that. Imperfectability was the lot of mankind; this, too, could scarcely go without notice. But men could also be immensely kind and goodhearted, full of unexpected generosity and sweetness. Also pathetic in their pretensions. Of pathetic pretensions Felix had seen more than his fill as a university teacher, where he daily noticed scores of little snobberies as he watched his colleagues skate perilously across the fragile ice of their thin status. Perhaps they sensed his amusement at this spectacle, for in his own department, that of comparative literature, he had no close friends. He was able to succeed not through academic politics — after Buchenwald, taking academic politics seriously was not possible for him —

but because he had a reasonably high standing in the world of international culture.

Perhaps it was owing to his priding himself on the absence of snobbery that Felix had decided to move into the North-wood Apartments rather than one of two other retirement homes in the neighborhood: Hamilton House, which had no Jews that he knew of, and the Walter Roebuck Home, which was all male. Northwood Apartments was all Jewish, chiefly *Ostjuden* as far as he could tell, and lived in by both men and women, mostly widows and widowers. Its advantages included its being less expensive than Hamilton House, closer to the home of Connie and Moritz, and, as it seemed to him on his two inspection visits before moving in, livelier. It was bad enough being elderly and ill, Felix thought; one didn't have to be stuffy and dull into the bargain.

But no sooner had Felix moved into the Northwood than he began to wonder if he hadn't perhaps made a serious mistake. Part of the problem was living so exclusively among the old. Would he ever grow used to it? So many osteoporotic women, humped and bent forward; one woman, in a crueler trick of na-ture, was bent backward, each of her steps seeming perilous, as if she were permanently backing away from the edge of a cliff. Every second person at Northwood seemed to wear a hearing aid, and some wore two — Felix's own hearing was not so good, though thus far he had resisted getting such a device — with the result that people seemed not to talk but to yell at one another. Because of bad hearing, too, few people answered to knock-ing on their doors. Metal canes with thick rubber bottoms were everywhere. One man, who Felix learned had had three strokes, trudged about on a walker, a piece of hideous alumi-num scaffolding the mere sight of which never failed to lower Felix's spirits. No shortage of toupees among the men, nor wigs

among the women. Eyesight everywhere was damnably dim, and it was common to see people reading the newspaper or letters with their heads two or three inches from the paper. Conversation, at least much of it that Felix overheard, seemed to be chiefly about health, when it was not about death and the dead. The old women complained about the present, Felix noted, while the old men tended to lie about the past. Such — as Felix recalled hearing Miss Iris Godkin, the social director of Northwood, often call them — were "the golden years."

So many little Jewish women, Felix thought when he came down to his first dinner at Northwood; they seemed, on the average, to be about four foot ten. But then Felix had long before noticed the propensity of age to shrink the small and make the tall blurry. He was one of the tall, six foot one, and before his illnesses he had weighed 210 pounds. He assumed that he had himself become somewhat blurry, as if someone had fiddled with the contrast dial on his face, though, perhaps mercifully, his eyesight was not good enough to know for certain. When checks came to him in restaurants, he could not always make out their sums, even with his glasses on. Still, Felix stood out among his fellow residents at Northwood as a veritable giant. The only one in the place taller than he was Miss Godkin, blond and buxom, a real Wagnerian heroine, Felix thought, remembering that he never felt any regard for Wagner, no matter how much so intelligent a man as Thomas Mann may have struggled to come to terms with him. Wagner represented for Felix the worst of Teutonic culture: heavy, vastly overstated, grossly overdone, bloated, tinged all over with anti-Semitism.

Miss Godkin, walking about with a walkie-talkie of some sort in her hand, bright capped teeth always flashing, was unrelentingly, almost brutally cheerful. Miss Godkin felt it her duty to enforce a spirit of happiness among the denizens of Northwood Apartments. She would have smiled through an earth-

quake, Felix thought, perhaps planned on her deathbed to say to whoever it was who gathered around her, as her last words, what she said to everyone she encountered at Northwood: "Have a wonderful day!" It took considerable restraint on Felix's part not to respond to one of Miss Godkin's "Have a wonderful day"s by saying, as it often occurred to him to say, "An uneventful one will be sufficient, thank you all the same, madam."

But Miss Godkin was only one of the obstacles at Northwood. There was also Morris Manzelman, at whose regular table Felix had sat at lunch his second day at Northwood. The first time they met, this Manzelman, a short man with white hair and a carefully groomed white mustache, held out a small, manicured hand. "Morry Manzelman," he announced, "used to be Arrow Transport."

Felix did not at first pick up that Arrow Transport was the name of the trucking company Manzelman had begun and worked at his entire life. His two sons, Arnold and Irwin, ran the company now. When Manzelman learned that Felix had taught in a university, he ever afterward referred to him as Professor. Manzelman had a taste for jokes, but regrettably it didn't usually match Felix's taste in jokes. At breakfast, the third full day that Felix spent at Northwood, Manzelman, over a meal of bran flakes, stewed prunes, prune juice, and hot chocolate, announced that he heard a good one the other day from a friend, Al Bergman, used to be a union agent, now retired in Florida.

"It seems, Professor, this fella, a widower, maybe he's sixty-five, moves into a retirement home. Pretty soon he sees that he's one of only three guys in the joint, the others being in their nineties and a bit gaga, if you know what I mean, and all the rest is women. A man who uses his *kop,* he sees there's a chance for a bit of extra cash in a situation like this. So he puts up a sign on his door, 'Sex for Sale.'"

Manzelman paused for a long draught of prune juice.

"Pretty soon a little old broad knocks on his door. 'I saw your sign,' she tells him, 'and I wonder how much you charge.' The fellow hadn't really thought about it before, so he says, on the spur of the moment, you know, he says, 'Well, five dollars for on the floor, ten dollars for on the couch over there, and twenty dollars for on the bed.' The lady opens a small change purse and takes out from it a twenty, which she hands to him. 'You want to do it on the bed, then?' the fella asks. 'No,' she says, 'four times on the floor.'"

Felix was not a rude man. But he found it difficult to respond properly to this joke told at eight in the morning. Manzelman seemed not to mind. The joy for him, Felix concluded, was as much in the performance as in the response. A pure kind of artist, this Manzelman.

That morning at breakfast they were joined by three other men. Felix later learned that two, like Manzelman, were widowers; the third had divorced his wife long before moving into Northwood. Apparently they met regularly at this table for meals. Felix, owing to his having sat with Manzelman two days in a row, was now considered a regular along with them, which meant that they expected him to eat all his meals at Manzelman's table. Wishing to avoid awkwardness, Felix went along.

"Professor," Manzelman said, "I'd like you to meet Sam Karzen, used to be Turner and Hess Menswear; Harry Feldstein, used to be Linoleum City on Cermak Road; and Max Schindler, used to be Schindler and Rabinowitz Plumbing. Boys, meet the Professor."

"Felix Arnstein," Felix said, putting out his hand, thinking perhaps he ought to add, "used to be Central European Literature."

Over their breakfasts, they carried on what Felix surmised must have been their normal conversation. "How 'bout those

Cubs?" said Feldstein. "Do they stink or what?" Sam Karzen mentioned seeing a building for sale in the morning paper's real estate section that was going for $8.5 million. "You're not going to believe this, but I could have bought that same building, in 1938, for sixty-five grand," he said. "But in those days sixty-five grand looked like serious dough."

"Tell me about it," said Manzelman. "You could have had it for a song, but at that time who could afford sheet music? Right? Same old story."

Schindler said less than the others. He was a smallish man, with a nose that depended well over his upper lip, on which he had a dark but wispy mustache. He had large, fleshy ears. The expression on his face had a striking sourness, which gave him a look of perpetual discontent. Felix would later learn from Manzelman that the great event of Max Schindler's life was an acrimonious lawsuit against his deceased partner's sons — he himself had no children — for control of his and their dead father's plumbing company. It was a protracted lawsuit that, according to Manzelman, had cost Schindler hundreds of thousands of dollars and that he finally lost, forcing him out of the business.

"You boys heard about the widow Schwartz?" Manzelman asked. "She called the *Tribune* to place a death announcement for her late husband. The fella on the *Tribune* tells her that they charge by the word. 'O.K.,' she says, 'make it "Schwartz dead."' 'No, madam,' the fella from the *Tribune* says, 'there's a fifty-dollar minimum, and for that you get five words.' The widow thinks a minute, then she says, 'O.K., make it "Schwartz dead. Cadillac for sale."'"

Yes, Felix thought, moving into the Northwood Apartments may have been a serious mistake, but it was too late to do anything about it. This was, he knew, to be his last move but one, and that ultimate move was probably not all that far in the future. More than once Felix had told his sister that he didn't mind death so much as dying. But now, surrounded by the aged and the infirm, he realized that this was a cheap attempt at aphorism. Dying and death — the truth was, he minded both.

Felix never quite caught on to the rhythm of the almost ceaseless activity at Northwood. Miss Godkin was indefatigable, not only in her cheerfulness but in her determination, as Felix put it to himself, to enforce gregariousness among the residents. She planned endless events, requiring only the least excuse and sometimes doing without that. There were Halloween parties and Hanukkah parties and New Year's Eve parties; there were also Victorian teas, Hawaiian luaus, an Africa Safari Day, an Evening in the Orient, a Roman Orgy Supper. There was something called a Spring Change Over, in which hairdressers came in and changed the hairdos of any woman at Northwood who was in the mood to do so. They were ready, too, to provide hairstyling for any of the men who wanted it, and a few did (for the first time in his life Felix felt himself fortunate to be bald). There was even a St. Patrick's Day party, for which Miss Godkin had decorated the large dining room and the other public rooms with cardboard shamrocks and leprechauns and green bunting and at which she arranged to have served a lunch of kosher corned beef and cabbage.

When the men met that morning at their regular table, Morry Manzelman, looking at all the green decorations, said, "This broad is really pushing it." Harry Feldstein, who tended, Felix noted, to take a somewhat simplistic view of human nature generally, added, "What this dame needs, all the goddamn parties in the world ain't going to provide. One good *schtup* and maybe she'd calm down and we'd have a few less parties and a lot more peace and quiet around here." Felix noted that lots of women, in Feldstein's view, seemed to need one good *schtup*. It was his single idea, his *idée fixe*. A bit of a hedgehog, this man Feldstein, Felix reflected, remembering Isaiah Berlin's little essay "The Hedgehog and the Fox." Felix knew Isaiah Berlin from his year at Oxford: a man full of interesting anecdotes and a love of gossip; Felix had sat with him more than once at high table at All Souls. Now dining regularly with Manzelman, Karzen, Feldstein, and Schindler, Felix could scarcely be said to be quite at high table any longer.

"An old guy, maybe ninety-six, ninety-seven," Manzelman began at breakfast, "announces to his friends that he is going to marry a girl twenty-five. 'At your time of life, sex with a girl that young could be fatal,' a friend tells him. 'Look,' the old guy says, 'what can I do? If she dies, she dies.'"

Perhaps it was not the best morning for such a joke, for two weeks before Sam Karzen had had a stroke. He was in his early seventies, younger than Felix. Formerly in the clothing business, Karzen always dressed dapperly, but for another era. He put together fancy color combinations, matched up ties and socks with the handkerchiefs that flounced jauntily out of his jacket pocket, wore monogrammed shirts with French cuffs, had a gold key chain with the letters of his first name pending from his alligator belt with its initialed gold buckle, kept a dazzling shine on his buckled loafers. Karzen's stroke was not fatal — he was out of the hospital a week afterward — but now the left side of his face sagged, his jaw tended to go slack, and he had temporarily to use one of those wretched walkers. He resumed his seat at what Felix now thought of as the Manzelman table. Since his stroke, Karzen stared out vacantly during conversation; his speech was slightly slurred. The old Jewish dandy had looked death in the eye, Felix sensed, and it had clearly left him stunned.

A strange way to live, Felix often thought since his move into Northwood. Everyone was waiting around for the inevitable. Cancer, stroke, heart attack, or, worst news of all, Alzheimer's disease. If you had the good fortune to reach your late seventies or early eighties, these were what awaited. Not even Miss Godkin's fierce smile could put them off. One day one of the familiar little women would not appear at her table in the dining room, and the word would go around that an embolism had taken her. The fellow who always wanted to talk about the stock market, and whom Felix one day heard shouting at another resident that if he didn't use the *kop* God gave him, what the hell good was he, now this man's own *kop* was permanently stilled by a heart attack he suffered while sitting on the toilet in his apartment on the seventh floor. The rather handsome Mrs. Fay Bernstein, always so neatly dressed and coifed — still on the attack, still looking for a husband, Felix thought when first he saw her — was now out of the game, taken by a cerebral hemorrhage. Teitlebaum, a small, red-faced man, pudgy and robust, always a ready audience for Manzelman's jokes, used to be in the wholesale meat business, was swept away three weeks after he was found to have cancer of the pancreas. What awaited himself, Felix wondered. He hoped for a clean, quick end. A heart attack in his sleep, or perhaps a swift stroke while reading in his chair — what he yearned for was a gentle *schtup* from God, as Harry Feldstein might have put it.

So much thought about death reminded Felix of his years at Buchenwald. Altogether too facile to compare this life with that, except to say that in both places the population was all Jewish and thoughts of death dominated and concentrated the mind. Who said that the knowledge that one would hang in a fortnight concentrated the mind? Samuel Johnson or Hobbes? Felix could not just now recall. But he did recall that it was Pascal who said that the human condition was everyone gathered in a room awaiting being called to be garroted in the next room, without knowing which among them was to be called in next. Just so. Here at Northwood everyone knew he or she would be called into that room fairly soon.

The comparison between the Nazi death camps and old age in a retirement home was ridiculous, Felix knew. Everyday terror was absent, for one thing; and for another, here at Northwood one came and went as one pleased. Felix had dinner at least once a week — usually on Sunday — with Connie and Moritz. Sometimes they went to concerts together on Friday night at the symphony downtown. He would occasionally accept an invitation from a former colleague and his wife at the university. Felix had met Manzelman's two sons, who picked up their father for Jewish holidays and for his grandchildren's birthdays and other family occasions. They were nice boys with ambitious hairdos, worn long in the back. Karzen sometimes spent a weekend with his daughter's family in the northern suburbs. Feldstein was taken by a nephew to baseball and football games; the day after, at breakfast, he would regale the table with accounts of how the games were fixed; another of his obsessions, evidently. Felix, having no interest in athletics, could not follow these conversations. He was hesitant and finally chose not to ask who a man frequently referred to — and always with vehemence — as "Ditka" might be.

The only man who never left Northwood was Max Schindler. No one ever picked him up. He never spoke of relatives. He seemed without friends outside the Manzelman table. Even at the table he was not particularly friendly. Felix felt that there was something permanently dark about Schindler — dark and disappointed. Schindler did not much join in with the others at Manzelman's table and seemed less to participate than to observe from the sidelines. Manzelman once told Felix that Schindler was extremely well balanced. "Do you think so?" asked Felix, not realizing he was falling for a joke. "Yes," said

Manzelman, "he has a chip on both shoulders." Felix sensed that Schindler was thoughtful, but what he thought about was far from clear. Felix recalled that Schindler had had an apparently bitter divorce, had gone through long and expensive litigation that had cost him his business. For an American, Felix supposed, Schindler's life had not been easy.

Felix, too, had remained aloof at Northwood. He had tried to do so without seeming in any way unduly distant or cool. Among these retired businessmen, lawyers, physicians, and the widows of businessmen, lawyers, and physicians, he — the Professor — was doubtless considered something of an oddity, but not so much of one as to make anyone uncomfortable in his presence, or so Felix hoped. He shared with Max Schindler the quality of being a bit on the sidelines, of not being able to join wholeheartedly in the general atmosphere of Northwood, either in its aspect of false gaiety imposed by Miss Godkin or in its aspect of amused knowingness about the world — of having heard everything before — lent by Morry Manzelman.

It was on the night of Rosh Hashanah that Felix went down to the dining room to find Schindler alone at their usual table. Manzelman, Feldstein, and Karzen were spending the evening with family. Schindler had no family, or at least none that he ever spoke of. And Connie and Moritz, secular Viennese Jews that they were, did not celebrate Jewish holidays. The dining room was nearly empty. A buffet of soup and sandwiches was set out. Felix approached the table with his food on a tray. Schindler was already eating, somewhat noisily, his soup.

"Sit down, Professor," he said. "Just the two of us here tonight. We'll get by fine without Manzelman's jokes, eh?"

"Good evening, Mr. Schindler," said Felix. "The quiet is a nice change, I agree."

"I have to tell you, Professor, I tried to read your books," said Schindler, his nose no more than two inches above his soup. "I took two of them out from the local library, but I have to report it was no-go."

"I am sorry to hear this," Felix said. "What seems to have been the problem?"

"I tried to read the one about this philosopher. Neetsy, is it?"

"On Nietzsche, yes."

"Too complicated, too abstract for me. I couldn't follow the damn thing, though I did understand that this Neetsy wrote about serious stuff. But tell me, do you only write about what other writers have written?"

Felix tried to ignore the condescension implicit in this description of his work, though he had to admit that as pure description it was accurate. "Yes, I suppose that is all I do," he said. "But you tell me, Mr. Schindler, do you find much time for reading?"

"Not that much," said Schindler. "I find writing much more interesting."

"Really?" said Felix. "And what do you write?"

"I've written a book about my life, an autobiography, I guess you'd call it, though it is maybe more about my thoughts about life than about my life itself."

"Sounds most interesting."

"Do you think so?"

"Yes, yes, of course."

"I've got a Xerox copy. I'll drop it off at your apartment later tonight."

Felix realized that he had made a significant error. Among academics it was understood that when you said that you thought the next person's writing was "most interesting," it certainly never for a moment meant that you wished to read it. In Schindler he was not dealing with an academic but instead with someone who apparently took words for what they said. He would have to be more careful in future. Too late now, though.

When Felix left his rooms the next morning, there at the door in a brown grocery bag was a Xerox copy of a 376-page manuscript, written in rather schoolboyish handwriting, with the title *Dog Eat Dog: My Life and Thoughts* by Max C. Schindler.

Breakfast a few days later began with Manzelman telling the story about a man who reports to his wife that, even though he wasn't able to produce his birth certificate, he was able to convince the bureaucrats at the Social Security office that he was old enough to collect benefits by opening his shirt and showing them the white hair on his chest. "'Oh, yeah,'" said Manzelman, imitating the high and whining voice of a long-suffering wife, "'while you were at it, you should've opened your fly — you could've claimed disability.'"

Felix, still very much the literary critic, always looking for patterns in thought, wondered why so many of Manzelman's jokes seemed to be about impotence or excessive potency. Nothing on the surface funny about either subject, surely. Or was this some American craziness that, like many another, he had no hope of ever grasping?

Schindler, meanwhile, made no mention of his dropping off his manuscript. Nor did he mention it at lunch or at dinner. Felix sensed that Schindler didn't want the other men at the table to know that he had written a book. Felix fully understood this. But he began to feel a certain pressure to read the manuscript, which he didn't look forward to doing. Plowing through all those pages written in longhand, for one thing. For another, what sorts of lies would he have to tell Schindler after he read it? Schindler, he sensed, was not a man whom one could put off with gracious evasions. He would have to find a way to tell him the truth without hurting him. But first he would have to read it.

Felix avoided Schindler's manuscript for more than a week. It sat there in its brown bag, like a sack of tomatoes first ripening and then going bad, on the floor beside his small desk. Merely to look at it gave Felix a bad conscience; and in his small apartment at Northwood, he could not evade looking at it for long. Yet, Felix said to himself, it remained easier to feel guilty about the manuscript than actually to read the damn thing. Schindler, meanwhile, still made no mention of it.

Finally, Schindler's stoicism and his own bad conscience got to Felix. One evening after dinner, up in his sitting room, he removed the thickish pages, and, exhaling deeply, like a man setting out to swim in a cold and choppy sea, he plunged in. Schindler's handwriting was far from illegible. And his manuscript, Felix found, was far from unreadable. It was, in fact, immensely readable without being particularly good. Perhaps Felix had lingered too long in his professional life over Kafka and Kraus, Musil and Mann, but he had developed a taste for the dark in literature, even though his own temperament tended toward the sweet and sunny. And if you liked dark, then you had to be interested in what Schindler had written, which was unrelievedly dark.

Dog Eat Dog turned out to be Max Schindler's *apologia*. It was an *apologia*, however, with an interesting twist. Schindler's defense of his own life was not that he was better than the rest of mankind, but that he was merely no worse, if only because it was impossible to be worse. The saga began with Schindler's parents, who he felt had betrayed him. His younger brother, he early discovered, was their favorite child. He, Schindler, was put to work once he had completed high school, while both parents sacrificed to send this brother to college and dental school. (The brother died, of a heart attack, in his forties.) Behind his parents' religion Schindler found nothing but fear; he found their yearning for respectability pathetic. Outside the home, going to school, he everywhere ran into anti-Semitism: among the Irish and Polish children with whom he went to school and among his Protestant teachers, who he now confidently felt had held him back. Accounts were offered of various bosses who cheated and insulted and humiliated Schindler in his youthful jobs.

And then sex entered Schindler's life, or at any rate his manuscript, and things promptly became worse. Schindler described without embarrassment the blistering heat of his adolescent urgings. These, as he wrote, "found no surcease" in his young manhood. However great his attraction to women, just that great, it seemed, was their revulsion from him. In Schindler's pages — and Felix felt that he could not read more than fifty or so of them at a sitting — all men were beasts, all women whores. But the greatest whore of all was the woman he eventually married. She, before the second year of their marriage was out, cuckolded Schindler with his brother, the dentist, and later with other men, thus setting him forever outside his own family. After his divorce, Schindler never again entered into anything resembling a serious relationship with a respectable woman, but instead, once a month or so, took his trade to prostitutes, who, as he recounted in *Dog Eat Dog,* were "a good deal more honest or straightforward than any respectable woman I was likely to meet." In his manuscript, he talked of his visits to prostitutes as having "his ashes hauled." Felix wondered what the etymology of such an expression might be.

Apart from the few prostitutes he frequented, the only other person in his book for whom Schindler had a good word was his business partner. Here though, Felix, a close reader, could not help but notice that, while he said that his partner was a relatively honest and dependable man, he, Schindler, never referred to him by anything other than his last name, Rabinowitz. And many more pages in *Dog Eat Dog* — a venomous forty-three-page chapter, in fact — were devoted to Schindler's lengthy lawsuit with Rabinowitz's sons. These included attacks on lawyers, on municipal corruption, on the unfitness of judges, on the inaccessibility of justice through the courts, and on the venality and greed of young and old alike.

When Felix set the last page on his lap, he felt a mixture of relief and admiration for the man. Schindler was often ungrammatical and sometimes pitifully awkward in straining after grandiloquent effects ("no surcease"), but one had to recognize his manuscript's relentless bleakness of tone. In 376 pages Schindler had not once lapsed into humor (except of the bitterest kind), affectionate feeling, or, so far as Felix could tell, dishonesty. Somehow, while recounting the ghastly treatment he had met with throughout his life, Schindler never set himself up as someone whose own splendid virtues deserved better of life. On the contrary, he made it plain, this was the way life was. This was human nature. Men were pigs, women and money were the filth they rolled in. What more could one expect? It was quite a performance.

The question that soon occurred to Felix was, Why had Schindler given him this book to read? Did he think that Felix might help him to get it published? That was not a possibility; apart from its literary crudities, libel laws alone ensured the book's being unpublishable. Did he want Felix's admiration? Perhaps, though if so, then only in a limited way, or so Felix thought. He may have wanted Felix to know that he, too, was a highly sapient fellow, a writer of a sort, and not merely one who wrote only about other men's writings — odd, Felix reflected, even the slightest insult stuck in one's memory — but out of hard, direct experience. Felix knew enough about writing to know that no one writes merely for himself, no matter how unregarding he may claim to be about the rest of the world. What Felix concluded was that Schindler's book was a cry from the heart; and that though until now Schindler had no one to cry out to, with the advent in his life of Felix Arnstein, himself obviously a thoughtful man, there was finally someone who would understand both the pain the world had inflicted on Max Schindler and his need to leave some record of it, but for whom and to what purpose it was, again, far from clear.

The question that confronted Felix was how to answer this cry for understanding from this sad yet otherwise altogether unattractive man, a man who had gone through life quite loveless and without any of the world's small rewards of achievement, recognition, simple pleasure in daily activity, a man whose only victory, if victory it could be counted, was survival. Felix could not in good conscience greet Schindler as a fellow human sufferer — *mon semblable, mon frère* — for even though, by most measures, Felix had been given a larger bowl of the world's bitter provender, he did not find life anywhere near so dread an affair as Schindler. Yet he could not go on living in the same building with this man, taking most of his meals with him, and not formally recognize that he, Max C. Schindler, used to be in the plumbing business, had been allowed a look into the darkness of the human heart.

"An old guy," said Morry Manzelman at breakfast, "maybe he's a hundred and four, maybe a hundred and five, he complains to his doctor that he thinks he's slowing down sexually. The doctor, amazed that the old guy has a sex life at all, asks him when he first noticed this. 'Oh, last night,' says the old-timer, 'and then again this morning.'"

Felix looked at Schindler when Manzelman had finished his joke. He was smiling politely, Felix felt, perhaps even perfunctorily. What could Schindler possibly think of a man such as Morry Manzelman? Or Sam Karzen, dressed up with his mouth gaping slightly from his stroke. Or Harry Feldstein, with his sex panacea for all the world's troubles. What did he think of Felix himself? Not easily known, of course, but Felix suspected that he thought the men he dined with dupes, fools who preferred not to look life in the face, as he had done, and take it for the horrendous business it was.

Another two weeks had gone by and Felix had still not told Schindler that he had read his book. Yet, having read it, he viewed Schindler differently. For how long could a man carry such a load of disgust and loathing for the world? Schindler, according to his book, had done so for some decades. What was behind all the hatred for life in *Dog Eat Dog*? Felix, when he thought about it, had perhaps greater reasons for sustaining a permanent grudge against life: there was his enforced exile from the country of his birth, the true horrors he had seen and lived with at Buchenwald, his congenital inability to lead a normal family life. Felix did not think that he underestimated the difficulties and darkness that life was capable of putting before a man, but next to Schindler he was almost childlike in his cheerfulness.

What Felix and Schindler shared, or so Felix concluded, was their singleness, their detachment, their condition, as the French called it, of *célibataire,* which meant finally their aloneness in the universe. Here Schindler far outdid him, Felix knew. But neither of them, the old literary critic in Felix also knew, propelled any plot; each existed in a state of nearly total inconsequence. Whatever they did, including the discourteous yet inevitable act of dying, the world would in no serious way be altered. Felix did not believe in God, even though he would on occasion invoke his name; the best he could manage by way of a position on the question of God was the rather boring one of hopeful agnosticism. Yet the oblivion in lieu of an afterlife that was the most likely outcome promised by this position held its own terrors. But there were no satisfactory answers to such a momentous question, not for Felix there weren't. He had long ago decided, against the advice of the poet, to "go gently into that good night," though he wished he could be more certain about how gentle how his going was figured to be. Schindler, on the other hand, as his book made plain, intended to go screaming into the same night. In the end, of course, go they both would, and each would be lost in the darkness. Perhaps Schindler and Felix shared more than he, Felix, had at first realized.

Normally, Felix made it a point to avoid Miss Godkin's special events evenings, but he often forgot to check the bulletin board in the main lobby of Northwood, where notification of them was always posted. So when he came down to his evening meal, he was surprised to discover that he had walked into Viva Mexico Night. He was greeted at the door to the dining room by the Brunhild-like Miss Godkin.

"Hello, Professor," she exclaimed in a rich singsong voice. She was wearing a long black gown, very décolleté, revealing an enormous shelf of bosom, with a rhinestone-studded mantilla and a rose in her blond hair. "Or should I say *Buenos noches?*" and she twice clicked her heels against the parquet floor.

Felix was flustered. He blinked at all the color in the usually subdued and sedate dining room. Bright-colored crepe paper festooned the walls, with papier-mâché birds and little burros hanging at various places from the ceiling; also a piñata hung from the chandelier at the center of the room. Two pudgy Mexican musicians, mustachioed, wearing wide sombreros, short black embroidered jackets and trousers with stripes up the sides, boots, and what Felix took to be toy revolvers in holsters around their waists, were singing a song with a refrain that sounded to him like "Wonton and mayo." Miss Godkin, the hem of her lavish black gown sweeping across the floor, led Felix to his regular table.

"*Muchachos,*" she said, "may I present Don Professor Arnstein?" And then, as Felix, still a bit stunned, fell into his chair,

Miss Godkin, kicking up a large leg backward, left, calling out *"Adiós."*

"What do ya mean, *want* to marry her?" Manzelman was saying, ending yet another of his jokes. "The old coot *had* to marry her."

Felix looked around the room. Many of the women, who seemed to have more enthusiasm for these evenings of Miss Godkin's than the men, were got up in garish clothes: peasant blouses, red and green scarves, long dangling earrings, flowers in their hair. But many of the men, committed no doubt to the idea of being good sports, went along, too, and wore bandannas around the loose skin of their necks; a few had turned up in large sombreros, which sat awkwardly on their bald heads or thinning gray hair. Looking around the room, Felix felt a stab of sadness for its occupants, once serious people whose usefulness was now considered exhausted and who were passing their last years in this pitiful charade.

One of the two Mexican musicians now abandoned his guitar for a large drum, which he carried supported by a strap around his neck; the other musician joined him with a trumpet. Miss Godkin, in the middle of the floor, encouraged everyone — *"señores, señoritas!"* — to join her in something called "The Mexican Hat Dance." The music of the drum and the trumpet was very loud; a number of residents, most of them women, joined Miss Godkin on what was now the dance floor. The five men at the Manzelman table were unable to hear themselves talk, though Felix thought he saw the word *schtup* form on Feldstein's lips. Schindler, looking at Felix, nodded his head, pointing toward the door in a signal that he join him in avoiding all this racket. Felix rose from the table and did so.

The early autumn air was clear and cool. After the noise in the dining room, the relative silence of the streets seemed luxurious. The crepuscular light had a calming effect. Without either man saying a word about their destination, both turned at the corner and headed for the park along the lake. Felix was six or seven inches taller than Schindler. Odd, he felt, but he seemed to think of this man only as Schindler, never as Max, even though he had shared so many meals with him, even though he had read of his endless humiliations. Something there was about Schindler that resisted intimacy without encouraging formality.

At the park, they sat on a bench facing a small lagoon and the lake to the east of the lagoon. A jogger ran by, a heavyset man in orange pants and a chartreuse sweatshirt, red in the face and listening to a radio through earphones. Then a couple, a young man and woman, wearing black spandex shorts, sped by on green-wheeled roller skates, their arms swinging vigorously. Four men in helmets and wearing colorful tops and shorts, also of spandex, cycled past. They looked to be in their fifties.

"Trying to evade death," said Schindler.

"A new American pastime, I believe," said Felix.

"Can't be done," said Schindler. "Still, you can't stop people from trying."

"I suppose not," said Felix.

"Tell me, Professor," said Schindler, "have you had a chance to read my book?"

"I have. It is very powerful, Mr. Schindler, very powerful indeed."

"Powerful is good?"

"Yes, powerful is good. Not that you can hope to publish such a manuscript. It would invite yet more lawsuits, as you must know. But then you must have known that when you wrote it."

"I didn't really write it with publishing in mind," said Schindler. "I wrote it because I felt I ought to say what I thought about the world before I left it. If someone reads it, good. If not, not. Either way, I guess it don't matter that much. Still, I'm curious to know what you thought."

"They are dark, very dark, your thoughts about life, at least as you set them down in your book," Felix said. "Does life really seem so unremittingly bleak to you?"

"Only," said Schindler, a rare smile playing across his mouth, "when I think about it."

"What of acts of kindness?" Felix asked. "Or of self-sacrificing heroism, such as occur in war or even on the street? Do not such things lead you to believe that not all life is so dark?"

"I consider things like that exceptions that prove no rule, brief intermissions from a cruel comic show that always goes on. Life, Professor, is no picnic, as you may have noticed, but a stern test that everyone fails. That's how I, at least, have come to look at it."

"I am sure that you must have asked yourself why we are all put through this test and why it is prescribed in advance that all must fail."

Schindler ran his hand through his thin hair. "I think there may be a God or gods or some such being — who knows, Professor. But I also think that it or him or they don't give a damn. I think someone may be laughing at us. That we are all the butt of some big joke. A bigger joke than our friend Manzelman ever dreamed of. That, since you ask, is what I think."

"And what of a mother's love for her children? Of the disinterested kindness of people toward one another? Of charitable impulses? This means nothing in your view?"

"I haven't known any of that personally, you see. What I have known — actually experienced — is very different. Maybe, Professor, your own life has been easier than mine. You've never married. You have been a teacher all your life. I don't mean to be insulting, but maybe you've been better protected from the bitterness of the world than me."

As if by an impulse over which he had no control, Felix pushed up the sleeve of his suit jacket, unbuttoned his shirt cuff, and showed Schindler the tattooed number on his forearm.

"I underestimated you," said Schindler. "You have seen the devil." He looked at the ground.

"Perhaps I have," said Felix.

"How, after the Nazis, could you go on living?" asked Schindler.

"Perhaps because I like life," said Felix, "and am not unduly fond of the unknown alternative to it. Who knows, maybe each of us brings his own darkness into the world with him. Also his own light. I continue to see life as a gift. You, I gather from your book, see it otherwise."

"I am too old now to see it any other way," said Schindler. "I have encountered mostly fools. I have known too little kindness. I have drawn my conclusions."

Felix wished he could say something even mildly comforting. This conversation had gone deeper than he planned, or cared, for it to go. And now it had nowhere else to go.

Schindler rose from the bench. A slender, beautiful young woman in a purple sweatsuit with a red headband encircling long blond hair jogged by at a good pace. Run, young lady, Felix thought, let your mind linger on thoughts of love, on your own beauty, on all the delights of life. One day you, too, will know decrepitude. Your mind, too, will have little to think about but its own extinction. He, too, rose from the bench. Wordlessly, the two old men, one tall, one short, shuffled slowly out of the park to return to the party in celebration of the people and culture of Mexico.

Felix did not go down to breakfast the next morning. Around ten o'clock the fire department's emergency vehicle, siren screaming, pulled up at the main entrance of Northwood. Felix heard it from his room, where, after reading that morning's newspaper, he was treating himself to a bit of Rilke's *Die Sonette an Orpheus,* which he loved. Nothing unusual about the siren. Some days the fire department vehicle pulled up at Northwood two or three times, to resuscitate someone with breathing trouble, or take a heart case off to the hospital, or remove the corpse of a resident who had expired during the night. It was at lunch that Felix learned that the fire department had come this time for the removal of another corpse, that of Max Schindler.

Schindler, Morry Manzelman explained, had taken his own life. He had run a hot bath, put himself in it, then opened the veins in his wrists and ankles. Or so Manzelman learned from the Puerto Rican maid who found Schindler's body when she came in to do his room earlier this morning. Manzelman reported that Schindler also left a $50 tip, with a note saying that it was for whoever had to clean up the mess. He left no other message.

"A handsome gesture," said Manzelman. "The fifty-buck tip, I mean. You fellas know the joke about Mrs. Goldberg?" Manzelman continued. "Goes on a cruise as a slave where they imitate all the conditions of a Roman slave galley. They aren't out of port ten minutes, she asks the woman seated next to her, Mrs. Silverman, who has been on this cruise before, 'Tell me, Mrs. Silverman, when this cruise is over, how much do you tip the whipper?'"

"He died in the manner of Seneca," said Felix, aloud but to no one in particular. "A philosopher's death." And then, to himself, he thought: Max, dear fellow, bon voyage, Godspeed, rest at last in peace.

Artie Glick in a Family Way

ARTIE GLICK, emerging from his therapist's office on Michigan Avenue, was more puzzled than usual. He thought Dr. Lieberman would have been pleased at his announcement of his decision to marry. True, Artie was fifty-seven; true, too, he had failed at marriage once before, though that was eighteen years ago. Lindsey Connors, the woman he planned to marry, was, at thirty-eight, nearly twenty years younger than he. Until now this hadn't seemed to Artie a complicating factor. Until now neither had her Catholicism. Lindsey's Catholicism, it turned out, had forced Artie's hand. She was what she herself called a cafeteria Catholic, picking and choosing what she liked from the religion in which she had grown up. Church doctrine against contraception — no, she felt she didn't have to live with that; the doctrine against abortion — yes, emphatically yes, that she felt she must live with.

The evening Lindsey told Artie she was pregnant she also told him that she couldn't bring herself to undergo an abortion. Which didn't, she quickly added, mean that he had to marry her. The carelessness that had resulted in her pregnancy was her responsibility, she told Artie, and she was prepared to live with its consequences. She was a lawyer, with a well-paying job at the firm of Sidley & Austin, one of the city's best, and money wasn't a problem. Neither was bringing up a child out of wedlock any longer the disgrace it once was. Besides, at thirty-eight, she might not have another chance to have a child. No, she told Artie, he needn't worry, unless he wanted to.

"But, baby," Artie found himself saying, "I want to worry. The responsibility is mine, too."

"Are you sure?"

"Absolutely," Artie answered, hoping she didn't notice him gulp before he said it.

This wasn't Artie's style at all. His style, at least with women, was one of hesitancy, noncommitment, deep caution. Gravely distrustful of his own instincts and of women's motives, he always held back, chose never to make other than the most deliberate moves. Dr. Lieberman once called him, in sexual relations, a passive paranoiac.

Dr. Monroe Lieberman, five years older than Artie, had himself been married three times and had had two children with each of his wives. As far as Artie could determine, none of these kids had had it easy; Lieberman's eldest child, Ariadne, was forty years old, fifty or so pounds overweight, worked in a vintage-clothing shop on Halsted Street, and she was the most successful of his children. Yet somehow none of Lieberman's own domestic disasters — he frequently used them to illustrate his advice — seemed to put the least dent in his sublime confidence. Artie began going to him thirteen years ago, not long after his father's death, at seventy-five bucks an hour; he was now paying him a hundred and fifty.

"So remind me, Arthur," Lieberman said when Artie told him about his forthcoming marriage, "how long have you known this young woman you now propose to marry?"

"About five months," Artie said.

"Not all that long, really," said Lieberman with a cool and warning distance in his voice. He was a pudgy man, with red-rimmed eyes under heavy black-framed glasses. He must have been a terrible athlete as a kid, Artie often thought.

"No," said Artie, "I suppose it's not."

"This is very unlike you, Arthur — you, who are usually so circumspect with women. We therapists tend to worry when our patients act in wildly uncharacteristic ways."

"She's carrying my child," Artie said.

"An old-fashioned phrase, Arthur, very Victorian actually. And can you be certain it's yours?"

A dirty mind never sleeps, Artie thought, especially a shrink's mind. Artie didn't much like Lieberman. Incomplete transference, Lieberman would probably call it; Artie had never gotten to the part about liking, let alone loving, him. But then, why had he remained with him so long, seeing him twice a week? That, Artie suspected, was probably why he was a sick guy.

Artie's problem, Lieberman continued to insist, was his father, dead fourteen years now but still haunting his son. The father was a ghost Artie had refused to bury, or so Lieberman claimed.

Herschel Gliksner had emigrated from Łódź at the age of nineteen, in 1928, arriving in America just in time for the Depression. In the attempt to Americanize himself, when he moved to Chicago he changed his name to Harry Glick, but never lost his greenhorn's accent. He drifted into the dry-cleaning business, much of which, in those days, was run by Jews. He worked long hours, saved, and by the end of World War II had five shops, nine trucks on the street, and a plant with eighty-five workers on the payroll. A smallish man with a low hairline, all muscle, he drove himself hard and drove his sons no less hard. Artie's brother, Barry, managed an early escape: he went to medical school and soon after graduating set up a practice in Tiburon, in Marin County, California. Artie, who briefly attended Roosevelt University, went to work for Top-Notch Cleaners with his father.

In all their time together, when he was a boy through the twenty-two years he worked with his father at Top-Notch, Artie could not recall a single calm conversation between them. His father lectured, hectored, badgered; argued, screamed, cursed; he lived in a state of continuous irritation. Nor could Artie remember a time when the old man gave him credit for having any judgment. Once, when he was already a married man and thirty-five years old, Artie heard his father, in his office at the plant, say over the phone to one of his pinochle cronies, "Go on vacation? Whaddya kiddin' me? Who'd run the place? For help I got nothin' but idiots." Artie felt his stomach turn over. He probably should have quit right then. But he was married — had, in fact, a childless and rocky marriage — and no place to go. All he knew was the dry-cleaning business.

When Harry Glick had had his second heart attack, and his physician had practically forced the old man to take time off, from Florida he'd call Artie at least once every two hours, reminding him of this, telling him not to forget that, assuming always that his now forty-three-year-old son had no brains, no common sense. Always behind his father's questions, instructions, advice, there was a barely hidden anger. Was it, Artie wondered, directed at him or at the world? He never felt he could ask. He never really found out why his father was always so ticked off.

His father's bypass surgery was done at St. Francis Hospital in Evanston, where the head of the coronary unit was a tall, lean surgeon named Tom Murphy. When Artie first saw him, he thought Dr. Murphy ought to be wearing a white silk scarf, for he looked more like a test pilot than a surgeon. Dr. Murphy told Artie that the surgery was very iffy; the two attacks had greatly weakened his father's heart, yet there was no choice but to operate.

Artie was in his father's room when the orderlies came to take him down to surgery. He called Artie over to his bed, beckoned him to lean over so that he could whisper in his ear. Artie thought his father had something deeply personal to tell him. Instead he pointed to the slender bronze crucifix on the wall above his bed and, in his accented English, whispered, "If I don't come out of dis alive, take dat cross off the wall and shove it up dis guy Moiphy's *tuchis.*" His father died on the operating table. So far as Artie knew, those were Harry Glick's last words.

In the years since his father's death, Artie had built up Top-Notch to ten shops with twelve trucks on the street. He had acquired exclusive rights to a process for cleaning suede and leather, so that dry cleaners all over Chicago sent problem garments to him. His payroll was just under two hundred people. He often wondered what his old man would have thought of all this.

The Koreans were taking over the dry-cleaning business in Chicago, and a syndicate headed by a family named Kim had made Artie an offer of $4.5 million for Top-Notch. He assumed that that number meant they would close for $5 million, and he took it to an old high school friend named Larry Engel, who was a partner at Sidley & Austin. Engel, who specialized in trusts and estates, passed Artie along to Lindsey Connors. She was blond, small-boned, authoritative, had a winning sense of humor. After the first time they slept together, following two business lunches and a dinner at Kiki's on Franklin Street, she said, "That was so nice I don't think I'll even bother to bill you for it."

They went to lots of movies. Artie learned that she had four brothers, all athletes, so that when Artie took her to Bulls games she knew what was going on. She grew up in Newton Centre, outside Boston; had gone to Mount Holyoke, then to Northwestern Law School. Not yet a partner in her firm, she worked the twelve-hour day. Artie saw her mostly on weekends. Sometimes they would spend all day Sunday at his apartment on Scott Street, off State Parkway, he shuffling through the fat *Trib*, a Bears game playing like Muzak in the background, she tapping away at her laptop on his dining room table. There was no talk about their moving in together. Artie had never told her he loved her. And now, it seemed, he had committed himself to marrying her.

"Tell me, Arthur," Dr. Lieberman asked, "why would you do this?"

"Because," said Artie, "I feel I have a responsibility toward the child."

"Forgive me if I question your motives here, Arthur," said Lieberman, "though you know questioning your motives is one of the things you pay me for, isn't it? This young woman, and maybe even her baby, do they really need you? Maybe things work the other way around. Do you, by any chance, I wonder, need them?"

"What the hell for?"

"Well, to put it gently, Arthur, to make a life for yourself."

Up yours, fat boy, thought Artie. "I have a life," he said.

"Do you really?"

Artie usually arrived at the plant around seven A.M. Most days he hung around until six P.M., when he drove over to the McClurg Court health club. There he played racquetball or got into a half-court basketball game; he might swim afterward or sit for twenty minutes in the sauna. He was on the periphery of the McClurg Court regulars, as he thought of them, Jewish bachelors and divorced guys roughly his own age, and some five or ten years older. Ex-athletes, they had gone to Senn or

Sullivan, Von Steuben or Roosevelt high schools. They talked stock tips, sports, sex. Over the years Artie had met a number of women at McClurg — enough so that he didn't yet have to sink to Jewish singles dances. He took them to dinner; he met them for breakfast; sometimes he scored, sometimes not. Three times a year he went down to Miami to visit his mother, who at eighty-two — knock wood — was still in pretty good shape. Once every couple of years he would spend four days on the Coast with his brother and his family. Add in two fifty-minute sessions each week with Lieberman. Wasn't that a life?

"And marriage, Arthur," Lieberman continued, "marriage, wouldn't it be fair to say, hasn't exactly been your strong suit, has it?"

"That was nearly twenty years ago," Artie replied.

Artie had to admit that his marriage, which had lasted seven years, was the worst goddamn time of his life. Judy Levy was his age. They had both gone to Sullivan. Why they married in the first place wasn't clear to Artie — everyone in those days seemed to marry in his early twenties, so why not him? — and became less clear as time went on. They began life together as two people who really didn't know each other and ended by hating each other. She couldn't have children; he didn't want to adopt. In the end, Judy caught him cheating on her with a Polish receptionist at the plant, which she was able to use to stick it to him for a handsome divorce settlement. ("Schmuck," said his father, when he found out, "you don't got enough sense not to piss in your own inkwell.") Judy, Artie had heard, had moved to Los Angeles and remarried. They had lost touch. Three or so years ago he saw her shopping at Field's — she must have been in town visiting her mother — and felt absolutely nothing. He didn't even bother to walk up and say hello to her.

"'Affectlessness' we call it, Arthur," said Lieberman. "An inability to feel and show emotion in the right proportion. That's part of your problem, Arthur. That's part of the rich inheritance from your father."

Lieberman liked to bang away at the dead Harry Glick. Artie sometimes imagined a meeting between the two. "I sense deeply repressed rage in you, Arthur," Lieberman had said to Artie on more than one occasion. In Harry Glick, Lieberman could have seen rage all right, the real thing, out on the surface, on full display. As for Artie's father, two minutes with Monroe Lieberman and he would have turned to Artie and said, "Dis son of a bitch — what is he, crazy? And you, you're paying him hard-earned money to listen to your troubles. Maybe you're crazier than he is." One of the nice things about his father, Artie thought, was that after him life seemed pretty easy.

Yet if life was so easy, why, Artie asked himself, now so long after his father's death, was he still in therapy? He told himself that he felt an emptiness in his life — something wrong, something missing. Artie was not proud of being in therapy. He never told his brother about it, though the two of them often talked about growing up with the old man. Oddly, a month or so after he had begun to go out with her, he told Lindsey that he was seeing a shrink.

"Oh," she said, "Jewish golf."

"Jewish golf?"

"Psychotherapy is what Jews have instead of golf," she said. "Gentiles try to improve their backswing, Jews their past. I'm not sure that either, after great expense and effort, have much luck." She told him that half the Jewish kids she knew at Mount Holyoke were in therapy. Others had been bonkers about contemporary painting. Still others put their faith in radical politics. Some went in for all three. "They hit the trifecta," she said.

Lindsey's conversation was filled with such stuff. It came of growing up with four brothers and working around aggressive men at Sidley & Austin. She had a strong sense of reality and a comic view of those who, out of self-deception, didn't. Between college and law school she had taken three years off and worked in a fish-canning factory in Australia, as a waitress in Tel Aviv, as a secretary in Manhattan. She seemed to have no fear of life, none whatsoever.

"How did you get to the age of thirty-eight without marrying?" Artie asked her one night in bed.

"Just lucky, I guess," she replied.

"Really?"

"Truth is," she said, "I think even brave men are a little afraid of me."

"How so?"

"They sense I can see through them."

"Can you?"

"Usually, yes, I think I can."

"What about me? What do you see in me?"

"A moderately screwed-up guy," she said, "but not a bullshitter. And decent. Also gentle. And in the current market, friend, a decent, gentle non-bullshitter is fairly rare."

This conversation had taken place before Lindsey had announced her pregnancy and before Artie had asked to stay with her and their child. Now that he had asked, it made more sense than ever that he sell Top-Notch. The child, his and Lindsey's, would need him, or so he imagined. If he got $5 million for the business, by the time he paid his mother and brother their shares, took care of taxes and fees, he'd still get away with a little more than $2 million, which, along with his own savings and investments, meant he wouldn't have to work again. Would he miss it? He doubted it — it was dry cleaning, after all, not portrait painting or pro basketball — though you never knew. Having a serious hand in bringing up a child seemed O.K. — more than O.K., it seemed damn nice.

Artie assumed Lindsey would want to return to work after the birth of the child. Her career was still ahead of her. Artie hadn't really had a career, but his life, he began to feel, might just be in front of him. Time to begin. With a little luck, he hoped to be able to live long enough to see his child out of college. With a little more luck, he might see him or her settled in life.

"Arthur," said Lieberman, leaning in and removing his glasses, "I'm not going to shit you here, this marriage is a big mistake. Don't make it. This is all sheer fantasy formation on your part, believe me."

Artie didn't want to believe him, but the fact was that he had of late taken, in dreamy moments, to thinking a lot about his life with Lindsey and their child. He imagined a daughter. He would like her to be named Anna, after his maternal grandmother, whom he could barely remember but whose favorite grandchild he was supposed to have been. He imagined her small and fair, like her mother, but otherwise Jewish, in her instincts, outlook, general smarts. (Would she be raised Jewish? Artie hoped so, but had not yet brought the matter up with Lindsey.) He saw himself taking her to the park, buying her toys and clothes, playing with her, later teaching her what he knew about life. He imagined her a good athlete, a tennis player maybe, like her mother a whiz at school, goodhearted, affectionate, a sweet kid, a daddy's girl. Was this fantasy formation or just pleasant dreams? There must be a difference between the two. What was wrong with dreaming anyhow?

"Look," Artie said, "first you tell me that I haven't really got a life, and now, when I have the chance for one, you tell me that I'm not ready for a life. That doesn't leave me with much room to maneuver, Doctor Lieberman."

"I don't think you follow me, Arthur. What I am saying is

that you have some unfinished business with your father, and until that is cleared up any significant relationship you enter into is doomed to failure."

"You know, Doctor, nothing personal, but sometimes I think you hate my father more than I do. Besides, I'm fifty-seven. At the rate we're going, you'll have me in perfect mental health just in time for death."

"How soon things get cleared away is entirely up to you, Arthur. It always has been."

"And if I disregard your advice?"

"As I say, I think you'd be making a grave mistake. And I'd have to conclude that you no longer need my advice and our relationship as doctor and patient would probably be at an end."

"I'll think about it and let you know," Artie said, getting up, looking at his watch, and deciding to spot Lieberman the twenty minutes he still had to go in the session. Let him use it to take a leak and have a coffee.

"See you Thursday?" Lieberman said.

"Sure," Artie said, "at noon."

Back at the plant, he had a call from Lindsey. She had just returned from her obstetrician and had something she needed to tell him. Was he free for dinner? They agreed to meet, at seven, in the downstairs room at Binyon's, across from the Standard Club.

When Artie arrived, Lindsey was already there, seated in a booth against the far wall, a glass of white wine before her, fiddling with the stem of the glass, looking, he thought, nervous. She was wearing a dark gray suit with a thin chalk stripe, a killer lawyer's suit. At any rate, she killed him in it. For some reason, this was one of those moments — there were many of them — when he thought of the difference in their ages. If he lived long enough, she might have to take care of him. He felt, not for the first time, that he was getting the better deal here. Well, at least she would have his money and the child.

"Greetings, counselor," he said, kissing her on the cheek, then sliding into the other side of the booth. He noted that she had already ordered him a drink, a vodka and tonic.

"Greetings, client and billee," she said. "How goes it?"

"All is quiet on the dry-cleaning front."

"Are there dry-cleaning jokes?" she wanted to know. "Unlike lawyer jokes, of which, as we both know, there are none."

"Dry cleaners, as you may not know, are famous for their wit. Yet in more than thirty-five years in the business, I've not heard a single dry-cleaning joke. Hard to account for this."

"It is, especially in light of the famous dry-cleaning wit. But rather than make up a dozen or so dry-cleaning jokes, let me tell you my news."

"It's not bad?" Artie said.

"I don't know," Lindsey said. "Maybe that's for you to judge."

"Now I am nervous," he said. "Out with it."

"I realize you're already sitting down, so hold on to the edge of the table."

"O.K.," he said, "hit me."

"First take a swallow of your drink." He did.

"Today I got the results of my amniocentesis exam. Hold on tight, Papa, everything's fine with Mama, but we're going to have twins. Boys, identical twin boys."

At the news, Artie wondered about the expression on his face. Confusion, disbelief, shock, a man going down for the third and last time, some combination of all of these; he thought he felt a muscle in his left cheek twitch. "You're kidding me," he finally managed to say.

"That's roughly what I said to my doctor. But she wasn't kidding, and I'm afraid I'm not."

"This is going to take a bit of getting used to," Artie said.

"I've known it for six hours now, and I can't get used to it my-self. It may take twenty or thirty years to get used to."

Artie thought of himself in parks, airports, restaurants, pushing one of those wide double strollers, two towheaded boys its passengers. People would no doubt take him for their grandfather. Would he have the energy to keep up with two boys, identical boys no less? All those diapers, two cribs, two highchairs, endless bottles of formula. Jesus, Artie thought, I am in the damn soup now, up to my lower lip.

"You know," Lindsey said, "you can still get out of this deal. No earnest money has been put down. No papers have been signed. You can still walk, friend, I want you to know that."

"Where would I walk to?" Artie said. "As it happens, I love you, girlie."

"You are screwed up," she said. "I happen to love you too."

Artie lifted his drink. "To the boys," he said.

"And to neurosis," she added. They clinked glasses.

That evening, alone in his apartment, Artie took out a sheet of paper and began a letter:

Dear Dr. Lieberman,

This is to let you know that I am to be the father of twin boys, due in December. I am marrying early next month. I would like you to know that I have thought over all you have said, and decided that, even if it is wise, it's wisdom I cannot use, cannot afford, at least not at this juncture in my life. I admire your confidence and sense of certainty about my life. I wish I had some of it myself, but I don't and probably never will. I am apparently one of those people who have to take things as they come. If any-thing, I feel I have lived all too carefully over the past years. It hasn't helped. I realize that, at my age, attempt-ing to raise twin boys is really putting myself in for it. But just now — I mean right at this very moment — it seems damn fine to me. It feels like life is calling out to me, one last chance not to live under someone else's tyranny (including, I hope you'll forgive me for saying so, yours) but in a sweet chaos of my own making. Screw it, Dr. Lieberman, but time is running out and if I don't get in the game now, I never will. Please cancel my appointment for next Thursday and for every Tuesday and Thursday thereafter.

Finally, I note that I owe you, for seven sessions, the sum of $1,050. I have decided not to pay. I've decided you have enough of my money as it is. Besides, I can use the money to buy one of those double strollers and spend the rest on diapers, which probably aren't cheap. If you want to attempt to collect this money, I invite you to turn it over to a collection agency. But I think you should know that I have a terrific lawyer.

Sincerely,

He signed the letter, in a large and bold hand, *Artie*.

The Third Mrs. Kessler

HER EYES — leaning closer to the magnifying mirror, Elaine could read the future in her eyes. Not so long ago one of her best features, they now seemed less brown, less deep, less alive with the hope and promise they once held. Despite ministrations with moisturizers and creams, the skin at the corners had begun to show crinkles. Her once lush lashes seemed thinner, even slightly scraggly, and needed lots of help. Pouches had not yet formed — be patient, she told herself, these, too, will arrive soon enough. The rims tended to redden, especially at night, a condition worsened by many years of wearing contact lenses. She had finally given up the lenses, to which she never quite adjusted, four years ago, just after the divorce from Jacob.

Had she been more beautiful as Mrs. Jacob Kessler, the third wife of the famous pianist, than as Elaine Goldman Kessler, the forty-four-year-old divorced mother of an eight-year-old son, or did she imagine it? Certainly, the world had been much more impressed with her as Mrs. Jacob Kessler. Hotel managers and maitre d's knocked themselves out to arrange the best tables, the most capacious suites, the quietest and most comfortable surroundings. Limousines awaited her exit from grand hotels; first class was the only air travel she knew. Except for the month they spent every summer at Jacob's place in Maine, near Castine, the details of cooking, cleaning, and other domestic chores were assumed to be beneath her notice — these days, working at a full-time job, she sometimes seemed to have time for little else — and even in Maine they had a cook four nights a week. The better part of her ten years as Mrs. Jacob Kessler had been quite magical — the most interesting part of her life, Elaine thought.

She had known about Jacob, of course, even owned some of his recordings, but had not met him until the first night she heard him play in concert. It was in Chicago, at Ravinia, in July, not under the pavilion but in the snug Murray Theater she so much preferred. She had been invited to meet him at a party after the concert at the Wasserburgs. Leonard Wasserburg was a former patient of Elaine's father, a very rich man and a major benefactor of the Ravinia festival. She wasn't at all sure she cared to go, but that night Jacob played the Schubert Impromptus, Mozart's Piano Sonata no. 25 in F, and the Beethoven *Pathétique*, whose second movement, the adagio, she particularly loved.

Elaine's seat was only five rows from the stage of the small theater. She noted Jacob's face, with its flared nostrils, fleshy ears, thick eyebrows, longish hair beginning to go silver at the temples, olive skin — the overall effect very Jewish yet aristocratic. Jacob Kessler was an aristocrat of art, Elaine formulated it to herself that night, someone who had been permitted knowledge of its inner secrets, one of the elect. For his encore, he played Ravel's *Pavane for a Dead Infanta*. He played it, as he seemed to play everything, without effort, his head and shoulders perfectly still, but with a beautifully controlled passion. She watched the slender strong hands returning to Ravel's plaintive theme and thought, in a flash of pure eroticism, of how they would feel playing over her body.

At the Wasserburgs' house on the lake, on the North Shore in Glencoe, amid the Matisse, the Motherwells, the Fairfield Porter, and the large Frankenthaler, he approached her. She was then twenty-nine, he forty-three. She had never married. He was recently divorced from his second wife. He was delighted, he claimed, to learn that Elaine wasn't a musician, hadn't even had any musical training.

"Forgive me," he said, "I took you for a cellist."

"Really? Why?"

"A little psychological vice. My world is almost completely bounded by music. I assume that anyone I meet at such evenings has musical interests, and I try to guess their instrument."

"But why the cello?"

"Deep strings, capable of passion and also darkness — I saw such things in you. I think you would be correct to take it as a compliment."

"I will," she said.

"In any case, I'm thrilled to be wrong."

"Why is that?"

"At least now I won't have to schlep a cello case on planes and trains."

Elaine didn't press him further. She had her car with her, the seven-year-old Honda Civic her father had bought for her when she graduated from Radcliffe, and two hours later he asked if she minded driving him the few miles to his hotel in Lake Forest. At the hotel, he wondered if she could be persuaded to stay for a nightcap. After a drink, he asked her to stay the night. Although it wasn't at all her way, she agreed without hesitation. They made love, fortissimo and pianissimo, and she fell asleep afterward in his arms, Ravel's beautiful pavane echoing in her head.

Her fear that she had been no more than a night's entertainment was put to rest when, two days later, he sent her a first-class plane ticket to Washington, where he was playing the same program at Wolf Trap the following weekend. He called the evening the ticket arrived, and she told him she would be there. In a calm, warmly reassuring voice, he said he was glad.

Elaine stayed in his suite at the Ritz-Carlton, near Dupont Circle. At breakfast Sunday morning in the Jockey Club, John Houseman came up to their table. Jacob had known the actor a long time, and they spoke as intimates.

"I'd like you to meet my fiancée, Elaine Goldman," Jacob said.

"How pleasing!" Houseman replied, not immediately releasing Elaine's hand. "My very best wishes, Miss Goldman."

When he left, Elaine, her fork playing with the strawberries on her plate, her knee touching Jacob's knee, was unable to look up.

"That's a funny way to go about it," she said. "I mean, learning you're engaged through conversation with a third party."

"I'm afraid I was using old John as a conduit, as they say in the CIA. But I really do hope you'll marry me."

"Do you usually move so quickly?"

"In these matters I do. It's only the small things in life — what tie to wear, what to order for dessert — that I agonize over. Important things never seem to detain me for long, or at least they never have."

"I hope you won't mind if I take some time to think all this through."

"Take all the time you need. I know you'll make the correct

decision and conclude, as I already have, that we belong to-gether."

Jacob went on to Boston for a performance at Tanglewood, and Elaine returned to Chicago. She had her job at Leo Burnett, the ad agency, where she was a media buyer; her apartment in Sandburg Village, for which her father had given her the down payment; her friends, most of them by now married and with children and living in Highland Park or Northbrook. But life in Chicago, after a long weekend with Jacob Kessler, suddenly felt a little unreal. Or was it the time, the quite magical time, spent with Jacob that seemed unreal?

When she told her father about it — Elaine's mother had died of a stroke two years before — at lunch at the Standard Club, he showed his usual unexcited reaction. Dr. David Gold-man, the noted oncologist, senior physician on the staff of Mi-chael Reese Hospital, was a careful man. He was too careful, in fact too subtle, to tell his daughter not to act rashly. He took a different tack, assuming, as he always had with her, that she had her own good judgment and subtlety.

"I know you've taken into consideration that you will be this man's third wife. You must have thought about your prospects of pleasing him when two women before you were unable to."

"I have thought about it, Daddy," she said. "And I'm afraid I don't have one intelligent reason for thinking that I can do better. I'm not under illusions that I possess some secret charm that'll change his character. What's worse, I'm not sure I want to change it. He's very dashing."

"There are children from the other marriages?"

"Two daughters, ten and eight, both from the first marriage. They live with their mother."

"Does he see much of them?"

"As much as possible, but, you know, he travels a good deal, both here and abroad, concertizing."

"I see," said Dr. Goldman. But from the way he said it, Elaine was pretty sure that he didn't see, not really.

The main dining room at the Standard Club was filled with men who reminded her of her father. They were solid, substantial men, earnest, responsible, serious — men with gravity. Elaine always felt she would marry a younger version of such a man herself: a physician perhaps, like her father, or a lawyer; in any case a professional man, with all that "professional" implied in the way of competence, command, control. And security.

Looking around at all these men in their various dark gray and blue suits and subdued neckties, she thought of Jacob's getup when he left her at the airport in Washington: soft Italian loafers, tan twill trousers, a buttery soft, blue cashmere blazer, a thick red-striped shirt with white collar and white cuffs from Turnbull & Asser — Turncoat & Asshole, he called them, when she asked — and a rich multicolored ascot from Charvet. Imagining him in this room, she had to suppress a smile.

"Well," her father said, "is there any great hurry about all this?"

"I think Jacob would like an answer before too long."

"What is it likely to be?"

"You know, Daddy, being married to a man like Jacob provides every opportunity for an interesting life."

"An interesting life?" Her father's quizzical look suggested that the concept was a fresh and strange one to him.

"By which I mean," she continued, "living for long stretches in Europe, meeting artists, a life surrounded by music and beauty."

"I can see where it all must seem very seductive," her father said. "But you won't truly be at the center of it, you know. Your claim will always be through your husband's talent."

"Life is very pleasing with this man, Daddy. It's more intense, exciting, richer than it's likely to be with anyone I've ever met or am likely to meet."

"What do you know about his family? Are his parents still living?"

"Neither is. He was brought up in Cincinnati. He was a piano prodigy. They weren't wealthy people. His father worked in the wholesale grocery business. Jacob's mother was the key figure in his life."

Elaine didn't stop to tell her father that, from the age of seven until he was seventeen, Jacob had had a patroness. A wealthy German-Jewish woman in Cincinnati, a Mrs. Loretta Binstock, put him on an allowance of $250 a month, to be used for lessons, private tutoring, clothes for recitals, and other expenses. She also paid his way to the Interlochen music camp in the summers. He was, as Jacob told Elaine, something like her house pet, invited to play for her guests, taught table manners, not infrequently humiliated for his youthful *Ostjuden* crudities. "Mrs. Binstock got her full money's worth" was his final word on the subject.

"So, like you, he's an only child?"

"Yes."

"Only children need lots of attention. I don't worry about where he's going to get his. But where will you get yours?"

"In good part from him, I hope. But do you think I need so much?"

"Truth is, you never did. You were always a good girl. Everything I wanted in a daughter."

"That means a lot to me."

"Sweetheart, you know I only wish you well. All I ask is that you retain your good judgment and remain as thoughtful as you've been all your life. What can the father of an intelligent woman hope but that she not make more than the allotted number of mistakes in a lifetime? You have my blessing."

"I knew I would, Daddy. In time I hope to have your complete approval, too. I hope you'll come to see the quality in Jacob that I do. I don't *hope*, really — I know you will." She covered his hand — his mottled, dry, veiny hand — with her own.

Dr. Goldman met his son-in-law only four times, for he died two years later of a heart attack, three years before the birth of the grandson who was named after him.

Elaine and Jacob were married, in London, a month after her lunch with her father. They had their honeymoon while Jacob played concerts across Europe. She sold her Chicago apartment, with everything in it, and moved into Jacob's large place on West End Avenue in New York. The apartment was dark, stuffed with books and records, and had two grand pianos. Nothing in the life she lived in Chicago had prepared her for life with Jacob.

Elaine soon came to understand that her husband wished to reside on the same august heights as Vladimir Horowitz. He thought of himself as Horowitz's spiritual heir: the pianist as performer, interpreter, creator, quasi-composer. Jacob imagined — he told her as much — that the line from Franz Liszt to Anton Rubinstein to Vladimir Horowitz ended with Jacob Kessler. True, a large number of his contemporaries were impressive in their way — Brendel, Ax, Perahia, and the younger (though no longer very) Serkin among them. Then there were the lesser figures: Dichter, de Larrocha, Watts, and scores of others about whom he need not worry. But none had emerged as the pianist of the age as, even in semi-retirement, Horowitz indisputably still was.

In the early years of their marriage, Elaine went on tour with Jacob to Brussels, Barcelona, Athens, Jerusalem. His easy cosmopolitanism thrilled her. This boy from Cincinnati, once roughly instructed in table manners by a German Jewess whose husband owned a downtown department store, was now utterly at ease in Paris, Rome, and London.

Wherever Jacob played, adulation followed. Audiences adored him; critics tended to agree. Vast applause, large quantities of lovely wine and excellent food, no money worries whatsoever — it was a fine life. "Ah, Mrs. Kessler," the Baroness Rothschild told Elaine one evening at a small dinner party, "your husband is a great artist, among the very greatest, and we are honored to have him here in Paris — and you with him, of course."

Not that life was perpetually so exhilarating. At home, back in New York, there was Jacob's unrelenting schedule of work. He had once told Elaine of a psychologist interested in artistic achievement who asserted that to become an accomplished piano soloist one needed to begin by the age of four and to have practiced ten thousand hours; to begin as late as eight and to have practiced a mere eight thousand hours condemned one to achieving nothing higher than the third rank. Jacob estimated that he must have practiced for something like twelve thousand hours. He had begun, under his mother's supervision, at the age of three. At six, he told Elaine, he had heard Franklin D. Roosevelt, in a radio address, formally declare war on Japan and Germany and announce that every American must now give his all. After turning off the radio, his mother had placed her hands on his little shoulders, looked him in the eye, and said, "Jacob, you have just heard your President say that everyone must help the war effort. What you must do, my son, is practice the piano more than ever."

Jacob practiced mornings, generally from nine to one. He always went reluctantly into the room he called his studio, dawdling over a third cup of coffee, asking for another piece of toast. He practiced in pajamas and robe. Elaine would listen as she moved around the apartment. Sometimes he would play compositions straight through, sometimes he would play a movement or a passage over and over and over again. On occasion, she would hear Jacob curse himself. "Stupid!" he would yell. "Idiot! Get the damn thing right!" One morning when his fingers lost their memory of the opening movement of the Mendelssohn Sonata in G Minor, she smiled as she heard him cry out, "Goddamn Clara Schumann!" At lunch, when she asked, he told her that it was Clara Schumann who had begun the tradition of playing in concert without musical notation, thus forcing all future virtuosi to do likewise. "It damn near drove poor Myra Hess to suicide, you know." Elaine did not know, but it didn't seem to matter.

She would sometimes look in on him during these practice sessions. Unlike in performance, during difficult passages he ground his jaw, waggled his chin, moved his lips. (When asked, he said he was talking to the long-dead composer, checking to see if he got it right.) During more relaxed passages he did a fine thing with his head, holding it high and off to the side. The utter seriousness of it all impressed Elaine immensely. She felt as if she had married a great athlete, but an athlete engaged in the world's most elevated sport. Watching him, she still couldn't believe she was married to this man, let alone was now pregnant by him.

They never really discussed having a baby. After a few years of being careful, they simply did nothing to prevent it. Elaine's pregnancy wasn't easy. Horrendous morning sickness attacked her well past her first trimester. She did not speak much about her illness to Jacob. He was nearly fifty years old, a man with adolescent daughters living on the West Coast and an important career in constant cultivation at home. Going to Lamaze classes with her was out of the question, not even a broachable subject.

How different this pregnancy would have been in Chicago,

Elaine thought. There would have been old friends who had gone through it before or were perhaps going through it now with a third or fourth child. There would have been lunches with much talk about baby clothes and plans for fixing up a nursery. There would no doubt have been a baby shower or two. Elaine missed having her mother to help her through this. Jacob was not unsympathetic, but she understood that — how exactly to put it? — his interest was not fully engaged.

With a career of the kind he had chosen, how could it be? In fact, it turned out that Jacob's agent had arranged a European tour for him during the time that Elaine was to deliver their child. He asked if she wished to travel with him and have the baby in Oslo or Stockholm or Copenhagen. She thought about it and decided, no, it would be better to stay in New York, where she had confidence in her obstetrician, a burly, smiling man who reminded her of one of her father's friends. Jacob offered to cancel the tour. Elaine said absolutely not, though she would have loved it if he had not merely offered but actually done it. When her son was born, Jacob, in Stockholm, sent two dozen long-stemmed roses and a magnum of champagne to the hospital. Elaine, from her hospital bed, wondered with whom he thought she might drink it. She was reminded, too, that he had had an unbreakable concert date in Los Angeles the day of her father's funeral.

Having understood the scope of Jacob's ambition — or at least believing she understood it — Elaine wished she could find a way to help him achieve what he wanted. But she hadn't the foggiest notion how. When she asked, he replied that merely being herself, being always there when he needed her, meant a great deal, really it meant everything. After David was born, she was able to persuade him to move from the West Side. She found a sunnier if slightly less roomy place on East Sixty-fourth, off Park. He agreed to give up his second piano so that a room could be turned into a nursery for their infant son. Elaine handled all the details of the move.

Jacob insisted they hire a nanny. Elaine didn't see the need for it. But he wanted his wife to have the freedom to travel with him when he required her to do so. She wanted to continue breastfeeding, but at the end of three months Jacob asked her to stop; it interfered with their travel plans and cut into their social life. Jacob was attentive to the child, but, after all, he was a man who had been through this not once but twice before with his own daughters. Children and artists did not go entirely smoothly together; in any case, in an artistic household, the needs of the artist, it was understood, came first.

On a day that Jacob was performing, for example, there was his special diet to be seen to: usually yogurt and perhaps a few strips of smoked salmon on very thin, lightly toasted bread. Coming out of his daily practice sessions, he was generally grumpy. Rather than giving him pleasure in his craft, practice reminded Jacob of all the things he wished to achieve at the piano but could not — not quite, or at least not quite well enough. He used to joke — it was barely a joke — that he practiced 364 days a year, and on Yom Kippur he read scores under the bed.

It was not until they were married more than five years that Elaine met Jacob's two daughters. Phoebe and Patricia were fifteen and thirteen, and had been brought up in San Diego, where Jacob's first wife lived. He had paid for their schooling and for most of the other expenses of raising them. Their mother, who played viola in chamber-music groups on the West Coast, had never remarried. The girls were in New York to visit an aunt. They were tallish and fair, thin and awkward. Patsy, as Jacob called the younger, wore complicated braces on both her upper and lower teeth. Phoebe, who had her father's good looks, also inherited some of her parents' musical ability; she played oboe well enough, apparently, to consider doing so professionally.

Both girls were shy, and neither was able to negotiate the menu at the Russian Tea Room, where the head waiter made a great fuss over their father. Jacob ordered blini and caviar for everyone, instructing the girls how to eat it and urging them to get used to the good things in life. Conversation did not flow easily. Elaine, feeling very much the outsider, attempted to question the girls about their schooling, about shopping in New York, and about anything else that came to mind — and not enough did. Their father braved his way through the meal with puns and less than successful jokes. My poor jokey Jakey, Elaine thought, trying so hard to convince them all that they were a normal, happy family. When the lunch was over, Elaine stood near the door of the restaurant as Jacob put the girls in a cab, not hugging but kissing each lightly on both cheeks. Their aunt was taking them to her summer place in New Hampshire and he wouldn't see them again this trip.

After this lunch, Elaine often wondered how Jacob could have walked away from these girls, so fragile, so vulnerable, left in the world to grow up without a father. Her own father, who had been no less preoccupied than Jacob, working with cancer patients whom in most cases he knew he had no hope of saving, had nonetheless managed to convey to Elaine that she made him proud, that at the end of another difficult day the sight of her refreshed him — that despite everything else on his mind, life without her would have been less good.

The two men, Jacob and her father, were of different generations. Men of her father's generation divorced only when they were driven to it. Without Jacob's divorces, of course, Elaine would never have come into his life, nor would their beautiful son exist. Still, there were those two girls, with their thin legs, shyness, and braces, who were being asked to pay the price for her happiness.

And she was happy. She had her son and she had her much admired husband. Mrs. Jacob Kessler was not at all a bad thing to be. On the stage, at his piano, Jacob Kessler had magic in his hands, and so abundant was it that some of this magic seemed almost to have rubbed off on her. The young woman at Vidal Sassoon who gave Elaine her manicures, and whose brother was taking piano lessons in Rego Park, one day asked that she autograph the liner notes of Jacob's most recent CD: "'To Jimmy,' if you don't mind." Embarrassed, Elaine nevertheless signed.

"*Ja,*" a sleepy voice on the other end answered.

"Jacob?" Elaine asked.

"One moment."

"Jacob?"

"Elaine?"

"Who was that who answered the phone?"

"That was the maid, dear, come to turn down the bed. It's nearly midnight in Amsterdam. How are you?"

"I'm fine, Jacob. Everything here's fine. How goes the week?"

"With Yervi all goes smoothly. The Concertgebouw remains a pleasure to work with. How's David?"

"He's fine. I hadn't realized it was so late. You'd think I'd have European times down by now."

"Not to worry, darling. Why don't I call you tomorrow?"

"Yes, do call. I love you."

"I you."

Elaine couldn't get that voice out of her mind. It had spoken only three words — "*Ja*" and "One moment" — yet in neither intonation nor logic did they seem the words of a chamber-maid. She played them over and over in her mind. Why did the voice sound so sleepy? Would a maid really say "One moment" and promptly hand the phone to her husband? Would a maid even answer the telephone when a guest was in the room? The more Elaine thought, the more dubious the whole thing became.

She decided not to confront Jacob with her suspicions — more than suspicions, really. She felt she had arrived at this decision in the name of peacekeeping, in the spirit of forgive and forget. Confronting Jacob would do no good — he would only deny it all, he would act hurt — and it might even end their marriage. Disappointed though she was, Elaine was not ready to write *finis* to this union. Besides, there was David to consider. Should she deprive her little boy of his father just because she couldn't bear the thought — the fact — of his unfaithfulness? Of course not.

Elaine also had to recognize the possibility that she didn't want the marriage to end for her own sake. Divorce, dress it up any way you like, always meant failure, and she wasn't ready to admit defeat. She wasn't ready to become the third Mrs. Jacob Kessler. She preferred being the current — make that the final — Mrs. Jacob Kessler. She never mentioned the Amsterdam call to her husband. But a few months later, when Jacob sat down at the piano with their young son to test his pitch, and afterward reported that David had no special gift for music, Elaine, for reasons not altogether clear to her, was secretly pleased.

Her marriage became a lie of convenience; a lie, at any rate, was at the center of it. Other marriages survived with other lies at their centers. Men and women grew disappointed with each other; passion grew stale; small, once mildly irritating habits over the years drove husbands and wives nearly crazy with distaste. Still, all these people stayed with what they had. They played on through. As, Elaine was determined, would she. If her husband felt the need occasionally to sleep with another woman, so long as he did so discreetly, well, let him. Jacob Kessler was not after all an ordinary man; his moods, his needs, his life — all were somehow different.

Elaine, then, was prepared to live with things. A kind of forbearance was called for; so were certain actressy qualities. She surprised herself at how many of these qualities she had. At the breakfast table, at social engagements, even in bed she easily enough pretended that nothing was wrong, nothing had changed. She discovered that she was more than a bit of an artist herself.

The evening Jacob played at the White House Elaine knew she had made the correct decision. It was still a good, an interesting, life. The First Lady, whom she sat next to at the concert, confided that Jacob Kessler was far and away her favorite among the pianists of his generation. She asked Elaine about her own musical background. "Me," Elaine found herself answering, "oh, I used to play the cello, but no longer."

Subtly, almost imperceptibly, the center of gravity in Elaine's marriage began to shift from her husband to her son. There was, after all, so little that she could do for Jacob and so much for David. She continued to take an interest in Jacob's career, sharing concern about his newest recordings, his concert dates, the scuttlebutt about other pianists — "the competition," as Jacob only half jokingly called them. But less and less did she travel with her husband, who himself seemed less and less to require her companionship. She assumed that on the road he found ways to look after his own needs, all of them. She didn't like to think about it. In the end, he returned to her and their son, that was the main thing. Things were under control. And so they remained for more than a year.

The morning after the night Jacob learned he had won a Grammy for his six-CD recording of the Beethoven sonatas, which critics were comparing to Schnabel's, a morning on which Jacob planned to celebrate by abstaining from practice and instead taking his son out to the park, began badly. It was nine-thirty. David was off in his room, his Filipino nanny, Mrs. Ramirez, helping him dress.

"Elaine," Jacob began, "I fear I have some dreary news."

"Which is?" she asked, looking up from the paper, a cup of coffee in her hand.

"Our marriage is over."

Her half-full cup slipped from her hand, the coffee sluicing off the table onto the Oriental rug she had picked out with such care. "I'm sorry," she said, "what did you say?"

"Over," Jacob said. "I've committed myself to someone else."

"What about your commitment to me and to your son?"

"There'll be money to take care of you both."

"I don't think money's the issue here, Jacob."

"No, the issue is my career, in which, it seems to me, you long ago lost interest."

"That's not true," Elaine said, not very authoritatively.

"I think it is. Besides, you must have known coming into this marriage what the arrangements were."

"I thought I did. Maybe I was mistaken. Repeat them for me, please."

"I'll give you the short form. My career comes first. You had to know that."

"Your sleeping with other women, in Amsterdam and God knows where else, is that also part of the arrangement?"

"An artist has certain needs. Whatever is good for his art is good for him. The world is organized for the creation of art, and nothing else matters. I know this idea is probably repugnant to you, but it's my view — and I'm stuck with it."

Elaine knew that the next utterance, should she dare make it, would mark the end of her marriage. She couldn't hold it back.

"But you just play the music," she said, hearing her own heart pounding, "you don't compose it. Faustian bargains aren't available to piano players, you idiot."

Jacob didn't answer. He turned away. At just that moment David and Mrs. Ramirez entered the room. David was wearing a sailor suit. Jacob swept the boy, who looked so much like him, into his arms and headed for the door.

"We'll return in an hour or so," he called, without looking back.

It turned out that the woman for whom Jacob left Elaine and David was Irish, twenty-three, and a flautist with the Bournemouth Symphony Orchestra. Her name was Meagan O'Donnell. As with Jacob's two earlier wives, Elaine never met her. She would from time to time see pictures of the two of them in the fashion press, at a charity ball or benefit.

Jacob gave her no difficulty about the divorce. She came away with the equity in the New York apartment and $7,000 a month in combined alimony and child support as well as an agreement that Jacob would pay the expenses for his son's education. This, added to the money she had inherited from her father, left her free from financial worry. Because of his traveling schedule, Jacob asked for no regular visitation rights and accepted Elaine's assurance that he would be able to see the boy whenever it was convenient for him.

It turned out not to be very convenient, at any rate not very often. After Elaine sold the apartment, she and David moved back to Chicago. They lived on State Parkway, near North Avenue, and David, when five years old, was sent to Francis Parker, a private school on the Near North Side. He was a cheerful child. Whenever his father played in Chicago, David and Jacob went off for an afternoon, and the boy returned a bit agitated but nothing worse. The effect on him of growing up without a father seemed to Elaine, in cooler moments, perhaps not so awful as she had expected — at least not yet.

When she first returned to Chicago, she thought she might involve herself in the musical life of the city: do volunteer work for the Chicago Symphony or the Lyric Opera, or get herself on the board of Music of the Baroque or one of the other institutions in town. But thinking further, she decided against it. When David was old enough to go to school full time, she returned to her job at Leo Burnett. She never again went to hear Jacob play.

From time to time she went out with men, most of them in their fifties or early sixties, the majority divorced or widowed. At work and elsewhere she was known as Elaine Goldman Kessler. Once, when a man named Sheldon Hefferman, who owned a number of car washes around the city, took her to dinner and asked her what her former husband did, she replied, "Oh, he was in the music business," and let it go at that. Although she never directly announced it to herself or to anyone else, Elaine sensed that she would probably never remarry. She had had her interesting life — more interesting than most — and now it was over.

Moe

"DINOSAURS," Lou Levin said. "Let's face it, we're a pack of goddamn dinosaurs."

"What's that supposed to mean?" Irv Brodsky asked.

"It means," said Levin, "that guys like us are destined no longer to appear on the face of the earth. We're soon to be extinct. The way we think, the way we act, Jesus, even handball, the game we play, is on its way out. Nobody under sixty plays this game anymore."

Slowly slipping off his knee brace, Moe Bernstein, though he didn't say anything, tended to agree. None of the sporting goods stores carried handballs any longer; you couldn't find a proper pair of gloves anywhere in the whole city. Only here at the Horwich Jewish Community Center was there equipment for the game he and his friends loved.

Once upon a time, handball was a game for serious athletes, real gym rats. You had to develop both your left and right hands, which not everyone, even the best athletes in other sports, could do. Most players were stocky, the better not to be pushed around on the court. Moe himself was five foot five and weighed 180 pounds, thick in the legs, barrel-chested, a real handball build. He still thought of himself as being in good shape, even though breathing came heavier now and he and his friends confined themselves to playing doubles, and for only an hour at that.

"Lou's right," Sid Melman chimed in. "It's another world. I was telling Sam Kantor, my broker, the other day about my niece. She announced she's converting to Catholicism. 'Don't complain,' he says to me. 'My own daughter, at thirty-three, last week tells my wife that she's a lesbian and is moving in with another broad. Next to lesbian, Catholicism is nice, Buddhism is nice. Shit, I'd take Islam before lesbian.'"

"That," said Levin, "is precisely why you're a dinosaur, Sidney."

"Up yours, Louie."

"Said like a true *alte kocker*," replied Levin. "Look, boys, the rules have been changed. We got caught in the switch. Everyone now can do what he likes. It's open season on everything. Delay no desire. Stop saving. Stick it anywhere you please. Walk away from any mess, any time. All this comes a little late for us, but whose fault is that?"

Stuffing his gear — jock, shorts, gym shoes, sweat socks, gloves, knee brace — into his gym bag, Bernstein could have contributed his own stories to the conversation, his own chronicles of the brave new world they all lived in, but decided against it. What was the point? Levin was probably right. They were dinosaurs, Moe included. He felt the calluses on his hands, mementos of half a century of swatting balls around YMCA and JCC courts all over Chicago. Even his hands marked him as a dinosaur — but at least he was a dinosaur who still had a great kill shot.

Bernstein drove his Buick, a Park Avenue, the five blocks from the JCC to his house on Fargo. He had kept the house after Sylvia died four years ago, though what he needed with three bedrooms, two baths, and a finished basement he couldn't say. It seemed like too much trouble to move. Besides, he didn't mind mowing the lawn in spring and summer; in the autumn there were the leaves to rake; and he still had the back muscles for shoveling snow, though this past winter he had begun to feel it.

The neighborhood was changing, but still safe. Korean families lived in the houses on either side of his, and an Indian physician, an anesthesiologist, lived across the way; his wife walked the neighborhood in saris. On Devon, once the main hub of shopping in the neighborhood, the Indians had taken over much of the retail business east of California Avenue — many sari palaces, as they called them — while west of California the ultra-Orthodox Jews dominated. The tonier Jews had long since departed, to Lincolnwood and Highland Park and Glencoe.

Nothing of interest in the mail: bills, catalogues, charity appeals, the usual junk. You want to get letters, Bernstein reminded himself, you have to write letters. Who today wrote letters? You called long-distance or faxed or e-mailed. He had decided to take a pass on the whole computer thing; at sixty-seven, he figured he was close enough to the grave to get away with it. He had thought about carrying around a cell phone, but decided not to.

He did have a VCR, which he used occasionally to record a Bears game when he was going to be out of the house. When he first got it, he rented movies, mostly the old ones he had grown up with, the Bogarts and Fred Astaires, William Powells and James Cagneys and Spencer Tracys, but he soon lost interest. Television news and the Cubs and Bears and Bulls gave him all the entertainment he needed. Most nights he went to bed before ten anyhow.

Bernstein popped a Stouffer's frozen lasagna into the oven,

then, gym bag in hand, walked upstairs. The room next to the master bedroom he had fixed up for his grandson, Nathaniel, soon after he was born, though the kid almost never used it. Bernstein had put Big Ten pennants on the walls along with a blown-up photograph of Walter Payton somersaulting into the end zone against the Packers and another of Babe Ruth finishing a home-run swing. In a bookcase were a few of his handball trophies, a copy of Abram Sachar's *History of the Jews,* and a plaque from the Israel Bonds office with Bernstein's first name, Morris, misspelled Maurice.

He had never bothered to redecorate the master bedroom after his wife's death, and so it remained essentially a woman's room, with gauzy curtains, prints of French ladies in gold frames, great lacy throw pillows over the flowery bedspread, and a frilly ruffle on the bed. His thick body slept alone in that feminine double bed. Whole days went by now when Bernstein forgot to think of Sylvia. They had been married forty-two years when she died. Sometimes, out in the car, at odd times of the day, he would try to recall her face and, concentrate though he might, he could not summon it up. After Bernstein himself died, there would be no one left to summon up his own. There was his son, of course, and there was his grandson, but he doubted he was likely to be on the mind of either for very long.

When the Stouffer's was ready, Bernstein fixed himself a salad of iceberg lettuce, which he covered with Kraft Thousand Island dressing, poured a glass of ginger ale, and took it all into the den. Setting it on a TV table before his favorite chair, he turned on the local six o'clock news and ate to the accompaniment of stories about West Side murders, South Side arsons, Northwest Side juvenile-gang warfare, and, for comic relief, political scandals. At the break after the weather, he returned to the kitchen to cut a slice of Sara Lee cheesecake, which he ate while watching the sports news.

After washing the dishes, Bernstein transferred himself to the couch to watch the Cubs-Mets game. It had, he thought, lighting a cigar, been a pretty good day. For the past thirty-four years Bernstein had been a salesman for Toledo Scale and had made a good living. Good enough, at any rate, to buy this house, send his son through college and law school, never drive a car more than three years old, and — himself a child of the Depression, and hence always a careful saver — live without any real financial worry. He no longer had to scramble for business the way he once did. He continued to service his old accounts, mostly butcher shops, looking after repairs and temporary replacements, updating old equipment, selling scale stickers and register tapes. He had notified the home office that he would take retirement at seventy, less than three years away.

Bernstein had started off the day by dropping in on Mikhail Petrovich, a Ukrainian butcher who had been using an antiquated machine, originally produced in 1948, which he took over when he bought the shop and which had finally broken down completely. With scarcely any effort on Bernstein's part, Petrovich had bought a $4,600 scale, the biggest-ticket item in Bernstein's line. After writing up the order, on the way out of the shop, he heard Petrovich, in his greenhorn accent, say to his assistant, "You know, I wake this morning, I never dream I buy scale."

Bernstein unlaced his shoes, put out his cigar, propped a pillow behind his head, and let his mind wander, the Cubs game playing in the background. His mind drifted to his son. He had never really approved of the kid's marriage to begin with. The girl wasn't his cup of tea. She was pretentious, hipped on psychology; he could never feel close to her. And the mother was even worse. Before marrying a woman, it's always a good idea to have a close look at the mother, so you see what's in store.

Much as he had wanted to alert his son to steer clear, Sylvia warned him against doing so. Besides, even though Norman was his only child, Bernstein had not been that close to the boy. He couldn't tell you why, but they never had the kind of relationship where the father could have slipped his arm around the son and said, "Look, Normie, you're in some pretty serious trouble here. These women are crushers. No one's got you in a hammerlock. Cut and run while there's still time. I'll cover you. I'll take some of the flak. Say your old man doesn't want you to marry so young. Make up any story you like. I'll back you all the way."

Of course, Bernstein thought at the time, he could be wrong. Nothing harder to figure than marriages. All begin in sexual attraction and most end in personal irritation. Yet sometimes the most impossible combinations, marriages you would have thought had no chance, worked out just fine. So Bernstein didn't say a word; he went along with the show.

And quite a show it was. The Shapiros must have spent no less than eighty grand on their daughter's wedding — like Norman, Deborah was an only child. Seymour Shapiro, a lawyer specializing in personal injury, turned a big buck. Bernstein would never forget the fuss Miriam Shapiro made when the rabbi showed up at the Drake Hotel without the *huppah*. He remembered the rabbi muttering something to the effect that the less religion people had, the more they insisted on the niceties. The bridal couple had written their own vows, of which Bernstein could now recall nothing except that he had shuddered while listening to them. He did remember that the rabbi, from a Reform temple in Glencoe, spoke with an English accent and seemed to get seven or eight syllables into his pronunciation of the word "Israel."

The kids, Norman and Deborah, appeared to get on well enough. Norman finished law school. Deborah taught "exceptional children," which Bernstein later learned meant that they had big problems. She called Bernstein "Dad," but it never felt quite right. Three years they waited to have a child of their own. When they wanted to move from the city to Highland Park, Norman came to his father to ask for a loan of twenty-five grand to help with the down payment, and of course Bernstein lent him the money, no interest.

Bernstein should have sensed trouble when Norman showed up one day wearing a mustache. It was brown and so luxuriously thick it looked as though it might be made of mink. Bernstein restrained himself from mocking the boy, but he couldn't take this seriously. "Norman," he wanted to say, "you planning to store that mustache with Traeger the furrier in the summer?" Soon Norman began to show up in Italian suits, double-breasted jobs, with ample shoulders; the suits went, Bernstein understood, for a grand apiece. He wore loafers with gold chains. A funny way for a lawyer to dress.

It was at the Passover Seder at the Bernstein home that Moe first realized trouble was brewing. Between the fish and the soup, his daughter-in-law began to cry and had to leave the room. His son excused himself, then came back ten minutes later to say he was sorry but they would have to leave, Debbie was so upset. In some panic himself, Norman told his parents he would call later to explain. Nathaniel was not yet two at the time.

What Norman had to explain was that he was leaving his wife and moving to Seattle with a young paralegal in the office, a girl named Lisa Podolfski. When Bernstein asked his son if he had thought this through, Norman replied, with some impatience in his voice, of course he had. When Bernstein next asked if he was prepared to accept his responsibilities as a father, Norman countered that he would do everything he could at a distance of two thousand miles. Why Seattle? Bernstein wanted to know. Because, Norman explained, he had lined up a job with an important law firm there. And besides, it was a beautiful city, one of the prettiest in America.

As a lawyer, Norman had to know that the Shapiros were a family that played hardball. Bernstein reminded him that no injury was more personal than divorce; they weren't about to let him off the hook. Miriam Shapiro would want to exact vengeance, see that her ex–son-in-law paid till it hurt. There were ways of fighting that, Norman replied. He wasn't himself a lawyer for nothing.

The long and short of it was that a year and a half after Norman left his wife, his new lady friend had left him. Two years later, he stopped coming to Chicago for his regular legal visitations with his son: a month in the summer, a week in the spring, another week at Christmas. As far as Bernstein knew, Norman kept up alimony and child support, but he had cut himself emotionally free. He claimed the visits with the boy were too stressful — that was the word he used, stressful. And besides, he said, Nathaniel's mother and grandmother had poisoned the boy against him.

At Sylvia's funeral, Norman told Bernstein that of course he had a bad conscience about Nathaniel, but what was he supposed to do? He brought along with him a young woman with blond hair flowing down her back named Yolanda with whom he was living at the time. He had a permanent and was wearing a gold chain around his neck. Norman, thought Bernstein at the time, Norman, my son and heir, you are a phony and a royal putz.

Bernstein awoke with a jolt and a sour taste in his mouth. Indigestion? Heartburn? He had difficulty swallowing. His left arm felt numb. Everyone knew this left-arm business was the first sign of a heart attack, so he had to be careful he wasn't imagining symptoms that weren't really there. He rose from the couch. He was all right on his feet, not shaky or anything. But the sour taste wouldn't go away, even after he had walked into the kitchen and rinsed out his mouth. The constricted feeling in his chest, caused by heartburn or heart attack or some hot peppers he had had for lunch or whatever the hell it was, refused to go away. Breathing wasn't easy. He slipped into his pants and, in some pain, bent over to lace his shoes.

The nearest hospital was St. Francis, in Evanston. Bernstein decided not to call an ambulance but to drive. He did so easily enough, though the traffic light at Western and Howard seemed to last for a goddamn ice age. He heard a voice say, in Petrovich's greenhorn accent, "I wake this morning, I never dream I have heart attack." He parked on the street and walked into St. Francis through the front door, asking the way to the emergency room. The numbness in his left arm and shoulder seemed so insistent as to be humming.

A resident and a nurse strapped him to an EKG machine, which revealed that his heartbeat was irregular, though only slightly so. They gave him some pills. They suggested he stay the night for more tests, which he agreed to do. The next afternoon a cardiologist named Arnold Meyers, a man in his forties who seemed too well dressed and who knew his son's former in-laws, recommended that Bernstein undergo a bypass operation. His heart attack — yes, it had been a heart attack all right — was a minor one, but a harbinger of worse to come.

"What if I do nothing?" Bernstein asked. He saw all those men walking around the Horwich Center with their elaborate, zipper-like scars: up the leg where the vein had been taken out, down the chest where it had been sewn in. He'd heard stories about the postoperative depression a lot of guys went through. And then there were the guys who died on the operating table.

"If you do nothing," said Dr. Meyers, more than a touch of

menace in his voice, "you are likely to die sometime within the next two or three years. You figure to have a number of these attacks, to grow weaker and weaker, and, owing to the absence of oxygen getting to your heart and finally to your brain because of your clogged arteries, a final stroke or heart attack will take you."

"How soon you want to do this surgery?" Bernstein asked.

"The sooner the better, of course. But it's probably best not to put it off for more than a few weeks. Fortunately, this last little attack — and there may have been others — did not do damage of a kind serious enough to prevent surgery."

"I'll get back to you," Bernstein said, buttoning his shirt and eager to be the hell out of the hospital.

Before he reached home — less, that is, than twenty minutes later — Bernstein had decided not to go ahead with the surgery. What did he need it for? He didn't feel like putting himself through the ordeal, and he didn't feel like changing the way he lived, which this young doctor claimed he would have to do even if the surgery succeeded. Heart attack or stroke, when you came to think about it, weren't bad ways to go. Both beat slow cancer deaths, let alone an extended nightmare like Alzheimer's.

Bernstein was alone in the world. Nobody depended on him. He'd had his innings; he'd had a pretty good roll of the dice. So he wouldn't get to eighty — the age at which his father died and which he had always thought he would reach. But he had a shot at seventy: three score and ten, the traditional biblical life span. No need to be a pig. He would settle for seventy.

At home, Bernstein popped in a Stouffer's Salisbury steak, opened a small can of corn Niblets, another of stewed tomatoes, which he set to warming on the stove. He checked the calls on his answering machine. Only one, from his former daughter-in-law, Deborah. "Dad," the message went, "I could use your help this weekend with Nathaniel. Please call when you have a free moment."

While his steak was still in the oven, Bernstein dialed Deborah.

"Oh, hi, Dad," she said in her slightly distracted way. "You got my message?"

"Of course," said Bernstein. "What is it? Nothing wrong with the boy?"

"Nothing at all. Why I called is that I've been invited to spend this weekend with friends in Wisconsin, at Green Lake, and there aren't going to be any children there. My parents are in Palm Springs. And I was wondering, if you're free, if maybe Nathaniel could stay with you."

"Sure," Bernstein said. "When do you need me to pick him up?"

"It would be great if you could come get him on Friday afternoon. I'll be back by early Sunday evening."

"No big problem," Bernstein said.

"Thanks a million, Dad. You're a lifesaver."

That Friday afternoon, on his way to pick up his grandson, driving out to Highland Park along Sheridan Road, the fine trees forming a tunnel overhead, the mansions on the lake side of the street seeming as impressive as ever, Bernstein thought about his death. Now that he had made the decision to forgo surgery, the weather, which he had never been all that concerned about, somehow seemed more important. His days, he now knew, were numbered, and he wondered what their final tally might be: 396, 582, 712? He hoped that when the moment came he might be at home, alone, no hospitals, no tubes in his nose or catheters up his gazoo. If he was lucky, he would expire without too great a struggle: a choke, a cough, a battle for breath, over and out.

His business was in order. He had a will. He had an insurance policy worth two hundred grand. He had another hundred and fifty grand and change in savings, mostly in CDs and Israel bonds. Bernstein didn't think the stock market was for little guys like him, and so had stayed away from it. His house was worth maybe another hundred and a half. All this would go to his son. It would buy a lot of Italian suits and loafers — buy lots of dinners for lots of Yolandas. Bernstein didn't much like to linger on the subject.

As for what waited on the other side, there was, Bernstein assumed, nothing. Lights out. Oblivion. End of story. He was someone who had honored his religion without observing it. He had put Norman through Hebrew school, just as he had himself gone as a boy, but the truth was he never could visualize either God or heaven. Yet, he now thought, he had always acted as if there were a God. He had tried to be hardworking, faithful, honorable, decent, within what you might call big-city limits. He was no angel, but neither was he a bastard. He tried to do what was right. What was disappointing, as he now thought about it, was that he hadn't made any real difference to anyone else's life. Not even to Sylvia, who was very self-sufficient and who, had she not met and married Moe Bernstein, would probably have had a similar life with someone else.

Bernstein parked his Buick at the side of his daughter-in-law's house, the same house for which he had lent his son twenty-five grand for the down payment. Two Mexicans were working in the yard. Deborah's red Toyota was in the open garage.

"Oh, hi, Dad," Deborah said when she came to the door. She

put out her cheek for Bernstein to kiss. They were a very kissy family, the Shapiros. Bernstein was not from the kissers and huggers, and always found greeting his ex–daughter-in-law a bit awkward.

Deborah, now in her mid-thirties, was starting to show her mileage, mostly around the eyes, which looked to Bernstein sad and tired. A woman raising a little boy alone had no picnic; Bernstein, though he did not care much for Debbie, allowed her this much.

"How go things with Norman?" she asked when Bernstein had come in.

"He's pretty well," Bernstein said, knowing this line of questioning was as unpromising as it was inevitable. "You know Norman."

"Yeah," she said, "I know Norman."

"Where's Natey?"

"Nobody ever calls him that," she reminded him.

"So what do I call him?"

"Nathaniel," she said. "Everybody calls him Nathaniel."

She called her son to come down, handing Bernstein a small suitcase she had packed for him. She also gave him a bottle of pills for Nathaniel's allergies and a piece of paper with a telephone number where, in case of a crisis, she could be reached. Bernstein had long ago been informed that Nathaniel was allergic to grass and dust. There wasn't much to be done about it. Apart from building the kid a cottage on the moon, or letting him live in an igloo, he was always going to be vulnerable.

Vulnerable is how Nathaniel looked as he came down the stairs. He was thin, he wore glasses, and as if — toss in his allergies — that weren't enough, this past winter he had had braces put on his upper teeth.

"Hi, Grandpa," the boy said.

"How are you, son?" Bernstein replied. "Ready to live the hard bachelor life with your grandfather?"

"I guess so." Nathaniel did not sound very enthusiastic.

"Kiss your mother goodbye," Deborah said, "and don't forget to take your allergy pills. Grandpa's got them."

Bernstein noted the boy's scrawniness, in his T-shirt and shorts, as he permitted himself to be hugged by his mother. Bernstein waited outside, a few steps down the walk, to avoid the awkwardness of another kiss from his former daughter-in-law.

"Thanks again, Dad," Deborah said. "I'm really very grateful."

In the car, Bernstein didn't have to tell his grandson to buckle up; the boy did it automatically. He was a withdrawn kid. On the way back home, Bernstein asked a number of questions that didn't seem to lead anywhere. Was he looking forward to going back to school in a few weeks? What were his current interests? What was the meaning of the turtles on his shirt? As Nathaniel explained the mysteries of the Ninja, Bernstein's eyes began to glaze. It occurred to him that he would not be alive to see this boy turn thirteen.

They stopped to pick up a few videos, and at home Bernstein put a couple of chicken pot pies in the oven. He asked Nathaniel if he'd like a glass of ginger ale, but the boy said he'd prefer milk, which Bernstein didn't keep in the house; he gave him orange juice instead. After dinner, they ate ice cream in the den, where the cartoon videos Nathaniel had selected quickly put Bernstein to sleep.

"Grandpa," Nathaniel said, "Grandpa, better get up. It's eleven o'clock."

Bernstein awoke in a daze. Nathaniel had already taken the videos out of the VCR and removed and washed their ice cream dishes. He was, Bernstein began to sense, used to looking after himself. His mother, who had long ago left teaching and now worked as an interior decorator, wasn't always home when he returned from school.

Nathaniel slept in pajamas, Bernstein in a Lawson YMCA T-shirt and his boxer shorts. He put Nathaniel in the bedroom with the Walter Payton and Babe Ruth photographs. Tucking the boy into bed, Bernstein wasn't sure whether or not he was supposed to kiss him goodnight. But as he put his grandson's glasses on the night table, he leaned down and kissed his forehead.

"Night, Grandpa."

"Night, kid," Bernstein said. "Don't let the bedbugs bite."

"What's that mean?"

"It's a long story, kiddo. It goes back to when people were poor and didn't always live in the best conditions. I'll explain in the morning. Sleep well."

At 2:37 by his digital clock, Bernstein awoke to the sound of sobbing. He found his grandson crying in his sleep. Instead of turning on the light, he picked the boy up and brought him into his own room, setting him down on the bed as gently as he could so as not to wake him.

"O.K., sweetheart," said Bernstein, lightly patting his grandson's back with his callused hands, "it's O.K., nothing to worry about. Your grandpa's with you. Nothing bad's going to happen."

Soon the sobbing stopped. Bernstein lay down next to the boy and slipped his arm around him. His thick hairy arm touched the boy's ribs. God, the kid is thin — this was Bernstein's last thought before he fell off to sleep.

Next morning Bernstein rose at his usual six o'clock and, before showering, ducked out to the Jewel to pick up some milk, hot dogs and buns, and potato chips. He also bought a pound of corned beef and a rye bread in the deli section.

When he returned home, Nathaniel was awake. "Grandpa," he called out as Bernstein came in through the back door. He was sitting in front of the television, watching cartoons in his pajamas and robe.

"How did I get in your bed last night?"

"I was wondering that myself," Bernstein said. "I'll bet you sleepwalked. I was glad to have you there, though. It was cold for a summer night. Now what d'you want for breakfast? How about I scramble up some eggs for us? Or make French toast? Your grandma taught me years ago to make very good French toast."

"I've already had my eggs for the week," Nathaniel said.

"How many do you have?"

"Mommy doesn't think it's a good idea to eat more than two eggs a week. She watches our diets."

"What can you eat?"

"How about some juice and toast and yogurt?" said the boy.

Nathaniel ate his toast without butter. Bernstein had no yogurt in the house. After they both showered, Bernstein asked his grandson to help him mow the lawn, but soon saw that the boy didn't have much strength or endurance. When Bernstein asked if he wanted a Coke with his lunch, Nathaniel said he'd prefer Perrier, which Bernstein didn't have. The kid just nibbled on the corned beef sandwich Bernstein made. His stomach was easily upset, he confided, and he wasn't supposed to eat spicy foods.

The Cubs were out of town, but through his friend Irv Brodsky, Bernstein had been able to get a couple of tickets to the White Sox game that night. Nathaniel was not exactly thrilled at the prospect. Bernstein knew the kid wasn't much of an athlete, but now he learned he had no interest even in watching sports. The only things he played, it seemed, were computer games.

"Your dad is a big sports fan, you know," Bernstein told him. "When he was a kid he knew everything there was to know about every active player in both leagues and a lot about some players long dead."

"I guess I didn't know that," the boy said.

Bernstein remembered that Norman had left when Nathaniel was only two. His other grandfather apparently hadn't spent all that much time with him either, and after the divorce Bernstein, too, had drifted away, the ambiguities of dealing with your son's ex-wife being too complicated for him, especially after Sylvia died. He sent his grandson a birthday gift, gave him another at Hanukkah, and saw him at most four or five times a year. Sometimes he would have a guilty conscience and would telephone, but the conversations were always unsatisfactory. Like the other men in Nathaniel's life, Bernstein, too, had checked out.

"Look," he now said. "We don't have to go."

"It's up to you, Grandpa."

"No, Natey, it's up to you. I want you to enjoy yourself. How about we go out to dinner and rent another movie? Does that sound good?"

"Fine, Grandpa," the boy said, looking up through his thick glasses. Bernstein had the feeling that his grandson was accommodating him, not the other way around, and felt a surge of love for the boy. He found himself wondering how things might turn out if he, Bernstein, were to raise him. He would do a damn sight better than his mother or than he himself had done with his own son. He imagined taking the boy with him to a place like Arizona, where no one knew either of them, and teaching him all he knew about being a man and surviving in a tough world. But this was pure fantasy, not something Bernstein normally allowed himself to indulge in.

They ate at a Greek restaurant on West Devon, in Lincolnwood, after stopping to pick up an old Lassie movie. At dinner Bernstein told Nathaniel about all the great animal movies he remembered from his youth: *Rin Tin Tin, Lassie, My Friend Flicka,* and others whose names he couldn't now recall. At home, he was surprised to learn that the hero of the video they had rented was a young Peter Lawford — in later life, apparently, a stooge for Frank Sinatra and a procurer for President Kennedy. Wonderful English accent, though.

"Grandpa, Grandpa," Nathaniel said, rousing Bernstein gently. Once again he had fallen asleep, and once again the boy had rewound and taken out the cassette.

"Did things work out O.K., Natey?" Bernstein asked. "Lassie get home all right?"

"Yeah, Grandpa," the boy reported seriously, "it all worked out fine."

Upstairs, they brushed their teeth together, the boy in his pajamas, Bernstein in a T-shirt that read *B'nai B'rith Handball Championships, Men's Seniors, 1979.* Nathaniel asked for dental floss, but Bernstein had none. He made a mental note to stock the joint with yogurt, Perrier, and dental floss for his grandson's next visit. He wanted to ask if Nathaniel would like to sleep in his bed, but decided not to lest the boy think his grandfather was babying him.

Bernstein awoke on Sunday morning, the sun shining into his room, the acrid smell of urine in his nostrils. Nathaniel's room was empty, the sheets stripped from the bed. He called out his name, and the boy answered from the basement. There, in his Jockey shorts, a sharp bone protruding in a little bump from each of his shoulder blades, Nathaniel stood near the washing machine, trembling. A wash was already churning away.

"I had an accident, Grandpa," he said remorsefully.

"I see that," Bernstein replied. "Are you O.K.?"

"Yeah," said Nathaniel. "I'm O.K. I'm sorry I made a mess."

"Don't worry about it," Bernstein said. "C'mon upstairs, I'll give you something to wear."

Back in the kitchen, Bernstein poured orange juice for the boy, who was swimming in his grandfather's Detroit Senior Nationals T-shirt.

"Natey," said Bernstein, "does this happen to you often?"

"Just every once in a while," said the boy. "Dr. Holtzman tells Mommy it's nothing to worry about."

"Dr. Holtzman?"

"She's Mommy's therapist. Mine, too."

"You see a therapist?"

"Yes."

"For how long has this been?"

"Three years."

"How often?"

"Just once a week."

"What do you talk about?"

"Mostly about my missing not having a father and stuff."

"But you have a father."

"You know what I mean."

Again Bernstein had a desire to pick the boy up, load him into the Buick, and just drive off. They'd buy clothes later. He'd take over the job his own son had quit. Toward this child with his glasses and braces, this bed wetter and sobber in his sleep, worried at age eight about his diet and already seeing a therapist, toward this small bundle of bones and anxieties, not the sort of grandchild he would ever have imagined having, Bernstein felt a stab of protective love such as he had never felt be-

fore in his life. Listening to his grandson recount his sessions
with the therapist, Bernstein went foggy in the eye and had to
hold back the desire to weep.

A handball game had been scheduled that afternoon, and so
Bernstein took Nathaniel along with him to the Horwich Center. He introduced him to Levin and Brodsky and Melman.

"How are ya, Nate?" Brodsky asked. "Gonna be a handball
player like your grandpa?"

"Probably not," the boy answered humorlessly.

"I suppose a handball genius like your grandfather comes
along only every four generations or so," said Lou Levin.

"He's teasing me, not you, Natey," Bernstein said. "I'll make
him pay for it on the court in a minute or two."

The four old athletes suited up for their game, slipping into
their jocks and sweat socks, shorts and sneakers, putting on
their special bandages and supports: Bernstein his knee brace,
Melman a pad for his left elbow, Brodsky an Ace bandage
around the thigh, Levin his corset for a back that tended to go
out on him.

After whapping the ball around for a half-hour or so, Bernstein took one low off the back wall with his left hand and
zapped it crosscourt into the crease of the front wall on the
right — a zinger, a winner, a beauty. He looked up to the bal-
cony where his grandson stood watching. Bernstein waved,
the boy waved back, flashing a dark smile with his wired-up
teeth. "Great shot, Grandpa," the child yelled. Bernstein's heart
jumped.

Later that afternoon, driving Nathaniel home, impressed as always with the lushness and wealth of Sheridan Road along the
North Shore, Bernstein could not help thinking of all the secret miseries, small and large, that must reside in these vast
homes with their tennis courts, German cars, and healthy-look-

ing daughters with suntanned legs. People passing his own ex–
daughter-in-law's house, with its manicured landscaping, could
not know that it sheltered a sweet and sadly screwed-up little
boy.

"You know, Natey," Bernstein said, "I was fourteen when my
father died. So I know a little bit about living without a father.
Maybe not as much as you, but a little bit."

"Did you love him, Grandpa?"

"I guess I did, but you know, Natey, I never really saw all that
much of him. He was from the old country, Russia, and he
worked in the produce market on Fulton Street. He used to go
to work at four in the morning. When he'd come back at four
or so in the afternoon, he was pretty tired. He had a strong foreign accent, my father, your great-grandfather. He worked very
hard. He didn't have a lot of time for his children or for anything else but his work."

"Did you miss him when he died?"

"I did, Natey, but I knew that life had to go on. Just like it has
to go on for you. You drew a terrible card, having parents who
couldn't live together, and then another bad one when your dad
moved to Seattle. But, you know, you can't let that knock you
out. You've got to be tough. You've got to survive so that someday, when you're a father, you'll never do anything to cause
your own son or daughter to feel all the sad feelings you've had
to feel."

The boy didn't reply. He was looking straight ahead. Bernstein silently cursed the seat belt, which prevented him from
pulling the boy closer, slipping an arm around him, kissing the
top of his head.

"I can't promise you things are going to work out, Natey. I
wish I could. Life's a tough pull, if you know what I mean. But
you can't let it beat you. Sooner or later, everyone is called on to
be a man. Your problem is that you've been called on much ear-

lier than most guys. But you've still got to try. You've got to give it your best shot. Know what I mean, Natey?"

Bernstein's words suddenly sounded hollow to him, a combination of psychotherapist, rabbi, and Knute Rockne. In the end, after preaching to the boy, he, too, would drive away. Another bullshitter. Words weren't going to help his grandson. This was a boy whose life was missing something no words could ever give back. If the sins of the fathers are supposed to be visited on the sons, Bernstein thought, maybe it also worked the other way around, and this was his turn to pay.

"Natey," Bernstein said as the Buick pulled up in the driveway before the boy's house, "would you by any chance like me to teach you to play handball?"

"Would you have time?"

"I'll find time. It's a great game, and I'd really like you to learn how to play it."

"I'm not sure I can do it, but I'll try."

"You can do it, Natey. It's in your blood. Suppose I pick you up next Sunday morning. You'll come with me to the Center and we'll work out for an hour before my game with the boys. You'll warm your grandpa up. How's that sound?"

"It sounds like fun."

The boy released his seat-belt buckle. Bernstein got out of the car with him, handing him the small suitcase from the back seat. He put out his hand, then pulled the boy toward him and hugged him, patting him gently on the back.

"Next Sunday at eleven. Bring your gyms and a pair of shorts."

Holding his suitcase against his thin leg, the boy waved as Bernstein backed out of the driveway.

On Monday, at ten of twelve, just before breaking for lunch, Moe Bernstein called Dr. Arnold Meyers from a pay phone on

Roosevelt Road to announce he was ready to schedule bypass surgery.

"No doubt about it, absolutely none, Mr. Bernstein," the young cardiologist said in a somewhat smarmy voice, "you've made the correct decision."

A good deal less than certain himself, Bernstein hung up and stepped around the corner into Manny's Delicatessen, where he ate a four-inch-high pastrami sandwich on a kaiser roll, a potato latke the size of a cake dish, and a heaping serving of rice pudding, all washed down by two cups of black coffee. Sure, O.K., all right, let them cut out his whole heart. But if they thought they could change Moe Bernstein, they had another think coming.

Love and *The Guinness Book of Records*

WHEN VIVIAN CALLED to ask me to take her to the memorial for Charlie Fairfax, I said of course I would. She doesn't get around all that easily anymore, and besides, I hadn't had a chance to say goodbye to Charlie in life and this would be a way to say goodbye to him in death. Charlie Fairfax was a strange guy, what in the old days we used to call a character. Running a saloon, I think I've met a character or two in my time, and Charlie, I believe, qualifies.

I knew Charlie off and on for more than thirty years, and I can't say that I ever came close to really knowing him, let alone to figuring him out. What I couldn't figure out in particular was him and Vivian. Charlie was married, had three kids, all daughters. He had dough. He lived in the western suburbs, in Hinsdale, which, in Chicago, is about as suburban as you can get. As a physician, even though he wasn't in private practice, he was pretty well settled in life. What did he need a love affair with the same woman for something like thirty-three years, and with a woman — though I feel a little dishonorable for saying it — who, for something like a third of that time, I'm not sure he was all that crazy about? Something here in this maybe for *The Guinness Book of Records*.

The reason I feel I oughtn't to be putting down Vivian is that she has been sick in recent years, suffering from emphysema, and then, too, she and I go back a long way. We went to high school together, to Von Steuben, in Albany Park, on the Northwest Side. Last two years in high school we were a thing, Vivian and me. As I think back on it, Vivian was a courageous kid, way ahead of her time — the time then being the early 1950s — not afraid of sex or of much else. I suppose it's no big news now, but Vivian was the first girl I knew who made no bones about enjoying sex. This came as a revelation to me in those days, and a very useful reminder in later life.

Vivian and I were, in our small way, rebels in our high school, which was very Jewish, mostly lower middle class, and pretty conventionally competitive in a Jewish lower-middle-class kind of way. Vivian wasn't Jewish. Her father had been killed in World War II, and her mother worked as a legal secretary in the Loop. My mother was Jewish but my old man wasn't, and he and my mother divorced when I was nine years old. He took off for the Coast and eventually dropped out of my and my younger brother's lives. Vivian and I had an absence of fathers in common, also non-Jewish names, which, at our high school, put us on the outside of things — or at least made us feel a little odd and outside. Among ourselves we used to make fun of the other kids at Von Steuben, with their ambitions to go on to medical and dental and law school, to move out to the suburbs, to live the good and careful life, which I guess most of them long ago succeeded in doing.

That life wasn't for us. Vivian and I, we thought of ourselves as different, above all that, much deeper and more daring. We

loved jazz, Charlie Parker especially. We tried everything together that there was to try then: drinking, smoking a little
grass (this was in 1954), sex. Perhaps the only thing to be said
about our sex is that, fun and exciting though it was at the time,
we never conned ourselves into thinking we loved each other.
To have done that would have gone against our general feeling
about ourselves as rebels.

Vivian kept up the notion of being a rebel long after I
dropped it. For her it took the form of becoming interested in
art, in painting and dance and music and theater. I suppose she
was what in those days used to be called a bohemian. This was
long before everyone in the country became a bohemian. For
a while she tried to make a career as a painter, but for whatever reasons — I suppose lack of talent among them — it didn't
pan out.

Neither of us went to college. On my side, the money wasn't
there, and the truth is I wasn't all that good a student. I suppose
I could have gone to Wright Junior College — "You can't go
wrong with Wright," kids in the neighborhood used to joke —
but I didn't see much point in it. Instead, I went to work, lived at
home, and helped out financially. My mother's salary from selling housewares at Marshall Field's wasn't much, even in those
days, though people used to make a big deal of the ten percent
employee discount on all merchandise. I tried out construction,
selling home improvements, finally bartending. I liked the bartending, its odd hours, its limited responsibilities, the opportunity it offered to meet girls; I wouldn't be surprised if even its
lack of respectability wasn't part of the attraction. Anyhow I
stayed with it long enough eventually to buy Flaherty's, the
joint on Halsted Street I own now, a pretty successful joint, if I
do say so myself, thanks to the gentrification of the area that
took place fifteen or so years ago, which turned a neighborhood
bar into an upscale watering hole for the young.

Vivian, who took the commercial course at Von Steuben, became, like her mother, a secretary after high school. Only she never for a minute thought of herself as a secretary. She moved to Hyde Park, sat in on an occasional course at the University of Chicago, hung around the bar called Jimmy's on Fifty-fifth Street, and worked at secretarying just enough to pay for her apartment, a two-room basement flat on Blackstone off Fifty-third Street. She worked at the medical school, which is where she met Charlie Fairfax. When they met, he was thirty-two, she was nineteen. The year was 1956.

As Vivian once explained to me, those were the days when the brightest guys in medical school, especially at places like the University of Chicago, became research physicians. The possibilities for big dough hadn't yet come into play for doctors. Charlie was apparently considered one of the brightest of the bright. He was also from a good family. He was already long married, had two kids, a third one on the way. But he fell for Vivian, and she did for him, too. In Albany Park she never met a guy even remotely like Charlie Fairfax. I don't suppose Charlie ever knew anyone quite like Vivian, either.

The memorial for Charlie was held in a lecture hall at the university's medical school. Charlie's specialty was public health medicine — his interest was in epidemics, and I guess he was an important guy in his field. At one time, in his late fifties, Vivian told me, Charlie was being considered for the job of U.S. surgeon general. I myself can't see him as surgeon general. Charlie didn't seem, or even look much like, a doctor. He had none of the self-importance, none of the pompousness, of most of the doctors I have known. In fact, I was once in a bar with Charlie where he was taken for a cop. "What's yours, Lieutenant?" I remember the bartender asking him. I thought it was pretty funny, and so did Charlie, in his sort of subdued way.

Charlie was thin, tall, with a high forehead and close-cut thick black hair. He always wore a blue suit, striped button-down-collar shirts, variations on a red knit tie, plain-toed cordovan shoes. He wore a raincoat, no lining, right through Chicago winters; never wore a hat. He had no hobbies — unless you count Vivian as his hobby — and he didn't have much small talk. For some reason, he knew a lot about Broadway musicals: Cole Porter, Gershwin, Rodgers and Hart, that kind of stuff. He would smile, but I don't think I ever saw him laugh. He must have had a lot on his mind, Charlie, what with his job, his teaching, and what I need to think of as his two wives.

I sure as hell would never have recognized Charlie from what was being said about him in this hall at the University of Chicago. It seemed that he was a mystery to most of the guys who worked with him. One guy got up to talk about how valuable Charlie was when, many years ago, he worked at the Centers for Disease Control in Atlanta. Another guy talked about how effective Charlie was in meetings with the other professors at the university, and this was mainly because he was respected for being so reasonable. Someone else talked about his mastery of details and willingness to take on the tough jobs no one else wanted to deal with at the medical school. One guy spoke of Charlie's work as a teacher, a researcher, and an administrator, and said that we really ought to consider Charlie's life and *careers*. (I thought it made more sense the other way around: his career and his lives.) Another guy got up, a neighbor of Charlie's in Hinsdale, also a physician, and talked about how Charlie hated to rake leaves. Everyone laughed. Big joke.

As I listened to all this crap, sitting toward the back of the hall, I thought to myself, Charlie, baby, you fooled them all. Quite a performance, Charlie, very impressive. You had them all faked out of their socks, my man. These guys droned on, professors making their little jokes, but none of them had a clue to the man they thought they were talking about. None of them knew diddly about old Charlie, dead at sixty-six of a heart attack, even though some had worked with him for thirty-five years. Anyhow, this is what I thought as I sat there listening to these dummies gabbing away, their clueless talk accompanied by the heavy breathing of the woman sitting beside me, Vivian — Charlie's unknown, undeclared, but in every other way true second wife.

Vivian's breathing, from her emphysema, was made more difficult than usual by her struggle against tears. It occurred to me that she was enjoying all this stuff said about Charlie, taking it all in, in her own mind secretly playing the widow. Meanwhile, Charlie's actual widow, seated on the stage with her and Charlie's three thick-legged daughters, also seemed to be enjoying the tributes to her husband, laughing in all the right places. I had never seen her before and always wondered what she looked like. She was a birdlike woman, small and churchy-looking and, like her daughters, thick in the calves — not the kind of woman I would have figured Charlie to have married. But then, go figure Charlie.

Among the many things I didn't know about Charlie and his amazing life was if his wife — Susan was her name — knew about Vivian. Vivian of course knew a lot about Susan, but I don't think she had seen her for twenty-eight or twenty-nine years, when she, Vivian, briefly worked as Charlie's secretary at the medical school. Charlie never talked about his wife around me, though he knew I knew he was married. It was a subject we left alone. When we'd go out, Charlie and Vivian and me and another woman, usually a different one each time, it felt to me exactly as if Charlie and Vivian were married — and, toward the end, not too happily married at that.

I myself have been married once, for roughly eighteen months, in my late twenties. It was long enough for me to recognize that I wasn't cut out to be a husband. A guy comes into my joint one night, he's just off a divorce after a long marriage, and he tells me that the thing about marriage is that it's one year of flames and forty years of ashes. That, for me, about gets it, except that I could only take about six months of the ashes. But not Charlie, who must have liked being a husband enough to want to do it twice, with two women, simultaneously.

If I keep referring to Vivian as Charlie's second wife, it's because it wouldn't make sense to call her Charlie's mistress. Having a mistress to me implies paying a broad's rent. Charlie never did that; besides, Vivian didn't need it and wouldn't have wanted it if she did. A mistress also implies ownership, the woman being there at the guy's convenience. Charlie and Vivian's arrangement wasn't anything like that. Toward the end, it was closer to the truth to say that Vivian was there for Charlie's inconvenience. She drove him crazy sometimes. She relied on him, yes, but never for money. By the time she was in her mid-twenties Vivian had given up on trying to make it as a painter, and took a series of jobs at art galleries on Michigan Avenue and, later, along the Chicago River. She never made a fortune, but she did all right. Her high opinion of herself seemed to get her decent-paying jobs.

In the early years, Charlie would occasionally take her with him on his trips to Atlanta, and later on he might buy her something extravagant — a watch for a grand or so, maybe, or maybe some French luggage — but money was never at the heart of their relationship. In the beginning, I always assumed, sex was at the heart of it, and love — why not? — and maybe it gave them both a way to escape the lives they were supposed to be living. Sex was no small thing to Vivian. She had theories about it. The leading one was that a person shouldn't go too long without it. She was also very good at it, ready to act on her curiosity. When I think back to our little fling in high school, in our sex it was Vivian who led, as if we were on a dance floor, who called the turns, who was the teacher.

Vivian's views on sex, I realize now, were essentially those of a man. She wanted a lot of it, and she didn't have much conscience about whom she did it with. She was also ready to go out and get it. In the same way a man goes after a good-looking unescorted woman in a bar, she was capable of going after a good-looking man. She was herself less good-looking than interesting-looking. She had these hooded eyes, deep and very dark brown, that were powerful with suggestion; hers was a face filled with promise, or so anyway I always felt. Did her sleeping with so many different guys have any effect on her? I really don't know. Why did she do it so easily? What the hell, she must have thought, why not, you only go around once.

I saw little of Vivian in the early days of her affair with Charlie. In my twenties, I was struggling to get started in life myself. We would talk on the phone once a month or so, but three or four months might go by when we wouldn't see each other at all. I do remember the night she first introduced me to Charlie. I had been working behind the bar at Flaherty's maybe two months. Vivian walked up with him. Both of them seemed out of place in the joint, which was strictly working class, but Charlie more so than Vivian. She introduced him to me as Dr. Charles Fairfax.

"Charlie'll be fine," he said, reaching across the bar to shake my hand.

He drank a martini, of which we didn't sell too many at Flaherty's in those days, didn't talk much, let Vivian gas on about him and his interests. He seemed a little humorless to me. Maybe meeting Vivian's old friends — like me, a bartender who hadn't gone to college — was more than he'd bargained for. I thought maybe he was a snob, but I was wrong. What I did learn at this first meeting was that he didn't give a damn about sports, local politics, or most of the other things that interested me or the other jokers at Flaherty's. I couldn't be sure what interested him, except his work, and I was in no position to talk with him about that.

You knew as soon as you met him that Charlie was one of those lucky people who other people want to like them. Your liking him wasn't of all that much interest, or so everything about him seemed to suggest. I remember thinking that it would be nice if I could have this guy's respect, though I wasn't sure how to go about winning it. I thought that somehow if this guy liked me, I would maybe be elevated a little in my own eyes.

I didn't yet know that Charlie was married. Vivian told me about that later. When she did tell me, she also told me that he was very serious about her. Having been involved in lots of casual affairs, she knew, she said, when a man was serious.

"What does serious mean?" I asked. "Is he going to leave his wife and kids for you?"

"No," she said, "and I wouldn't want him to. When I say he's serious, what I mean is that he's going to stick around. He's not an ordinary guy, Charlie. He's nuts about me. And he takes responsibility."

I wasn't sure what was behind that last sentence. What did it mean for a married man, father of three kids, to take responsibility for a woman when he had no plans to leave his wife for her? I asked Vivian what she meant.

"All I know," she said, "is that Charlie will be around whenever I need him. That's all I really need to know." How she knew, I never discovered. But she was dead-on right.

Did Charlie know what he had gotten himself into? Did he ever want out? What did he think on those late-night drives on the Eisenhower or Stevenson Expressway from one of Vivian's various apartments on the Near North Side back to his house in Hinsdale? I used to wonder how Charlie brought off his schedule. What did he tell his wife when he returned home at two-thirty in the morning on a Wednesday? He was a scientist, so maybe he told her that he was working late in some lab. Or maybe, early in his marriage, he had established that his comings and goings were not to be questioned. Maybe he told his wife that he traveled more than he did, and maybe many of the nights that he left Vivian's, he returned to his office in Hyde Park to grab a couple of hours' sleep. Who knows? It wasn't something I ever felt close enough to Charlie to question him about. But I always thought it was a damn impressive piece of work, his bringing all this off for more than three decades.

I suppose Charlie was what a guy in the joint the other night, referring to someone else, called "a chaos merchant" — someone who can put up with tremendous amounts of tension and confusion in his life and keep on going. I've seen the type myself. Guys who are in trouble with the IRS, are cheating on their wives and business partners, have cancer, serious debt, the Mafia on their tail, are being blackmailed, and yet still find time to dress well and, when out for an evening, try to pick up a young waitress. Amazing characters — how they do it, I don't know. But guys like this do exist.

What made Charlie different is that, in spite of the disorder that his relationship with Vivian brought to his life, you could see in everything about him — in his manner, the way he dressed, the cars he drove (a series of very dull Dodges) — that he longed for order. He used to take Vivian shopping for groceries, he picked up her dry cleaning, he did her taxes. He tried, without much success, to get her to cut down on her smoking. Vivian, a bohemian for life, cared little for the everyday details of living, even as she grew older. With Charlie around, though, she didn't have to worry too much about them; he looked after them for her.

I remember Vivian was living in a studio apartment on Division Street, just off Rush Street, the night she and Charlie had me up for dinner. It was a simple meal — steak, baked potatoes, a salad, a bottle of Chianti — all prepared and served by Charlie in his usual getup of blue suit, striped shirt, red tie. I recall him slipping his jacket on after serving us and then sitting down to join us.

"He's a good cook, Charlie, no?" said Vivian.

"A terrific cook," I said. "I'd marry him myself," I added. A pretty bad joke under the circumstances.

"Sorry, sport," said Charlie, "but I'm afraid I'm already spoken for."

"Yes," Vivian put in, "Charlie here's a happily married man."

I had sailed us into dangerous waters, that much was plain. I hoped to sail us out of them, as best I could, with the tact learned behind the bar.

"I'm not too expert on the subject of marriage and happiness myself," I said, "so I think I'd like to change the subject. Charlie, where did you buy these steaks? They're terrific."

"Why change the subject?" Vivian said. "Happiness and marriage is a great subject — one of the greatest, though Charlie is the only one at this table who can tell us anything of interest about it."

"True enough, Vivian and I have touched on it a time or two," Charlie said. "But never with very felicitous consequences, wouldn't you say, Vivian?" Charlie had a way of raising his left eyebrow when asking a question that could be a real conversation stopper. That eyebrow said, Ah, want to be unpleasant, do you? If you do, you've come to the right place, friend. This was the first time I had seen him make use of this eyebrow move, and it worked beautifully. "The steaks," he said, "come from Stop and Shop in the Loop. They are good, aren't they?"

The subject of marriage never came up again when I was with Vivian and Charlie. They did, though, have a number of arguments — not quite full arguments, maybe skirmishes is the better word — in my presence that made them seem, I don't know how else to say this, very married. But it would probably be a mistake to think that Vivian felt herself a disappointed woman, that she pined away for the marriage that never happened. Near as I could make out, she liked her arrangement with Charlie. It gave her the fairly steady attention of one man and, with it, all the freedom of a single woman.

Vivian took every advantage of that freedom. I said earlier that she was like a man in her sex interests. Maybe I ought to qualify that by adding that she was like a man without very good taste. Vivian could be reckless. Over the years at Flaherty's I've seen her go off with some real dogs; studs, maybe, but dogs nevertheless: weightlifters, guys with ponytails, every kind of phony artist type, half-in-the-bag ad-agency pricks, frauds of one kind or another. Usually nothing much came of it, nothing more than a quick roll in the hay, or so I always supposed. Vivian never went into details, but for some reason she didn't hide any of this from me either. Maybe she looked on me as family. In a way, I guess that's how I look on her, even now.

Once, though, about ten years ago, a guy named Leslie Weiss moved in with her. He was five or six years younger than Vivian. He was handsome, with thick hair that went over his ears. I never saw him wear anything but Levi's and work shirts, which was a funny getup for a guy who didn't seem to do much work. He claimed to be writing a novel. He never finished it. He was a drinking man, pretty well hooked on the sauce. Vivian would bring him into my joint and often we'd find ourselves scraping him off the bar at the end of the night. I'm not sure where Vivian thought this was going, but it was evident to me that in this guy Leslie she was doing charity work of a kind that wasn't exactly tax deductible.

During her Leslie days, which went on for nearly a year, I found myself worried more about Charlie than anyone else. Naturally, with this guy Leslie camping out in Vivian's apartment — she was living on Oak Street at the time — Charlie saw very little of her. But he came into Flaherty's a lot during that year. Charlie wasn't a guy to cry in his beer, so he didn't tell me what he was feeling, but you could see he was hurting. It was like his wife was cheating on him, except that Vivian wasn't his wife, and he was the one who had been cheating for years.

It also must have hurt Charlie to think of Vivian with so inferior a character as Leslie Weiss, though he never knocked him to me. On those nights when Charlie came into the joint, he would ask me if I had heard from Vivian and if everything was all right with her. I would tell him that, so far as I knew, she was fine. She, meanwhile, if she planned to come into the joint with this Leslie guy, always called first to check to see that Charlie wasn't there. Once, when Vivian was there with Leslie, Charlie showed up late and Vivian had to introduce Leslie to him. There wasn't much conversation among the three of them. As I remember it, Charlie's left eyebrow seemed up most of the time. I was behind the bar that night. At one point, Leslie returned from the men's room and asked Charlie where Vivian was. Charlie took a sip from his martini, set the drink down, and said — it isn't a line you forget, especially since I never before or after heard Charlie use the word — "She's attending to her cunt just now. She'll be along presently. Have another drink."

When Leslie finally cut out — I think he claimed he had a job teaching at a community college in New Jersey — things between Charlie and Vivian went back to what they once were.

Maybe not quite back to what they once were. Vivian moving Leslie in with her must have seemed an act of serious infidelity to Charlie. They were still together, but something was different. Charlie was as attentive as before — running Vivian around for groceries, picking up her cleaning, doing her taxes — but when they were together his eyebrow seemed to be up more than I had remembered.

Vivian is one of those people who, if you're going to like her, you got to agree to allow her to say stupid things, otherwise you'd spend all your time arguing with her. She might, for example, call some cluck brilliant who obviously isn't, but, you figure, what the hell, she wants to think of this schmuck as a genius, let her. She had a need to appear young, Vivian did, and so she claimed to enjoy the junky music of the moment, or she would defend what seemed to me goofy plays or paintings, or say that she thought a man wearing an earring was sexy. I always took a pass when this kind of thing came up, let it slide off my back. Charlie used to do the same, but no longer.

"Tell us, Vivian, what it is you find so fetching about the male earring," I once heard him say. "I'm sure you have thought the subject through thoroughly and have fascinating ideas about it."

Once the singer Bobby Short was in town, at the Park East, to play an evening of Gershwin songs. It was Vivian's birthday, and Charlie arranged for a table for four; I joined them with a woman I was seeing at the time. There was a kind of tension in the air. Bobby Short wasn't as good as he was on records. He seemed to be shouting the songs. The service was lousy, the drinks worse. Charlie and Vivian missed few opportunities to zing each other. Quite an evening. I felt like I had brought a woman along so that we could both watch an old married couple go at each other and be pleased that at least we weren't married.

"Well," said Charlie, after paying for our drinks, "Bobby Short may not have been much, but Gershwin still has a little something. He's almost up there with Mick Jagger, wouldn't you say, Vivian?"

"Go to hell, Charlie," she answered, turning her head away to exhale a cloud of cigarette smoke.

In recent years, I saw Charlie and Vivian less often. I opened another saloon, and had to be on the premises there more than at Flaherty's, and so sometimes missed them when they came in to the old joint. I would see them for dinner maybe two, three times a year, and sometimes we would meet to listen to some new jazz pianist or cabaret singer Charlie had discovered. But whenever we did meet, it struck me that Charlie's left eyebrow was in action a good part of the time. "Jesus, Charlie," Vivian said to him one night when we were listening to some guy play and sing Cole Porter in the lobby bar of the Knickerbocker Hotel, "if I need a lot of criticism, I'll read the fucking Sunday *New York Times*."

Vivian didn't need any more criticism than life itself had given her. A customer in my new joint the other night said that, after forty, a woman could keep either her face or her figure, but she had to lose one or the other. Vivian, poor kid, seemed by fifty to have pretty near lost both. She had grown heavy and now had a puffy look. The sixty or so unfiltered Pall Malls she smoked every day gave her face wrinkles that makeup couldn't hide, though it seemed she was using more and more of it, which only made matters worse. She always dressed dramatically, but now her clothes called attention to the fact that she was too old for them. Like a lot of people who work hard at staying young, Vivian was aging badly.

Charlie hung in there, though. Near as I could tell, he wasn't seeing Vivian any less. He was still running errands for her, still trying to bring some order to her life. He was driving his Dodge at all hours up and back from Hyde Park, the Near North Side, and Hinsdale. Meanwhile, of course, he had his own suburban family. His oldest daughter, who had married and was living in Boston, had made Charlie a grandfather. He was flying fairly frequently down to the Centers for Disease Control. He had complications to attend to at the medical school, where, because of the neighborhood, he once told me, it was no longer easy to get the best young men to take teaching and research jobs. But still he found time to take Vivian shopping or pick her up at the dentist or remind her to put her fur coat into storage. With Vivian, Charlie was nothing if not dutiful. He was, I thought, a model of a Jewish husband, without being Jewish or, in Vivian's case, a husband.

My own guess is that some of the things that kept them together for all that time were not so different from what keeps many long-married couples together: laziness, fear of the unfamiliar involved in finding someone new, the power of sheer goddamn stubborn habit. But in Charlie's case I think it was something else, too. I think maybe Charlie felt a deeper responsibility for Vivian than a normal man would feel even for a wife of many years. If he left a wife, at least she could sue him, come away with a little dough. If there were children, they could look out for their mother. A broken marriage, no matter how bad the feeling, at least usually leaves something behind. But a love affair that goes on longer than most marriages nowadays — what does that leave?

I have no idea how Vivian's life might have turned out without Charlie on the scene, but maybe he felt that, without him, she would have had a more settled life. I don't know. Her contempt for the lives now led by the people we went to high school with was pretty strong. If she yearned to be married or a mother, she never whispered a word of it to me. You never know for sure about these things, but my sense is that, without Charlie, Vivian would have been a lot worse off.

That wasn't the way Charlie saw it. The only time we talked about it, Charlie and I, was after his first heart attack — it was his third attack that killed him — and I visited him at Billings Hospital. Before the visit, I called first to see if the coast was clear. I didn't want to run into Charlie's wife or any of his kids; I had to remind myself that I was part of his secret life.

It was one of those gray Chicago days in March. A layer of dirt-darkened ice was on the ground, with candy-bar wrappers, dog crap, even a few coins frozen underneath. Black guys walked by with knitted Chicago Bears caps pulled down over their ears.

"So what're they telling you about your condition?" I asked soon after I found my way to Charlie's room.

"There's not much they have to tell me. My father died of coronary failure when he was fifty-two. I had an older brother who died of the same thing at fifty-five. I suppose I have to consider myself ahead of the game."

"What about taking good care of yourself, Charlie, diet and exercise and all that?" I chose not to mention tension and stress.

"I long ago decided that I intend to die as I've lived. People who wrap themselves in cotton after a heart attack generally peg out soon after anyway. I think what'll happen now, no matter what I do, is that I'll undergo a few more heart attacks until, sooner or later, the finisher comes."

Not much to say in answer to that. Charlie was the physician; it wasn't my place to give him a pep talk about careful living.

"When I'm gone, it may not be so easy for our friend Vivian," he said. "I wish I could tie things up better than I'm going to be able to, but under the circumstances there isn't going to be much I can do."

"For example?"

"For example, there'll be no mention of her in my will. And I haven't made the kind of money that would make it possible for me to leave her a decent sum. I wish I had."

"My guess is that she doesn't expect anything like that."

"Do you think that, without me, Vivian would have married, had children?"

"I don't think so, Charlie."

"Still, if I hadn't interceded in her life, it would have been much different today."

"My own opinion is that maybe it would have been worse."

"No way of knowing that. Meanwhile, I did intercede, and when she was just a kid. I have a responsibility."

I told Charlie that, allowing that it even existed, I thought he had more than fulfilled that responsibility. I told him that he had been, along with everything else, a dear friend and like a brother to her. I told him a good deal more that I can't remember now. But what I can remember is that he didn't seem to buy any of it.

Charlie never really recovered from that first heart attack. Thin to begin with, he suddenly began to seem thinner, almost emaciated. And gray — not just his hair, which had already gone gray, but his skin began to take on a grayish look. The skin of his face seemed to sag; the bounce had gone out of his walk. And there was a new look in his eyes, not a look of terror exactly, but a look that implied that death, his own death, was not far off, which in Charlie's case it wasn't.

After his first heart attack, Charlie seemed more gentle with Vivian. He no longer felt the need, evidently, to straighten her out all the time when she fell into what he considered bad tast or damn foolishness. None of that mattered much now.

In his weakened condition, late-night drives back to Hi were out for Charlie. Still, he would pick her up every two after work, run the old round of her errands, and then they would have an early dinner together. I joined them once, for coffee and dessert, at the end of one of their early dinners, this one at Convito, on Chestnut just west of Rush, a few weeks before Charlie died. He looked awfully tired; his shirt collar seemed too large for the loose skin on his neck. Vivian remained Vivian, jabbering away about some avant-garde play she'd seen the night before at the Steppenwolf Theatre, an unfiltered Pall Mall in her fingers wreathing her in a cloud of smoke as she pitched into a piece of amaretto cheesecake. Charlie sat there, letting her rattle on. At that moment he seemed less like her lover than a father who was tolerant though not altogether pleased at how his daughter had turned out.

I was the one who called Vivian to tell her about Charlie's death. I knew she didn't read the paper, and when I saw the announcement on the *Trib* obituary page, I thought maybe it would be better if she heard the news from me.

"Oh, shit," she said, "poor Charlie. There was so much I wanted to tell him. I wanted to tell him one last time how much I loved him. We'd been through so much. I wanted him to know how much I loved him."

"Charlie was a pretty smart guy," I said. "He must have known."

"Do you really think so?" Vivian said.

"I know so," I said.

Did Charlie know? Did he give a damn? Was love the point of his thirty-odd years with Vivian? What the hell was? Well, Charlie, I thought, as I hung up the phone after this conversation with Vivian, it's done, all over. You did what you could. Nothing more to be done now. It's quits, Charlie. You're off the at last.

Family Values

APART FROM your brother," my father used to say, "money is your best friend." He said it to me early, and he said it more than once. He made a good amount of it, too, especially for someone who never finished high school. Money was the source of much of the pleasure he took in life. "You know," he said to me repeatedly in his later years, "it's a source of satisfaction to me in my old age to know that I don't have to worry or depend on anybody else for anything."

Money could also be the cause of regret in my father. He would often point out some handsome old office building and tell me that, in 1934, he could have had it, as he always put it, for a song. When he died, he left an estate worth just under $2 million, not bad for a man whose business was printing menus, stationery, and clothing labels, and who never had more than eight people working for him at any one time.

I may have been less impressed with money than my father was, but I certainly never thought it a trivial matter. Even as a boy, I noticed many of the things money could do: among them, gain you respect and give you confidence. In my father' small circle of friends, the man with the most money could usually be depended upon to do the most talking, his authority extending to all subjects, from balanced budgets to birth control.

I could see where money might be your friend, if not quite your best friend, but the problem I had with my father's maxim was the introductory bit about my brother. I never came near to thinking of my brother, Lou, as my best friend, though there were times when I would have liked to. We never fought, Lou and I, but neither did we get along all that well — not, I suspect, that Lou ever noticed.

Lou is four years older than I. Four years is a funny chronological distance for brothers. During school days, it meant Lou was always leaving places I was about to enter: high school, college, the army. As soon as I'd had a common experience with my brother and therefore something to talk about in a close way, he was gone, on to something else, off to somewhere else. The other part of the problem was that, after Lou, I was viewed as something of a disappointment. It wasn't as easy for me to admit this when I was a kid as it is now, but I always knew it was true.

When we were kids I envied everything about my brother. He was dark and came into his physical maturity early; I got our mother's fair skin and light brown hair and didn't shave daily until I was past twenty. At only five foot ten, Lou was the star his junior and senior years on the Senn High School basketball team, second team All-City the year he graduated. A dead shot, my brother picked up the nickname True Lou, sometimes reduced to just True. I wasn't there myself, but once, against Amundsen High, the Amundsen kids, mostly from working-class German and Swedish families, took up the Senn High chant of "True Lou, True Lou," changing it to "Jew Lou, Jew Lou." My brother, in response, scored thirty-seven points and blew them off the court.

In our apartment on Talman, in the two-flat my father bought just after the war, my brother and I shared a bedroom. I recall waking early one summer morning — I was fourteen, Lou eighteen — and looking over at the next bed, and there was my brother, sleeping on his back, dark and muscular in his boxer shorts, his handsome face in perfect repose.

Tell me, Lou, I remember thinking, where do I get courage? How do I talk to girls? How do I make kids admire me? You know all about these things, Lou. Please, let me in on them. At that moment, my brother groaned and turned over on his side, his back now to me, and fell into deeper sleep.

I was pre-med at the University of Michigan until I ran into something called organic chemistry, which put an end to my plan to become a physician. I finished with a degree in zoology, but with no real interest in going on to graduate school. So I returned to Chicago, got a teaching certificate, and began teaching high school in the Chicago public school system. My father always used to say that a man has to love what he does for a living, but I think he must have been disappointed by my choice of work. He never said anything about it to me, but teaching in the public schools was to him, I would guess, like working in the post office: it showed a serious want of ambition.

I sensed he thought his son Louis was closer to the right idea. A business major at the University of Illinois, after graduation Lou became a stockbroker. I once asked him why he didn't go into our father's business. "Are you kidding, Aaron?" he said. "Our old man uses up all the oxygen in the place. There's not enough air for anyone else down there to breathe." Lou was right, of course.

Our father was too conservative to play the stock market, even when his son wanted to let him in on a sure thing. ("The only sure thing in this life, Louis, is death," he used to say. "Everything else is in doubt.") Our father loved control. "Something doesn't sell, I can change the price, I can create movement. But with stock, I'm helpless. I'm in the hands of the big boys, who don't give a good goddamn for my lousy few bucks." Yet, despite all this talk, I still think our father was pleased to have a son so clearly in on the action.

I know our mother was more than pleased about Lou's marriage. Dotty Kagan was a catch. Her father was the biggest Buick dealer in the city. A large bluff man with silver hair, Solly Kagan was connected — in every way. Five hundred–odd guests were at the wedding at the Drake Hotel: sports, show business, Mafia people, everyone was there, more than twice as many Kagan as Rabinowitz guests. I was a groomsman. A guy named Howie Bloch, who played basketball for DePaul, was Lou's best man. My father came up to me, in a rented tuxedo, a glass of champagne in his hand — a far from usual sight — and, slipping his arm around my shoulders, leaned in and whispered, "Did you ever see so many four-flushers in one room?"

I suppose Lou could have gone into business with Solly Kagan, but selling Buicks wasn't what he had in mind. Not long after his marriage, he left his stockbrokerage and, with his father-in-law's help, bought a seat on the Board of Trade. Wild stories floated around in those days about the lottery-like fortunes being made in pork bellies, soybeans, corn, and the rest of it. Urban young men who had never seen a farm outside the movies were said to make hundreds of thousands in the course of a few days, bidding this or that grain or vegetable or slaughtered animal up or down. At the end of a good week on the commodities market, guys would stop on the way home to order a Rolls-Royce or get on a jet bound for Vegas or Acapulco with a girlfriend and return Sunday night, so as not to miss Monday's action.

The commodities market closed in the early afternoon, when Lou and his pals departed for the McClurg Court Health

Club. They played basketball and racquetball and, after a day of gambling on the market, turned their attention to betting on ball games. Sitting in front of one of the club's television sets on a Tuesday afternoon, watching a Cubs-Cards game, Ken Holtzman going against Steve Carlton, a friend of my brother's named Lloydie Franks, taking the Cubs, bet his current-year Jaguar against a guy named Norm Friedman's current-year Mercedes. At the end of the game, which the Cubs lost in extra innings, Lloydie flipped his car keys over to Friedman and took a cab home. "I never liked the goddamn maroon on that Jag," he said. The next morning he ordered a new XKE, in dark blue.

Wild success stories on the commodities market were pretty standard. This guy had a half-million-dollar week, that guy had a two-hundred-grand morning. Stories of guys tapping out were talked about a great deal less. My brother Lou's was such a story. After holding his own for two years or so, Lou went belly-up. Carloads of wheat did him in. Completely busted out, he lost his seat and his wife's savings.

Lou must have heard a good deal about it from Dotty. To shore himself up, maybe to rebuild his confidence, Lou started in on some serious skirt chasing. He may have been cheating on his wife long before — it wasn't the kind of thing he would have told me — but suddenly I would hear stories about my brother on Rush Street with one or another knockout woman. "I saw your big brother at the Orange Tree last night," my friend Mel Rosen told me, "with a blonde who was off the charts." Dotty was a brunette.

I didn't see much of Lou and his wife except when they came to my parents' apartment for Passover and high-holiday dinners. They had a two-bedroom apartment on Sheridan Road, in The Berry, near Belmont. Dotty worked part time for her father. She had had a miscarriage three months into a pregnancy. It was hard not to sense that she held herself above our family.

At my mother's dinner table, she acted as if she were visiting royalty. I once met her with two of her girlfriends, coming out of Saks on Michigan Avenue, and she introduced me as her brother-in-law "Arthur." I decided not to correct her. I mean, what would have been the point?

"Let's count our blessings," my father said when the divorce was announced. "At least there weren't any kids."

Not long after his divorce, Lou moved to Florida. Buddy Lansfield, a friend of my brother's from high school, was selling real estate down there, a big condo development at Delray Beach, and told Lou to get the hell on a plane, there was a fortune to be made. After that, I would hear about my brother from time to time from my father.

"Heard from your brother Louis last week," he would say. "Apparently he's doing a nice job in Florida. It's not the gold mine he thought it would be, but he's making a good buck, or so he says."

I had been teaching biology and general science at Mather High for nearly eight years when Lou remarried. (I never married. Until forty-five, I considered myself single; now, at fifty-three, I think of myself as a bachelor for life.) Lou's second wife, Ginny, was a large redhead, Gentile, a runner-up in a Miss Florida beauty pageant.

"Oh," she said, the first time Lou had brought her to Chicago to meet our parents. "Lou's little brother. How sweet!" And she enfolded me in a warm, fleshy, perfumed embrace. "Lou's told me so much about you, Aaron." What, I wondered, could it have been? What did Lou actually know about me to tell?

"Welcome to the Rabinowitz family, Ginny," I said rather lamely, still mildly disoriented from my new sister-in-law's hug.

I neglected to mention that Lou had legally changed his name from Rabinowitz to Rabin. When I asked him why, he said that Rabin was a hell of a lot simpler all around. Our father

was a little put off by this. "It isn't elegant, the name Rabinowitz," he said to me not long after Lou had told him about
shortening his name, "but at least it is what it is, if you know
what I mean."

If I had guessed that Lou's second marriage wouldn't last
long, I would have been wrong. He and Ginny stayed together.
They had two kids: a daughter, Ashley, and a son, Scott. ("Your
brother gives his kids names that sound like streets," my father
said.) Unlike Dotty, Ginny thought she was marrying up, and
she always made a great fuss when my parents flew down to
Delray to visit their grandchildren. Although they weren't at
first too crazy about their son marrying a non-Jew, they came to
appreciate that their second daughter-in-law had a good heart,
which meant a lot to them. It was Ginny who insisted that Scott
be sent to Hebrew school and go through a bar mitzvah.

Whether Lou played around on Ginny I haven't any idea. I
went down to Delray five or six times, especially when my parents hit their late seventies and didn't travel so easily on their
own. But even there I didn't see all that much of my brother.
He had become a golfer, a good one, with a two-stroke handi-
cap, and much of the time he seemed to be on the course at his
club. In Florida, Lou ran with the same type of crowd he had
run with in Chicago: former athletes, high rollers, guys with a
taste for all kinds of action. He played in golf games where at
the end of a round two or three thousand dollars might change
hands. Ginny gave Lou a wide and very tolerant berth. If my
brother didn't come home for dinner, even when his parents
were visiting, well, that was all right; he was probably at the
club, playing thirty-six. "You know Lou," Ginny said, with a
smile, to my mother.

Back in Chicago, I happened to be with my father when Sam
Kaufman, his neighbor on Talman, after greeting me, asked my
father how his son in Florida was doing.

"What can I tell you," my father said. "Fifty-five years old and he's still chasing balls. Once basketballs, now golf balls. Near as I can tell, he's playing games all day and farting in silk."

After my mother died — of congestive heart failure; she had, for reasons she chose never to tell, refused a pacemaker — I began to see more of my father. He was seventy-eight and without the woman who had been with him for fifty-seven years. A senior citizens' home of any kind was out of the question for my father; he planned to stay in the apartment on Talman. His mind was good, his health, except for high blood pressure and a touch of rheumatism in the right hip, not bad. He now joined me in the bachelor ranks. We began to have dinner together twice a week, on Wednesdays and Sundays.

Wednesdays we went to The Bagel, on Devon, where the crowd was geriatric and where my father invariably ordered salami and eggs; Sundays we went to Pekin House, on Western, where he liked the chicken chow mein and the egg foo yung and where the Chinese owner, after so many years of catering to his Jewish clientele, had himself begun to look Jewish. Conversation wasn't always easy. Having closed up his business three years before, my father had lost his major source of stories. He also had a taste for capping sentences, for closing off a big subject. When Communism fell, for example, all he said was "What did you expect? It was doomed by impracticality from the start." So much for worldwide Communism. Once — only once — did he say, as if it were an astonishing revelation, "You know, I miss your mother." I assured him that there was hardly anything unnatural about that.

Always laconic, after wandering alone and perhaps talking to himself in his apartment all day, he became less expansive than ever. Occasionally, he would regain his old bleak incisiveness. One night at The Bagel, searching for topics of conversation, I complained about the relentlessness of the commercials on television. Mildly stimulated by this, my father set out the three main ways of doing business in America. At the upper levels, he said, you supplied customers with national advertising and public relations; at the middle level, you bought them liquor or theater tickets or women. And then there was his level. "What's that, Dad?" I asked. "Oh," he said, "I cut prices. I always thought it was much more honorable."

Our positions in life had subtly altered. I was now closer to the parent, he to the child. "Dad, there's a bit of rice on your chin," I would catch myself saying. "Dad, you have enough milk and everything in the apartment?" I would ask. Yet, despite this, I continued to regard him as having superior wisdom. Every time I drove over to Talman to pick him up, I felt a slight thrill of anticipation. Perhaps tonight he would tell me what he had been thinking as he came to the end of his days. Perhaps tonight he would fill me in on the meaning of his life, with clues about the meaning of my own. Perhaps tonight he would tell me what he really thought — about me, about my brother, about what he counted as significant in life.

He never did. My father died eighteen months after his wife — in his sleep, of a stroke. I didn't, finally, know what my father thought of me. Whatever it might have been, I couldn't help but wonder if it would have been different had I made it to med school and become a physician. Would he have shown a pride in me that he never came close to showing in my being a high school science teacher? When I was with him, even in those last eighteen months, I always felt a little, I don't know, insignificant, as if I were his driver or male secretary or employee. He never even asked me why I hadn't married. When your son becomes a man, I read somewhere, make him your brother. I know my father never regarded me as anything other than his younger son, a kid, even though I was past fifty and tell-ing him to remove the rice from his chin or that dab of egg from the corner of his lip.

What if I had been the older brother? I used to wonder. What if there had been no Lou at all? What if I had been al-lowed to go about things in my own way, without always being compared to my brother or feeling that I had to go at things in another way? Where is it decreed that only one brother sleeps with beautiful women, feels no responsibility other than for himself, gets to wear the peach-colored golf pants?

One of the things my father and I did sometimes discuss at those Bagel and Pekin House dinners was his finances. He never bragged about how well he had done in business, but it was clear that he was pleased by the fact that, living by his few tight moral maxims — keep your overhead low, don't live be-yond your means, always put something away for a rainy day — he had come out a winner.

Always a methodical businessman, my father wanted me to know the details of his finances, so that in the event of his death there would be no surprises or loose ends. Whenever he trav-eled, he reminded me where he hid the key to his box in the bank vault. He showed me where he put the small brown note-book in which he kept a record of his various mutual funds, certificates of deposit, Israel bonds, and savings accounts along with the dates on which his interest checks arrived. One night before going out to Pekin House, we sat at the dining room ta-ble and he went through each page of this notebook with me. When he came to the last page on which he had any notations, he shuffled to a page in the back on which, in light pencil, he had written: "Louis — $100,000."

"One thing more," my father said. "About six years ago I lent your brother a hundred grand. He was in some sort of dif-ficulty. I never asked what it was. He hasn't paid it back."

"You never asked for it?"

"That's right. I'm sure when he has it, he'll repay me."

"I see," I said, though I didn't, not really.

"Anyhow," my father said, "I thought you ought to know about it, just in case."

"In case of what?"

"In case I check out a little early," he said with the practiced coolness with which he always mentioned death.

This conversation took place a little more than a month before he died.

Our father died on a Monday night, and Lou and his wife arrived from Florida Tuesday night. The burial was scheduled for Thursday morning. ("Jews don't screw around," my father used to say. "They get the corpse in the ground quick. Right thing to do, too.") I thought they would stay at my father's place, but instead Lou and Ginny checked into the Ritz-Carlton on Michigan Avenue.

Lou was supposed to meet me at Weinstein Brothers to make funeral arrangements on Wednesday morning, but was late. I dealt with one of the Weinstein grandsons, a short fellow with an expensive haircut wearing a double-breasted suit whose lining, when he unbuttoned his coat at his desk, matched his yarmulke. Quite a touch, I thought. He was showing me around the casket room when Lou walked in.

"Sorry I'm late, Aaron," he said. "I had a tough time getting a cab."

"Morning, Lou," I said. "This is Mr. Arnold Weinstein."

After they shook hands, Weinstein said he would leave the two of us alone to make our choice of caskets.

My brother, I have to say, looked terrific. He had his year-round tan. His hair was still black and thick. (Mine was thin and gray, what there was left of it.) He wasn't wearing glasses; I never saw him in glasses. He didn't wear a necktie, but an open-collar, deep blue silk shirt. He had on a light gray suit and black loafers with gold buckles. He wore a thin, black-faced watch with a heavy gold and silver band. He was still True Lou, and he looked as if life had never laid a glove on him.

"Dad told me that we weren't to undergo any big expense," I said. "His instructions were to keep it simple."

"What's 'simple' mean?"

"Near as I can tell, it means about eleven hundred bucks," I said, and pointed out a plain oak coffin that had a Jewish star carved on its lid. "That's the same casket we had for mother."

"Our father drove Oldsmobiles all his life," Lou said, "and it looks as if he's going out in a Chevy, and not top of the line, either." He put an arm around my shoulders — I don't remember his ever doing that before — and we walked together to Arnold Weinstein's office, where the figures were added up and the final documents signed.

When I drove Lou over to the Talman Avenue apartment, he explained that Ginny was doing some shopping downtown. Scott was flying in from the University of Florida in Gainesville later this evening. Ashley had just started a new job — something to do with making travel arrangements for large corporations — and felt it was a mistake to take time off, even for a few days. He knew I would understand. When I drove up in front of the old two-flat, I greeted Harry Becker, who lived two buildings down and who paid his condolences.

"You remember my brother, Lou," I said.

"Of course," he said, "the basketball player. How're you doin'?"

When we were inside, Lou asked me who Becker was, and was surprised when I told him that he had been in the same house since we were boys. I had made a start at going through our parents' things, and had left two boxes of old photos out on the dining room table. I suggested to Lou that he might like to go through them and take what he wanted. Lou didn't seem much interested.

"All this old furniture has really had it," he said, looking around. "I suppose we can have an estate sale and get rid of it in one shot."

"Anything here you think Ginny might like? Ma's good dishes maybe? Or her silver?"

"I'll check with her," Lou said, dropping onto the white couch in the living room. "Sit a minute, kid. I know the load of all the detail has fallen on you. What can I do to help?"

"Not much, really. Dad left things in very good order. He was a tidy man."

"Good order was one of the things he valued," my brother said.

"He left us a lot of money," I said. "And he set up trusts for your children. All this goes through Kornfeld, his lawyer. He's an old-timer but at least he's not going to charge us two hundred fifty dollars an hour."

"Our old man wouldn't pay two-fifty for an hour in the sack with Rita Hayworth and Marilyn Monroe — together."

"Sounds accurate to me," I said. "He once told me that if other men were ready to lie, cheat, and kill for money, the least he could do was respect it. Anyhow he always did."

"And now it's ours to piss away any way we like," Lou said. "Must be a moral in there somewhere."

Lou said he was hungry, so I drove him over to The Bagel, whose customers seemed, on this day, particularly decrepit. Every table had someone with a walker or a bad case of osteoporosis or a vacant look in the eyes. The rest were vastly overweight.

"Jesus, this joint makes Florida look more youthful than the winter Olympic tryouts," Lou said.

When our food came, Lou asked me what I knew about the financial details in the will. I explained that, apart from the benefactions to his kids and a few donations to Jewish charities, everything was to be split evenly between us. I told him that the estate came to just under $2 million, and the sale of the two-flat on Talman would put it well over that. He showed no emotion. I made no mention of the hundred grand he borrowed from our father.

"What'll this money mean to you?" he asked.

"Don't get me wrong," I said, "I'm damn glad to have it, but it's come a little late for me. Maybe I'll use it to travel. Buy a fancier car. I've always wanted a convertible."

"What're you waiting for? Do it."

"Maybe I will."

"I have business plans for this money," my brother said. "There's new development possibilities on the west coast of Florida. This money will make it possible for me to be a player — not a major player, but at least I'll be able to take a hand. I've made a decent living over the years, but I'd still like a chance to break the bank."

"What do you suppose our father had it in mind for us to do with this money?"

"Probably sit on it," Lou said.

"Did you love him, Lou?"

"I'm not sure love enters in. He never did me any harm. A couple of times he was there for me when I was in a tight spot. He sure as hell wasn't the kind of guy you'd turn to if you had any kind of emotional problem. He provided. He did the best he could by his own lights."

"He was a lonely man."

"Lonely, I don't know. He was certainly a loner. Except for our mother, he was never close to anyone I know about."

"I admired him. He did his duty."

"I suppose you're right," said Lou, picking up the check and dropping two singles for a tip. "I better get back downtown."

"I'll drive you."

I took Peterson down to the Drive. We passed Senn High School, that monumental gray structure, the scene of True Lou Rabinowitz's greatest glory. Woebegone-looking Hispanic and black kids were standing on Ridge, waiting for a bus. Lots of graffiti in black paint were splattered on the walls of the school building.

"Christ," said Lou, "it all looks so dilapidated."

"That's only because it is."

Lake Shore Drive, with its grand buildings, revived his spirits.

"You know, Aaron, I once asked our old man why he never moved to the Drive. I think Mother would have liked the luxury of it. Do you know what he told me? He told me, 'What do I need it for? So every time I want to use my car I have to tip a guy a buck to fetch it for me?' Case closed."

"Maybe it's such thinking that allows you to save up a couple of million bucks."

"Maybe so."

Lou and Ginny had a date for dinner with some old friends of Lou's. We'd meet at nine-thirty the next morning at the funeral home.

"Oh, one more thing," Lou said in front of the hotel, holding the car door half open. "A few years ago Dad loaned me ten grand, which I never got around to paying him back. Don't forget to mention that to the lawyer when it comes to closing accounts."

My brother leaned closer, shook my hand. I can't be sure

what expression, if any, was on my face. "Take care, kid," he said, patting me on the knee, and walked around the car and into the Ritz-Carlton.

"Ten grand," I yelled into the windshield, driving away from the hotel. "Off by only ninety, bro." Back on the Outer Drive, the lake gleaming sapphire blue on my right, I thought, All these years my brother Lou ignores me, and now he plans to screw me. What a prick!

The funeral went off smoothly. In his eulogy, the rabbi concentrated on our father's contributions to Jewish charities and on his love for his family. It was a bright October day. Two high school buddies of Lou's, both now bald and paunchy, and four men who taught with me in the science department at Mather served as pallbearers.

Back at the apartment, a few old friends of my mother's, Sam Kaufman, Harry Becker, and three or four other old neighbors showed up along with the pallbearers. Ginny ordered much too elaborate a lazy Susan tray, which, with all its uneaten chopped liver, corned beef, salami, cole slaw, pickles, olives, and potato salad, now sat there forlornly: the funeral meats growing cold. When everyone had left, Lou, Ginny, and I sat in my parents' living room. We were all dressed in black, cups of coffee in front of us.

"If ever there was a time for a cigarette, this is it," Lou said.

"How long ago did you quit?" I asked.

"Your brother stopped smoking a little more than two years ago," Ginny said.

"And a day hasn't gone by when I haven't thought about it. Did you ever smoke, Aaron?"

"For twenty years, two packs a day toward the end," I answered, once again freshly amazed at what my brother didn't know, or never bothered to notice, about me.

"Your brother and I are very grateful to you, Aaron, for watching out for Dad and now for seeing after the funeral and the lawyer and the real estate and everything," Ginny said.

"No big problem," I said. I wondered if Ginny knew about the $100,000 her husband had borrowed, and decided that guys like Lou didn't tell such things to their wives.

"Still, we owe you," Lou said.

About ninety thousand dollars more than you're ready to acknowledge, brother, I thought of shooting back, and this was the perfect time, the golden opportunity, to land the shot that kills.

"Don't think twice about it," I said, and thought, Well, a great chance blown? I could've nailed Lou right there in front of his wife. God knows he deserves it.

"Lou," I said, "there's something we have to talk about. Do you mind taking a walk around the block with me?"

"Sure, Aaron," Lou said, shooting back his cuff so that he could look down at his black-faced watch. I noted the thickness of his wrist, the hairiness of the backs of his hands. He wore a ring with a blue stone on the little finger of his left hand.

We were out on Talman Avenue, my brother and I, in the crisp autumn air. I remembered this block, our block, more than forty years ago when people were still allowed to burn leaves in the gutter. I remembered the fine smell of burning leaves and the glow of small fires in the twilight. In winter, I would come home from Hebrew school in the dark down this block, carrying my book cradled in my left arm like a football, using my other arm to fend off would-be tacklers, whom I dodged in the style of George McAfee or J. R. Boone or one of the other great Bear running backs of the time.

"What's on your mind, kid?" Lou said.

"A hundred grand, Lou," I replied.

"Whaddya mean? What hundred grand?"

"The hundred grand you borrowed from Dad."

"What do you know about that?"

"Dad told me he lent you a hundred thousand dollars. He made a notation in his records about it."

"Did he? Did he note that I returned the money roughly a year ago?"

"No. He didn't say anything about your having returned it. And he first mentioned it a month ago."

"Well, I did. And then, later, I borrowed another ten grand from him, which I mentioned to you yesterday in front of the Ritz-Carlton."

My brother looked straight ahead. He picked up his pace. I would have bet the entire hundred grand that he was lying.

"You have any proof you paid it back?" I asked.

"You have any proof I didn't?" he replied.

"Dad would have told me."

"How can you be so sure? The old man's memory wasn't so great."

"A hundred-grand payment he wouldn't forget."

"Well, I'm telling you I repaid him. The burden's on you to prove otherwise. Maybe you want to go to court about it."

"Dad would've loved that."

"The decision's yours, Aaron," he said without looking over at me.

"There really isn't any goddamn decision, and you know it, Lou."

My brother stopped. Turning to me, he said, "I'm telling you, I gave the old man back that hundred grand. Believe it or not. Either way, I don't give a fuck."

"You're a liar," I said, feeling myself slip out of control, "and a jagoff." The last, strangely, was a word I hadn't used since high school.

Lou grabbed me by the upper part of my necktie. He

brought back his fist. I felt myself wince. My own fist was in the air. I saw us, two men in their fifties, rolling around on the ground on the corner of Talman and North Shore. Were we supposed to be Cain and Abel, or Esau and Jacob? Two of the Three Stooges seemed more like it. Lou, too, must have been struck by the ridiculousness of it, for he lowered his fist and let go of my tie.

"You're a fool," he said. "You know that? A damn fool."

I didn't answer. We walked back to the apartment without speaking. As I turned to the door, Lou, again looking down at his watch, said, "Tell Ginny I'll meet her out here."

Ginny was washing dishes, wearing one of my mother's old aprons. I told her Lou was waiting outside and eager to get going.

"Let me at least help you put away all this deli," she said.

"No need," I said. "I'll get it after you take off."

Lou was sitting in the silver Lincoln Town Car he had rented for the day. I walked Ginny around to the passenger side and held the door open for her. Before she got in, she hugged me and kissed me on the cheek.

I walked around to the other side. My brother was seated behind the wheel, the window closed on his side. He had on sunglasses. He looked straight ahead. He drove away without a word. It struck me that, with my father dead, I might never see my brother again.

I stood on the curb watching them drive off down the street on which Lou and I had grown up. As the car turned east at the corner, for some reason I muttered, "Sail on, silver bird," a line from some old song that had stuck in my mind.

I returned to the apartment. In the kitchen I found some aluminum foil and began to wrap the corned beef, salami, and the rest to take back to my apartment. I never eat olives, but I wrapped those, too. I gazed through the dining room to the front of the apartment, which contained so many of the things my mother once loved. I had to sit down in one of the dining room chairs and take several deep breaths, exhaling through my mouth. It was all over, done.

You're only free when both your parents are dead, or so I've heard it said. I suppose it means that with your parents gone there is no one left who can still regard you as a child. Or maybe, as in my case, with no kids of my own, it means that family responsibilities are over at last. I don't really know. All I know is that I was now without any family whatsoever, and it wasn't freedom I was feeling but an emptiness that went deep down and that I knew I would never completely be able to shake.

The Executor

HEN PAUL BERTRAM asked me in 1959 to stay on at Princeton as his graduate assistant, I felt as Walter Lippmann must have felt when, many decades earlier, he was asked a similar question by George Santayana at Harvard. Lippmann turned down the job — as the most promising young man in America, he didn't need it — and I sometimes wish I had done the same. My six-year involvement with Paul — I came to call him by his first name only in the last two years of his life — was to leave such lasting effects that I have often wondered, in the way (I suppose) of a man who marries young and starts a family, what things would have been like had I remained clear of any relationship with Paul and Julia Bertram. Yet my life is unimaginable without them.

I say "them" because people thought of the childless Bertrams more as a couple than as two distinct individuals. In some very loose sense — in some vulgar sense, Paul would no doubt have interjected — they were rather like Virginia and Leonard Woolf, with Paul, the more talented of the two, cast in the role of Virginia. He was also like Virginia in seeming the more sensitive, the more vulnerable. But they were indubitably a pair, if not quite, as I was to discover, a team. In conversation, they were never Paul Bertram and his wife, or Paul and Mrs. Bertram. One spoke of inviting the Bertrams, or one wondered what the Bertrams would think of something or other, or one would drop their names as a single unit: "Yes, last night at Morris Bishop's I finally met the Bertrams." Julia, who wrote short stories and what is called cultural criticism, seemed habituated in print to using the first-person plural, so much so that a clever journalist, considering something Julia had recently written, once asked, "Who is 'we'?" But everyone knew who we was — we was the Bertrams.

Paul Bertram was of course the famous critic and the author of that exquisite single volume of poems, *Lapis Lazuli,* which his friend W. H. Auden had extravagantly called "perhaps the only volume of poetry produced in the twentieth century likely to be read well into the twenty-first." When I decided on teaching as a career, I remember Paul saying to me that Shaw had got it wrong when he observed that those who cannot do, teach. "The way it should really run," he said, "is that those who cannot accept less in life than true greatness have no place to turn but teaching." I always took this to mean that Paul had once touched the stars and knew he would never do so again, and so had resigned himself to a life of criticism and teaching.

How else explain a man who had written eighteen or twenty perfect poems but who never afterward continued in the line of his genius? It would, I thought, be very much like Paul to accept his own limitations, in art as elsewhere. If a single word described his manner, character, even style, that word was resignation. He was resigned to the cards life had dealt him, to life as it was, to the brevity of his time on earth, to the distinct possibility of oblivion at the end of a dependably less than smooth road. I knew that Paul, many years earlier, had undergone a long psychoanalysis. He was still a Freudian in the larger, philosophical sense — a *Civilization and Its Discontents* Freudian. In Paul, though, the accent was quite as much on the civilization as on the discontents; or, to put it somewhat differently, he made the discontents seem worth putting up with, if only one could attain to civilization of his deeply admirable kind.

I first encountered Paul when I walked into his senior seminar on Keats. Like every undergraduate at Princeton studying English, I had heard of him. Along with the volume of poems, he had written three books of critical essays, each of which had helped to define the period in which it was written: the fatal utopianism of our revolutionary 1930s, the callowness of our liberalism after the war, the inadequacy of our conservative 1950s. As a critic of culture, Paul seemed to be telling us that we hadn't grasped life's essential lessons, at least not with anything like the complexity of response they required.

A small man with gray hair combed straight back, green eyes with dark pouches underneath, dressed always in a beautifully cut dark gray suit with a white button-down shirt and a black knit tie and plain-toed black shoes, Paul Bertram seemed less academic than other teachers I had come across at Princeton. He looked as though he could have succeeded outside a university setting: as a subtle high-court judge, an eye surgeon, an architect working with the entire history of European culture under his belt.

That first day of class Professor Bertram slipped into the classroom at Pyme Hall, wrote his name and the course number on the board, took a seat at the head of the table, withdrew from his shirt pocket a periwinkle-blue packet of Gauloises and from his suit-coat pocket a small gold lighter. Before speaking, he lit up. I have never seen anyone smoke quite the way Paul Bertram did. He inhaled deeply, as if the cigarette were connected to an oxygen tank he required to stay alive. Removing the short French cigarette from his mouth, he slowly, very slowly, released a quantity of smoke so vast as to make our classroom seem a back room in war-torn Europe where matters of life and death were being discussed and no small talk was allowed.

He began: "A man of twenty-five, of stunted growth, a physician by training, lies in a bed in a dampish room in Rome. He is dying of tuberculosis, then known as consumption, and he is aware of it. He also knows that he has written a number of poems that have a distinct chance of living forever. He ponders his fate. Was it worth it? Was it a fair bargain? Would *you* agree to it: to have your name live forever through your work when you yourself will be jerked abruptly from life before you have really begun to live it?" Here Bertram, exhaling, released yet another immensity of smoke. "Well," he asked, "would you?"

He went around the room, asking each of the eleven of us, all males of twenty-one, if we would accept the bargain that had been given to John Keats without his ever having consented to it. Allowing for variations in articulateness, almost everyone in the class answered the question in the same way. Forty or fifty fewer years of life in return for eternal fame? None of my classmates had the slightest hesitation or doubt.

I was the lone dissenter. I remember saying, more emphatically than I generally spoke in any classroom, that I thought it a bad deal from start to finish. If, at the end of a reasonably long and rich life, I were to arrive in heaven, what difference would earthly fame, even eternal fame, make? Arrival in hell would not change things. Nor would the bargain be any better if the atheists were correct and oblivion was what awaited me. Honor, yes; but fame, I concluded, was not among the very limited number of things for which one ought to be ready to give up one's life.

Professor Bertram timed yet another cloud of smoke to coincide with my finish. "An unpredictable point of view, Mr. Hopkins," he said, squinting. "I won't, just now, detain the class to ask what besides honor you would be ready to give up your life for. But some other time I just might."

He never did, but, as I say, Paul was a subtle man, and I have no doubt he divined what was on my list, which hasn't changed much since that afternoon in Princeton. It was an afternoon that transformed my life. I had always been a good student — at the top of my class at Dalton, at the top again at Groton, and near the top at Princeton. But I would work for Paul Bertram as I worked for no other teacher. He would disdain the word, but he really did inspire me. I read everything I could about Keats: all the biographies, all the memoirs of his contemporaries, nearly all the criticism. I had the great poems by heart; I came pretty near to memorizing the key letters. I yearned to excel in Paul Bertram's eyes even more than I did in my father's — and I admired and loved my father a great deal.

If I yearned for Paul Bertram's approval, he, I now understand, took me up in turn. He was not someone who wished for disciples; his thought was not so clear-cut, so hard-edged, that disciples could hope to follow it — to become, in effect, Bertramists. The notion was absurd. The only way to do that was to become copiously cultivated. I'm not sure what he saw in me, and I've thought fairly long about it. Perhaps he felt that, having ignited the flame of intellectual passion, he should keep me in a state of permanent conflagration. Or perhaps he had other things in mind.

In class or in his office, he never addressed me as other than Mr. Hopkins — Kenneth would come later. But I could sense that his expectations for me were higher than for my classmates, and I saw it as my job not to disappoint him. I had grown up with my father's lucid, lawyerly mind, a mind that could parse the cause-and-effect relations of an intricate problem, diagram it, and return it to you with its certain, settled solution. But so enraptured had I become by the very style of Paul Bertram's thinking, which somehow took things to a level above cause and effect, beyond right or wrong, to where the meaning of life itself seemed at stake, that I became — I don't know how else to say it — intellectually drunk in his classes. I worried not at all about the reactions of my classmates, who must have despised me for making them seem shallow, but often these late-afternoon classes in Pyme Hall came down to conversations between the two of us. The deep pleasure of it thrilled me.

Toward the end of the semester — the fall semester — Paul invited me to his house for dinner. I was more than a little nervous. My awe for him had not abated; familiarity only bred greater respect. And Julia Bertram, by reputation, was a different but no less formidable personage. Preparing for this dinner as I might for a final exam, I read every item in her slender output. I wondered what Bertram had told her about me, sensing that her standard could well be as severe as, if not more so than, her husband's.

When Julia was young, I later learned, Allen Tate and Richard Blackmur were both supposed to have proposed marriage to her. Unlike Paul, she was not Jewish, but came from a Boston family that had suffered an irredeemable setback during the Depression, thus putting an end to what must have seemed a promising musical career: she had begun life as a violin prodigy.

Julia Bertram greeted me at the door of a rather small house on Hun Road. In the manner of a great diva, she accepted the flowers and bottle of wine I had brought and said, "Thank you, Mr. Hopkins. My husband is still upstairs. Let us have a glass of sherry before he joins us."

She led me into a small living room, modestly furnished. Books and magazines were set out on a coffee table and on lamp tables. No bookcases were in sight; Bertram's study must have been upstairs. Moving aside copies of *Poetry* and *Partisan Review,* she set a not very appealing plate of crackers and cheddar cheese on the coffee table and handed me my glass. Although a slight woman, Julia Bertram had thick, muscular calves. Evidently not a leg man, I thought irreverently to myself of my professor.

She sat across from me. "So tell me," she said, "do you too love my husband?"

"Sorry," I said, "I don't understand."

"Don't you? Regrettable. Many of his students do, you know. They seem to find in him the ideal father for whom they long."

"Actually," I said, "I'm not searching for a father. I have a quite good one at home in New York."

"Then what do you find appealing about him? I assume there must be something or you wouldn't be here."

"He's taught me a way of thinking I hadn't known before," I said. "He has a handsome mind."

"An interesting notion," she replied. "Yes, I suppose he does."

"How long have you and Professor Bertram been at Princeton?" I asked, hoping to change the subject.

"More than a quarter of a century. Your professor was the first Jew to teach full time in the English department at Princeton. But perhaps you already knew that."

"I didn't, though I knew there was a lot of anti-Semitism here until well after the war."

"Paul was — maybe he still is — what used to be called a white Jew. He comes across as so very distinguished, you know, that his being Jewish can be set aside. Anyway, Princeton must have recognized that sooner or later they would have to acquire a Jew for the English department, so why not a superior one?"

Professor Bertram's entrance saved me from having to consider why she was telling me all this. He was wearing the same getup as in class, and he had a Gauloise going. He looked weary. Had he been in his study, devising one of his slightly oblique, inevitably brilliant essays? Napping? Or was it that life with this woman was, at best, never easy?

"Sherry, dear?" Julia said.

"That would be lovely," he said, sitting down next to me on the black leather couch. He leaned forward and put a small wedge of cheese on a cracker. His wife handed him a glass.

"Mr. Hopkins here is thinking of going to law school," he said to his wife. "A grievous error, at least in my view."

"Oh? Why so, Paul?" she asked.

"Because he has a talent for literature and, my guess is, will soon enough develop a sense of vocation for it, too."

"Is your father a lawyer?" Julia asked.

"Yes," I said. "He's at Sullivan and Cromwell in New York."

"Isn't that John Foster Dulles's old firm?"

"It was," I answered, "but Dulles left for the State Department just before my father arrived."

"A talent for literature is all very well," said Julia Bertram, holding her glass before her as if to inspect it for cleanliness. "But a talent for life is rather better, don't you think, Paul?" A look passed between them, but what its significance was I couldn't fathom.

"Lots of lawyers in the world," he said, "but very few people who can read with the perceptiveness of Mr. Hopkins."

"What are you proposing, dear?"

"I'm proposing that Mr. Hopkins stay on at Princeton and do a doctorate, which I would be willing to supervise." Bertram was known to be contemptuous of graduate students as well as of graduate studies; that he was willing to see me through a Ph.D. was no trivial matter. It was an enormous compliment.

I remember that dinner was drier than the sherry. Julia served a boned chicken breast, small red potatoes, and asparagus. With a mere student as a guest, she had not bothered to hire any help, and so had to get up to serve each course herself — with, it seemed to me, a slight edge of irritation. Conversation was a bit strained. After asking about my family and grilling me on other professors at Princeton, the Bertrams talked, for the most part between themselves, about contemporary novelists, poets, and critics. They were none too charitable.

"The only real thing about Robert Lowell," I remember Paul saying that night, "is his madness. The rest is contrived, artificial, phony."

"Quite right, dear," Julia replied. "Another dish of ice cream, Mr. Hopkins?"

Much to my father's chagrin, I rejected Harvard Law and remained at Princeton. For the next five years I did graduate work and then wrote a dissertation about Henry James as expatriate. I do not expect ever to know a better time. Reading and discussing James with Paul Bertram elevated me as nothing else had done, or, I suspect, will again. He read the major novels with a delicacy of judgment that I could not have imagined existing, and the novelist's own character with no less refinement. Clearly Bertram understood James so deeply because he himself possessed the sensibility of a true artist, only without the vast outpouring of solid work that James — at a staggering price in loneliness, as my teacher made plain — achieved, to his everlasting renown.

The question I eventually had to ask myself, though, was whether Paul Bertram was in fact a stunted artist. As his student and then his assistant, I came to learn things about him. His odd cautiousness, for example. Without ever mentioning it to me — and I saw him nearly every day — he had produced a slender volume to which he gave the title *Culture & Confidence*. I first became aware of its existence when a chapter appeared in the English magazine *Encounter*. Complimenting him, I made the mistake of referring to it as the opening chapter of something that seemed to me marvelously promising.

"Thank you, Kenneth," he said, "but I'm afraid that what you read is the last chapter."

My mistake, I now see, was not entirely due to ignorance. Paul Bertram's prose style, always carefully measured, had become toward the end of his life more tentative, hesitant, even costive than before. Intended perhaps as an amalgam of T. S. Eliot and E. M. Forster, it was laced, if not overloaded, with Paul's own grave dubiety, so that between his genuine subtlety and his no less genuine doubt, his meaning became like a code that had to be broken to be understood. Reading *Culture & Confidence*, I kept asking myself, What does he really mean? and then, toward the middle of what was after all a short book, Why the hell doesn't he just say it?

I had finished my dissertation and accepted a job at New York University — Princeton had no place for me — when one day, over coffee in his office, Paul announced that he would like me to function, along with Julia, as an executor of his estate. He was nearing seventy, Julia was two years older than he, and such things needed looking after.

"I would be honored," I said quickly.

"Before it's all over," he said, exhaling, "you are likely to be more than honored. You may well be irritated, frustrated, and put into possession of knowledge you would have preferred to live without."

"Still, just now I'm honored."

"You are, Kenneth, a solid citizen. Probably something you

got from your father. My own father would have called you a *fayner goy*, an upstanding Gentile."

"Aren't there any upstanding Jews for this job?"

"None quite so upstanding as you, my boy. And you know, don't you, Kenneth, that I have come to think of you as my boy. Had I the good luck to have had a son, I should have liked him to be as you are." He took a deep drag on his Gauloise and looked away.

"Thank you" was all I could manage, fearful my throat would catch.

That evening I drove Paul back to Hun Road. He had agreed to give the T. S. Eliot Lectures at Trinity College, Dublin, in the autumn, but now he said he hadn't a clue what to give them on. I suggested Eliot himself, a figure whom he had known personally and for whom he had great and (as always) complex regard.

"It's a thought," he said, bending down to wave goodbye at the closed car window. I watched him walk up to the house, a small figure, slightly bent. From behind he seemed an old man. He stopped at the door to light a cigarette, as if needing the fortification to get him over the threshold.

Paul never lived to give the Eliot Lectures, but died of heart failure in his sleep a month after our last meeting. In her call, Julia said I would have to come to Princeton to talk with their lawyer.

It all seemed simple enough. The Bertrams held everything in common ownership, so there was really no property to be concerned about, aside from Paul's personal effects. (I asked Julia if I might have his gold-tipped Parker 51 pen and his Dunhill lighter, and she gave both to me.) Julia and I were to be in charge of all decisions having to do with Paul's papers, and I would take over in the event of her demise. Pretty standard stuff, or so I thought at the time.

I had never felt quite comfortable with Julia. Sometimes I thought she viewed me as a rival for her husband's affections, though reflecting further I rejected this as altogether too egotistical and self-gratulatory. After all, was I ever anything more than his favorite student? He never reposed any important confidences in me; the closest we came to intimacy was that afternoon in his office when he told me that he would have wished for a son like me. For my part, I felt I couldn't ask him why he and Julia had never had children. Was it a conscious decision? Was one of them incapable? Was it Julia's wish?

After the lawyer, I drove Julia home. She asked me in for coffee. The little house, with its magazines and books covering just about every flat surface, seemed, as always, half shabby-genteel, half bohemian–graduate student. As she sat sipping her coffee, Julia appeared to me to be in good shape for someone who had just lost a husband. Was it possible that Paul's death had freed her, not only from the weight of his complexity but from playing second fiddle? Now that Paul was dead, would Julia give up that first-person plural?

"There is a great deal you couldn't know about my husband," she finally said, setting down her coffee. "Much that might disappoint you."

"I agree with your first point," I said, "and I'm sorry to hear about the second."

"Paul, you see, was a depressive," she continued. "Not a clinical depressive. No physician ever diagnosed him as such, no one put him on a regimen of pills, nothing of that sort, but it came to the same thing. He was very dark most of the time; his was what I came to think of as a spiritual depression. It was, as you might imagine, not all that easy to live with."

"Over what, precisely, was he depressed?"

"Over his life. He had come to regard his work as second-rate. He was very lonely. He felt himself without true peers." Here she paused. "And he had come to regard his marriage as empty."

"Did he tell you these things?"

"Not directly."

"Then how can you be sure?"

"Some of them I sensed. I knew Paul always wanted a child, but we weren't able to have one because of difficulties with my own female arrangements. But I thought he had long ago become resigned to it, as I had."

"How do you know he wasn't?"

"Because of this," she said, reaching over to pick up a manuscript on the lamp table near her chair. She handed it to me over the coffee table.

I looked at the sheaf of pages — fewer, I estimated, than a hundred. The top page bore a title, *The Parched Garden*. I could see it was a manuscript of poems.

"I found them among my husband's effects," Julia said. "It broke my heart to learn he was writing these poems behind my back. There are forty-six of them here. Did you know about their existence?"

"Paul never mentioned them to me," I said truthfully.

"I want you to take them with you and read them. Be careful, by the way; I have made no copies. You will discover that I do not come off very well in them. It turns out I am a dry and grasping person whom false ambition has turned sour. I am the wrong road taken, the principal, the overarching, and the irrevocable mistake of Paul's life."

"That is difficult for me to believe," I said, my voice not sounding as reassuring as I hoped.

"The poems do not lie," Julia said quietly. "If they weren't so damnably beautiful, I probably would never have shown them to you. But you are my co-executor. I want you to read them and tell me what you think we ought to do with them. Because I am so — how to put it? — implicated, the decision should probably be yours exclusively."

I thought at this point Julia might break down, but she didn't. As she walked me to the door, I told her I would call her after I'd read the manuscript and had a chance to think a bit. She put out her hand. I grasped it. Standing on the threshold, a cool dusk wind blowing, I wondered if she would extend her cheek for a kiss. She didn't.

The first thing to be said about the poems in *The Parched Garden* is that they were technically exquisite. Tossing off one form after another, using the most delicate and intricate meters, Paul showed that he had all the moves of a great craftsman, and was still capable of giving deep pleasure to anyone who understood the nature of true poetic achievement. The second thing to be said is that the poems were *very* dark — in some places bitter, in others positively poisonous. It would be pleasing to make the distinction between form and content in Paul's manuscript, yet how many times had he told me that any such distinction was nonsense, that the two were inseparable, inextricably intertwined?

To do a turn on Wordsworth, the poems seemed to me like nothing so much as emotion recollected in hostility. "A Book of Grievances" might as aptly have been their title. And Julia was right: the greatest grievance was against her. Without her, the poems made quite plain, Paul would have gone on to be the artist he wished to be. It was Julia who brought him back into the world, grounded him. Without her, he might have flown.

Reading those poems, I changed my view of Paul Bertram almost completely. The writer whom I had thought resigned to life's limitations turned out not to have been resigned to anything. He turned out to have hated his life, with its little compromises and its large deceits. Civilization, he was testifying, was not worth the discontents; far from it.

But what would publication do to Paul's reputation as a critic of superior subtlety and, in *Lapis Lazuli*, a poet of small but sublime creation? Wouldn't it put in doubt all that had come before? And where, then, did my own responsibility lie? Suddenly I recalled an anecdote Paul had told me about a man named Rosenthal (or was it Rosenberg?), a businessman of serious intellectual interests in early-twentieth-century Prague. Although he himself did no writing, this Rosenthal (let me call him) was much respected by all the writers and intellectuals of the city. One day in 1924, he ran into a worried-looking Max Brod.

"Ah, Rosenthal, I have just returned from the deathbed of my dear friend Franz Kafka, and he has asked me to destroy all his writings."

"Unfortunate," replied Rosenthal, "but a deathbed wish is a sacred thing."

"I know," said Brod, "but how can I destroy the works of Franz Kafka, the greatest writer of German prose of our time?"

"If you feel so strongly about it," replied Rosenthal, "then you must not do it."

"But it is a deathbed wish!"

"Very well, then you must."

"But how can I?"

They went around like this three or four more times, until finally, losing all patience, Rosenthal said: "Look, Brod, here is the solution. You must defy Franz Kafka's deathbed wish. Do not destroy his manuscripts. But in penance, my dear Brod, you must destroy your own."

And here Bertram, smiling faintly, remarked that, having

read a fair amount of the all-too-prolific Brod, he thought Rosenthal's idea not bad at all, with or without the deathbed wish of Franz Kafka.

I tried to remember when Paul had told me this anecdote. Was it four years ago? Five? Could he have known at the time that he would put me in the Max Brod hot seat? As the author of a single work, a dissertation on Henry James turned into a book currently being considered by the University of Chicago Press, not even the Rosenthal solution was available to me.

I read through the manuscript fully five more times before calling Julia Bertram to arrange another meeting. I had come to a decision, but I wanted to check it with her before acting. She was not eager to meet, and wondered why we couldn't discuss the matter over the phone. I said I thought it was too important for that. Somewhat grudgingly, she relented.

"I told you," she began, sitting in the same wing chair as when I had first met her, "that this decision is yours."

"I know that," I said, "but it does affect you, too. Surely you realize that."

"Of course I do. The discovery of Paul's poems puts not only my private life but such literary reputation as I have in an altogether different light. Since my husband's death, I have become a perfect villainess, or I will once these poems are made public. Behind every successful man there is a woman, they used to say; they neglected to add that behind every failed man there is also a woman. Apparently I am now to go down in the footnotes of literary history as one of the latter. It will not surprise you to know, Kenneth, that this is not at all what I had in mind."

"Tell me," I asked, "why didn't you destroy the manuscript after you read it?"

"First, because it is my husband's, and I am not in the habit of destroying anything belonging to Paul. Second, because, hateful though I find it, I recognize that the writing is beautiful, and I am also not in the habit of destroying beautiful things."

"What would you have me do?"

"I believe I've told you that I am the last person to advise you on this."

"I've come to a decision," I said, "but I wanted you to know what it is."

"And what have you decided?"

"I have decided not to publish the poems while you are alive, assuming of course that you die before I do. This way Paul's poems, and the views that may be read into them, will not cause you any pain on earth."

"Very considerate of you, Kenneth," Julia said. "I shall feel the pain only through eternity."

"What do you mean?"

"What I mean, dear boy, is that my husband has betrayed me, and betrayed me sorely. He has made it clear that my own life has been without meaning, unless its meaning is that I have existed solely in order to make life worse for a man named Paul Bertram. Whether the world knows about this while I am alive or after I am dead scarcely matters, does it?"

"No," I said, feeling profoundly my own insensitivity. "I suppose it doesn't."

It was a windy day, and at the door, as I was leaving, Julia told me that she was thinking of moving to Arizona. She had a younger sister, also widowed, living near Tucson. The eastern winters were beginning to get to her, and her sister was all the family she had left in the world. Once again we shook hands, this time with the tacit realization that we might never meet again.

Getting into my car, I placed Paul's manuscript on the front seat next to me. I saw Julia Bertram standing in her doorway, staring but not waving as I pulled away, the once formidable figure now frail and vulnerable. Driving out of Princeton, I thought about Paul and what he would have wanted done with this manuscript on which he had worked with such obviously painstaking care. Although the poems had the polish of finished work, there was no way of knowing when he had written them. Had he, I wondered, completed this manuscript years ago and felt unable, or unwilling, or insufficiently courageous to publish it during his lifetime? That he would have wanted it published at some point I was sure. Was I now recruited to be his accomplice against his own wife, against his own life? Was that what he had meant in calling me a *fayner goy* — that I could be relied upon to carry out a job like this? And what, in such a situation, did upstandingness consist of, anyway?

On the New Jersey Turnpike the wind rocked my car. I leaned over and removed the rubber band that held the manuscript. The first poem, executed in tercets, was titled "The Millstone." Keeping an eye on the road, I could barely make out the words, though the elegance of the form on the page exerted its own small seductiveness.

I must have drifted out of my lane, for a driver coming up on the left gave me three sharp blasts of his horn. I pressed a button, and the window on the driver's side slid down with a deep purr. Holding out Paul Bertram's single surviving manuscript, and taking a deep breath, I released it, all of it, into the wind. Through the rear-view mirror I could see nothing but perfectly made poems scattering over the New Jersey Turnpike. Had a cop been around, I suppose I might have been stopped for littering. Fair enough. The fine would have been worth it.

Saturday Afternoon at the Zoo with Dad

EVINE'S HEART sank when he heard the honking siren —
just like the Gestapo in that old Anne Frank movie — and
then saw the red lights twirling atop the police car behind
him. "Please turn right at the light," instructed a voice
over the speaker. Levine moved his green Jaguar off Sheridan
onto Granville. Dammit, there goes another twenty minutes.
He was late as it was. A heavyset black cop approached. "May
I see your license and insurance card, sir?" Removing them
from his wallet, Levine passed the documents through the open
window.

"Did you know that you were speeding, Barry," the cop
said. "Doing forty-three miles an hour in a thirty-mile-an-hour
zone."

Levine considered responding, "What's this Barry bullshit,
officer, do we know each other? Just give me the ticket and
let's both get going." In the good-old, bad-old Chicago days,
he would have kept a ten-dollar bill in the plastic window of

his wallet along with his driver's license, the cop would have slipped it out, returned the wallet, and everyone would have gone away happy. No longer. Levine decided to go with the honesty ploy. "I wouldn't be surprised, officer. I'm already late to pick up my kids for my weekend visit, and I guess I was pushing it. I'm awfully sorry."

It worked. "I'm a divorced father myself," the cop offered in return. "I know how it is."

"Yeah," Levine said, "it's not so great."

"I'm going to let you off on this one, Barry." The cop handed back Levine's documents. "But watch it. The next officer stops you may just be a happily married man."

"Not too many of those," said Levine with a smile, "but thanks a lot. I appreciate it."

Nice cop, decent guy, a good sign, lucky day maybe. Levine could use the luck. He had been living in dread since he first heard from Sandy on Monday.

"Barry?" she had said over the phone, and at the sound of her voice, Levine froze. "Barry? It's Sandy." Her casualness blotted out the fact that she and Levine hadn't spoken for more than four — Jesus! — it would soon be five years.

"Sandy, good to hear from you," Levine lied. "What's doing?"

It turned out she was coming from Los Angeles to Chicago for her twentieth high school reunion, and she was bringing the kids. They were going to stay for three days, and she had all the bases covered except for Saturday afternoon, when a class picnic was planned and she had no one to watch Jonathan and Jennifer. Could he take them off her hands for five, maybe six hours?

Had he been faster on his feet, Levine would have claimed an out-of-town appointment, a golf date, exploratory surgery, some damn thing. But somehow he lost it. He heard himself saying, in a dopey, unbelievably saccharine voice: "Sure, Saturday afternoon will be great. Where can I pick them up?" What a schmuck!

Mrs. Sandra Goldstein Levine Kravitz, Levine's first and former and only wife, had been remarried for nearly eight years now, and thank God Kravitz had come along when he did. Ten years older than Levine, never married, a lawyer who worked in trusts and estates with a big Jewish firm in L.A., Harvey Kravitz had gotten him off the hook in more ways than one. Because of him, Levine did not have to think about his ex-wife with pity, anger, or guilt. He didn't have to think of her at all, and in fact he almost never did.

Soon after marrying her, Kravitz also told Sandy they needn't bother with child-support payments. Although Levine put up a feigned protest, this was dandy with him. Two grand less a month going out, and not an easy check to write — two G's for the maintenance of children he no longer saw and to help out a wife he'd just as soon didn't exist. He could find better uses for the money.

Jonathan had been three and Jennifer a year and a half when Levine and Sandy divorced. In their generally acrimonious separation, visitation was one of the biggest bones of contention. Marty Spivak, Levine's attorney, had fought for Levine to get the children every weekend and — once they were in school — during spring and Christmas vacations and for a full month each summer. It sounded good at the time. But what was a bachelor, then in his early forties, supposed to do with two toddlers for a full weekend?

Levine's parents were still alive, and at first he brought the kids over to their place. They were very good about it, doting and generous in the way of Jewish grandparents. But for him, hanging around his parents' apartment in Winston Towers, with its lime-colored wall-to-wall shag carpeting, the weekends stretched out interminably. Pushing his daughter in a stroller around the streets of West Rogers Park, carrying his son piggyback, he often went to a nearby playground to put Jonathan on a swing or play with both children in the sandbox. Each weekend came to seem like a long winter — a bad fiscal quarter.

Levine began to skip occasionally. Then his mother got liver cancer and, with her chemo treatments, became too weak to help look after the kids. By the time Harvey Kravitz came along, Levine was ready — relieved — to let him move Sandy and the kids to Los Angeles. Two years later, after a couple of notably unsuccessful visits — he stayed at a Ramada Inn in Westwood, mostly watching pay-per-view movies in his room — Sandy announced that Kravitz wanted to adopt Jonathan and Jennifer, and Levine was ready to concede that, too.

"Barry," his father told him, "don't be crazy. They're your children, your flesh and blood, they should carry your name." But Levine felt he had no leverage. The children had never come to Chicago, and his Los Angeles visits were a complete bust, demoralizing in every way. What the hell, he thought, Kravitz pays all the bills, and they seem to like him. Let them be Kravitz's kids, let them take his name. In the end, what really does it matter? After a year or so, he ceased calling every few weeks, then he stopped sending birthday gifts. Finally, he no longer even thought of himself as a father.

When they were married, there was nothing that Sandy and Levine couldn't find to fight about: her parents, his parents, his friends, her friends, money, child-rearing methods, food, and of course sex. Levine was thirty-five when he married — no kid —

Sandy twenty-four. He had felt it was time for him to call an end to single life. A serious error. The problem probably wasn't even Sandy; it was marriage. He, Levine came to conclude about himself, was just one of the world's natural bachelors.

After the divorce, he moved into an apartment on Scott Street, on the old Gold Coast. He left the commodities market each afternoon at two P.M., and by two-thirty he was on the treadmill at the East Bank Club, or shooting baskets in a pickup game, or sitting in a Jacuzzi, checking out passing women, of whom, for a man with money and leisure, there seemed to be no shortage. Most evenings, when not with a younger woman, he would have dinner with a few guys from the club. They would talk sports or stocks or funny adventures with broads.

He liked things the way they were. One Friday afternoon at the East Bank a guy named Earl Berlin asked if he was free for the weekend. Berlin had just invited two girls on a high-rollers' junket to Vegas; he needed to make a foursome, but they had to be on a plane at O'Hare in two hours. Levine looked at the woman he was to escort — Debbie was her first name, Berlin hadn't quite caught her last — a racquetball player at the club, nice body, thick dark hair, and thought, Why not, let's go. He boarded the plane with nothing but the clothes he was wearing and his American Express card and bought everything, even socks and underwear, at Caesar's Palace. Debbie turned out to be a very accommodating young lady; Levine won more than $3,000 at craps and blackjack; and as a souvenir of the weekend he still had two pairs of cashmere socks for which he had paid $50 a shot.

When Levine went out with a new girl — and most of the women he went out with he thought of as girls — he would tell her that he was divorced but never mention having had children. If they asked, he lied and said no. He wasn't likely to be with the girl that long, so the lie was unlikely to catch up with him. And thus far it hadn't.

It was 11:10 when Levine's Jaguar pulled up in front of the North Shore Hilton. He was forty minutes late, and Sandy and the two children were waiting at the entrance. He felt an urge to accelerate and keep driving. From the car, he could see that the girl, now ten and a half, had her mother's fair skin and light hair — dishwater blond, it used to be called. He noted, too, the braces on her teeth. Jonathan looked more like a Levine, dark, small, with curly hair; he looked, in fact, astonishingly like Levine at the same age. Sandy, who had put on a few pounds, seemed exactly what she was, a rich attorney's wife and a mother who had fought, successfully, to keep her family together. A brief and unexpected flare of admiration shot through him.

Pulling the car over, Levine left the engine running and walked up to them. He had neglected to prepare an opening line.

"Sorry I'm late."

"Hello, Barry," his ex-wife said, all business. "I'd like it if you could have Jonathan and Jenny back here at the hotel by five."

"Shouldn't be a problem."

"Great," she said, "and thanks for helping out." Was there a touch of sarcasm in her voice, or was Levine imagining it? His radar wasn't working so well this morning.

"Maybe we'll have a chance to talk later," Sandy said, turning back into the cool dark of the lobby.

Levine and the children had not yet spoken. Both kids got into the back seat. As Levine pulled out, he caught a glimpse of them in the rear-view mirror sitting close together, almost huddled. It occurred to him they might feel even more awkward than he.

"What do you say to lunch and a trip to the zoo in Lincoln Park?" He had nearly six hours to kill. Although it was early June, the Cubs were out of town, and besides, it might be a mistake to take a girl to a ball game, though for all he knew his daughter might be one of those girl athletes. He didn't know about the boy. Maybe he was a video-game nut.

"Whatever you want," replied Jonathan.

"O.K.," Levine said, sensing a long afternoon, "the zoo it is."

He took McCormick over to Devon, thinking the kids might be interested in the neighborhood where he and their mother had both grown up. Of course, it had all changed drastically since those days. Indian and Pakistani shops now dominated Devon Avenue. "West Rajah's Park," his friend Shel Reisman now called the neighborhood.

"Your mother and I grew up here," Levine said. "Has she ever told you anything about it?"

"She said that people didn't think too much about crime," the girl piped up. "Not like now." To Levine, studying her in the mirror, her braces made her seem all the more vulnerable.

"That's true," he said. "When I was younger than you, Jonathan, my parents let me go downtown on the El by myself. My father — you probably don't remember him — grew up with two guys who owned a gym where boxers trained. They let me hang out there. You care about sports?"

"Pro basketball," the boy said.

"Me, too," Levine agreed. "Follow the Bulls?"

"Who doesn't? Michael Jordan, Scottie Pippen, crazy Dennis Rodman."

"I like Rodman's hair," the girl said, "but Mommy says his bleaching it so many colors is going to ruin it."

"He can rebound like crazy," Jonathan put in. "But he can't stand up to Shaq in the low post. In the low post Shaq would take him on tour."

"You're both right," Levine said. So he had a son who knew sports. His own boyhood was dominated by them: playing, watching, fantasizing. Something nice about this discovery.

On the Outer Drive he passed Weiss Memorial Hospital, where both his parents had died. Best to leave this unmentioned. Through his divorce, he had deprived his own parents of the pleasures of their grandchildren. Neither had ever said anything to him about it. He doubted that he himself would ever be a grandfather, except in the most remote and technical sense. Right now that didn't seem to him much of a deprivation. Different generations, different views.

At a Greek restaurant on Halsted named Demi's, he ordered an omelet made with egg whites, while the children had cheeseburgers with fries and Cokes.

"You like growing up in California, Jennifer?"

"Nobody calls her Jennifer," Jonathan said. "Everybody calls her Jenny."

"Sorry."

"It's fun," the girl said, "though maybe I'd like to see snow sometimes."

"California's all we know," Jonathan added. "We've got nothing to compare it to."

"When you were little, of course," Levine reminded them, "you lived in Chicago."

"You mean when you were our father," Jenny said.

"Right." Past tense noted.

Halfway through lunch Jenny knocked over her Coke, half of which spilled onto her brother's fries and uneaten cheeseburger. Rising to wipe up the mess, Levine noticed a redhead, maybe in her late twenties, entering the restaurant; impressive rack but, in his judgment, a little short in the leg. Not, just now, a good time to make a move. He must have seemed like a divorced father out with his kids for the weekend, or a guy giving his wife a break on a Saturday, but certainly not what he was — a professional bachelor, perpetually on the attack.

Apparently a visit to the zoo on a sunny early-summer day was not an altogether original idea. Three times Levine drove around the streets before finally pulling into a garage on Clark, where a sullen Mexican took a $12 fee without any thanks.

At the entrance to the park, Jenny wanted a great blue bouffant of cotton candy being sold by a Pakistani.

"She's not supposed to eat candy because of her braces," her brother said, a note of satisfaction in his voice.

"Yes I can," the girl protested, "if I rinse after."

"Where are you going to rinse here, dork?"

"None of your business, moron."

"O.K.," Levine said, "let's take a pass. We'll get some ice cream and peanuts inside. How's that?"

"But I *love* cotton candy," Jenny said, "and I can rinse out at one of the fountains."

Screw it, Levine thought, I see these kids for one day; am I supposed to be responsible for her character as well as her dental hygiene? He shelled out two bucks and handed Jenny the blue cloud of sugar.

The zoo was teeming. Lots of kids being wheeled around in strollers. Many grandparents, plus some middle-aged guys with younger wives and little kids — second-family men. A band was playing: blacks in dreadlocks clanged away on steel drums while a woman with a shaved head sang a combination of African and Caribbean melodies. Levine took Jenny's hand. Jonathan walked a few steps ahead. They joined the crowd around the seals, which were darting in and out of their pool and hooting as they slapped themselves dry on the rocks.

Levine looked around for Jonathan, but he was gone. The seal exhibit had an underground walkway with windows that allowed you to view the animals from beneath. Probably the boy had gone down for a look.

"Jenny," Levine said, letting go of her hand, "wait right here. Don't move. I have to find your brother." He trotted downstairs to the walkway, the blue of the water giving off an eerie light in the darkish corridor. Three kids in NBA jerseys with baggy shorts, big shoes, and baseball hats worn backward stared into one of the windows. At the end of the walkway Levine found Jonathan peering through another. He thought briefly of scolding him but instead took his hand and walked him back outside. When they got there, Jenny was gone. "Shit," Levine said aloud. "Now what?"

"She sometimes just goes off by herself," the boy replied, "like in a department store or something. She can get kinda dreamy. My mom and dad always find her." Dad, of course, was Kravitz.

The sun was shining with particular radiance. People seemed happy to be out with their children, gazing at animals, drinking soda, eating lemon ices, listening to music. Calm seemed everywhere but in Levine's heart. He wasn't sure in which direction to begin. There had to be a central lost-and-found somewhere, but would Jenny know where to find it and have the good sense to wait for him there?

He steered Jonathan into the nearby big-cat house. Most of the lions, leopards, and tigers were out-of-doors, lazing, along with a solitary cheetah, in the sun. Searching the nearly empty building, he noted only a single panther padding slowly around its cage. The muscles in the beast's chest, the cold look in its eyes, sent a shiver through Levine. These days the press was full of child molestation stories. Block it out.

They tried the snake house. No Jenny. Then the ape house, a new building. The large gorillas were napping. The orangutans seemed idiotic, the baboons even lewder than he remembered. Where the hell was she? C'mon, sweetheart, Levine pleaded silently, don't put me through this. Outside, back in the beaming sun, Levine took Jonathan's hand. They passed the giraffes with their gentle, quizzical looks, the zebras swishing their tails, shaggy bisons and wildebeests seriously in need of a bath. Finally, they came upon a building marked *Information Center*.

"Excuse me," Levine said to the young woman inside with a diamond chip under her lower lip. "Is there a lost-and-found for kids? I want to report a little girl missing."

"It's at Gateway House," she said, "at the east gate. Would you like me to call to see if she's there? We could also have her paged."

"Please," Levine said. "Her name's Jenny Kravitz. She's ten, and she's wearing a red T-shirt and jeans. Braces on her teeth."

"No problem."

Maybe for you, Levine thought. He had a pretty good imagination for disaster, and right now it was envisioning Mexican street gangs, old perverts, canny kidnappers, ransom notes; the possibilities were practically endless.

"I'm sorry, your daughter's not at Gateway House," the girl reported, hanging up the phone. "But she could show up at any moment, Mr. Kravitz, and in the meantime I'll do a page."

"Thanks," he said. "But it's Levine, not Kravitz."

"I thought you said her name was Kravitz."

"It is, but mine's Levine. It's a long story."

"I see," she said, not looking as if she did. As they left the building, they heard Jenny's name over the PA system.

"I'm thirsty," Jonathan said. "Could I get a Coke or something?"

The closest spot was Café Brauer, a bit of a walk, but Levine thought he ought to accommodate the boy. They sat for a few minutes at one of the tables along the lagoon.

"What will you do," Jonathan asked, "if my sister's dead?"

"Jesus," said Levine, "she's not dead. Don't even talk that way."

"No, I mean, what would you do if she was?"

"I'd feel terrible," Levine said. "Wouldn't you?"

"Yeah, sure, but I mean, I'm her brother. I'm supposed to."

"Well, I'm her father."

"Not really."

"What do you mean not really?"

"I mean, you're only sort of our father, but not really. Isn't that right? I mean, you don't see us, you don't talk to us. Do you think about us?"

"Of course I think about you," Levine said. "All the time."

"Then how come you never call or anything?"

"I guess I think it makes it easier on everybody if I don't. You live far away and everything."

"I once asked my new dad what he would do if he didn't live with his children, and you know what he said?"

"No," said Levine.

"He said it would kill him if he lost his children. But then he said that everyone is different and we shouldn't judge you. Maybe you have your reasons." The boy paused.

"I do have reasons," Levine said, beginning to sweat. "The main one is that I didn't want to make your lives more complicated. Your mother and I didn't get along so well when we were married, and I thought it would be easier if I just sort of disappeared."

"I see," Jonathan said, dropping his eyes and putting the straw in his mouth.

"Look," Levine said, "we better get to Gateway House. Maybe your sister is there waiting for us."

"Maybe," the boy said, noisily draining the last of his drink.

Levine thought they should check the petting zoo, which was in a nearby barn. As he and the boy walked through the door, he saw Jenny standing near a small black goat. A flash of anger was quickly swallowed by relief. He watched as the child made a tentative approach to the little goat. Hard to believe she would be a woman one day, exciting to men, with her own plots and agendas. As they walked up to her, she turned and smiled as if nothing in the world were wrong. God, Levine thought, those braces! He put his hand on her head, about to pet her just as she was petting the goat. Then he remembered his anger.

"Where have you been?" he said, hearing the sternness in his voice. "You had your brother and me worried sick."

"I'm sorry," she said. "I just got tired of waiting for you at the seals."

"Mom would kill you if she knew what you did," her brother lectured her.

"It's none of your business."

"It's my business," Levine interjected. "I'm responsible for you, at least for this afternoon. And Jonathan's right. Your mother would be furious with both of us if she knew you just took off on your own the way you did."

"You know she would, too, Jenny," Jonathan added.

"Look, let's get out of here," Levine said. "Let's get out of the zoo and get an ice cream or something."

They made their way out, Jenny's hand tightly folded in Levine's, Jonathan walking alongside. The Lincoln Park neighborhood seemed very youthful on this summer day. Lots of young women in spandex, their hair pulled back in ponytails, out for a run. They found a Baskin-Robbins on Clark, near Fullerton, where Levine stood in line behind a gay couple roughly his own age, two bald guys in tank tops. He bought double-dip sugar cones for the kids — rocky road and cherry vanilla for Jenny, two scoops of pistachio for Jonathan — and a nonfat chocolate frozen yogurt for himself. A booth opened up, and they grabbed it.

"Are you gonna tell Mommy about my getting lost?" Jenny asked.

"Would you prefer I didn't?"

"Yeah," she said. "I think she'd only get mad — I mean, really mad."

"What do you think, Jonathan?" Levine asked. "Can we keep it a secret just between the three of us?"

"O.K.," he said, "I won't tell."

"Bet he does," Jenny said.

"Bet I won't."

"If Jonathan says he won't tell, he won't tell," Levine said. "He looks to me like a man who keeps his word, and I believe him." Levine put out his hand; Jenny took it. He then reached for Jonathan's hand and put it on top. "So it's our secret then," he said.

Driving home, brother and sister once more sat in the back seat. Passing Weiss Memorial again, Levine, feeling like a chauffeur in his own car, said: "See that red brick building on the left? That's where my mother and father died. They were your grandparents, you know."

"Were they nice?" Jenny asked.

"Very nice, fair and kind and goodhearted, and they loved you both when you were babies, though of course you can't be expected to remember them."

"What did they die from?" Jonathan asked.

"Cancer. Both of them. Your grandmother first."

"Why did you and Mommy get divorced?" Jenny asked. "Mommy said you stopped loving each other. Is that true?"

"Sort of," Levine said. "But maybe it's just as true to say that I didn't like being married that much."

"Does that mean you didn't like being our father?" the girl asked.

A tough question. "I wouldn't put it that way," he said, looking at the kids in the mirror. He was glad to be sitting where he was, where they couldn't see directly into his face. "I would say that I wasn't that good at being a father."

"Is that a good reason for leaving us?" Jonathan put in.

"No, I suppose not. But your new father's good to you, right? He loves you, right? So maybe it worked out for the best."

"It's not the same thing," the boy said. Had Levine himself at twelve been as relentless as this kid?

"It's not the same thing as what?"

"It's not the same thing as having your real father," Jonathan said.

Levine, turning off the Outer Drive and onto Sheridan Road, didn't answer.

"Do you love us?" Jenny asked.

"What a question. Of course I do." He was passing the place where, earlier today, the cop had stopped him for speeding. No response from the back seat. After another block or two, the silence seemed chilling. At the corner of Sheridan and Devon, Levine thought to tell them about the great Granada movie theater that once stood here, an Aladdinish place, huge and wildly ornate, where he went every Friday night through high school. Going to the Granada as a boy to watch Cary Grant and Gary Cooper and Tyrone Power, he never thought he might one day become a father who would abandon his children. Life had its tricks, all right. Not that they had been left to poverty, hunger, or anything like that. They were probably living better with Kravitz than they would if he had stayed married to their mother. Maybe if they hadn't moved to goddamn California he would have managed to keep in touch. But they were two thousand miles away, for shit's sake. What was he supposed to do? Sneaking another peek in the mirror, Levine realized he couldn't quite successfully suppress what he knew was the correct answer to that question.

It was 5:05 when the Jaguar pulled up to the door of the Hilton. Sandy, waiting inside, came out and opened the back door.

"Did you have a nice time?"

"Yes," Jenny said. Jonathan said nothing.

"The zoo was crowded," Levine offered. "We had an ice cream about an hour or so ago. Hope it won't spoil their dinner." A bit nervous, he wasn't clear about the choreography of his departure.

"Want to come in for a cup of coffee?" Sandy asked.

"Thanks, but I'd better be off. Besides, you probably want to get going."

"I suppose we should."

"It was fun," Levine said. "They're good kids." He put out his hand to Jonathan, who shook it without looking at him. Turning to Jenny, he found himself pulling the child to him and kissing the top of her head. "Bye, baby," he muttered.

"Goodbye," she said. It occurred to him that neither of them had called him anything all day long.

In a slightly jerky movement, Sandy quickly leaned in, brushing his cheek with hers. "Thanks."

Somehow Levine managed to get back behind the wheel, lower the window on the passenger side, and try his best to smile and wave as he pulled away. In the rear-view mirror he saw his ex-wife, her free arm around the shoulders of her daughter, the two of them waving back; her son made no movement at all. For once, Levine was glad he had nothing on for the evening. Maybe he'd grab a sandwich, watch a ball game on television, hit the sack early. It had been a long day.

Freddy Duchamp in Action

O
N THE MORNING the letter — it was a form letter, actually — arrived from the warden at Joliet prison, I had a lunch date with Max Schecter. Max had retired from the Chicago police department two years earlier. He had been a flier in World War II and had flown for the Israelis in their war of independence. His business card read *Colonel Max Schecter,* and, under that, a single word: *Mercenary.* He was a single-idea man, Max: the idea was that the world was still out to get the Jews and that most Jews were all too ready to connive in their own ultimate destruction. He wrote lots of letters to the Chicago papers and to the Jewish press, naming the politicians who were really friends of the Jews — almost none qualified — and those who weren't, a multitude.

Max had no distaste for violence — his language bristled with it — but he didn't look anything like the fighter pilot he had been. He was almost aggressively bald (he had taken to wearing caps indoors), short, not particularly muscular, and with an emphatic limp. Most of his old power was in his face and especially in his teeth: his smile hinted at the hope that you might make the mistake of trying to mess with him. Even now, Max was not a man to fool with. His voice, with its metallic ring, carried in public places, and given some of his remarks, this sometimes caused me to wince.

Max and I didn't meet often, usually once or twice a year, though he always sent a card on the Jewish holidays. When my wife died, he wrote me a letter about life being little else but a series of losses, which I found touching. All the more so, I suppose, because as far as I knew, Max was himself quite alone in the world.

"So, David," he said with one of his knowing smiles as I came up to the table at the Belden Deli, "how's it hanging?" He had already set up office. Newspaper clippings lay on the table, also a few photocopied items, some recent letters he had received, a few he had written, and a mangled copy of the *Chicago Sun-Times.*

"By the same few threads," I answered. "And with you?"

"I could complain," he said, the teeth flashing, "but who would listen?"

"Max," I said, sitting down, "I need your advice. I just got a letter from the warden at Joliet, asking permission for an inmate to write to me. I'm guessing he's read one of my books. Can you think of a good reason not to say yes?"

"None at all," said Max with his sly smile, "as long as you stand ready to do this guy a big favor someday."

"Such as?"

"Begin a correspondence with a con and eventually he's going to ask you to write a letter to the parole board or lend him money or, if he gets out, he'll ask to stay with you for three or four days. Or more. If you're ready for that, what've you got to lose?"

In other words, if I was prepared to be taken advantage of by a crook — a thief, maybe a rapist, possibly a murderer — sure, go ahead. After all, whatever else the guy had done in the world, at least he had the excellent taste to admire my wonderful writing.

"Thanks, Max," I said, "that's helpful."

But not helpful enough, apparently. Because after I returned home and considered the cogency of Max's words, I still wrote to the warden and said O.K. It wasn't that I didn't believe Max; it was, I told myself, that even though I was past sixty, I still believed it was important not to close your heart too quickly. Besides, if the guy asked one of the favors Max predicted, I could always turn him down, couldn't I?

His first letter, which arrived roughly a month later, was in a small and careful hand, with no grammatical or spelling errors:

> Dear Mr. Ross,
>
> This is just to let you know that I enjoyed your novel *The Argyle Boys.* I grew up in the neighborhood you wrote about. I went to Senn High School like the guys in your book. I also hung out like them at Zeitkin's drugstore. My parents lived on Sheridan near Foster. I was born in 1934, so I'm three years older than you. Was the character you call Bronco Levine by any chance based on a guy named Buddy Levitz? Thanks for writing a good book. And thanks also for giving me permission to write to you. Someday I'd like to read some more of your other books.

The letter was signed Fred C. Duchamp; somehow the comic dignity of that C., from prison, made me a little sad. I wrote back to thank him for the letter and told him he was right about Buddy Levitz, who, I reported, had died four years ago of lung cancer. And I sent him another of my novels, *West Rogers Park,* which also had characters from Senn High School and was set in the time of our boyhood. I took care not to ask him any questions, including the most interesting one of all, which was why he happened to be in prison. I didn't want to make him think I was looking for a pen pal.

A few weeks later in the Loop I ran into Lou Stein, who had become one of the chief chroniclers of our youth, and asked him if he remembered a kid named Fred Duchamp. He did: a smallish guy, according to Lou, with an air of tidiness about him. Played center field in softball games at Clarendon, a good ballplayer, covered a lot of ground, a punch hitter, something of a loner, not sure if he was Jewish or not. I tried hard but I still couldn't place him.

In six weeks another letter arrived from Joliet. It seems the prison guards were in no hurry to get packages into the hands of prisoners, and so it had taken a while before he'd gotten my book. But he had now read it, and it, too, reminded him of the old days. West Rogers Park tended to be more solidly middle class and also more Jewish than his own part of town, along Sheridan Road and Marine Drive. He himself, he volunteered, came of a mixed marriage: his mother was Jewish, his father not — which, in those days, was scandalous. His mother's family had sat *shiva* when she married Earl Duchamp, a car salesman who, his son confided, had been a skirt chaser and never made much of a living. Fred, an only child, grew up sleeping on a studio couch in the family's one-bedroom furnished apartment. "Luck of the draw who you get for parents," he wrote, "and only a chump would blame them for his fate in life, unless they regularly beat the hell out of you or something." He ended by asking if I knew whatever had become of a kid named Frankie Winters, whom he remembered as a good athlete — great arm — and a sweet guy.

Frankie I remembered very well. He was small, with the build of a gymnast, a fine smile, and I recalled hearing that he had married his old girlfriend, Nancy. They were the last of the jitterbuggers; at high school dances, the floor would clear — as in a forties MGM musical — and Frankie and Nancy would dance alone, everyone else forming a circle to look on. He had become a physical therapist, which was a good bit below the aspirations of most of the Jewish boys I had grown up with, and had long since moved to Peoria.

I decided to call Frankie Winters. Claiming to remember me, he asked what I did for a living, which meant he had not known of my books (he was the model for a minor character in *The Argyle Boys*). More important, he remembered Fred Duchamp.

"An odd guy, Freddy," Frankie said. "He kinda went off on his own. His old man was an operator, a salesman of some sort. Freddy liked to gamble. They used to let him play in poker games at the Somerset Hotel when he was still in high school. High stakes. Pretty big stuff in those days."

"Did he ever marry?"

"I don't know. After high school I lost touch with him. What's he doing now, you know?"

"I don't," I said, feeling it wasn't my place to tell anyone that Freddy Duchamp was in jail. "I only heard about him through a cousin of mine who met him somewhere."

Before hanging up, Frankie informed me that he and Nancy had two daughters, now in their late thirties, and five grandchildren. I sent off a postcard to Freddy Duchamp with this news, allegedly gleaned from someone I'd run into who was in touch with Frankie Winters. On a return card Freddy wrote, in his careful hand: "I liked Frank. I remember him as a kid with no bullshit about him." And there was a postscript: "Have you ever heard of a writer named Theodore Dreiser? Am starting to read a book of his. He seems to know the score."

Don't ask me why, but in Powell's used bookstore in Hyde Park I bought a copy of W. A. Swanberg's biography of Dreiser and shipped it to Joliet. Three weeks later, Freddy wrote to thank me and to announce that he was up for parole in two weeks and expected to get it. ("Knock wood," he added in parentheses.) Then he was planning to be in Chicago for a few days, on his way to the West Coast to visit his daughter in Sacramento. Would I mind if he called? He'd like to take me to lunch to pay me back for my kindness. Of course, if I didn't want to have lunch with an ex-con, he'd understand.

"And, by the way," he added, "I never told you why I am in Joliet. I was sentenced to ten years for armed robbery. I'll have served a little more than three of them. I was arrested in Schaumburg for putting a plastic bag in a night depository. I was guilty as hell. I did this three times earlier before getting caught. My big mistake was that the time they caught me I was carrying a gun. Dumb, especially since I've never shot a gun in my life. When we meet — if we meet — I'll be able to explain it all. I still don't think of myself as a thief. But that's a long story. Maybe everybody's got a long story. Thanks again for your letters and for the books."

Well, at least Max Schecter was wrong about one thing: I wasn't going to be asked to support Freddy Duchamp's request for parole. I can't help it, but I like it when guys like Max, in their certainty, are wrong. I sent Freddy my unlisted phone number, and said yes, I hoped he'd call.

When he did, his voice was slightly high-pitched and had a refined quality to it. He planned to be in town for two, maybe three days on family business before taking off for California by bus, and was staying at the Lawson YMCA on Chicago Avenue. He had a taste for deli. Was there a good one nearby where we could get together? I proposed The Bagel, on Broadway, the last Jewish deli in Chicago not owned and run by Greeks. We agreed to meet the next day at noon.

"I'm small," he said when I asked what he looked like, "with white hair, but not a lot of it left. Don't worry, I'll find you from the photos on your books."

I had beat him to The Bagel, where I took one of the front booths with a view of the door. Freddy entered exactly on time: about five foot six, small-boned, with thinning white hair brushed straight back. He looked as if he had just emerged from a shower. He wore a blue windbreaker over a white shirt, tan pants neatly pressed. His plain-toed black shoes and the transparent frames of his glasses looked as if they might be prison issue. He carried a small gym bag. I waved.

"Fred Duchamp," he said, extending a hand while sliding smoothly into the booth.

"David Ross." I shook his hand, which was small, the skin dry but soft. The nails on his slender fingers, I noted, had a coat of polish. What had he done in prison, I wondered, made license plates, worked in the laundry, maybe in the library? All I knew about jail was what I had seen in the movies. Had he been — every man's nightmare — raped? His experience of the world was a lot wider than mine.

"So," I said, "it must feel good to be out."

"Very good," he said. "Amazingly good, in fact."

The waitress came to take our order, and I asked for a turkey sandwich and coffee. He ordered corned beef on a kaiser roll, with french fries, three pickles, and a Coke.

"I used to worry about cholesterol." He smiled briefly. "Prison food takes your mind off it."

"Was it as tough as advertised?"

"You get used to it," he said, "and you meet some extraordinary types."

"This your only time?"

"I once did eight months, in Sandstone, in Minnesota, for kiting checks. Next to Joliet, Sandstone was a piece of cake, a rest home."

"How'd you happen to get caught carrying a gun?"

"You want the long version or the short version?"

"You have a medium version?"

"I'll invent one."

Our food arrived. Freddy took a small bite of his enormous sandwich, chewing slowly, savoring it as if it were a rare wine, which, after years at Joliet, it must have seemed.

"After I graduated high school, I decided that I didn't need college. School bored me, even though I wasn't too bad at it. Through my old man I got a job working as a flunky for a guy whose territory was Chicago, selling Hart, Schaffner and Marx clothes. Very big firm in those days, you may remember. After a couple of years I was given a territory of my own. It included Iowa and the Dakotas, northern Minnesota. Ever been in Grand Forks, North Dakota, in February?"

"I haven't had the pleasure."

"I soon had enough of such pleasures myself. It was time to get off the road. Hart, Schaffner controlled a number of stores around Chicago, one of them in South Shore — this was before the neighborhood changed — and I worked out a deal to take it over."

"What year would that've been?"

"Winter of 1959. It was called the Pickwick Shop, on Jeffrey just off Seventy-first Street. The plan was for me to own the joint outright in seven years. Meanwhile, I got married, had a kid, and went off to my store six days a week."

"Sounds like you were a good citizen."

"Absolutely. Except that after maybe three years of this I'm going out of my gourd. I'm down on my knees adjusting the break on the trousers of old men, worrying that I've bought too many long-sleeved knit polo shirts that I can't move, hating every minute of it, and at the same time thinking maybe I ought to be looking into opening a second store in the new shopping center in Flossmore. And I probably would have, except for a little move I made one Tuesday afternoon when I called four bookies in town and bet a combined ten grand on the Cards to beat the Cubs, and won. It was a completely nuts thing to do. But I did it and came out winners."

"A nice afternoon's work."

"You know how many pairs of socks or Hathaway shirts or Hickey goddamn Freeman suits you have to sell to clear ten grand? Anyhow, for the first time in my life I felt like I was my own boss. I was in action, like the gamblers say. As a kid in high school, I used to play the football parlay cards, and I would sit in on poker games at the Somerset. I was a strong gin player, too. But this was different. This was flying."

"What did your wife say?"

"Whaddya kiddin' me? Why would I tell my wife? Every gambler keeps three sets of books: a fake one for his wife, a fake one for the government, and a real one for himself."

Signaling the waitress, he ordered another Coke and a piece of cheesecake. I had a refill on my coffee.

"I don't know what you must have felt when you decided you could write, but maybe it's the same. My mind was never at rest. I was always worked up, but happily worked up, if you know what I mean."

"I know exactly what you mean," I said.

"I was always thinking about angles, odds, deviations, possible scores. I started betting baseball games regularly. I studied pitchers. I looked into streaks, weather conditions, the effects of minor injuries."

"Were you making more ten-grand bets?"

"No. Never. Every so often I would take a flier and bet a grand, but mostly it was two or three hundred bucks a game, depending on what I thought of the line. I was doing O.K., making an extra grand or two on the side every month. Anyway, there wasn't much to do at the store now that the blacks were coming into South Shore and the whites were leaving in panic. You didn't see too many black guys in Harris tweed sports jackets, plaid shirts, and khaki pants with a little belt in the back. I opened the joint in the morning mostly to study the *Sporting News* and call in my bets."

"Sounds like the Pickwick Shop was a front, without your meaning it to be."

"Yeah, I guess it was. But to get on with the end of my days as a haberdasher, one day around noon I'm on the phone, calling in my bets, when in walk three black guys, maybe in their early twenties. Two of them pull guns, and the third tells me to get on the floor, face down."

"What did you do?"

"I'm not sure you'll believe this, but I remember being mainly ticked off because I thought I had a good thing going in the Pirates-Dodgers game and now I might not get my bet down in time. They go over to the cash register where they get about eighty bucks, and another twenty-two hundred in my money clip, and my watch and wedding ring off me. Then they're about to leave, and they tell me to count to a thousand before I get up off the floor, when for some crazy reason I hear myself saying, 'How're you boys fixed for socks and underwear?' This brought me a kick in the side of the head from the guy who wasn't carrying the gun. Six weeks later I locked the place and never looked back. Even today, I hear the word 'inventory,' I get nervous."

"What did your wife say?"

"She didn't say anything because she didn't know anything. Rochelle assumed I was looking for a location for another store. What I was really looking for was someone to beat the Celtics at long odds. By the way, she's married to a dentist now, lives in Highland Park. I gave her a tough time."

"Because of the gambling?"

"Because of having to hide the gambling. To put her off what was really going on, I pretended to be having love affairs — the last thing a real gambler is interested in. I'd do things like leave condoms in my pockets or smear lipstick on a shirt collar. When she confronted me, I made a full confession and promised never to do it again. She wanted me to go into psychotherapy. I said I would consider it. This was when the Lakers were on a thirty-three-game streak, and I had them almost all the way, most nights easily beating the spread. I was on a roll. I could've afforded a team of shrinks. It lasted three years before I started to lose. But then I lost big-time. I couldn't have won a bet on the outcome of World War Two. I was completely bombed out, my credit was cut off, tap city."

"And then?"

"Things dragged on for a while. Shelley eventually found out about the gambling. She wanted me to go to her father to get money for therapy. I agreed to see some guy. He had an office in the Loop, but at our first meeting I saw that he didn't have a clue. He said my gambling was self-destructive, which didn't seem very interesting. What this guy didn't understand was that gambling wasn't a substitute for something missing in my life. It *was* my life. I never felt guilty about it. The only guilt I feel is for making a stupid bet."

"What about your wife? No guilt there?"

"None. She remarried — the right man this time. True, I missed out on raising my daughter, but she seems to have survived in good shape. The thing about a gambling life is that you only got to take care of yourself. I have no family, no bills outside of having to provide food and shelter for myself, no inventory. I travel light. There're some jobs that make it wrong to marry and bring someone else into your life, when you don't have time for them. Gambling's gotta be one of them."

Perhaps I had been around too many writers, academics, lawyers, people shuffling one kind of paper or another, but I found Freddy Duchamp's direct experience of life impressive, and that he had also thought so clearly about his choices in life made him seem somehow attractive. I knew that I hadn't the courage to operate so wholly on my own.

"I'm sure you've heard it before, David — O.K. to call you David? — but life is a gamble. You get up every morning hoping you don't find a funny little lump in your gonads when showering, or a throbbing in your left arm when driving to work. You turn onto the freeway and wonder if some hopped-up punk in an old beater isn't going to smash you to pieces. You come home at night and hope your wife hasn't taken off with the nice-looking guy that runs the produce department at the supermarket. It's all a gamble, right?"

"From a certain point of view," I said, "I suppose it is. But most of what you're calling gambles are really out of a man's control: the cancer, the car crash, the wife running off. Doesn't a full-time gambler like to *court* danger? He's asking for it — he can't live without it."

"Can you live without writing?"

"Probably not, but if I don't write, or if I start a book that flops, it isn't the same as losing twenty grand in Vegas."

"I don't go to Vegas. I don't go to racetracks, either. The crowds at both places, so many losers under one roof, make me sadder than hell. But I'll tell you something you might think crazy. A good loss every now and then isn't such a terrible thing. Take my word for it: I've had some high-voltage jolts in this business. But a big loss can put the world in perspective. After you're tapped out you can sometimes see things a lot clearer.

You know you have to stir yourself, rebound, not let defeat get the best of you. Don't get me wrong. Between winning and losing, winning is always a lot better. But even losing isn't, if you get my drift, a total loss."

"Forgive my asking, but is doing time at Joliet part of losing?"

"No, that shouldn't have happened. But I did something stupid. I got in the hole with the boys. I made the mistake of borrowing from Guido to pay Dominic. I'm talking juice. Guido started to lean on me. One day a few of the boys picked me up outside my apartment on Marine Drive. They knocked the windows out of my car — windshield and everything — with a baseball bat, an aluminum one. They promised to do the same to my head if I didn't get up-to-date on my payments. I bought a gun, which I began to keep in the glove compartment."

"So that's why a nice half-Jewish boy like you was packing heat?"

"Heat? I see you go to the movies. Well, carrying a gun by itself isn't going to get you into much trouble. A warning, a slap on the wrist, usually nothing more. My problem was that the cops in Schaumburg found the gun in my car the night they picked me up fishing out the plastic bag I had planted in the night depository. This gave them the opportunity to turn robbery into armed robbery, and that meant hard time at Joliet."

I wanted to ask him details about life in prison, but thought better of it. "Where do you go from here?" I asked instead.

"Right now I need to find a hotel or motel, something for under fifty bucks a night, for tonight and Thursday night."

"I thought you were staying at the Lawson Y."

"I checked out this morning. Couldn't take it. At least in Joliet they lock the inmates up at night. The noise in the halls there is wild."

Never smother a generous impulse, my mother used to say,

and now I heard myself saying, "Look, I have an extra room. It's got a foldout couch. Not the most comfortable thing in the world, but it's yours for the next two nights if you want it."

"That's nice of you," he said. "Really nice. But I need to be in touch with someone first. A guy promised to drive me out to Rosehill on Thursday. I want to visit my parents' graves before I leave town."

When he got up to use the phone, I sat wondering if I'd done the right thing. Well, I reassured myself, at least he isn't a killer or a rapist or a child molester. Gambling — it's practically a white-collar crime. Is it even a crime? Where's the victim? He was a neat-enough-looking guy. If my wife were still alive, of course, I'd never have invited him to stay. But I could save him a hundred bucks, which might come in handy when he was with his daughter. I wondered if Freddy, like me, was by now a grandfather. No place for a *zayde,* prison. Nor was the Lawson Y.

When he returned, the waitress set down the check. I reached for it, but he grabbed it from under my hand.

"This is mine."

"Can I at least leave the tip?"

"No," he said, floating a $5 bill onto the table, and adding with a quick smile, "But a better tip, in my opinion, is to take the Packers on Sunday and give the Lions the seven and a half points."

As we drove to my place on Belden, I told Freddy I wouldn't be able to spend much time with him over the next two days. I had a family dinner that night, and the next day I was involved in a panel at Loyola University that figured to take up most of the day, with a dinner in the evening as part of the deal. But he would have a key and could come and go as he liked, and he could help himself to anything he found in the refrigerator. I was an instant-coffee man; I hoped he didn't mind.

"After Joliet," he said, "instant coffee is luxury to me."

At the apartment I showed him the room with the fold-out couch. He looked around. Then he asked, rather shyly, I thought, "Excuse me, but do you have an iron I can use? Right now I just own these pants, three white shirts, and a couple of sets of socks and underwear. I can wash the stuff out in the kitchen sink if it's O.K. with you."

There was a washer-dryer in the apartment. I showed him where it was and how to use it. An extra robe, blue terrycloth, was hanging on the back of the bathroom door; he was free to use that, too.

"Thanks," he said, "this is gonna help a lot. What time you figure to leave tomorrow?"

"I have to be at Loyola by nine-thirty," I said.

"My friend won't be picking me up for the cemetery till ten. So if I don't see you tonight, I'll catch you in the morning."

"Great," I said. "Take it easy. Take care of yourself."

Returning home that night at around eleven-thirty, I looked into the open door of his room. The light from the hall cast eerie shadows over my guest, who lay sleeping on his back, the covers tossed off, arms up and behind him, head resting on his locked hands. Although when awake he displayed the easy coordination of the former athlete, I saw that Freddy, in his undershorts, had an old man's body, bony and white, the skin crepelike on the underside of his arms, his chest and legs hairless. A plate of dentures — lowers, I thought — soaked in a glass on a nearby lamp table. The hollows of his eyes were deep, the skin around them veiny, purplish. Life, his body declared, hadn't been easy.

I walked into the kitchen at six the next morning. Freddy was at the table in my old blue robe, a cup of coffee and the *Trib* before him.

"Another dumb Bears draft," he pronounced, looking up from the sports section. "Dumbest team in pro football. Dumbest management, dumbest coaches, dumbest players. Betting against them since 1964, a man would be rich today."

"No argument," I said. "Even as a kid I always thought George Halas one of the great horse's asses. The old line about him was that he threw nickels around like manhole covers. Tremendously pompous, too. Certain he was going to get a seat on the fifty-yard line in heaven."

"Nobody in the organization seems to realize that wide receivers are where the money is in the NFL. All the great teams have had great wide receivers."

"Not quarterbacks?"

"Wide receivers make quarterbacks, not the other way around. Look at the record. Look at the Vikes. They don't always have great quarterbacks, but they always have great wide receivers and they're always contenders. I made a nice bundle for years betting on the Oakland Raiders because of Fred Biletnikoff. Biletnikoff could catch a bobby pin in a hurricane. I made out so well on him I used to send him a giant-size tube of Stick-Um and a card on his birthday."

"More coffee? Some breakfast? Cereal? Toast? A bagel?"

"A little later maybe. It's kinda hard getting used to living like a human being again. What time are you supposed to give your talk?"

"I have to be there by nine-thirty. It's not a talk, by the way, but a panel. There're five of us. On the subject of the responsibility of the writer."

"Yeah? What is the responsibility of the writer?"

"Not sure I've figured it out yet," I said. "Maybe it's to be no more of a son of a bitch than anyone else, which leaves a lot of leeway. That, and maybe a writer is under a greater obligation to keep himself open to new experience. Not to close the gate

too soon, if you know what I mean, not to become too confident that he has all the answers."

"You getting paid for this?"

"Two thousand dollars," I said.

"Pretty good scam, sounds like to me."

"Some days are better than others."

"I'd better get into the shower," he said. "What time you figure to be home tonight?"

"Not much before ten."

"I have to be on the bus for Sacramento leaving Harrison
Street at eight in the morning."

"I'll drive you to the station if you like."

"That would be great. But I already owe you a lot."

"Don't worry about it. Let's just call it the writer's responsibility."

"Maybe on your panel you can mention the fact that you
helped out an old ex-con and get them to push up the fee another five bills."

My day at Loyola seemed only slightly longer than a full day's
root canal. On the panel were an angry feminist, a young black
poet who had recently become a Muslim, a middle-aged man
dressed in black who taught Queer Theory at Northwestern,
and the gray-ponytailed editor of a local literary quarterly that
probably had more would-be contributors than readers. Contemplating the people sharing the platform with me, I wished
I had gone into the used-car business.

At ten-thirty that night, exhausted, I turned the key to my
apartment, reminding myself that whenever I'd expected something to result in easy money, it never worked out. The place
was dark. Freddy, I assumed, was already asleep. I flipped on the
light switch in the hall to find the apartment empty — stripped
of its belongings. Furniture, prints on the walls, Oriental rugs,

stereo system, books: everything was gone. Or almost everything. My clothes were still in their closets, and the shirts, socks, underwear, and other things once in my large bureau in the master bedroom were piled neatly on the floor. My computer and printer lay on the floor of the room I used as an office, the papers from my desk and file cabinet in piles. Food was still in the kitchen cabinets; the refrigerator was still humming. Otherwise the place had been cleaned out. I thought of Susan, my wife, who had lovingly acquired all the furniture in this apartment, and the only thing that came to my mind was the old sports cliché: "We wuz robbed!"

In the kitchen, taped to the refrigerator, was a sheet from one of my yellow legal pads, folded in half. I removed and opened it:

> Dear David (if I may),
>   I got $4,500 for the furniture and books. It's probably worth a lot more, but I didn't have much time for haggling, especially on a cash deal. I needed the money to get myself back into action. Maybe one day I'll get it back to you, though I suppose the chances are somewhere around 11–5 against. By the way, I don't have a daughter, in Sacramento or anyplace else, so no point in looking for me there. Life's a gamble, pal, and I guess you lost this one. Sorry.
>
>   Fred C. Duchamp

I looked around the empty apartment and felt so stupid I could have sat down and wept, except that there wasn't a chair to sit down on.

"So, Max," I said at the Starbucks on Diversey two weeks later, "am I a damn fool or what?"

Max had already informed me it was too late to put out an

APB on Freddy Duchamp, and he thought the likelihood of my recovering my furniture and books rather small.

"What you are is another guy who fell for a wolf in wolf's clothing," Max offered. "Happens all the time. People think they can change other people. Ain't going to happen."

I didn't argue with Max. But in fact I didn't think he had it quite right. Part of my job as a novelist was to investigate other people's motives, and while I might not always get them right, I liked to think that at least I knew my own. Right after Freddy cleaned me out, I felt the way he said he had felt after a serious gambling loss. Foolish maybe, but somehow my place in the world seemed clearer than before.

And now I realized that my offer to correspond with Freddy Duchamp and then to help him out had not arisen entirely out of large-heartedness. I'd thought I could make use of him; I'd thought he'd furnish me with material — that the story of his life could become, once I wrote it, my story. He had picked me out as a potential mark, and I had done the same with him. There had been corruption enough, then, to go around. From me Freddy got the money to put himself back in action. I lost my furniture but got my story. In the end it was what gamblers call a wash.

"More coffee?" asked Max, rising from his chair.

"Sure," I said. Watching the old warrior limp to the counter, I slid his *Sun-Times* to my side of the table and turned to the middle pages. I'd heard there was a big furniture sale at Marshall Field's.

Don Juan Zimmerman

IN HIS TERRYCLOTH robe, over his morning coffee, Donny Zimmerman read the *Chicago Jewish Chronicle*. Sometimes it contained an item about a guy he had gone to high school with. Norm Lippman, who owned a coast-to-coast chain of sporting goods stores, was a big figure in the United Jewish Appeal. Ronnie Saltzman had made a killing in real estate, and every so often a story would surface about his being a possible buyer of the Chicago Bears. Dave Gordon, who at first went into his father's glazing business, then made a fortune selling glass insurance, was a partner in the Bulls and White Sox with Jerry Reinsdorf. A guy named Friedkin, three years older than Donny, had directed the movie *The French Connection,* and the other day Donny read that this Friedkin was claiming to be five years younger than he was. What a world, he thought; even the successful were four-flushers!

He turned to the back page with the personal ads, guys looking for broads, broads for guys. He read the "Women Seeking Men" section with a practiced eye.

> Wanted: one special, professional, caring gentleman, over 50, to be a special friend to this attractive, full-figured Jewish female professional. Seeking a person to relate to the emotions one experiences during this time of life.

"Full-figured" was one giveaway; those "special"s and that "caring" another.

> Friends first! Seeking a divorced/widowed Jewish man, 35–60, of good character, for divorced, young-looking, sincere Jewish female, two children. I'm moral, stable, attractive, disease-free. Seek honesty, open communication. Prefer nonsmoker.

Donny, who enjoyed a good cigar from time to time, poured himself another half cup of coffee, composing in his mind his own never-to-be-sent ad for the *Chronicle:*

> Man in middle fifties, balding, not in very good shape, fairly well-to-do, not previously married and probably unmarriageable. Seeks easy sex of an uncomplicated kind. (Offers of oral sex not refused.) No taste for open communication. Limited range of interests, art and culture not included. Poor dancer. Gastronomically unadventurous. Not comfortable with children. Values less important than good looks.

That ought to draw a fine response. Donny lifted himself out of his chair, carrying his coffee into the bathroom to consider himself in the full-length mirror. The prospect, even he had to recognize, did not entice. At fifty-four, he was roughly twenty pounds overweight, his teeth were capped, his skin tended toward the blotchy, a lot of his hair was gone, and what was left of it was gray and frizzy. He wore glasses. He looked, in fact, much as his father had before his death, at the age of sixty-four, of a massive single-shot coronary. The old man was at his desk going over some papers when, pow!, he just went down. Two years later, Donny's mother followed.

Donny had taken each of his own minor physical setbacks in something like reasonable stride — what the hell choice did he have? — though every once in a while he was amazed by their cumulative effect. In restaurants and bars, he preferred to avoid seats facing mirrors. Sometimes he would be walking down a street in the Loop, catch his reflection in a window, and fail to recognize that this slightly portly middle-aged man was, of all people, Donny Zimmerman.

If he weren't a bachelor, maybe the question of physique wouldn't enter in. But the fact is that Donny was still in the hunt. He had been in it, if anyone was counting, for nearly forty years. He liked women. True, not enough to marry one, but he enjoyed their company, liked sleeping with them, liked their odd perspectives on the world, liked them to like him. When he didn't have a woman to take out to dinner, or for Sunday brunch, or for a weekend in Wisconsin, life seemed less pleasing. Yet somehow it could never be the same woman for long.

Donny: he still thought of himself by that boyhood name, and so did friends from high school he would run into on LaSalle Street. But the figure in the bathroom mirror didn't look like a Donny. It looked more like a guy named Louis or Morris or Irv or Sam, one of the men of his father's generation who used to come over to play pinochle. Would any of them have understood his life? He doubted it. His own father did nothing to hide his disappointment at his only child's failure to marry and provide him with grandchildren. "No woman good enough for you?" Sidney Zimmerman said on more than one occasion. When Donny protested that he wanted to play the field for a while, his father replied: "I got some news for you, kid — you're no Don Juan. Find the right girl and settle down. You'll save a lot of wear and tear all around."

Most of Donny's high-school friends had married, bang, right out of the gate — by twenty-three, by twenty-seven at the latest. This was something he never understood. What was the hurry? Lots of lovely ladies out there, why harness yourself to only one? When his friends' marriages went down the tubes, Donny couldn't help feeling just a touch reconfirmed in his own wisdom. Then there were the guys in their late forties or early fifties who had children with second or third wives. Why would a guy want to keep that kind of pressure on himself, especially when there was a good chance he wouldn't be around to see the kids out of school?

Yet women, Donny found, were still a big part of his thoughts, not to mention his conversation with his pals at the East Bank Club. He would go there after work — a successful if small-time lawyer, he did DWI cases, real estate closings, minor personal injury, the occasional easy divorce — slip into a Fila running suit, maybe shoot twenty free throws, try twenty-five or so sit-ups, ten or so minutes on the treadmill, take a *schvitz*, twenty minutes in the Jacuzzi, then sit in the lounge, checking the action.

"Men are not by nature monogamous," said Bert Silverstein authoritatively. He ought to know. Sixty-one and never married, Bert had a mistress of thirty-two years' standing. But there was also a series of young Polish girls, newly arrived in Chicago, whom he had installed in an apartment he owned in Jefferson Park, at the cost of roughly $1,500 a month each. He would drop in on them once or twice a week to get, as he put it, his pipes cleaned.

"Silverstein," Donny's high school friend Lenny Friedman needled, "still cheating on your mistress, I trust?" Then, turning to Donny, "Bert here's my role model, you know."

Like his pals, Donny believed in the double standard, not so much in the justice as in the fact of it. Things were different for men and women. Donny once went out with a good-looking woman who had a limp. It turned him off. The same limp on a good-looking man might be thought distinguished. A man in his fifties — himself, for example — was still in the ball game, when all but the most extraordinary women of his age were not. This was merely the way things were set up — unfairly, but there it was.

Why should a woman want to sleep with him? He was no beauty; with the passing of the years he was uncomfortably closer to the beast. "No romance without finance," Art Rosen used to say, meaning that, for guys like them, if they were to have any measure of success with attractive younger women, they needed expensive cars (Donny drove a year-old blue Mercedes), good tickets for games and plays, the best tables, and, Donny felt, the appearance of urban mastery, of knowing their way around.

At the same time, a certain ruthlessness was required. You had somehow to make plain that a bartering arrangement was in effect, in which niceness was traded for niceness. Yet how much longer could this game go on? More and more, young women seemed a little too young, their fund of common knowledge smaller with each passing year. It felt odd to sleep with a woman and, the next morning, over breakfast, discover that she had never heard of Mussolini or Claudette Colbert or Louis Armstrong.

Then there was the physical end of things. "The first time you can't do it twice is what is known as disappointment," his friend Lenny once announced at the East Bank coffee shop. "The second time you can't do it once is what is known as despair." Although he wasn't about to admit it, Donny was long used to disappointment, and he was not entirely free of despair, either. Sometimes, climbing into bed with a thirty-two-year-old tootsie — who would never, by the way, have even heard of the word "tootsie" — he felt like some old player who couldn't hit the fastball any longer but was just putting in another year toward his pension.

Sometimes, too, feeling a little callow, he asked himself why he had never married. Maybe the problem was that he had grown up in the 1950s, and so the very illicitness of sex, then in such short supply, still excited him, the way certain men who lived through Prohibition could never get over the excitement of alcohol. But there were times he thought things went deeper — or at least farther back.

At Senn High School, Donny had never been at the center of things. He was an uninterested student and only a mediocre athlete; he didn't run with the most admired kids. Socially, he was never on the first team — maybe not even on the second. What he most remembered about those years was a relentless yearning. Donny's life with the girls of Senn, all those Jackies and Shelleys, those Sues and Nancys and Dianes, was restricted to thoughts, fantasies. His few attempts at dating were a fizzle. He drove off a few times with friends to the cathouses of Braidwood and Kankakee — the speakeasies of their Prohibition — but of club and fraternity dances, drive-in movies, balls at the Edgewater Beach Hotel and the Palmer House, he knew little. Was he getting his own back now, making up for his lost youth?

All this came to him one late afternoon when, across the coffee shop at the East Bank, he saw two women seated at a table along the wall, one of whom he was almost sure was Bobby Goldman. He pictured her at Harry's, the store outside Senn where the Jewish kids used to gather in the morning, at lunch, and after school to socialize, smoke, flirt, joke around. He remembered the girls from Lake Shore Drive or from West Rogers Park, in their cashmere sweaters or club jackets, notebooks clutched to their bosoms. In late May or early June, they would wear white sleeveless blouses. Viewing from the side, one might make out a camisole or the elastic of a bra strap. Donny could get pretty worked up by such oblique sightings of the promised land — though never promised, in those days he knew all too well, to him.

In the final semester of his senior year, Donny took a course in typing — someone had said it might come in handy if he went to college — and found himself seated next to Bobby Goldman. She was one of the most popular girls in the school, which was to say one of the most admired. Smallish, dark, slightly pudgy but in a way that to Donny seemed only sexy, Bobby wore either cashmere or angora sweaters, usually under a blue-and-gold club jacket (the club was called the Chicitas). She went out with a guy named Mark Springer, a champion swimmer, backstroke and freestyle, who had his own car, a two-tone green-and-cream Chevy Bel Air, hardtop convertible, current year's model. Mark Springer's father was chief of surgery at Michael Reese Hospital, and the family lived on Lake Shore Drive. Bobby lived in West Rogers Park. Her father was in used auto parts, but in a big way.

The high point of Donny's school day that year was typing, which met, he remembered even now, during seventh period. He turned out to be a terrible typist, and he made lots of jokes to Bobby Goldman about his ineptitude with the clunky old Royal with no letters on its keys. She seemed to enjoy them all, flashing a smile that made him want to send her a thank-you note each time. Donny sensed a natural sweetness in her generous response. He wanted to protect her, even though, as far as he could make out, she didn't in the least need his protection.

In those days Donny was able to imagine himself in wonderfully complicated sex play with various girls at Senn: in the back seats of cars, in their beds (never, for some reason, in his own), in Lake Michigan, in open fields and meadows (a fine pastoral touch, this, for a city kid). But with Bobby the only fantasy he could sustain was one of marriage. He imagined their living together; he imagined their children; he even imagined their dog (a wirehaired terrier named Bernie). Although he often thought about asking her out, invariably he lost his nerve. Had she refused, everything would have been spoiled. And why shouldn't she refuse? Once, getting up his nerve, he called her at home. Her mother answered, asked who it was, and Donny, trembling, his mouth gone dry, hung up. At the end of the semester he got a D in typing. Bobby, after graduation, went downstate to the University of Illinois.

Looking across the East Bank coffee shop, Donny was now absolutely certain it was she. Her face showed lines at the corners of the eyes and a bit more around the mouth, but she still had that heart-stopping smile. Her hair was mostly dark with streaks of silver — frosting, he thought it was called. She was wearing a velour running getup. When the check came, he noted that she took half-glasses out of her purse to read it; with his bachelor's instinct, he also noted that she wore no wedding ring.

"Hi," Donny began awkwardly that evening when he finally tracked her down on the phone — she lived in Lincolnwood and her name was Mrs. Roberta Levinson. "Am I talking to the former Bobby Goldman?"

"Yes," she answered, a little warily.

"I hoped so. I'm not sure you'll remember me, but my name is Donald Zimmerman. We went to high school together. We sat next to each other in typing, senior year."

"Forgive me," she said, "but I'm not sure I do."

"It was a while ago," Donny offered. "But when I saw you in the East Bank Club today, I thought it was you, and I wondered if you'd like to meet for coffee or a drink or maybe dinner, you know, to talk about the good old days."

"They weren't too bad, were they?"

"The older I get, the more I'm inclined to believe they were pretty damn swell," said Donny.

The conversation picked up a decent flow, and they talked about the small but growing number of classmates who had died, mostly of cancer and heart attacks. Donny learned that she had been twice married, once divorced, and was now a widow. They arranged to meet two nights later, for an early dinner.

Driving up from the city, Donny wondered if he hadn't made a bad choice. He had last been at Myron & Phil's steakhouse about two years ago, with Lenny Friedman. "This restaurant, which has been in business for more than sixty years, if you count its days on the old West Side," Lenny said as he slathered chopped liver on black bread, "is probably responsible for the deaths of more Jews than Martin Bormann." What if Bobby was a health-food nut? Nor did you have to live on seaweed to find Myron & Phil's objectionable. Waiting for Bobby at the bar — he had arrived twenty minutes early out of nervousness — he thought the joint was especially thick with cigarette smoke. A feeling of passionate intensity, all directed to the serious activity of eating, dominated the room. Cutlery clattered against china; everyone was a little too tanned or a little too burnished, probably from high blood pressure. The scene before him, Donny felt, was red meat devouring red meat.

He saw her come in, stand by the table near the hostess's podium, look around. She wore taupe-colored trousers, brown suede shoes with low heels, a red polo shirt under a white cardigan. Clutching a brown suede purse, she seemed smallish, vulnerable, kindly — still the girl he had adored more than thirty-five years ago. He slipped off the bar stool and made his way over.

"Bobby Goldman," he said, holding out his hand. "Donny Zimmerman."

"Of course," she replied. "Now I remember you."

"Well, I had more hair and less flesh. But you haven't really changed all that much."

"What did you say you do? Con man? Or is it used cars?"

"Really. You haven't changed all that much. You are beyond any question Bobby Goldman."

"Levinson, actually."

"Look, is this the wrong place? Should we go someplace else?"

"No, it's fine," she said. "I'll just spend my full year's cholesterol budget on one meal. No big deal."

They were taken to a table near the back. To one side, three men in thick, colorful sweaters were at work on large strip steaks. To the other side, an elaborately coifed woman with hyperthyroid eyes held a rib bone aloft, making a point; her husband, a bald, heavyset man in white pants and a light blue linen jacket, was mournfully contemplating a devastated T-bone.

Bobby told him she still saw some of her old high school friends. Jackie Weiner, Sue Shapiro, Lee Silverman, Judy Pollock — each name caused a little ping of nostalgic longing in Donny. Many of them had had tough lives: divorces, mastectomies, dead husbands. Her old boyfriend Mark Springer had committed suicide; it turned out he was a clinical depressive, but in those days, she said, who ever heard of depression? When Donny volunteered that the only friend he still saw from high school was Lenny Friedman, Bobby said she didn't remember him. They had traveled in different circles in those days.

Then she gave him her own story. Her first marriage, to a man named Jerry Goodman, with whom she had a daughter, fell apart in the sixties. "He was a player, Jerry," she said with a weary sadness. "If he could get into a woman's bed, he felt he shouldn't let the opportunity pass. It became an embarrassment. My father, who was still alive then, said it wasn't likely to get better, so I filed for divorce. I was thirty."

After the divorce, she had to go to work — Jerry was irregular with his child-support payments, her father's business had suffered reverses. It was at the firm where she worked as a legal secretary that she met her second husband, Marty Levinson. He was twenty years older than she, divorced, with children already grown. He had been very good to her, Marty — generous, a sport in the old-fashioned sense. When he died three years ago, he left her financially well taken care of. She still lived in his house.

As Bobby was recounting all this, Donny could not help hearing the voice of Bert Silverstein: "One of the benefits of younger women over older women is that they have shorter stories." Then Bobby told him about the death of her daughter, Jenny.

"She was twenty-six, and she was killed in a car crash coming back from Ann Arbor, where she was a graduate student. It was less than a year ago. Jenny was not only my daughter, she was my dearest friend. We'd spent the eleven years between my marriages alone together. She's left a hole in my life that I don't expect will ever be filled."

Bobby looked down at her purse on the table. Donny, murmuring "I'm sorry," fell silent.

"I suppose no one gets off scot-free," she said finally, looking up.

Except me, Donny realized at that moment; except me. The reason was that he had kept himself clear of entanglements. For an instant, he felt he had missed something — he wasn't quite sure what — essential.

When the attendant brought Bobby's Lexus around, Donny held the door for her.

"Would you like to do this again?" he asked, leaning in at the window.

"It would be nice," she said. "Please call."

His own car arrived as she drove off. He tipped the kid a fin, got in, and drove home wishing he were seventeen again and just returning from his first date with Bobby Goldman.

"Still good-looking?" Lenny asked the next day at the East Bank when Donny told him about the previous evening.

"I'd say so," Donny said. "And nice. I had a kind of crush on her in high school."

"Didn't she used to go out with a swimmer, a guy named Singer maybe?"

"Springer. He committed suicide. A depressive, apparently."

"These days who isn't? People who aren't are either in chemotherapy or waiting for a bypass. Did you ever think growing old would be such goddamn fun?"

Lenny had his own aggravations. Five years ago, Lois, his wife, was discovered to have multiple sclerosis. It was just now starting to hit her hard, and the doctors said she would eventually have to live in a wheelchair. Lenny, who had been cheating on her for years, had recently stopped — or so Donny supposed, from Lenny's silence on the matter.

"You going to see her again?"

"I think so," Donny said. "Sure. Why not?"

"What's the attraction?"

"You aren't going to believe this, but part of the attraction is that she hasn't had so easy a life. She had a first husband who screwed around on her. Another husband died. She lost a kid, a daughter, in a car accident."

"That makes her sexy?"

"It makes her interesting."

"You intend to do anything about it?"

"What's to do? I hope to see her again."

"Careful, Donny. Up to now, you know, you've led a blameless life."

"What's that supposed to mean?"

"It means that you've stayed in the chase but out of the wars."

"Meaning?"

"Meaning that when you get beyond screwing, life becomes stickier. I've always admired your coolness in this line."

Donny remembered that the man he was talking to had a wife with multiple sclerosis. "Jesus, Lenny, I've been out with her once."

"If I were you, friend, I'd watch my step. In this field, land mines are everywhere."

One of the *nice* things about being with an older woman, Donny thought, was that she knew the words to the same songs you did. Coming back from the men's room, he noticed Bobby faintly lipping the words to "Tenderly" along with the pianist in the bar-lounge of the Knickerbocker Hotel. But mainly he couldn't get over the fact that he was in the company of Bobby Goldman — that she was, in some sense, his girl, though "girl" might not be the most precise word.

Things progressed even faster than he had hoped. He had taken Bobby out to brunch the Sunday following their first dinner together. The next week they went to a movie at the Wilmette Theater, saw something called *The Unbearable Lightness of Being:* a mistake, too sex-ridden, people humping away in what seemed like interminable slow motion. Sitting there, he found himself vaguely embarrassed. He sneaked a look at her; she seemed to be watching the proceedings painlessly.

A week later, at Bobby's place in Lincolnwood, Donny was at first edgy, then astounded at where life had landed him. He lay in her queen-size bed, on very good sheets, the antique quilt with geese on it pulled back, in his boxer shorts, waiting for her to emerge from the bathroom. He always felt this an odd moment, a moment of slight confusion when the hunter suddenly wonders whether he isn't after all the prey. He heard water running, jars opening, atomizers hissing. He didn't know what to expect, hoped to hold up his end, speculated on the need, at his age, to offer up a prayer for sexual performance.

It went pretty well. No rockets on either side, or so Donny judged, but for him his mere presence in this bed was fireworks enough. He stayed the night. The next morning, in a light pink velour robe, she served him breakfast: coffee, orange juice, bagels with Scottish marmalade. Lovely light flooded her blue and white kitchen. Passing one of his tests, Bobby looked even better in the morning. She said he was the first man she had been with since her husband's death three years ago, and he decided — what the hell — to believe her. He felt great.

Driving into the city on the Kennedy Expressway, Donny thought that if this had taken place thirty-odd years ago, by now he would probably be the U.S. senator for Illinois or sitting on the Supreme Court. The golden-oldies station was playing "Love Is a Many Splendored Thing," and in an off-key voice, very loud, he sang along, his head out the window of the Mercedes, until the driver of a garbage truck behind him honked to indicate he was out of his lane, passed him on the right, and gave him the finger. City life, thought Donny with a smile. Not half bad.

He was fifty-four. With luck he might get to eighty, which meant maybe he had twenty-five or so years left. Suddenly, living alone seemed bleak, a hardship. Chasing women after sixty was already pushing it; after seventy it would be obscene. He thought of Bobby in her nightgown — a prospect, he mused, he wouldn't mind waking up to in the years remaining.

But what did *she* want? He, all things considered, was a less than lovely prospect to contemplate. She evidently didn't need his money; Levinson had probably left her with more than Donny could supply. The only thing he had to offer, really, was himself, Donald Lawrence Zimmerman, a lumpish man of middle age who had earned his livelihood on the edge of the civil courts. That, plus a thirty-odd-years-delayed crush. Not much of a bargain.

"How is it you've never married?" she asked one night in the Cape Cod Room at the Drake.

"I think it was because I valued — maybe overvalued — my freedom. I loved the idea of staying loose, traveling light, not being tied down. It's a masculine ideal, I suppose. Probably a dumb one."

"Didn't you ever want children?"

"This will make me sound cold, but I never did. I looked around and saw all the people who seemed to make a botch of their kids, or who only wanted to get away from them when they were young, or couldn't wait to be free when they grew up."

"Having a child is the best thing I've done," Bobby said. "Nothing else compares."

"I can see why you'd say that."

"It's also why losing my daughter is something I can't hope ever to get over. Not finally. Not really."

"Would you marry again?" Donny asked nervously.

"It's too soon," she said. "I'd like to live with my loss a while longer. But let's get back to you. Ever been close?"

"Can't say as I have."

"Saving yourself for the senior prom?" she asked, smiling.

"I never went to ours."

"A big night. I went with poor dead Mark Springer."

"I wish you'd gone with me," Donny said, "but I'd never have had the nerve to ask you."

"You seem to have acquired the nerve now."

"You've made it easy for me."

"Do you know that the women's magazines say that men like you are the worst of all possible risks."

"How so?"

"Men who've got beyond forty-five and never married. They're supposed to be fundamentally unserious about women. Even men who've divorced twice are a better bet. Widowers beat men like you hands down."

"I didn't know I was such a disaster."

"Sorry to bring you the news."

"Truth is, you're bringing me lots of news," Donny said. "Being with you makes me think I've wasted a lot of time, like maybe three decades."

"Didn't you ever think of the future?"

"Not much beyond the weekend."

"I think about it all the time," she said, "and I don't want to ruin what's left of it. I envy you. You seem to feel no pressure."

"I've never had a grand plan. The future, I figure, will take care of itself."

Four days later, Donny visited his internist, Harry Berger, for a follow-up on the physical he took every two years. Harry made him feel that the future would take care not only of itself but of him, too. He was saying that he didn't like the feel of Donny's prostate, and a blood test showed that his PSA count, the main indicator of trouble, was unnaturally high, up around seventeen. He wanted him to see a urologist. He was going to order a biopsy.

Donny liked Harry Berger, a rabid Bulls fan, fiftyish, with none of the authoritative pomposity of most physicians. He used to tease him about being the youngest man in America named Harry. But now the doctor's seriousness as he talked about Donny's prostate was somehow the most alarming symptom of all. There would be other tests to take; there was the danger that the cancer — and cancer it looked to be — had spread to the bone or to other organs. All this they would know in the next few weeks.

Donny walked out of the Pittsfield Building in a daze. The sun brightened even dreary Wabash Avenue, with its El tracks and tired office buildings. It was Indian summer. A black guy in a dashiki, leaning against the Mailers Building, was playing "Mood Indigo," not very well, on a saxophone. Donny dropped a ten into his open instrument case; maybe it would bring him luck. He was in no pain of any sort, except for shock and heartsickness. The world, through which he usually strode so easily, suddenly made no sense. Maybe he wasn't going to get off scot-free after all.

He took a cab to the East Bank Club, staring into the back of the Paki driver's neck. He would have traded lives with him, even-up. When he got to the club, Lenny was sitting in the locker room, schmoozing with Bert Silverstein, Art Rosen, and a guy named Howie Harris, who thirty-five years ago had been a basketball star at Von Steuben High. They were talking about some hot stock tip, a company that sold telephones you could take into the shower. Donny signaled Lenny that he needed a word in private.

"What're you going to do, kid?" Lenny said after Donny told him the news.

"What I'm going to do is everything I can to avoid checking out. I was counting on another couple of decades. I somehow hadn't imagined cancer. I thought maybe a heart attack, like my father."

"Snake eyes don't care who's holding the dice. Besides, lots of guys beat prostate cancer."

"Maybe so. I hope to God I'm one of them. I don't want it said that I lived by the sword and died by the sword."

"I'll do the jokes around here, buddy. Who else're you planning to tell?"

"There's no one else, except maybe Bobby. I guess I can't really not tell her."

When the biopsy proved positive, Donny decided he couldn't delay much longer. But he was in a tough position. He and Bobby had been together maybe twelve or fifteen times over the past five weeks. Their intimacy had grown. Did he love her? Who knew? He felt comfortable and at ease as he had around no other woman he had ever known. Did she reciprocate the feeling, whatever it was? He didn't know that, either. What he did know was that Bobby owed him nothing, and that she had already seen enough of desertion and death. He put off telling her a while longer.

At Weiss Memorial, a youngish urologist named Stuart Kalinsky told Donny that he would have to schedule a CAT scan, an MRI, and a bone scan. After that, unless the cancer had spread, there would be the question of whether to fight it with hormone therapy, radiation, chemotherapy, or surgery. But all this would be decided in due time. Kalinsky thought they had caught it early. He seemed an unusually cheerful man, especially for one whose patients, or so Donny assumed, must have croaked at alarming rates.

Three weeks later, he got what he supposed was good news. The prostate cancer had not spread, and Kalinsky thought surgery made the most sense, though he welcomed Donny's obtaining a second opinion. The surgery itself wasn't all that dangerous, but the recuperation and aftereffects could be difficult. One thing he had to look forward to was months of incontinence, which could even be permanent. Another possibility was impotence, though something like eighty percent of men in his condition regained limited potency. Donny didn't want to know what was behind the word "limited"; for now, he would settle for staying alive.

"I guess I'm prepared to go through with the surgery," Donny said, "but you have to promise to tell me, Dr. Kalinsky, if the time comes when I no longer have to keep flossing."

Kalinsky, with a smile, promised.

Donny had a date that evening with Bobby. They had agreed to meet Near North, at Mei's, a little Chinese restaurant on Clark Street they had been to once before.

He arrived first and took a booth near the back of the still empty restaurant. Bobby had been visiting her tax lawyer, settling some matters in her husband's complicated estate. As he watched her enter and search briefly for him, he once again appreciated her delicacy and elegance. She was wearing a blue suit with a single-strand necklace of small pearls and pearl earrings. He seemed never to tire of looking at this woman. It wasn't exactly passion he felt, but something calmer, reassuring.

He rose from the booth, and as she walked up to him she held out her hand and offered her cheek.

"Ah, Chinese, the food of our people," Donny said as the young Chinese waitress presented the menus.

Midway through the meal, after the appetizers, soup, and moo shu chicken, Donny made his announcement. "I have something sort of sad to tell you. I learned for certain today that I have to have surgery for prostate cancer."

"Oh, my God!" The genuineness of her emotion, he was pleased to note, left no doubt.

"I know," he said.

"When does it happen?"

"In ten days."

"What can I do?" she asked.

"Stay with me," he said, hearing a tremor in his voice. "I'm frightened."

Bobby touched the top of his hand, left her fingers there. He felt tears dribble down his face. He wasn't crying because he was afraid of death; it was life he didn't want to leave.

Although the surgeon claimed to have gotten all the cancer, eighteen months later — months filled with every physical indignity — it returned, this time attacking the lymph nodes, and metastasizing from there to bone cancer. He and Bobby continued to live separately until, when the end was no longer deniable, she suggested that he move into her house in Lincolnwood. He wanted to ask her to marry him, but he knew there were good financial reasons against it, and so he didn't.

Besides, Donny thought, what they had was just as good as marriage, except for never having had a child together. When they were apart for more than a few hours — and now they rarely were — his life seemed to empty out and then fill up with fear at his imminent death. Under the pressure of his sentence, he felt himself getting wiser, but somehow not quickly enough for it to matter.

His illness made Donny tired, and most nights they watched the VCR in Bobby's den. She had stocked up on the movie candy of their youth — Jujyfruits, Dots, Milk Duds, Good & Plenty — and every night she popped corn, not sparing the butter. In his own mind, Donny tried not to dwell on the time he had wasted in his life. But what was left was leaking away all too quickly.

When it looked as if he would have to go into the hospital, Bobby arranged for a hospice program to allow him to remain at home. She had a hospital bed put into the den, and Kalinsky instructed her on giving Donny his morphine. Toward the end, as he flitted in and out of consciousness, a round-the-clock nursing service was hired, but he only wanted to be near Bobby. She held his hand, massaged his feet, set cool cloths lightly soaked with bay rum on his forehead. He would look at her, smile, mutter thank you.

He died, slipped away really, with his hand in hers. Five days later a lawyer named Max Liebman called Bobby to say that Donny had left his entire estate — after deductions for final expenses, it came to some $650,000 — to the Jennifer Levinson Foundation, an institution he had set up to give scholarships to deserving students at the University of Michigan. It was only after making an appointment to go over the details and hanging up the phone that Bobby began — quietly, with an almost pleasing sense of completion — to weep.

Dubinsky on the Loose

MANNY DUBINSKY had been fifty years in the scrap metal business, a buyer, before he retired at the age of seventy-five. Why scrap? Because when he got out of the army — the better part of his time he had served as an orderly-room sergeant on Guam — he was offered a job at H. J. Kramer Metals, Inc., owned by his mother's brother Henry. Going to law school would have meant another three years before he could marry Grace, and after the four years they had already waited for the war to end, that was precisely three years too long. Dubinsky went into scrap metal because he wanted to marry without further delay, and so well had the marriage turned out that he never, not for a minute, seriously regretted it.

When his Uncle Henry's two sons and their brother-in-law Herb Cohen took over the top positions in the business, friends said to him, "Manny, why don't you go in for yourself?" "I'd be glad to" was his answer, "as soon as you can arrange the three million dollars for my first crushing machine." It was big business, scrap metal, not for little guys; and though Manny

Dubinsky always made a good living — and some years a damn good living — when it came to million-dollar machinery, he had to count himself a little guy.

Everybody loved Grace. And why not? She was an extraordinary woman. Dubinsky never tired of telling people that his wife had majored in physics at the University of Illinois — and this was in 1937, when she was the only female in the department. She was, in his phrase, the "playmaker" of their social life. Somehow or other, at home or on one of their vacation cruises, she found couples who were perfectly simpatico. Until Ruthie went off to college — she was their only child after a tricky first, and last, pregnancy — Grace remained at home, devoting herself to her family. When she returned to work she became a science editor at a Chicago textbook firm, turning the opaque writing of physicists and chemists into readable English. But even with her full-time job Dubinsky never felt any lessening of her wifely ministrations. He couldn't remember a bad meal; where clean shirts came from was knowledge kept from him; and never once did he pack his own suitcase for his many buying trips.

There was no one, it seemed, that Grace couldn't get along with, including the Bermans. Al Berman, an insurance man, was Ruthie's father-in-law, and as complacently boring a man as Dubinsky had ever met. Estelle, Al's wife, was a female bully, only happy when she got her way, no matter how trivial the point of contention, and with Estelle everything was in contention. As for their son, Larry, a lawyer who managed to strike a note of insufferable knowingness in everything he said, Dubinsky tried not to be around him any more than was absolutely necessary.

Shortly before the wedding, the Dubinskys had gone out with their friends Irv and Anne Ellmann, and Anne asked Manny how he felt about his much-loved daughter's match. "I'll tell you how I feel," Dubinsky heard himself reply. "I feel like I'm about to hand over a Stradivarius to a gorilla." Grace kicked him gently under the table. "We have to live with these terrible people, Manny," she said in the car on the way home. "It won't do to knock them, even to our dearest friends." That was Grace.

Dubinsky's seventy-fifth birthday nearly coincided with his fiftieth anniversary at Kramer Metals. Herb Harris, now president of the firm, had let him work past normal retirement age, and although he was still carrying his share of the load, even Dubinsky knew the time had come to hang it up. A lunch was given in his honor at the Standard Club. The place had once been strictly for German Jews, and his Uncle Henry, like every other successful Eastern European Jew, had had to settle for membership in the old Covenant Club, on Clark and Madison. But through what Grace once called "mixed marriages" with their coreligionists from Eastern Europe, the ranks of German Jews in Chicago had so thinned out that the Standard now took in anyone able to ante up the hefty entry fee.

At the lunch, with all the officers and buyers present, Herb Harris spoke of Manny Dubinsky's long service. Everywhere, he said, the mutual pact of loyalty between business institutions and the people who worked for them was breaking down, but not yet at Kramer Metals. Thanking Dubinsky for his efforts on the firm's behalf, Herb presented him with a Rolex watch and a check for $20,000, which, he said, he hoped Manny would use to take his wife on a first-class vacation to Europe.

Dubinsky was much moved. Driving home to Evanston, he felt his years had not been wasted. He remembered Herbie Harris as a kid, coming into the firm in the early 1960s. He'd led it through some rocky patches, and turned out to be not only a clear-headed businessman but a *mensch*. Dubinsky glanced at the large new watch on his wrist, felt the check resting in his suit-coat pocket. Grace, he thought, would be pleased. Maybe they would take that trip.

Parking the Buick in the garage of his apartment building, Dubinsky let himself in the door and called his wife's name. No answer. He called again. She must be out. He went into the kitchen to get a glass of ice water and found the refrigerator door open, Grace, face down, on the floor. He knelt to feel her forehead. Cold. He called 911 and, while waiting for the ambulance, gave his wife his best shot at CPR. Sitting on the floor, he rocked her in his arms, chanting "No, God, no, please God, no." He had no recollection of it, but later he was told that the paramedics had to pry him loose from her. The cause of death was massive cerebral hemorrhage; the time was fixed at an hour before Dubinsky arrived home. On one and the same day he lost his work and his truest friend.

Now, three years later, Dubinsky had yet to recover from the combined blow.

Much sooner than that, he realized he was helpless when it came to operating the washer and dryer in the basement. Although he thought he knew how to cook an egg, one day he put in six to boil and went out briefly on an errand. He returned home to a terrible smell, egg on the kitchen ceiling and wall behind the stove, and a burned-out pot. Apart from breakfast, he tried eating all his meals out, but discovered he was unbearably self-conscious sitting alone in a restaurant. He began bringing dinners back from the Pine Yard, the nearby Chinese restaurant.

At Grace's funeral service — it was at Piser's in Skokie — there had been a huge turnout, but going over the names of people who had signed the book, Dubinsky saw that the vast majority were his wife's friends, not his. After her death he was occasionally invited to dinner by the Ellmanns or other couples he and Grace used to see together. But before long the invitations, not all that many to begin with, had dropped off. Grace, not Manny, had been the real draw of the Dubinskys.

A month or so after the funeral, Dubinsky began to notice something else: he was developing a tendency, quite new to him, to tell people off. One day in the Golden Parthenon, a local greasy spoon — a Grecian spoon, Grace had called it — the waitress brought his check along with the lunch and he barked out, in a voice he didn't recognize, "What the hell's the rush act here? You can't give me the check after my coffee? Maybe you'd prefer I eat in the goddamn car?" In the express line of the supermarket, to the young checkout girl with a diamond chip in her nose and an earring in her lip he snarled, "What's all this extra jewelry about? You want to make sure you don't get ahead in life?" In line at the bank, he advised the man ahead of him, who looked to be his own age and who had white hair pulled back in a small ponytail, "Excuse me, pal, are you aware that your hairdo makes you look like a complete schmuck?" As if avoiding a lunatic, the man turned away.

The worst came one evening at his daughter's in Highland Park. Since Grace's death, Dubinsky had a standing invitation to Friday-night dinner, which gave him a chance to see his grandchildren, Tyler and Justin, both now in high school. An only child himself, Dubinsky hadn't any other family. His sister-in-law, Marian, had died a year before Grace, and Grace's brother, Ben, was in a nursing home with Alzheimer's in Boca Raton. Ruthie and the children were all he had.

Dinner that Friday went reasonably well. Ruthie cooked a brisket, her mother's recipe, and they were eating their dessert, flourless chocolate cake with raspberries. The boys had already gone off. Dubinsky's mistake was to ask his son-in-law how he liked the Bulls' chances in the Eastern Division finals against the Knicks. The series was in its fifth game.

"Bulls in seven," Larry said. "You have to know that, Manny. Too much money is at stake — ticket sales, television revenues, concessions — not to make sure it goes the full seven games."

"I would have thought," Dubinsky said, "that too much was at stake even to consider fixing a pro basketball game."

"Manny, c'mon, you've been around. With the right people at the controls, there isn't anything can't be fixed. You know it and I know it."

"I don't know anything of the kind," Dubinsky said.

"Well," his son-in-law put in, "maybe you should."

"You telling me I'm naïve?" Dubinsky asked. "Is that what you're telling me? Where the hell do you get off saying something like that?" He saw his daughter wince, but it was too late. He couldn't stop; the train had already jumped the track. "You know-it-all son of a bitch. No one can tell you anything. You've got all the answers. I'll tell you something, son-in-law, you're just another low-grade con-man lawyer, of which this country could use about half a million fewer than it has." He looked again at his daughter, who didn't know where to put her eyes.

There went Friday nights.

Dubinsky asked his friend Murray Kaplan if he remembered his having had such a violent temper in the past. Murray said no.

"Then what's going on?"

"Forgive me if I'm wrong, Manny," Murray offered, "but I wonder if maybe you're angry at having lost Gracie the way you did. Maybe you're taking it out on everyone else. I mean, it's just possible."

Dubinsky had to admit the possibility. He would have to control himself — and he also would have to control another habit he had developed, that of delivering little lectures on the superiority of the past to the present. Suddenly, as if out of nowhere, he found himself exclaiming to people he hardly knew that when he was in his twenties he hadn't known a single divorced couple — outside Hollywood, of course. Or he would launch into a sermonette on how young couples seemed to want everything these days, whereas when he was first married it was assumed that life's luxuries were well in the future. Or he would attack today's athletes, with their insanely large salaries, as unappreciative pigs. Or regale his dentist's technician with an account of the Depression, when just to have a job was to consider oneself blessed, whereas today . . .

This, too, had to stop.

A year or so after Grace's death, friends, mostly other women, had begun to try fixing Dubinsky up. So strong was his loneliness that he went along with it, at least at first. Murray Kaplan's wife, Lillian, knew widows she wanted him to meet. At Beth Emet, the synagogue where Grace had been more active than he, though he went to services on occasion, other opportunities presented themselves.

Dubinsky wasn't looking for a tootsie. He was now seventy-eight, and most of the women he considered eligible were in their middle to late sixties or early to middle seventies. Yet everyone seemed wrong. Many had health problems; others had been married to wealthy men and were looking for someone to maintain them at the same level of luxury.

But to Dubinsky the most astonishing thing of all was the high number of women he met who, as grandmothers, brought with them wildly dysfunctional families. At least he considered them dysfunctional, which he understood was the new word for screwed up, totally out of control, deeply *meshuggeh*. One night at dinner, a woman named Ida Baumgartner broke down in tears. She had learned just before meeting him that her favorite granddaughter had been deserted by her lesbian companion of three years and was going through hell. Another, Louise Siegel, casually mentioned that her physician son-in-law had turned himself in to the Illinois medical board for cocaine addiction. Gladys Schwartz's grandson had AIDS; Faye Bernstein's son Marvin was leaving his wife, which didn't seem too terrible until Dubinsky was told that the son was planning a sex-change operation. My God, he thought, while I was living quietly with my wife and shopping around metals, the world was going mad.

He pulled back. Enough with these women and their crazy families. Better to live alone, quietly, sanely. Still, the loneliness got to him. For about eleven seconds he considered a retirement home, where something like a social life would be provided. But, although he suffered some of the memory lapses of age, his health — knock wood — was still excellent, his mind clear. He could make it fine on his own, with luck maybe for a good while longer.

Time lay heavily. On a typical day, Dubinsky awoke at six — go break the habits of a lifetime — had coffee, juice, and cereal, read through the *Chicago Tribune,* and was showered by seven-thirty. He had joined the Evanston Athletic Club, and five days a week he went for a one-hour workout: a bit of walking around the track, time on the stationary bicycle, the rowing machine, the treadmill, some light weightlifting. He was usually finished by nine o'clock. The rest of the day hung there, like a punishing desert sun, bearing down on him.

Some mornings he would go food shopping, having learned by now how to put a frozen dinner in the microwave and warm up a can of soup on the stove, though his doctor told him to watch the sodium. He could also boil hot dogs. Then there was the occasional medical or dental appointment, and every other Thursday, Krystyna, the Polish woman who cleaned the apartment, appeared at nine-thirty. His accountant he saw once a year, at tax time. He wasn't much on movies. He watched television, mostly the news on CNN or PBS and some sports, but the so-called prime-time stuff left him pretty cold. He met Ruthie for lunch, though less often now that he'd told off her husband. He was saddened to discover they hadn't all that much to say to each other.

Dubinsky had always been a reader. Thank God for that. He began using the Evanston library, where he took out two or three books a week, mostly on current history and especially on the war — his war, World War II. He was also a sucker for books on Winston Churchill, the greatest man, he thought, of the twentieth century. The library, recently rebuilt, was a large, comfortable place, clean and well lit, and Dubinsky spent a good deal of time on the third floor, in the periodicals section. He began reading the *Wall Street Journal, Fortune, Business Week, Forbes, The Economist.* He wasn't a stock market man, nor was he familiar with the intricacies of economics, but he did like to think of himself as a businessman, even in retirement. Besides, he preferred the library to the isolation of his apartment with its sometimes overwhelming weight of memories.

In the periodicals section the main librarian was a small woman, pudgy, with long hair beginning to turn gray, given to extremes of moodiness. Sometimes she made Dubinsky feel that he was part of the family, at other times that he was an old bum using the library for shelter. Another woman, a light-skinned black, maybe a mulatto, also worked in the section part time. Her cheerfulness was perpetual, her smile winning. She was tallish, slender, and wore soft dresses and gauzy scarves in vibrant colors. She knew his name from the slips he filled out when he needed to see a back issue of one of his business magazines. "How are you, Mr. Dubinsky?" she would say, or, "Nice day, isn't it, Mr. Dubinsky?" He didn't know her name.

On the day that would have been his fifty-third wedding anniversary, Dubinsky got out of bed with a pain in his left knee. Murray, two years older, had once warned him about such signs of age. "The morning you wake up free of pain," he had said, "watch out. You're probably dead." Dubinsky limped into the kitchen, poured juice and cereal, put up the water for instant coffee. He decided to take a pass on the health club. Skimming through the *Trib*, he wondered what the day would have been like if Grace were still alive. Would they have had a party with their friends to celebrate? Would they have gone off on a trip together, maybe New York to see some shows? God, he missed her.

He went into the den to pay some bills, taking out his checkbook, his Cross pen, the packet of stamps. He was signing a check to the gas company when his eyes fogged. Jesus, Dubinsky thought, I'm crying. On the couch now, facing the television set, he felt the tears come faster. "Grace," he said to the empty room, "I should have gone first. It would have made more sense."

This was a new low, and it wasn't his style. Quickly, leaving the bills on the desk, Dubinsky showered and dressed and left for the library. He made his way through the *Wall Street Journal,* then forced himself to read most of the current *Fortune*. This being his wedding anniversary, he decided to treat himself to lunch at an Italian restaurant across the street, where a young waiter announced that his name was Howard and proceeded to recite the chef's specials for the day at a level of detail Dubinsky had no hope of following. He ordered a grilled chicken sandwich and an iced tea. The noise level in the place seemed very high, and Howard must have returned four times to ask if everything was all right. Scanning the room, Dubinsky decided he was the oldest person there by twenty years.

After buying a few toiletries at the drugstore and browsing at Barnes & Noble, Dubinsky returned to the library at two. He took from the shelf *Churchill's Generals* by John Keegan and began to read in one of the comfortable leather chairs until he felt a jerk of his neck and realized that he had fallen asleep. For more than two hours, it turned out. Old-man stuff, he thought, this nodding off in public places. Had his mouth been open, had he been snoring? No one was in sight except for two high school girls, working on their homework at a nearby table.

Dubinsky gathered up the Churchill book along with his small plastic bag of toiletries and walked slowly down the long, steep staircase to the first floor. At one of the automatic checkout machines, he removed his library card from his wallet and put the book through. As he was picking it up, the pleasant woman from the periodicals section walked past.

"Hello, Mr. Dubinsky," she said, flashing her smile.

"Nice to see you," said Dubinsky, still a bit dazed from his nap. He stared at her as she walked off, then took his book and left.

The phone rang at a little after seven P.M., as Dubinsky was finishing his microwaved Stouffer's veal parmigiana followed by a dish of vanilla ice cream, washed down with decaffeinated coffee.

"Hello, this is Olivia Hampton." The voice was familiar, but not the name.

"I'm sorry, who?"

"At the library."

Of course. "Sorry," said Dubinsky. "What can I do for you?"

"Well, it seems you left your wallet in the library, and I have it with me now. I would have called earlier, but I've been on the run."

Dubinsky's hand went to his back pocket. Empty. Gone.

"My God," he said, "I hadn't even noticed it was missing. Where'd you find it?"

"It was on the table at the checkout machines. Someone turned it in. When would you like to pick it up?"

"I guess I could get it at the library tomorrow," he said.

"I'm not planning to go in to work tomorrow," she said. "Maybe you could pick it up here. I'm on Madison, in southeast Evanston. Or I could drop it off for you if you like."

Dubinsky thought for a moment. He didn't like to drive at night if he could avoid it, but he also didn't want to ask this woman to come out.

"Are you by any chance free to meet me for lunch tomorrow?" he asked.

"I guess I could be," she said.

The Italian restaurant came vaguely to mind. "How about the Roxy, at noon?"

"I'll see you there," she said, and hung up.

Standing in the foyer — he arrived ten minutes early — Dubinsky wondered if he'd made a mistake. Until last night he hadn't known this woman's name. What the hell would they talk about? How would he get through this lunch?

"Miss Hampton," he said as she entered though the revolving door. She was wearing a cream-colored dress and a bright red scarf with lots of blue and yellow in it. Her shoes were red.

She held out her hand. "Nice to see you, Mr. Dubinsky," she said. "By the way, it's Mrs. Hampton."

"You're married?"

"Was. I'm a widow. My husband died nine years ago."

A woman in her twenties, in black pants and top, hair pulled back from her face, showed them to a table against the wall. The restaurant didn't seem quite so daunting as before.

"Do you come here often?" she asked. What wonderful teeth, Dubinsky thought, strong and white. He himself wore a partial bridge. She must have been in her early sixties, maybe a touch older.

"Not too often," he replied.

"Hi," a young girl announced. "I'm Kelly, and I'll be your server today. May I tell you about our specials?"

Dubinsky and Olivia Hampton exchanged glances.

"Sure," said Dubinsky, "let 'er rip," and Kelly went through her spiel: "just a touch of tarragon," "a light coating of pesto," "a slight hint of balsamic vinegar."

Again they looked at each other, smiling.

"Look here, honey," Mrs. Hampton said, "I think you can stop with all that talk now. I'm going to have the grilled chicken sandwich and some iced tea."

"Same for me," Dubinsky said, ordering yesterday's lunch.

"Strange world we're living in," she said. "Perhaps you've noticed."

"Afraid I have. It's become one of my subjects — one I've had to steer myself away from. I get a little crazy on it."

"Me, too," she said. "I find I have to bite my tongue all the time. Especially at the library. The other night I went to a movie, and when I came out I said to myself, 'I don't ever want to see another movie I haven't already seen before — maybe thirty years before.' Oh, before I forget." She reached into her purse. "Your wallet."

A delicate moment, Dubinsky thought. He considered offering a reward, but then, afraid of insulting her, thought better of it.

"There's sixty-eight dollars in it," she said. "Nothing important's missing, I hope."

Dubinsky checked for his credit cards, his driver's license; everything seemed to be there. "This is a first for me, leaving my wallet," he said. "I'm glad to have it back. Thanks."

"I've left my purse in different places more than once. It's part of getting older, I suppose."

"You haven't hit that age yet," he said.

"I'm seventy-two."

"Really," Dubinsky said. "I hope you don't think I'm conning you, but you seem a lot younger."

"I do think you're conning me, but feel free to do more of it." She flashed her smile again. "Tell me, Mr. Dubinsky, how long have you been a widower?"

"Three years, but I don't remember saying I was a widower."

"You didn't have to," she said. "It shows."

"How so?"

"The way you carry yourself. The sadness around the eyes, the bereft look."

"It's that obvious?"

"To me it is. But then, I still see it in myself, and it's nearly ten years since my husband died. I think the only penalty you pay for a good marriage is that you never really get over its coming to an end. I still get up some mornings disappointed that Charley isn't next to me."

"Then it doesn't get any easier?"

"You lose something that can't be replaced. At the same time, you know, life goes on. It has to go on."

Dubinsky wondered what Grace would have thought of this woman. He wondered, in fact, what she would have thought of his being at lunch with a black woman who sounded, if truth be told, as if she were Jewish.

"My wife also happened to have been my best friend, so it was like losing two key people at once, if you know what I mean, Mrs. Hampton."

"Forgive me, but if we're going to talk about such things, maybe you'd better call me Olivia."

"I'm Immanuel — Manny, if you like."

Through the rest of lunch he filled her in on his family, and learned from her that she had a son who was a dentist living in South Shore and a daughter in Washington, D.C., with three kids and a husband who sold municipal bonds. Her own husband, like her son, had been a dentist. She herself had gone to the University of Chicago but didn't finish her degree, which she much regretted. She had begun working at the library a year after her husband died. Nothing dysfunctional here.

She was very funny about her co-workers. She told him about a librarian on the second floor, a woman in her fifties, who hated to put new books into circulation, claiming that the patrons would only wreck them eventually. "I mean," Olivia said, "she actually used the word 'eventually.'" The mood swings of the woman in periodicals she attributed to her relationship with a man she had been dating for some twenty-three years, who was himself under the thumb of a psychotherapist and who didn't feel he should marry or do anything to alter his life until he completed therapy. "And that," Olivia said, "figures to be around the time vaudeville comes back. Poor Kathy, I'm afraid she's just not a good closer."

Dubinsky was having a good time. They rehearsed their common view that the world was growing nuttier and nuttier, dumber and dumber. Dubinsky confided his opinions on men's ponytails, purple and other colored hair, earrings inserted in places other than the ear. He mentioned what seemed to him the madness in the families of the few women he had gone out with after his wife died. He discovered he was able to make her laugh.

"My motto," she said, "has become, Take the world as you find it, but in your own fashion try not to leave it that way. Does that make any sense?"

Dubinsky didn't want to answer too quickly. "It does," he said after a pause, "it really does."

The restaurant was beginning to empty. He looked at his watch: they had been together for more than two and a half hours.

"I suppose we ought to let this young woman go home," she said, nodding at the waitress.

"I suppose so." Dubinsky left the money for lunch and a thirty percent tip. When they emerged the sun was strong and he experienced that sweet sensation of return that he used to feel seventy-odd years ago coming out of the Granada movie theater into the sunlight. Then, as now, he had to adjust, and then, as now, the adjustment was to a slightly richer reality.

"Olivia," he said, shaking her hand, "I would like it if we could do this again."

"I would, too, Immanuel," she said. "Call when you feel like. My number's in the book."

"I will," he said. "Maybe fairly soon."

"That would be fine. And thanks for lunch."

"Thanks for my wallet."

Driving home in a haze of elation, Dubinsky looked down at the speedometer and noted that he was doing 50 in a thirty-mile-an-hour zone. He braked gently and wondered how many days he was required to wait before calling her for dinner.

Coming In with Their Hands Up

I'M STANDING in line for a Coke and a hot dog during half-time at a Bulls-Pistons game when I can't help eavesdropping on two guys in line just ahead of me. They're "Canadians," as my father, in a helpful code word, used to call Jews: "Not many Canadians here tonight," he'd say as we entered a restaurant. They're in their forties, expensively dressed. One of them has what looks like a $100 haircut, lots of well-curried black curls running down the back of his thick neck onto the collar of a $1,200 Armani suit. The other guy's short and mostly bald, but with a little ponytail; he's also wearing at least three grand in clothes. They take good care of themselves, these boys; they have that East Bank Health Club look. Both are wearing clunky Rolex watches and soft black leather loafers. Maybe they're in the commodities market, maybe they inherited golden businesses from their fathers.

"Kimmy's going ahead with the divorce," the guy with the haircut says to the guy with the ponytail. "She tells me she's had it. She's gone to a lawyer."

"Who'd she go to?" his pal asks.

"A guy named Allen Bernstein."

"Jesus!" the guy with the ponytail says. "Allen Bernstein takes no prisoners. Might as well come in with your hands up and hope you can come away with your Bulls tickets and a couple of extra sets of underwear."

"Really? No shit?"

"No shit. Allen Bernstein's a fiend, a killer."

I'm Allen Bernstein. I've been a divorce lawyer in Chicago for thirty years, and I listened to this conversation with calm but deep pleasure. I considered it a fine piece of free advertising. To be a lawyer is bad enough, but to be a lawyer specializing in divorce, let's face it, is to incur double enmity: to be despised by most people for your profession, and by your fellow lawyers for your specialty within the profession. When I started out and someone asked me what I did, I used to have to steel myself before saying. No more.

Nobody sets out to become a divorce lawyer. I got into it because of the limited possibilities open to me when I graduated from DePaul Law School in 1962. My father was a union plumber, the first licensed Jewish plumber in the city. After I graduated from Von Steuben, in Albany Park, I thought about acquiring a license myself, but at the last minute decided instead on Wright Junior College, mainly because I wasn't ready to go to work. After Wright I went on to Roosevelt University, on Michigan Avenue in the Loop, but I remember less about what happened in the classroom than about the never-ending gin games in the student lounge: a penny a point, Hollywood-Oklahoma, spades double, big stakes in those days. My major was political science, please don't ask me why.

When I graduated, I still wasn't ready for work, so I applied to DePaul Law and was accepted. I took odd jobs — selling shoes at Maling's at night, construction in the summer — to pay my way. The big goal at DePaul was to pass the bar. The time the teachers gave you for answering questions on exams was limited to thirteen minutes — the exact amount allotted on the Illinois bar exam.

Graduate, pass the bar, start making some dough. Sights were set no higher, which was fine by me. The big law firms weren't interested in guys from DePaul unless maybe you had a political or family connection, and I didn't have either one. I finished around the middle of my class. No one was recruiting me; I'd have to make it on my own. I wasn't particularly interested in any specialty, except that I didn't want to be stuck behind a desk doing estates or trusts or some dry crap like that. I was also pretty sure I didn't have the skill or the instinct to be a full-time litigator. After passing the bar I was officially a "professional man," but unemployed.

I had an Uncle Bernie, my mother's brother, a bookie, and among his clients were some of the Jewish high fliers in the Chicago of those days. They included two brothers, Marvin and Jack Brent — "originally Brodsky," my uncle volunteered — who were divorce lawyers. They were said to have made a ton of money. They were also said to be very tough. My uncle used the same phrase about them that the guy at the Bulls game would use about me — "Your wife hires the Brent brothers in a divorce suit, you might as well come in with your hands up" — which may be why it pleased me so much to hear it again, this time about me, after all those years. Anyhow, Uncle Bernie arranged for me to meet the younger Brent brother, Jack.

When I phoned, Jack Brent said he couldn't clear time in the office, but we could talk that night at the Raphael Hotel, on Delaware east of Michigan, where he lived. He could give me fifteen minutes, no more. I was to meet him in the lobby at six-thirty. I would recognize him, he said, and hung up without bothering to say goodbye.

*   *   *

I was fifteen minutes early; he was ten minutes late. But he was right about recognizing him. His suit was the giveaway: lush gray, a three-piece job, nipped in at the waist, with sharp, exaggerated lapels. It looked simultaneously soft and armored, and flashed extremely expensive. (Jack and Marvin, I later learned, had these suits made by a guy on Michigan Avenue named George Mashbitz, who used to make bespoke suits for the actor Forrest Tucker, the gossip columnist Irving Kupcinet, and others who kept a locker for their cigars in the humidor room at Dunhill's.) He carried a chesterfield coat over his arm, and in his hand — you'll have to believe me on this — held a pearl-gray homburg. He was tall, very erect, bald, with a blotchy, pinkish-purplish complexion. The effect was pure shyster.

"I'm running late, kid," he said after I introduced myself. "But I can give you a few minutes. Sit down over here." He pointed to two facing couches.

"So whaddya want?" he began, gingerly setting down his chesterfield and homburg.

"I want to know about the opportunities in divorce law."

"Mostly they're opportunities to see human beings at their most disgraceful. Also to be widely despised — by your adversaries, your colleagues, and usually, in the end, your clients. And there are opportunities to show the highest contempt for the law, which in this field is pretty goddamn disgusting, by forcing everyone to lie, cheat, and do what he can to screw the other party. Those are the opportunities. Next question."

"Why are you in it?"

"For the money, which, if you cull your clientele carefully, can be staggeringly high. Next question." He looked at his watch, a wafer-thin gold job with small diamonds for numbers.

"Do you and your brother have any other lawyers working for you?"

"Why? You looking for work?"

"I am."

"How hungry are you?"

"Very," I heard myself say. Strange, but not until that precise moment did I realize that I wanted to be rich — not making a decent living, not being "comfortable," but rich, really rich.

"I'll talk to my brother. Maybe we could use a young guy to run errands. You'd be strictly a gofer at first, you understand. Low pay, maybe a hundred a week. Just because the Brent brothers make a lot doesn't mean we like to give it away." He looked at his watch again. "I gotta be somewhere," he said, gathering up his coat and hat. "My brother's in New York till late next week. Call me at the beginning of next week and I'll see if we have anything for you."

When I called, I got the job. Only they paid me not a hundred bucks a week but sixty-five: no George Mashbitz suits for me. Marvin Brent, three years older than Jack, had even darker views and less in the way of a sense of humor. The Brent brothers, bachelors, kept adjoining suites in the Raphael and drove matching black Fleetwoods. They had no interest in politics or even the news, didn't care about food, saw no family. Each took a one-week vacation — never together — and went to New York to see musical comedies. (For reasons I could never figure out, they had this thing about musicals.) During the five years that I worked for them, neither, so far as I could make out, had anything approaching a serious relationship with a woman. I assume they availed themselves of expensive hookers.

As I soon discovered, they used the services of these ladies fairly often in their business. In those days, before no-fault came into being, divorce in Illinois could be obtained on four grounds only: adultery, desertion (technically, for a year), physical cruelty, and mental cruelty. The Brent brothers' clients were almost exclusively Jewish, and Jews didn't do physical cruelty, at least not in those days. To get a divorce for mental cruelty, you had to come up with tortures more exquisite than Alfred Hitchcock's — it practically couldn't be done. Desertion was an option, but many people didn't want to wait out the full year or more — especially the men, who often had a lady in the wings to whom extravagant and urgent promises had been made.

That left adultery. We staged lots of adulteries, usually at the Bismark Hotel on Randolph. The guy caught in bed with a naked woman, the schlocky private detective, the photographer — the whole comic bit. I served as director, if not yet producer, for many of these farces.

The hookers got $50 for the assignment. (We billed the clients $500 and put it under the category of clerical services.) They tended to be big and brassy, in the pinup style of the day, with names like Rusty, Pam, or Babs. I paid them in cash, and would occasionally take them out afterward to O'Connell's on Rush Street for coffee and a sandwich. The conversation often touched on celebrity tricks they had turned. Some had slept with guys who played for the Bears. One girl was a regular stop for Desi Arnaz when he came to Chicago. "What's he like?" I asked her. "Desi?" she said, putting down her coffee cup and dragging on a cigarette. "A real pig."

As a rule, the Brent brothers preferred women to men as clients. It made more sense to sue the men, since they had the money. "We'll gently squeeze his nuts" was a favorite expression of Marvin Brent's, "then add the serious pressure later." (I could never hear him say this without feeling a stab in my groin.) Most of these clients were sent over by larger firms that declined divorce cases because they didn't want what used to be called a reception room problem — some broad sitting there crying, red-faced, Kleenexes all over the joint, while corporate clients were waiting on heavy-billing business. It was undignified. Marvin and Jack Brent didn't care about dignity.

I was surprised at first by how comforting they could be to these women. Once they decided to take a case — and the only ones I ever saw them turn down involved husbands without enough money to be worth their while — they made it plain that the husband was the enemy and the Brothers Brent were ready to nail the son of a bitch to the wall. Who knows, right now the guy was probably holding back, spending it on a girl-friend. The main thing was to listen to their advice and not soften in any way. In the end, their client would be able to live as well as when she was married, maybe a little better. Nothing they hated more than reconciliations, and they did everything they could to prevent them. Women who went into Marvin or Jack Brent's office with Kleenex in hand came out smiling — the sly smile of vengeance anticipated.

The husbands, on the other hand, had blood in their eyes. In court, they would mutter — sometimes, more than mutter, hurl — the roughest insults they could come up with at Jack or Marvin. Occasionally an anonymous caller threatened to beat up or even murder one of them.

One day I'm sitting in the reception room waiting to meet a friend for lunch when a man named Louis Schoenwald, a little guy, dapper, in his early sixties, comes in and asks to speak to Jack Brent.

"May I inquire on what business?" says Rhona, our reception-ist.

"Mr. Brent is representing my wife, Nancy," he says calmly.

"I'm sorry," Sylvia answers, "but Mr. Brent doesn't see the husbands or wives of clients except by appointment."

"Very well," says Mr. Schoenwald. "I can understand that. I'll call for an appointment." He turns toward the door and begins to walk out when suddenly he pivots and races down the hall. Next thing I hear is a door slamming, and Jack calls out, "Get this bastard off me, goddammit." I run down the hall to find

Schoenwald on the desk, on top of Jack, his hands around his neck, Jack's face turning from his normal purplish red to pure maroon.

After a struggle I manage to pull Schoenwald off, walking him out of the office in a hammerlock. "I'll kill him," he's screaming. "The cocksucker doesn't deserve to live." That's what I mean by a reception room problem.

Marvin and Jack Brent died roughly six years later, within seven months of each other, both of massive coronaries. I had left them two years earlier, to go in for myself. They threw me a bit of work, fish too small for their expensive nets. I sent them kickbacks. Marvin died first, and an obit appeared in the *Trib*, complete with picture, in which he looked, as in life, menacingly well groomed. No services were held, no request for contributions to the Heart Disease Research Foundation or anywhere else. I sent Jack a note of condolence, but never received an answer. When Jack died, the obit in the *Trib* was smaller, again no service announced. What could possibly be said about him, I wondered, and then remembered the old joke about the guy no one was willing to eulogize at his funeral until finally some geezer gets up and announces, in a strong Yiddish accent, "His brudder vas even woise."

As for me, by the time I opened my own office — Allen Bernstein & Associates — divorce law in Illinois had begun to change, and so had the clientele. No-fault, with its assumption (sensible enough in theory, I suppose) that there isn't always a clear villain in the breakup of a marriage, opened the floodgates to some peculiar characters. Where before divorce tended to be a game for the rich, now everyone wanted to play. With the craziness of the late 1960s, there was a feeling in the air that everything was possible.

It was all very good for business. Suddenly people began ap-

pearing in my office wanting to get out of marriages because
. . . well, they weren't really sure why. In the vast majority of
cases I could have told them: they thought they were missing
out on better screwing elsewhere.

Too crude? You wouldn't think so if you heard their stories.
One Friday afternoon a woman in her late thirties, her name's
Susan Blumenthal, comes in for help. Her husband, his name's
Howard, he's a CPA. They live in Highland Park, which sug-
gests he's a pretty good provider. They have two kids, a boy and
a girl, both under ten. She doesn't work, has never held a job.

"Is Howard cheating on you?"

"Not that I know of," she says.

"Is he beating you up, or maybe he's what is called mentally
cruel?"

"Neither," she says.

"Is he incapacitated in any way?"

"No."

"Well, what precisely is your complaint?"

"When Howard takes off his glasses for sex," she says, "I
want to laugh."

"I see," I said, not seeing at all. "Maybe you could tell me a
little more."

"I mean," she says, "how can I make love to a man when I
want to laugh at him?"

"Let me get this straight. You want to leave your husband because he takes off his glasses to make love to you, and without
his glasses on he makes you laugh? This is your complaint?"

"Yes."

"What about contact lenses?"

"It wouldn't be the same," she says, finally getting to the
point. "Besides, I'm in love with someone else."

It turns out the guy she's in love with is fifteen years younger
and plays in a rock band and isn't employed, at least just now.

But he's wonderful at tie-dyeing. She'd like to keep the house in Highland Park, and the Mercedes. She wouldn't mind working, she's thought about getting a teaching certificate, but jobs in the northern suburbs aren't easy to come by and, she figures, maybe it makes more sense to stay home with the kids, for whom these are important years.

I was able to get her just about everything she wanted, with the exception of the Mercedes. Poor Howard, I assume, recovered and is today happily blinking away in some other woman's bed.

But the ladies were nothing next to the men. When they came in with their hair grown over their ears, I knew it was unload-the-little-woman time. They had hundreds of different excuses, wild, elaborate, comic excuses. Most had other, much younger women lined up. One guy has the nerve to tell me that, since his wife's mastectomy, he can no longer perform in bed, and this being the case, it doesn't seem fair to her that they stay together. Then he goes on to outline a plan involving shifting his assets so as to leave his wife about enough for a studio apartment in a less than safe neighborhood near Wilson Avenue. I got him, too, what he wanted.

You don't have to be long in the business to understand that, once it becomes clear one party wants out, it's pig time. True, every once in a while some guy, out of extreme guilt over his outrageous behavior, comes in ready to give the store away. Then it becomes my job to discourage him. I paint his future — a bleak one if he allows himself to become hostage to the woman who will soon be his ex-wife. Before long, most of them come around. At the first strong demand, teeth flash and they're ready to take off the gloves.

I attribute my success to an understanding of my role as an absolute client's man. I'm no public-relations guy, and I don't mind being unyielding to the point of rigidity in my demands.

When I finally close up this practice, I don't expect to include goodwill among its assets; there isn't going to be any. No sportsmanship trophies in matrimonial law. What I learned from the Brent brothers is that it doesn't matter what other lawyers and their clients or even the judges think of you. There's only one point, winning, which means getting your clients what they want and making them pay you well for it. As the guy in the ponytail said, if your wife hires Allen Bernstein, you might as well come in with your hands up.

Why anyone would want to *marry* a divorce lawyer is itself something of a mystery, comparable in its way, I suppose, to a woman marrying a gynecologist. After dealing professionally with it all day, you can't expect a man to have too much enthusiasm for it in his private life.

I didn't marry until my fifties — fifty-two, to be precise. Leslee, eighteen years younger, hadn't been married before, so she wasn't a client — I had long ago made it a policy not to fool with a female client, though God knows the opportunities were plentiful. She was the only daughter of Ben Lerman, who had started out in life as a building contractor and made a fortune putting up cheap garages, then lost it when he expanded too quickly into lines of work he knew little about, including becoming a major stockholder in Arlington racetrack, which went under in a swamp of politics and corruption.

Like my old man, Ben was a working stiff, a dirt-under-the-nails man. Though in another age he probably would have preferred to keep her home, he had sent his daughter off to college — the University of Indiana — where she was a sorority girl. He and I got along. He was not so secretly pleased that his daughter, at thirty-four, was finally getting married, and to a Jewish guy, a lawyer, a professional man. I made a good living; that's all he needed to know. In marrying me, his girl, he figured, had come into safe harbor.

I'm not sure why Leslee was still unmarried. She's good-looking, *zaftig,* brunette, big eyes, with a gentle, feminine manner, a papa's girl. She taught third grade at Boone School in West Rogers Park. The kids in her class — Greeks, East Indians, Russians, lower-middle-class Jews — were crazy about her, and she about them. She would buy things at her own expense — art supplies, music tapes, books — to enliven her lessons, and three times a week brought pastries for the entire class. I used to joke with her that she was the only person in history who might have to declare Chapter 11 from a teaching job. When I first began taking her out she lived with two other girls, sorority sisters, on Surf Avenue.

I was forty-nine when we first met, and I had seen my run of Jewish women — from the nutsy all the way to those strictly in business for themselves. It was at a wedding: Leslee knew the bride, and the groom was a former client of mine entering into his third marriage. I was now living at the Raphael, on the floor above the Brent brothers' old suites. I was also billing somewhere in the neighborhood of $2 million a year, which, in an office with no partners, wasn't too shabby. I found myself attracted to this girl, with her appealing sweetness of nature: a case, I hear you saying, of opposites attracting. I decided to pursue her, but gently. A full-court press, I sensed, would be a mistake.

The first time I took Leslee out, we went to a movie and dinner. We began to go to Bulls games in the old Chicago Stadium. If there was a play in town, we might take that in. She asked me about my business, and I filled her in on the more outrageous cases, which I thought had a certain entertainment value. But she really didn't want to believe that people could behave so badly. She talked about her students in a way that made these little Jagdishes and Dimitris and Laliths come alive for me. Once, picking her up at school, I saw her help an Indian girl who had a fleck of something in her eye; her gentleness, the child's complete confidence in her, were something to behold. As Leslee got into the car she seemed exhilarated, and more beautiful than ever. I felt a flash of jealousy.

We didn't sleep together for the first three months. (Later, she told me she'd begun to worry about me.) When we did, things went fine, maybe even a little better than fine. Eventually, marriage became one of our subjects. A bachelor in his fifties becomes a very careful scrutinizer of female flaws. I felt too old to make a mistake, and I searched Leslee for things that, down the road, would make life with her a torture. The flaws I found, I decided, were of a kind I could live with, and some — her unworldliness, her hatred of confrontations, her weakness for all children — I found endearing.

What she saw in me, a guy almost twenty years her senior, no beauty, who'd been around the block more than a few times, I didn't know. One day I asked. "Because," Leslee said, "I felt you loved me more than any man I had ever met or ever would meet. And I knew that I could always count on you to protect me." Babe, I thought to myself, you're dead right on both counts.

The Raphael, loaded with well-off elderly Jewish widows, was no place for a married couple. We looked at a few townhouses in Lincoln Park, but Leslee favored a house in the suburbs. She wanted children of her own, and the sooner the better. No argument. Leslee without children never seemed a serious possibility, though I have to say I hadn't pictured myself a father. I'd probably seen too many clients ready to use their kids as weapons in divorce battles, or refusing to pay for their upkeep, or subjecting them to the humiliation of living together with new and often very temporary lovers.

Leslee agreed that I was too old for a big wedding, and besides, as I pointed out to her, only half joking, it would be a bad advertisement for my business. We put the money instead into a $900,000 house on Beach Road, just off the lake in Glencoe, a house with six bedrooms, a family room, a huge yard, space for lots of children, dogs — the full catastrophe, as I remember Anthony Quinn calling family life in that movie he did about that Greek.

Leslee's calm and sweetness played off strangely against the greed and emotional squalor of my clients' lives. Which was reality: my goodhearted, naturally refined wife, or the people making use of my services to elude their responsibilities or to tighten the screws on people they once claimed to love? Before Leslee, I would have said that reality was what went on in my office. Living with her made me a little less sure.

"Have you ever felt you wanted to practice another kind of law?" she once asked me.

"I don't know another kind, sweetheart," I said. "Besides, I'm good at what I do, and there's a lot of satisfaction in that. Not to speak of the income, which may just turn out to be useful to our grandchildren."

But before you can have grandchildren, you have to have children, and here we ran into a little glitch, an unexpected jiggeroo. We planned to have kids right away, or almost right away. Leslee's hope was to be in her seventh month in June, when school let out for the year, so that she could have her first child in late summer. She planned not to return to teaching, at least not soon. We never spoke about how many children we would have, but I always assumed at least two. I'm still not sure how many she had in mind.

The problem was that Leslee couldn't seem to get pregnant.

After a year, her gynecologist put her on pills and a careful sur-veillance of her temperature and body rhythms. During this pe-riod, called in at odd times from the sidelines, I felt like a field-goal kicker. When Leslee phoned in the middle of the morning to announce she needed the services of George Blanda, the old Chicago Bears kicker and our private name for my crucial func-tion, I would tell my secretary to cancel my appointments, have the garage bring my Porsche around, and speed home. It was fun for a while, but it began to get grim after nearly a year had gone by and nothing productive happened.

Our next step was a fertility specialist. I'll spare you the de-tails, but we eventually discovered that, even though my ap-petite and performance were normal, my counts were too low to produce a child. Although I was ready to adopt, Leslee put the quietus on any such idea. Her students were already her adopted children, she said, and she wanted to raise kids of her own — and mine. On this point she was adamant, absolutely in-flexible. There were other possibilities, and I was willing to con-sider any of them, but Leslee wasn't.

Never for a moment did she so much as hint that this sadness in her life was my fault. We rolled around in our large house, with its extra bedrooms that we both now knew would never be filled. She continued teaching. My practice filled out my days. In the summer we traveled, though I found I didn't like being away from the office for very long. One night, at the George V in Paris, I awoke to discover my wife weeping gently in her sleep. I thought of waking her, but there was, finally, nothing I could do to make things better.

In my business, I have seen too many older men who marry younger women and have to face the question of children. Of-ten these men have had kids with their first wives and have no interest in starting another family. Just as often, the women enter into an implicit bargain with them, a cruel pre-nup that never gets put on paper. In my opinion it's a bad deal — always a mistake for a young woman, leading sometimes to heartbreak, frequently to rancor, inevitably to disappointment. Leslee and I had made no such deal; quite the contrary. Still, having to go through life without children seemed to me a hell she shouldn't be made to bear. It seemed, somehow, impermissible.

After three years of marriage, I knew in my heart what I had to do. The question was how to go about it. In the old days, I might have called in the bimbos and staged a full Brent Bros. production at the old Bismark Hotel, with myself in the male lead and copies of the photos sent to Leslee. A campaign of mental cruelty — systematically ignoring her at home, humiliating her in public — would have taken too long, and I couldn't have done it even if I wanted to. Feigning impotence, given my feelings for her, was not in the cards. That left announcing that I'd found someone I loved more and I needed my freedom.

Of course I would make the actual proceedings as painless as possible, and I would see to it that she had enough money to live well and make her more attractive to the man who would give her children while there was still time — even more attractive, that is, than she already was. Leslee, sweetheart, my own, my true love, forgive me. I'm coming in with my hands up.

The Master's Ring

WHEN THE *New York Times* reported the death last year of Malcolm Gaynor, the literary biographer, at ninety-one, it made mention of the ring. A large green stone in a gold setting, it had lain on Malcolm's wedding-ring finger the day he came to Chicago to speak to the members of the Institute for Psychoanalysis. I thought it a touch gaudy for his otherwise understated manner, but I did not then know to whom it had originally belonged: the Master, the great American novelist who was the subject of the splendid three-volume work that had made Malcolm's reputation and given him his small but real claim to a place in literary history.

I did not know Malcolm all that well, having met him for the first time on that day in Chicago. Afterward we corresponded a fair amount, and I reviewed the second and third volumes of his biography, praising it and holding back my reservations, which chiefly centered on his rather heavy psychoanalyzing of his subject. I assumed he found me an agreeable enough younger man — there were more than thirty years between us — if not a brother under the skin, the two of us upholding the torch of literature in a mildly depraved and sadly deprecatory age.

I sensed but wasn't altogether certain that Malcolm was Jewish. He carried himself — how should I say? — somewhat tweedily, like an academic of the bad old days, the days when, frankly, types like Malcolm and me were not wanted in English departments. Only subsequently did I learn that at some point in the 1930s he had changed his name from Max Goldstein. As a young journalist, he had had a Communist phase, and I suspected — wrongly, as it would turn out — that it had been in order to improve his chances in the party that he chose an Anglicized name. But the change would have served him well even after he left the party, especially during his years in Paris, when his interests had turned literary and he met such figures as James Joyce and Edith Wharton, and later still when he encountered, and briefly became the amanuensis of, Bernard Berenson. Berenson, too, was a Jew, which didn't prevent him from being a bit of an anti-Semite — anti-Semitism being never so subtle as when wielded by one who has suffered at its hands.

Certainly Malcolm Gaynor stood a better chance of insinuating himself with the Master's descendants, now among the most *distingué* of American families, than Max Goldstein did. And insinuate himself Malcolm did. The family gave him permission to inspect all the Master's papers and, eventually, the right to edit his letters and notebooks. Malcolm, as they used to say about the guy with sole rights to a concession at the fairgrounds, had the X on the Master. Just as, for Lawrence of Arabia, the only way to Aqaba lay through the desert, so the only way to the Master lay through Malcolm; and, for his own good reasons, Malcolm did not trouble to smooth the way for other scholars.

A great theme of the Master's fiction is the dominance of one human being over another. Malcolm dominated the dead

Master. But he also needed him. Writing about him made Malcolm a better biographer and a keener and more penetrating critic than he would otherwise have been. Seven or eight years before he died, Malcolm produced a small book on the Pre-Raphaelite writers and painters: thin, snobbish, superfluous stuff. Somehow, the Master lent him authority and gravity — without him, Malcolm was merely one more, rather dim, academic biographer.

Another of the Master's great themes, playing through nearly all his works, is betrayal. Malcolm's sympathy for the Master was complete, yet he interpreted him through a Freudian filter that, my guess is, the Master himself would have found not just inadequate but utterly, quite hideously coarse. All artists despise Freud, or at least they should, for behind all great art is an unannounced protest against the overdetermination of character in which Freud, genius though he was, may be said to have specialized. Malcolm was not an artist; he was a critic and a scholar, and he had to use the tools at hand. But the Master, a consummate artist, would have found these tools woefully crude, if not, indeed, traitorous.

I began by invoking the Master's ring, which the *New York Times* duly touched upon in its obituary. I don't know how Malcolm came into possession of it. Perhaps he found it in a drawer in the old house in Sussex where the Master, having left London, spent the last years of his life before and during World War I; or possibly it was among his papers and effects kept by his family after death. But as soon as I read about the ring, I knew I wanted to own it. And the more I thought about it, the more deeply, urgently, passionately I wanted it.

My life is not driven by material possessions. I've craved a few things, but none of them has been that difficult to obtain. One was a gold Hermès lighter that, selling for $40 or so, seemed to me, in my early twenties, a great extravagance. For the better part of a month I was hardly able to think of anything else, and I finally bought the thing, if only to get my mind back on my work. Much later, I underwent a similar craving for a German fountain pen, a $300 Pelikan, and once again the only way to calm myself was to walk in and buy it, silly self-indulgence that it was. These little tales may make me seem trivial, but I hope they also reveal my honesty about a possibly pathetic but not completely disqualifying weakness.

As for the ring, the ring with its large green stone and gold setting, the ring worn by the Master, I found myself thinking about it at unexpected but insistent moments: standing in the shower, at meals, in the midst of teaching one of my classes at the University of Michigan or while working on wholly unrelated matters, after and sometimes even during lovemaking. How elegant that ring would look on the fourth finger of my right hand! The gold, as I remembered, was dull and only lightly burnished. ("I can stand a great deal of gold," wrote the Master, who had vainly hoped to acquire enough of it to remove the financial pressure from the writing.) The Master's ring — why shouldn't I have it? It oughtn't be allowed to sit in a vault, or even in a glass case in a museum. Besides, I knew the Master's mind and loved his work as much as anyone, and especially now that Malcolm Gaynor, the only man who knew the Master better, was dead, I felt in some odd way that I deserved it.

I decided to write to Malcolm's widow in San Francisco, where Malcolm had retired to write memoirs that he never completed. This was a second, late-life marriage; in his mid-seventies, he had left a wife of many years to marry a younger woman. Was she a former student? A younger faculty member?

A connection of Malcolm's through the psychiatric and thera-peutic world — the shrinkoisie, as I thought of them? I had no idea. I wrote to her cold, noting that I would be in San Fran-cisco in a few weeks to attend a meeting of the Association of Literary Scholars and Critics. As an old admirer and correspon-dent of her late husband's, I wondered if I might perhaps take her to lunch or meet her for an afternoon drink.

We met in the ornate lobby of the Fairmont Hotel on Nob Hill, where, off in the corner, an English tea was served. I had as-sumed that, like Malcolm, Angela Gaynor would be an Anglo-phile. I was wrong. As it emerged, nothing I had assumed about her was true. She was younger than I, perhaps in her early fifties; tallish (Malcolm had been five foot four at most and, with his carefully groomed white mustache and bald pate, looked like the *Esquire* man); elegant, without a trace of the dowdy style of academic women; blond, with eyes of almost periwinkle blue; and still striking — stunning, the women of my mother's generation would have called her.

"You must be Professor Shapiro," she said as she approached, holding out her hand. She was wearing dark blue trousers, an azure-colored silk shirt, no jewelry other than small gold ear-rings and a plain gold bracelet. Her hair was cut short. She had the high cheekbones and clean smile of a wellborn, well-cared-for woman of means.

"It's very good to meet you," I said, directing her to where I had reserved a table. "You must know San Francisco well."

"I love it," she said as we were seated. "Malcolm agreed to move here, to finish out his career at Berkeley, because of me."

"Was he spending most of his time on his memoirs?"

"Yes, but for the past two or three years his energy was so de-pleted that he couldn't give them much time. The sadness of his last years came from knowing he wasn't likely to finish his final project."

"How large is the manuscript?"

"That's the problem. It's more than four hundred pages, and it only takes him up to his twenties, the years he lived in France."

"Maybe parts of it," I said, "could be cut out and published as discrete pieces. I wonder if you'd mind my looking at it."

"Not at all," she said. "You'd know better than I. I'm not very literary. Malcolm used to be amused at the things I hadn't read. But then, I didn't grow up in a bookish home."

"The Master writes somewhere that 'women aren't literary in any substantial sense of the term,' implying, I think, that they're rather more attractive when not."

"I'll try to remember that. My parents lived in Libertyville, outside Chicago. My father was a vice president of Prudential, and I suppose we were pretty outdoorsy. They died in a plane accident in India, on an around-the-world tour, when I was twenty."

I remembered Libertyville as the home of Adlai Stevenson. Very horsy. Very rich. No Jews in those days. What would her parents, if they had been alive, have thought of their daughter's marriage to the former Max Goldstein? What did she see in him, I wondered.

"How did you and Malcolm meet, if I may ask?"

"At a lecture series where he was speaking on Jung and D. H. Lawrence. I didn't really care about either. I was with a friend who was a graduate student and was very big on Lawrence. Malcolm was dazzling. I'd never met anyone who seemed on such easy terms with culture — all culture. The therapists in the room were in awe of him. We met at the reception afterward. What he saw in me I'll never know."

I knew, and thought it unnecessary to reply. The remainder of our meeting went smoothly, and we made a date for the following morning at her house, where she would show me Malcolm's manuscript and other papers.

It was one of those mornings — sunny, in the low seventies, a light breeze blowing off the bay — when not to live in San Francisco seemed an act of genuine stupidity. I was a bit early, so I got out of my cab three blocks away and walked to Angela Gaynor's house, on Larkin Street near the top of Russian Hill. No one I passed appeared to be over thirty, and everyone was beautiful.

From the outside the house seemed modest, but indoors it was impressively Italianate, Venetian without the surrounding water or tourists: high ceilings, lots of good dark wood, arched entranceways. Turkey rugs, as the Master's generation called Oriental rugs, were nicely positioned in the rooms I passed through. Tapestries rather than paintings hung on the walls. I counted four small Degas bronzes, all of dancers, whether real or copies I did not know enough to say, but I would have been willing to bet they were real.

One could see the Master himself living comfortably here, as Malcolm could hardly have failed to note. It was here that he completed the final volume of his edition of the Master's letters, wearing, no doubt, the ring with the green stone as he put the last period to this monumental work. Gazing around, I wondered again about the extent of Malcolm's identification with the "great indefatigable alchemist," as a poet once described this most subtle of modern novelists. And was Malcolm's, I also began to wonder, a story that the Master himself ought to have written?

Angela Gaynor was in every way up to the beauty of the day and the grandeur of her house. She was in sandals and wore a loose skirt of a creamy taupe that swished and swirled splendidly as she moved about. Her otherwise mannish shirt, collarless and of a soft blue, played against the color of her eyes, and her hair was brushed back, emphasizing her good bones and high color. I could easily imagine her a hundred years earlier in a large hat and a light dress on the lawn of an English estate, at one of those aristocratic parties of which the Master never seemed to tire. The two most delightful words in the English language, he once said, were "summer afternoon." Angela Gaynor looked like a summer afternoon.

"Professor Shapiro, I've thought further about your offer to read my husband's unfinished memoir. I think Malcolm would have been pleased." She ushered me into a large room from which one could see the bay. "This was my husband's study."

The room looked familiar: the colors of the upholstery and rugs, the wall hangings, the furniture, the impressive arched window. And then it dawned on me — it was a careful reconstruction of the Master's garden room at his house in Sussex. The placement of the large glass bookcase, the desk against the wall, the small table and vases under the window, all were just as the Master had arranged them. The same du Maurier print hung on the wall. Even the escritoire, with its foldout writing surface where the Master composed his letters, was exactly duplicated here. It was a trifle eerie; perhaps more than a trifle.

From a lower drawer in the escritoire Angela Gaynor now removed an ample brown folder tied with a thick black ribbon. "Malcolm's memoirs," she said. "He had another copy made before he died, but I'd be grateful if you would return this one to me before you leave San Francisco."

"With pleasure," I said. And then I added, with, I hoped, the suggestion of an afterthought: "Whatever became of the Master's ring, which I remember your husband wearing?"

"Malcolm loved that ring. He would have wanted to be buried with it if he hadn't decided to be cremated. I took it to Sotheby's after his death. It was worth less than a thousand dollars. The remains of a great writer apparently do not command the prices of those of a Liberace or a Marilyn Monroe. Would you like to see it?"

"Yes," I said, trying to show no emotion. "Yes, I would, actually."

From another drawer she extracted a leather box. Along with the ring, it held a small silver container.

"It's a stamp box, a gift from the Master — forgive me, I seem to have picked up Malcolm's habit of addressing him that way — to that American woman novelist, the descendant of James Fenimore Cooper, I forget her name. I gather people now think she killed herself because of the Master's coldness to her."

"Constance Fenimore Woolson. What did Malcolm think?"

"I don't know, but my guess is that he wouldn't have believed it. For Malcolm the Master could do no wrong, especially in the line of thoughtfulness."

She handed me the ring. The gold was dull, just as I remembered, but it was heavier than I would have guessed, with the flat green stone running across the top. I balanced it in the palm of my hand. It had a splendid heft.

"Do you mind if I slip it on?"

"Of course not," she said.

The fit, on the fourth finger of my right hand, was perfect. Odd: the Master was a man of a certain bulk — he looked, several people noted, more like a sea captain than a novelist — yet his fingers must have been fairly thin if this ring could sit so snugly on my own rather slender hand. Perhaps spinning out those fine discriminations over five decades had kept his hands thin. I felt no talismanic power from having the ring on my finger, but I also didn't want to return it.

It would be a mistake, I sensed, to offer to buy it. But neither could I ask Angela Gaynor if she had plans for its disposition. Instead, I decided right there that I would have to devise a way to inveigle it from her. To be truthful, I suppose I had intended to do so from the start. My first thought was to ingratiate myself so thoroughly that it would naturally occur to her to offer it to me. Then again, I might have to come up with something more devious. Whatever it took, I felt I was up to the task.

"I envy you your possession of this ring," I said, slipping it off my finger and returning it to her hand. "I hope someday you'll find a proper repository for it."

"Perhaps you can help me think where," she said.

"That would be nice. But now let me take Malcolm's memoir, which I'm very eager to read. I'll report back to you in a few days."

At the door, as we shook hands, she thanked me again for spending time on her husband's work.

"Please," I said. "After all, Malcolm and I belonged to the same club." And then I quoted to her a characteristic sentence from one of the Master's stories that I had by heart: "'We're a numerous band, partakers of the same repose, who sit together in the shade of the tree, by the plash of the fountain, with the glare of the desert round us and no great vice that I know but the habit perhaps of estimating people a little too much by what they think of a certain style.'"

"I don't know that sentence, but I'm sure Malcolm would have."

"Beyond doubt," I said. "But then, Malcolm and I, as I say, belonged to the same club. 'The madness of art,' or at least the madness of the worship of art, and all that. You may be better off without it."

Back at my hotel, with clean San Francisco light coming in the windows of my corner room, I slipped Malcolm Gaynor's large manuscript out of its brown envelope, ordered lunch from room service — a hamburger and a half-bottle of white wine and a carafe of coffee — and began to read. I finished at eleven that evening, amazed at how far Malcolm had gone not only in reinventing himself (in the current cant phrase) but in convincing himself of the reality of his invention.

The memoir was written in a style all too reminiscent of the Master's last, major phase, with long looping circumambient sentences heavily laden with subordinate clauses and qualifying phrases. This elaborate style allowed Malcolm nicely to bury Max Goldstein and all his Jewish ancestors. In the memoir, he became a man of the world, a European if of no known country, a *flâneur* coming out of nowhere, a disembodied sensibility wandering among the cultural monuments and literature of the West. Nothing was said of Malcolm's difficult years as the son of Jewish parents — his father, I was later to learn, had been a tailor — growing up on Notre-Dame Street in Montreal; next to nothing about his days as a left-wing journalist, working for *PM,* the New York daily, covering strikes in New England; about his first wife, Marsha (née Mutchnik), not a word. A more complete job of erasure could scarcely be imagined.

What, I asked myself, was going on? Was it from the Master that Malcolm derived the need to eliminate Max? Implicit in reading every great author is the question of what *he,* the writer, would think of *me,* his reader. Did Malcolm sense that Max would never pass muster with the Master? (Muster with the Master. "I'm coming over from Dover," the Master once wrote in a letter to a friend, adding, "Over from Dover — what a language!") A case could be made that the Master was an anti-Semite — not a major league one, perhaps, but a player nonetheless. In one of his famous stories, a family of social climbers are described thus: "as good-natured as Jews before clothing-shops." Although he took the right line on the Dreyfus affair, when he returned to the United States in 1904 after a long absence the Master did not hesitate to express his fear that the hundreds of thousands of Jewish immigrants then crowding New York would defile the purity of his beloved English language. Malcolm's — my — ancestors could have been among those immigrants.

Almost all my cultural heroes, it now occurred to me, bore the stain of Jew hating, if not Jew baiting. Working backward, there was T. S. Eliot, with his wretched lowercase jew squatting on the windowsill, his Bleistein with the cigar; Virginia Woolf, who kept a cold spot in her heart for just about every Jew she ever met, despite having married one; Oscar Wilde, who, being cared for on his deathbed by his devoted friend Reggie Turner, at one point expostulated, "There, there, that will do, my little Jew"; Dickens, with his altogether too vivid figure of Fagin. And loop back to Shakespeare, the main man — the Franchise, as a black student of mine once referred to him in class — who gave us Shylock, the deadliest portrayal of a Jew yet.

What did we Jewish academics know of such men? For that matter, what could the various Howes, Kazins, Levins, Ellmanns, Blooms, Kaplans, Gaynor-Goldsteins, and others really know about Melville, Adams, Twain, Hardy, Joyce, Emerson, Lawrence, and the rest? We could make them seem more familiar, put them through our own dramas of alienation, anti-capitalism, Freudianism, and other intellectual dipsy-doos, but was this to understand them, or was it instead to turn them into a species of Jew themselves?

As for Malcolm's memoir, which toward the middle I began to skim, it was, as his wife suggested, too far from complete to be published as a book. But maybe I could get a portion or two of it run in, say, the *Virginia Quarterly* or the *Georgia Review,* where I had connections. I would report this to Angela Gaynor, hoping to soften her up a bit as part of my campaign to part her from the Master's ring.

That night, having fallen asleep with the television on, I had one of my infrequent dreams about losing teeth. But this time, instead of my own teeth coming loose, the Master's green ring fell from my mouth, in multiple copies. What were they doing there, I wondered, and why hadn't I choked on them? I awoke in a sweat, turned off the television set — it was 2:38 on the bedside digital clock — and managed to get back to sleep.

"I have to be candid," I said to Angela the next morning on the patio of her house. "I don't think there's a market for Malcolm's memoir as a book. I do think, though, that I can pull out a section or two that might interest a few literary magazines. There won't be much money, but it will keep your husband's name before the public."

"That's fine with me," she said. "Malcolm named me as his literary executor, and I'm not sure what my responsibilities are."

"I'd say they include doing all you can to protect his reputation, promote his work, and see that no one rips you off by using his writing without an acknowledgment or a fee."

"You make it sound so easy. To someone as deep in the woods as I am about all this, it's very confusing. Do you suppose I could call on you for help from time to time?" She was wearing a salmon-colored blouse that set off her lovely skin, and she seemed even more fetching when asking for help. Her posture, sitting on a metal ice cream chair, was perfect, her hands exquisite, the fingers long and delicate, her nails coated in clear polish. She wore a small round watch with a leather strap, and was utterly at ease in the world. Old Malcolm must have taken the keenest pleasure just in gazing upon her.

"Of course," I said. "I'll be happy to help in any way you wish. Whenever you feel troubled about anything to do with any of this, pick up the phone and call."

"I'm very grateful," she said, looking genuinely appreciative.

If we were in a story by Bernard Malamud, Saul Bellow, or Philip Roth, I thought, this was when I would make my move on the widow. I remember once discussing these writers in correspondence with Malcolm, who remarked, his Freudianism combining with his Jewish self-hatred, that he assumed they'd all grown up in small, crowded apartments that provided a fertile ground for the development of Oedipal complexes, leaving them all a little sex-crazed.

"Oh, one other thing, Professor Shapiro."

"Arnold, please."

"Arnold. I've discovered some notebooks of Malcolm's that go back a long way, to the early 1930s, actually. They have handwritten entries that I've tried to read but without much success. There are six of them. Do you have time?"

"I can make time, Mrs. Gaynor."

"Angela," she corrected me, with a smile.

When I left that morning I had under my arm Malcolm's diary — six black-and-white student notebooks with thick, falsely marbleized covers.

I began reading on the plane back to Detroit and finished the next morning in my office at Ann Arbor. Written in a small, not easily legible hand, the entries began in 1928, when Malcolm was twenty, and like the diaries and journals of many young men and women, they were much given to expressing anguish over the failure of the world to recognize their author's genius. But in this case there was a difference: Malcolm intended to do something about it.

From these diaries I learned that Malcolm, or rather Max, had been the first person in his family to attend a university, and over his father's objections (his mother goes unmentioned). Unlike the standard Jewish immigrant, eager to see his son advance in the new world through education, Oscar Goldstein preferred that Max not, in the words of the youthful diarist, "overstep himself." Although he did not expect Max to become a tailor, he foresaw something solid in retailing. What did a Jew need from literature?, the old man asked. The diary records harsh conversations between these small unbending men (as I imagine them), neither giving an inch.

Max, determined to study what he wished, went to McGill, though he continued to live in the family's two-bedroom apartment with his two sisters and an older brother. Since his father wouldn't contribute a penny to his education, he worked long hours at odd jobs — as a milkman's assistant, a bellboy at the Queen Elizabeth Hotel, a women's shoe salesman. During his four years at McGill, he never once talked about his life at the university in his father's presence.

It was the university that put paid to whatever ties Max retained to Judaism. They had never been very strong to begin with. The religion was a mystery to him, a dark and dampening one. Although the Goldsteins adhered to a Jewish diet and lit candles on Friday night, there was no spiritual side to any of it, at least none that Max, reporting to his diary, could see. When he was a boy, his father had taken the family for a week's holiday to a place called Kutenberg's in the Laurentian Mountains. Max, eight years old at the time, was fishing with baited hook and string at a small creek when he heard frightful cackling sounds, half beast, half human. Turning, he looked up the hill and saw an unshaven man in a yarmulke muttering a prayer before slitting the necks of chickens, one after another, and tossing them into the high grass where, with a gruesome death cackle, some forced themselves into a last apoplectic leap before expiring.

That, Max decided, was Judaism: scary and squalid, noisy and nauseating. The point of it all was lost on him — the more so since, as his diary also records, he had seen older Jews taunted and even kicked by French-Canadian boys. What he remembered from such scenes was a feeling of terror, terror at the thought that someday something similar could happen to him.

There was a small clutch of Jews at McGill in Max's time, admitted on a strict quota. They felt pleased to be there, although they remained outside the main life of the university. Except for those intent on a career in law or medicine, they tended to be bohemian, left wing, iconoclastic. They mocked Canada, their philistine business-minded parents, religion, everything that passed for bourgeois behavior. Max took up with this crowd, entered into its general outlook. He did well at school, so well that he determined to do graduate study, possibly to teach afterward. Yet when he proposed the idea to Ian MacGregor, the professor with whom he had done a tutorial on Tennyson, the old gentleman crushed his hopes under the guise of candor. I quote from Max's diary:

> "Mr. Goldstein," he said, "there is no question of your aptitude and affinity for the literature of England. But, I must be honest with you, I don't think your services as a teacher of the subject are likely to be wanted. Leastways not in North America. Not for a man of your religious persuasion [Max had underlined the last word]. I don't say it is fair, but it is the way it is, at any rate for the present, and not likely soon to change. I'd look for another way of going about things, if I were you, my boy."

Not long after, Max committed this thought to his diary:

> Anton Chekhov wrote that it is extremely difficult "to squeeze the slave out of oneself." I must find a way to squeeze the Jew out of myself. Why be hobbled by the detractions implicit in a religion I neither believe in nor feel the least affinity for? I must find a way out, and as soon as possible. I shall not breathe freely until I do.

Max was twenty-one when he wrote that. I don't know his biography in sufficient detail to say when, precisely, he changed his name, but by the time I met him, his speech had become correct, almost overly deliberate, and his accent, which he had somehow made mid-Atlantic, betrayed nothing of his origins. I suspect that many people took him for an Englishman, which is to say, a Gentile to the highest power. By the time I knew him, he had thoroughly Malcolmized himself.

Reading these distraught diaries, I suppose I came to despise the life of Malcolm. Whatever one thought of the worship-of-art club, the club of Jewishness, especially in the twentieth century, was one from which it seemed to me truly dishonorable to resign. Not that I was in a superior moral position here. Although I wasn't hiding my own Jewishness, I was greatly ignorant of my religion, and my wife, the mother of my two daughters, wasn't Jewish. So who was I to knock a twice-dead Max Goldstein for turning himself into Malcolm Gaynor?

And yet I did knock him, to myself at least, on that scoreboard we all keep to judge the way others we know have met life and its challenges. In discarding Max, Malcolm was posted on my scoreboard as a sellout. But then — I remonstrated with myself, going back and forth — into Jewishness Max/Malcolm had never really bought. Besides, so far as I knew, he had never denied he was Jewish; he just didn't, so to speak, lead with it.

He refashioned himself, did an ethnic makeover. What was it my business?, as my mother would have said.

My mother, it now occurred to me, was Malcolm's exact contemporary, both having been born in 1908. Unlike him, however, she, without the least scintilla of literary or any other overlay of culture, was untroubled in her Jewishness. The thought of trying to "pass" was beyond her imagining. She was, of course, vividly aware of the world's anti-Semitism; we never went by a neighborhood, country club, or restaurant during my youth in Chicago without her noting whether it was or was not restricted. She had no real Jewish education, she was not synagogue-going, she did not keep kosher, yet in every way she was contentedly, quite happily Jewish.

But then, my mother also accepted the world as she found it, whereas the young Max Goldstein did not. For him, that world, as long as his place in it was that of a Jew, was a blight. Or, more precisely, his own Jewishness blighted Max's world. And since, he figured, it was a blight easily enough removed, why not remove it? His ambitions, after all, were wider, higher than my mother's. They were ambitions on which his Jewish birth was a drag — and a drag with no discernible purpose or meaning. Better to cut it loose.

Was *that* right, though? Where did it all begin, and where end? I thought of the ancestors of Spinoza, who had risked their lives to perform the rituals of prayer, diet, and circumcision about which Max/Malcolm Goldstein/Gaynor wished he'd never heard. And then I thought about that much greater number who had their lives taken away from them not for practicing these rituals themselves but because their ancestors had done so. I had never felt comfortable talking about the massacre of the Jews of Europe: it was too large, too gruesome a subject, and besides, talking about it seemed to me to be drawing on a moral credit that wasn't really mine to draw on. Yet somehow it, too, made resigning from this club into a greater betrayal. In a small but personally significant way, it let the bastards win, and that could not be permitted.

Had none of these things occurred to the young Max Goldstein? To be fair, he probably changed his name before the European massacre became an event in history. At some point in the late 1930s, I would guess, he had turned Max into Malcolm, Goldstein into Gaynor. Was he relieved to feel the burden of his Jewishness fall from him? Did he sense that he could now soar into the universal empyrean? Did he feel joy? No one would ever know. The diaries were blank on the subject. The mature Malcolm never wrote about Jewish writers, and apart from his interest in psychoanalysis, he seemed successfully to have rinsed the Jew out of his prose style. Did he ever look back, have any regrets? Was he a happier man without the heavy historical freight of his ancestry? This, too, could not be known.

What I did know was that I owed a letter to Angela Gaynor. In it I said that I thought there might be some interest in her husband's papers at the University of Tulsa, whose library was buying up the papers of lots of American and English writers, sometimes paying extravagant sums. To judge from other purchases, they might offer $150,000 or so for Malcolm's manuscripts and letters. I volunteered to contact the appropriate person.

As for the notebooks that I still had in my possession, these, I told Angela, could do her husband's reputation no good. If I were she, I would burn them. I reminded her that the Master himself, in 1910, six years before his death, had a jolly little conflagration in the back yard of his house in which he put to flame what had been estimated as several thousand letters he wanted no one ever to see. If she had any questions about any of this, she was to call me back.

Four days later, as I arrived home from teaching an afternoon class, my wife told me that Mrs. Gaynor was on the phone. Without removing my jacket I picked up the telephone in the kitchen.

"Hello, Arnold," she said. "Your letter arrived this morning. Very helpful."

I imagined her in her Larkin Street palazzo, Malcolm's grand lady of the summer afternoon.

"I'm glad, Angela," I said. "Do you want me to contact Tulsa for you?"

"Please," she said. "And about Malcolm's notebooks? Do you still have them?"

"I do."

"May I ask you to burn them for me?"

"Of course," I said.

"Arnold, I can't tell you how important all this has been to me. I'd like it very much if you would accept, as a token of your help and your friendship to Malcolm, the green ring you seemed to like so much."

I hesitated. I swallowed. I heard myself say: "That is very kind of you, Angela, but I think I have to say no. That ring was Malcolm's. He somehow earned it, and might even be said to have paid a staggeringly high price for it. I couldn't wear it, or even have it around the house, thinking how much his devotion to the Master cost Malcolm. But I thank you, I thank you with all my heart."

"I won't press you," she said. "But please know that I'm very grateful."

"I'm even more grateful to you," I said, realizing afterward that this remark could not possibly make sense to her.

That same afternoon, in the cool Michigan autumn, a mug of coffee in my hand, I went out to the back yard and placed Malcolm's six notebooks in the wire trash basket near our grill. The pages burned easily, but the thick covers took a while and made a great deal of smoke. Standing there waiting, I had second thoughts about the ring. I still wanted it, though I also knew it was important that I not have it. Watching the smoke curl into the air, poking at the fire, sipping my coffee, I thought of the Master. If he were here now, reading my mind with his astonishing percipience, he would no doubt smile, perhaps less than distinctly but — to adopt his own penchant for the adverbial — subtly, amusedly, ever so Cheshirely.

Howie's Gift

RIVING UP the Edens Expressway, looking for the east-bound exit to Dundee Road, I wondered whether accepting this invitation had been such a hot idea. I hadn't seen Howie Rosen for at least five years, and before that, ever since he went off to medical school nearly thirty years ago, we had run into each other only sporadically, never by plan but usually outside a movie theater or in a restaurant or at a Bulls game. Nor had I ever been invited to his house in the suburb of Glencoe, or what the old anti-Semites on the North Shore used to call Glen Cohen.

It was against Howie, who tonight was going to celebrate his fiftieth birthday, that I had committed my last act of violence. I was eleven at the time, and my family had just moved to West Rogers Park, where my father, in a step up for us, had bought a two-flat. It was late July, school was still more than a month away, and I knew no one in the neighborhood. I would get up, eat breakfast, work on our small lawn, sometimes run an errand for my mother on Devon Avenue.

Most of my afternoons that summer I spent on roller skates, the old-fashioned kind with the key worn on a string around the neck. I skated in the street, where the asphalt was smoother than the lined and cracked sidewalks. Even now, forty years later, I can feel the pleasure of strong strides and long glides, the clatter of my skates on the street, the hum of the ball bearings rising from the bottoms of my feet.

I had just gotten an ice cream cone — butter pecan, double dip — from the fountain at Sanders drugstore on Pratt when I turned and bumped into the kid in line behind me, who had been standing too close. The ice cream fell from the cone and plopped, sickeningly, onto Sanders's none too clean floor.

"Watch out, stupid," I said, lightly pushing the kid. To my amazement, he fell backward, legs in the air, completely up-ended. As he tried to get up, I noticed that he was wearing a built-up shoe, a heavy brown one. His right leg must have been a good four inches shorter than his left.

"Sorry. God, I'm sorry," I said, giving him a hand up.

"My fault," he said. "I shouldn't've been standing so close. Lemme buy you another ice cream."

"No," I said, "it's O.K. You all right?"

"I'm fine," he said. "Really. I'm good. My name's Howie Rosen."

"Ben Cohen," I said, shaking the thin-fingered hand he held out to me.

We walked home together. He was taller than I, but his bad leg, which he had to drag along, caused his body to lean slightly forward and to the left. His black hair fell into his eyes, which were blue and very alert.

Howie's family, like mine, lived in a two-flat, three blocks away on Talman Avenue near Albion. He had two older sisters, Susan and Phyllis. His father, a small, dark man with great energy and high spirits, was a salesman for Abbott Laboratories. The dark hair and blue eyes came from his mother, a tallish woman who went about her housewifely work with a perpetual air of anxiety.

Once school began in September, it was Howie who discouraged me from ever taking seriously any ability I once thought I had in mathematics or science. Not that I did poorly in those subjects; only Howie, physically awkward as he was, was much smoother and faster in mental calculation. With his long, bony fingers he was also adept at building the most intricate model airplanes, using his X-Acto knife to carve balsa wood with what seemed to me, who always made an impatient botch of it, astonishing precision.

West Rogers Park turned out to be a neighborhood where, if you weren't a good athlete, you had better be witty. Howie's leg prevented him from playing, but he sometimes umped our playground slow-pitch softball games and occasionally, if we lacked a full contingent, he would pitch, though his heavy shoe made quick movements impossible. He knew a tremendous amount about major league baseball; no statistic, once locked in his powerful memory, ever escaped. The rest of us sometimes used him to settle arguments over things like how many home runs Swish Nicholson hit for the Cubs in 1944, or Luke Appling's record for the greatest number of foul balls in a single time at bat. His authority on these matters was indisputable.

Dragging his right leg, Howie managed to get on. Girls liked him, sensing his kindness and no doubt pitying him a little. Teachers recognized his gifts. Yet he never allowed himself to lapse into the role of teacher's pet. If he was no shakes at all on the playground and almost too adept at school, that was O.K. Rough though we kids were on each other, invoking any physical deficiency or irregularity to brand someone with a nickname — because of my stick-out ears, I was known as Juggy all through high school — no one ever dinged Howie.

We were never best or even especially close friends. But I would sometimes find myself at Howie's apartment, and you didn't have to be there long to realize that in his own home he was a privileged person. The youngest child, he was the only boy, and long awaited — especially by his father. Like most men in the neighborhood, Harry Rosen had come into his maturity during the Depression and never went to college. Yet he was determined that his only son would not only go to college but become a physician.

This was still the age when doctors were like gods, not least to a pharmaceutical salesman like Harry Rosen, who worked around them all day. My own father, a man with a healthy cynicism about human nature and a pretty tough guy generally, would go all fluttery in the presence of doctors. His voice seemed to rise a full octave when addressing his physician, a dull and, as I later learned, often medically incorrect man named Lewis Lerner.

The second time I visited Howie, he took me down to the basement, where his father had set up a lab for him: a Bunsen burner, seven or eight differently shaped beakers, lots of test tubes, a couple of dry-cell batteries, a half-dissected frog, two live white rabbits in separate cages. The full paraphernalia of the budding scientist was in place in that dark room on Talman Avenue. I asked Howie if Dr. Frankenstein ever came by.

"One doctor's enough," he said with his engaging smile, and from behind a collection of test tubes he took out a small mahogany rectangle with a dark metal placard that read, in gold lettering, *Dr. Howard I. Rosen, M.D.* "My dad had it made for me," he said, letting his eyes go upward, his thin arms shooting out, palms up.

"Pretty wild."

"I guess," Howie said. "My being a doctor is everything to my old man."

I remember thinking how nice it must be to be so tied to your father's dreams. Whatever my own father's dreams, I didn't appear in them. "You gotta love what you do" was his full text on the subject of my future, to which he would usually add, "What else can I tell you?" Although I would subsequently come to recognize this for genuine wisdom, at the time I wished he would be more specific. He himself sold auto parts, and seemed happy enough at it as long as business was good.

Growing up in West Rogers Park was not the Jewish upbringing I would later read about in memoirs by second-generation Jewish artists and intellectuals: all violin lessons, revolutionary politics discussed at the dinner table, *bubbe* in her room reading Tolstoy in Yiddish. In our neighborhood, politics, modern art, and psychotherapy played no role whatsoever. Fathers were too busy with their work as salesmen, owners of small businesses, or one-man law practices. Their horizons ended with making a good living and being excellent providers. As for their sons, most of the boys I knew in grade school and high school went on to the University of Illinois, where they majored in business; the rest, a small minority, aimed at dental or medical school.

Not taking any chances, Harry Rosen sent Howie to Evanston Township, the nearby suburban high school that was much better than Nicholas Senn, the Chicago public school the rest of us attended. At $600 a year for nonresidents, Evanston was a big ticket; in those days, a year at the University of Chicago ran just under $900. Howie flourished at Evanston. As a student manager of the baseball team he invited me once to a game his school was playing against New Trier. The game was predictably boring — all pitching, as high school baseball tends to be — but waiting afterward to drive Howie home, I watched him rounding up the equipment, dragging his built-up shoe across the base paths, unscrewing the three bases to put them away in the storage shed. Howie's lack of physical grace, even of normal mobility — how much, I wondered, did he think about it? To me it would have meant a substantial loss. Yet I never heard him complain, rail against his bad luck, or curse the world's injustice.

Howie's good mind was given a more than respectable workout at Evanston. In his senior year he won a Westinghouse science prize — his project had something to do with enzymes — which carried a full scholarship to Swarthmore. He was looking forward to it, but when Harry Rosen discovered that Howie could enroll in the medical school of the University of Illinois after only three years as an undergraduate there, Swarthmore was dead in the water.

I didn't see all that much of Howie when we were both students at Illinois. He was a Phi Sig, living in Urbana; I was a Phi Ep, living in neighboring Champaign. Like all pre-med students in those days, he was buried in four-hour labs or preparing for some crucial exam. The competition for medical school was fierce. A grade of B in a major science course could delay entry into med school by a year, a C or two could knock you out of the box permanently, forcing desperate application to schools in Italy or Latin America.

I would see Howie occasionally at the library or at Kam's, the beer hall on Daniel Street. Once we ducked in to split a pitcher, and after a couple of glasses he confided that if he had his way, he would drop the whole idea of medical school and do graduate work in biochemistry, the subject that really fascinated him.

"It's a much more interesting game, Ben," he said.

"Why not just do it?"

"I can't let my dad down. It would kill him. To him I'm already in my office at the Pittsfield Building. I wouldn't be surprised if he'd already ordered white coats with 'Dr. Howard I. Rosen, M.D.' over the pocket."

I had recently undergone something of a conversion of my own. Having begun at Illinois studying business like everyone else, in my second year I took an elective in introductory sociology. The notion that society was largely a human construct, that people had in effect made the whole damn thing up and kept it all going by playing their preappointed roles, elementary though it seems to me today, floored me then. Not long afterward, I changed my major. When my father asked me what possible use a degree in *sociology* could be, I lied and said I was thinking of going to law school, for which it would be useful preparation. Never having gone to college himself, he took my word for it.

The decision to study sociology changed my life, or so I believed at the time. I moved out of the fraternity, and I began to look in a more detached way at the culture in which I had grown up. I decided that there were things in the world more important than money and what it could buy — a thought that made me feel tremendously liberated. Eventually, I did a Ph.D. at the University of Chicago and, wanting to stay in the city, got a job teaching sociology at DePaul, which is where I am today.

I have to report that Harry Rosen died, of colon cancer, in his son's last year of med school, and so never got to shake his hand and say, "Congratulations, Dr. Rosen." A year later, Howie married a girl named Sandy Weiner, who had been a grade behind me at Senn. Thin, plain, she had lived on Lake Shore Drive and came from a well-to-do family: German Jews, I'm almost certain. Howie's M.D. must have made up in prestige for the four inches he'd been shorted in his right leg.

I wasn't — and didn't expect to be — invited to the wedding, which took place at the Standard Club.

"Kishkes," Howie told me when I asked him about his medical specialty a few years later. "Gastroenterology, Ben. I'm a big kishkes man." He was coming out of Joe Stein's Rumanian Steak House as I was going in, and was, I think, a bit drunk. He still wore the built-up shoe: medical science hadn't yet found a way to add several inches to a person's leg. The parking attendant brought up a tan-colored Mercedes convertible for Howie and his wife. She drove; he waved from the passenger seat.

I remember asking myself at the time if Harry Rosen's death by colon cancer had anything to do with his son's choice of specialty. Before attending this birthday party for Howie, I asked Bill Doyle, a colleague at DePaul whose subject is the sociology of medicine, about the earning capacity of gastroenterologists. Bill is amusingly dark in his view of doctors — "a Marxist with a dirty mind" is the way he describes himself.

"The trick to turning a big buck in medicine," he told me, "is to have that magic procedure: that little exam that you can do over and over again, almost in your sleep, which will bring in heavy green. The gastro gang's cash cow is the colonoscopy. On a good morning, doing six or seven of these puppies, an efficient guy can pull in fifteen grand."

I whistled softly.

"We're in the wrong field, Ben. Course, to do the job, you have to be able to stand a fair of amount of blood and shit, which, let's face it, is not to everyone's taste. But unless he's spending half his time bonking his nurses, a gastroenterologist ought to be able to bring in six or seven hundred G's per annum without working up a heavy sweat."

What, I wondered, would Harry Rosen have made of all this? He'd have been damned pleased, I'm sure. It was what he'd had in mind for Howie: nicely settled in life, a physician, a powerful moneymaker, well married with (I'd heard) two sons.

I myself drove a Ford Escort, seven years old.

Not that I'd ever doubted the rightness of my decision not to go for the money, even though by now it had become apparent that I would do no major work as a social scientist. I'm no Max Weber. My specialty is something called the "culture of poverty," and my work is chiefly statistical, having to do with welfare recipients on the West Side of Chicago. I prepare the ground out of which broader minds are supposed to build the monuments.

Still, sometimes I can't help wondering what my life would have been like if I had gone to law school. Would I, for instance, think a lot less about money than I do? The irony of my situation seems pretty heavy to me: forgoing money in my choice of career, only to be obsessed with money and status just about every day of my life. Would I be out of the financial wars, driving a car like Howie's, flashing a confident smile, if I hadn't taken that sociology course?

When Sandy Rosen called to invite me to Howie's party, she'd said it would be all right, if I liked, to bring a date. How she had heard I was divorced, I don't know; but I did bring a date, a woman in the anthropology department named Mary O'Brien, whose company I enjoy. Mary is a bit of a feminist — nowadays, almost every academic woman in her thirties is. She's smart, funny, with a taste for truth-telling that I find appealing. We enjoy each other's company without any impulse on either side to take things further. Mary knew nothing about Howie's and my background, but I did tell her that the evening might turn out to be her Trobriand Islands — she could plan on seeing some fairly exotic natives, and without having to spend the night on a cot in a bug-infested grass hut.

*   *   *

When we pulled up in my unwashed Ford, the Jaguars, Lexuses, Mercedeses, and gleaming SUVs parked on the street and in the driveway made me feel we had arrived not so much in a car as in a small slum. Every man at this party, I estimated, made at least a quarter million a year more than I, and many a lot more — as Mary, bright girl, would have no difficulty seeing.

I was wearing my standard outfit, blazer and gray trousers, white shirt with button-down collar, rep tie. Mary, whose background is lower-middle-class Chicago Irish, was in a long black skirt and white blouse, with a lightweight red cardigan draped over her shoulders. Since I expected to know a number of people from high school and the old neighborhood, I preferred, all other things being equal, to show up with a handsome woman. Mary qualified.

Sandy Rosen met us at the door, her smile revealing capped teeth that I figured must have priced out at around twenty grand. I introduced Mary — "Professor O'Brien" — and the two women shook hands. We confronted a large marble-floored foyer, high ceilings, views up a winding staircase, spacious rooms going off in three directions, the early light of a summer evening pouring in. The decorating, very much *House & Garden*, seemed in extremely good taste, no nutty sculpture or other surprises. I thought about the Rosens' dark apartment on Talman Avenue, with its three small bedrooms, one bath, and postage-stamp lawn, and I tried to imagine Harry Rosen, who used to spend a lot of time walking around in ribbed undershirts, in this house. Although Howie and I had started out in roughly the same circumstances, here he was living in grandeur while I had gone from three bedrooms on Maplewood to a one-bedroom, book-stuffed apartment on Belden, just west of Sheffield. Had it *ever* been in my power to acquire a house like this? I would never know.

"The party's out back," Sandy said. "The caterer has just set up. Dinner should be in less than an hour."

"Jesus, Benjy Cohen?" asked a large man, bald, with a neatly groomed beard beginning to go white.

"Sorry," I said. "I don't quite . . ."

"Just because a guy's lost his hair, gained sixty pounds, and has a white beard is no excuse not to recognize him." He smiled, adding, "David Aronson, you putz."

"David, forgive me." I introduced Mary, again as Professor O'Brien.

"Hey, Professor," he said. Turning, he smoothly slipped two fluted champagne glasses off the tray carried by a passing blond waitress, handing one to each of us. "Dom Perignon, Benjy. Nothing but the best for Dr. Howie."

We were soon informed that David had taken over his deceased father's business — bar and restaurant supplies — and that he ran it out of the same showroom and warehouse on West Jackson. David had two kids in college, one at Michigan and the other at Indiana. "What about yourself?"

I started to explain — my twenty years and more at DePaul, my divorce, my two daughters who (I did not say) lived with my ex-wife in northern California and whom I saw twice a year at best — when a short, pudgy guy walked past, his long, carefully layered hair falling back on a peach-colored jacket. David grabbed his arm. "Pauly, you recognize this turkey?"

"Benjy! God — like thirty years maybe? How goes it, Ben?"

It was Pauly Bernstein, who I'd heard had made a killing with a book called *Who's Who in Teenage America*, with spinoffs to follow. Other guys from what I was beginning to think of as the old country soon joined the circle: Larry Denenberg, a patent lawyer with Kirkland & Ellis and the first Jew to obtain a co-op apartment at 970 Lake Shore Drive; Burt Rudy, who played basketball for Loyola and now had a seat on the commodities market; Ronnie Graff, an orthodontist who had scored in real estate and was preparing for early retirement; an internist named Arnie Singer; Allan Greengoss, an investment counselor who told me — a touch sheepishly, I thought — that he had dropped the "goss" and was now plain Al Green.

We talked about the old days — the all-night poker games at Dicky Levinson's apartment when his parents were away in Florida; the dances at the Edgewater Beach Hotel, where we first heard the Four Freshmen; the day that Peter Pan, after getting caught serving horse meat, provided free hamburgers at its two restaurants. Had Mary not been at my side, there would have been talk about the rides to the cathouses in Danville or about visits to Doris, who kept an apartment two blocks from Chicago Stadium, and Iona, ex-wife to Bob Satterfield, the light-heavyweight champ with a glass jaw, who lived on South St. Lawrence.

"I miss the smell of the old Chicago Stadium," Pauly Bernstein said, "that fine confection of urine and frying onions." He was about to say more when one of the Nordic-looking waitresses announced that dinner was being served under the tent.

Following the crowd, I thought how much I enjoyed this talk, these guys, and yet how out of it I felt in this house. Had I betrayed them, had I betrayed my younger self, by living so very different a life? Or was I betraying my grown self with fantasies about the life I might have led? Already the evening was getting more complicated than I had expected.

The tent, with its yellow and white stripes, was enormous, though it took up only a small part of the Rosens' vast back yard. Under it I counted eleven tables, each set up for eight people. At one end, a small combo — guitar, bass, piano — played show tunes in an understated way; at the other, young men in tuxedo shirts and black bow ties from Gateaux Frères stood behind trays of lobster salad, boneless breast of chicken with wild rice, minuscule carrots and dried tomatoes, Dover sole with French beans and a white vegetable I couldn't identify but that Mary thought might be baby turnips. At the end of the table, a large black man wearing a white apron and a two-foot-high chef's hat was carving thick slices from a tenderloin of beef and serving small roasted potatoes and salad to go with it. Waiting in line for our food, I tried to fill Mary in on the men I had introduced her to and my memory of them as boys.

Most of the tables up front were filled, but we found two empty seats toward the rear with Sandy Rosen's father, a CPA, and his second wife. A younger associate of Howie's named Art Brodsky and his wife, who introduced herself as Kimmie, were also at the table, as were Sandy's younger sister Sara and her husband, a dentist named Mickey Schoenwald. Conversation did not come easily. Mr. Weiner wanted to know how I had come to know his son-in-law. Kimmy Brodsky asked Mary if she worked out, she was so slim. In the background we heard Cole Porter, Gershwin, Jerome Kern.

"Are you at least taking notes on this?" I whispered to Mary.

"No need to," she shot back. "I'm wearing a wire."

As we were finishing the main course a stocky man got up at the head table. Florid, with thinning gray hair done up in curls, wearing small round glasses, he was, it took me a moment to realize, Earle Berkson, who had played third base on our old softball team, sponsored by the Ashkenaz Deli on Morse Avenue. It took me another moment or two to visualize him off the hot corner, which as I remembered he had played with a fearless aggressiveness. Sandy's father leaned in to tell me Earle was now a plastic surgeon, very successful.

"Allow me to greet all the friends and family of my dear

friend Dr. Howard Rosen," Earle said with easy confidence. "Howie, schmuck, stand up."

Howie got to his feet. It was the first I had seen him this evening. He was handsomely turned out in a cream-colored linen jacket, dark gray trousers, a light blue shirt, and gold silk tie. His wife, I assumed, was dressing him, and doing a fine job of it. But he was still Howie. Tall, bony, he had retained his dark hair, which was starting to show gray at the temples and no longer fell into his eyes. I couldn't see his heavy shoe, but it must have been there.

"So, Howie, fifty big ones, baby," Earle continued. "Lots of lessening powers to look forward to, but I'm sure you're prepared. And lots of achievements to look back on. A quarter century of successful medical practice, a loving wife, two swell sons, this terrific house, expensive cars made exclusively by perpetrators of genocide, a condo in Boca. Goddammit, Howie, you've got it all. And richly deserved, too, my man."

Howie smiled warily, no doubt waiting for the bucket of ice water to drop from the ceiling, the trapdoor to open beneath him.

"When a bunch of your friends got together," Earle went on, "we wondered, What could we get Howie for his fiftieth? I mean, here is a man who has everything, right? What do you get this man that he doesn't already have? Only one thing, obviously." He signaled to his right; the combo struck up "Night Train."

"Ladies and gentlemen," Earle announced, "courtesy of happydreams.com, Ms. Reddi Flame!" From the left, a redhead, in G-string and tights, sequined, tasseled pasties covering her nipples, came shimmying over, stopped, and put her head on Howie's shoulder. She was tall, in her high heels nearly as tall as Howie. She looked to be in her late thirties, very *zaftig*.

"Happy birthday, Dr. Howie, darling," she said. Removing the pasties, shimmying again, she leaned in, rubbed against him, nuzzled his cheek. "Hmm, that was good." Then she looked out at the rest of us, sticking out her tongue in a manner that did not imply insult.

I had never before thought of a woman's breasts as dolorous. But so these seemed, and so at that moment did poor Howie. So, in fact, did we all. I glanced around quickly. Howie's mother-in-law had gone slack at the mouth; his father-in-law's face was red. The only one who seemed to be enjoying things was the black man in the chef's hat, smiling from behind his cutting board. The band, for some reason I didn't quite get, began playing "The Anniversary Waltz." To the left, whence the woman had made her entrance, I saw two men in ersatz black leather jackets, probably sent by the agency to look out for her. Mary, who had done her dissertation on gift-giving among the Navajo Indians, had rolled back her eyes. This, I thought, was one gift the Navajos never gave.

The entire tent seemed stuck, on freeze-frame. And then Howie did a wondrous thing. Turning to the woman, he stepped back, bowed at the waist, took her hand in his, and kissed it. Then, in a single, seamless move, he twirled out of his creamy jacket, made a brilliant, bullfighter-like *veronica*, and slipped it over her, bending to button it at the waist, covering her nakedness. Holding her hand in his, he announced: "Earle, what can I say? I thank you, Sandy I'm sure thanks you, my kids, and my in-laws, we all thank you for making this into what I now realize is going to be a truly memorable night. But I see from here that dessert is almost ready. Please, everyone, join me in devouring my birthday cake."

Still holding Ms. Reddi Flame by the hand, stopping to pick up his wife, whose hand he also grasped, Howie walked in his old leg-dragging way toward the back of the tent. I had to re-strain myself from giving him a one-man standing ovation.

After everyone had been served cake we sang "Happy Birth-day," and Howie thanked his wife and kids and everyone for coming and making it a special night. (In an otherwise graceful speech, I thought he overworked the word "special," but that's the pedant in me.) I looked over at Mary, who signaled it was all right with her if we made our exit.

There remained only to say goodbye to Howie, to whom I hadn't yet spoken. He was still eating his dessert, flanked by a teenage son who looked a lot like his grandfather Harry. The stripper must have quietly left; Howie had his jacket back.

"Ben!" he said as Mary and I approached. "Ben, it's great to see you. Glad you could come. How the hell are you?"

"Not as good as you, friend," I said, feeling the reassuring pressure of his large hand. "That move with your sport coat. That was impressive. Where'd you pick that up? In Barcelona?"

"Don't know, but it seemed to be there when I needed it."

He stood up, holding on to the table as I introduced him to Mary. "Hope these goings-on didn't upset you, Professor," he said.

"Nothing I haven't seen before, Dr. Rosen," Mary said. "Ev-ery morning in the shower, in fact."

"Nice girl, Ben," Howie said. "You gotta bring her around again."

"I'll do it," I said, though I knew it wasn't going to happen.

Back in the car, on the Edens, I asked Mary for her anthropolo-gist's-eye view of the night's proceedings.

"A most strange tribe," she began, with mock scientific pom-posity. "The men have a fetish for German motors and large, complicated wristwatches; possible talismanic meaning here.

They enjoy rehearsing stories of their days as young warriors, though none of these stories has anything to do with war. Women of the tribe make grand expenditures on soft fabrics, dentistry; much talk of diets with contradictory passion for food, especially miniature vegetables. No actual love practices among the natives observed, though some evidence of sex in the head. Kinship patterns need further investigation. United by religion though they are, it is less than clear what gods they worship."

"Solid report, Professor," I said. "Genius, as Schopenhauer said, is objectivity, and as a member of the aforementioned tribe I salute you. Now, can you tell me why, despite my own longing for objectivity and all my efforts at escape, I find I can't leave this tribe, and for some reason don't want to?"

"Perhaps because it contains people like your friend Howie Rosen."

"Ah, Howie."

"He really is a sweetie, your old pal. And outside all anthropological explanation."

"Other kinds, too, I'm pretty sure," I said.

Turning the Ford too abruptly at the Fullerton exit, I heard a Dunkin' Donuts coffee cup fall from the back seat onto the floor, and at that moment had an overpowering premonition that the rest of my days would be lived at an unhappy middle distance from the society I was once so pleased to think a pure invention.

A Loss for Words

TWO DAYS after my father's eighty-third birthday, it began: what Dr. Myron Spiegelman, the neurologist at Northwestern University Hospital, called "failure-of-word-retrieval syndrome." My father would be talking away in his confident manner when suddenly he would be stopped cold, the words "stock market" or "groceries" gone, unavailable, disappeared. For him it was sheer hell, for me a small torture to watch him going through it.

"Aaron," he'd say to me, "the trick to keeping an orderly . . . invalary . . . invidy . . . inev . . ."

"Inventory, Dad?" I would say, unable to stand it any longer.

"Yes, inventory, of course, thank you."

As predicted by Spiegelman, a small man with round tortoise-shell glasses, it got worse, and fairly fast. Soon my father ceased to stumble over the missing word; instead, he hadn't a clue as to its first letter. His face would take on a startled look, like a man inexplicably slipping on dry and level ground. Dementia was now on its way in earnest. How soon he would slide into full gaga, Spiegelman said, only God knew.

My father, Jack Feinberg, salesman extraordinaire, a man who had made his living — a damned good one — with his talk, who told jokes in perfect foreign accents and with no less perfect timing, whose tact was exquisite and whose reading of his customers' desires was flawless, whose powers of persuasion were legendary, who could sell anything anywhere anytime to anybody, my father was to lose his powers of speech. Worse, he knew it.

My mother had died three years before this business began. He had kept their old apartment, retaining the weekly services of Jessie Waters, the black woman who had cleaned for them for years. My wife and I had him over for dinner at least once a week, and the three of us went out together every Friday night. Otherwise he ate TV dinners and for lunch had corned beef sandwiches or hot dogs.

A year or so after my mother died, he bestirred himself to date other women, most of them from his building. He was still a good-looking man, my father, a dapper dresser with upright posture, a straight walk, lots of hair now turned white. But it was no-go. He once said that, having lived with the same woman for fifty-seven years, he still thought of her as the girl he had loved when they were both young. These others were now and forever old to him — as, he allowed, he was to them — and imagination did not suffice to bring back their youthful bloom.

Be kind to your children — one of his jokes ran — they choose your nursing home. His condition worsening, he knew he could no longer be alone, but he hated the idea of living exclusively among the elderly. This was why, I remembered, he had argued against my mother's desire to buy a condominium in Florida. "It's an elephant graveyard," he used to say. His own father, who had died at ninety-two, used to break into a run every time he passed a retirement community or nursing home. The old man was able to die in his own bed, and that was my father's ambition, too. Modest enough though the goal seemed, it wasn't going to happen.

My wife and I hunted around. Though my father could still manage daily chores pretty much on his own, soon he would probably need what was then starting to be called "assisted living." After that, well, I didn't want to think about after that.

Highland Hills was the place we settled on. Just under three miles from our own neighborhood in Winnetka, it had been built only twenty or so years earlier, was well kept up, and the food was quite good in the Jewish style to which my father was accustomed. Before signing a contract, I took him there alone, just the two of us.

A too perky young woman named Courtney Ginsberg gave us a tour, showing off the game and hobby rooms, the indoor swimming pool, the small gym, the dining room and coffee shop, and a vacant one-bedroom apartment of the kind my father would occupy, at least at the outset, overlooking the links behind the main building. Playing golf, my father used to say, was like taking a walk in a cemetery but without the monuments for distraction. He had no interest in any sports or games. He had no hobbies. He listened to lots of news radio, took two papers — the *Chicago Tribune* and the *Wall Street Journal* — and read books about World War II, in which he had fought, though he rarely spoke about it. He had a Purple Heart, and I remember from boyhood outings to Farwell Beach the angry, still-red shrapnel scars on his right calf.

Her tour finished, Ms. Ginsberg left us at the front desk. My father turned to me. "Well, Aaron," he said, "this is certainly . . ." His face took on that slightly stricken look as he put his strong hand around my forearm.

"Hell, Dad," I finished his sentence for him.

"Exactly," he said.

★   ★   ★

Five weeks later we moved him into Highland Hills. A good soldier, he took it well, without a trace of weepy philosophizing about what things come to in the end. He was able to stock the small apartment with some of his own furniture, and after helping him set up I wondered aloud about his new neighbors. My father handed me a directory of tenants. His apartment was 4L. A Mrs. Florence Kaplan was in 4K, and 4M was occupied by a Mr. Louis Holmberg. Could this be, I wondered, Lou Holmberg the tennis player, once ranked, if memory served, sixth or seventh in the nation?

It was eleven o'clock. I had been planning to stay for lunch, and as my father thought he wouldn't mind a brief nap, I told him I would roam around for an hour. In the hall, a small bald man fumbled with his keys next door. "Excuse me, sir," I said. "My name is Aaron Feinberg. I thought I would introduce myself. My father, Jack, is your new neighbor."

"Nice to meet you," he said, standing now with his hands in his pockets.

"Excuse me again, but are you Lou Holmberg the tennis player?"

"That's me," he said, a smile on his face. "Come in."

The floor plan was identical to my father's, but near the hall leading into the bedroom a glass cabinet held ten or twelve trophies of different sizes, all topped by little men getting ready to swing through on a serve. Having reached his highest ranking in the 1940s, Lou Holmberg was a man of what I suppose must be considered diminishing fame — that is, not many people younger than I could be expected to remember him, and I myself had never actually seen him play. I walked over to inspect the trophies. One was for the National Clay Courts Championship 1945, one for the Big Ten Championship 1942, one for the United States Doubles Championship 1948. Along the wall beside the cabinet were photographs of the youthful Lou

Holmberg in tennis togs, posing with other players. I recognized Jack Kramer, Pancho Segura, Bobby Riggs, Bill Talbert.

"I don't know this man," I said.

"That's Frank Sedgman, the Aussie," he said. "Hell of a scrapper."

"That's Don Budge, right? I'd recognize those white duck trousers anywhere."

"Yep," he said. "The same."

"You played against him?"

"Three times," he said, "never with a happy outcome."

"Did he really have the best backhand in the history of tennis?"

"That's probably true — and he also hit the heaviest ball I've ever had to contend with. Returning a Don Budge backhand could twist the racket out of your grip. It did mine." He paused. "These days, a Ping-Pong ball would do the trick."

He lifted his hands out of his pockets and I saw what he meant. At the end of his thick and powerful wrists his hands were like startled birds, trembly, agitated, out of control.

"Parkinson's," he said, returning them to his pockets. "But tell me, you play yourself?"

"As a kid," I said, "in local tournaments. I played for Cap Leighton at Senn High School."

"Cap Leighton. I haven't heard that name in forty years. He must be long dead."

"About twenty years."

"Is your father a tennis player?" he asked.

"No. He doesn't care about sports at all."

"Lucky man," said the ex-champion. "He's saved a lot of time over the years. What'd he work at?"

"He was a salesman of various things, from handkerchiefs to mutual funds."

"I sold insurance," he said. "I assume he's a widower, like me. But what's he doing here?"

"He has something called word-retrieval failure, which is an early warning sign of dementia."

"That's a tough sentence."

"He's a tough guy, my father, but also a nice one. I think you'll like him."

"A salesman who can't find the words and a tennis player who can't hold a racket. Sounds like we'll make a great team. What do you do for a living?"

"I'm a tax lawyer, in a three-man firm on Wacker Drive."

"I'm making a mental note never to tell you lawyer jokes."

"I'd be grateful for that. Also, if you could keep an eye out for my dad, Mr. Holmberg. He's going to need a friend."

"I'll do my best, Aaron. And it's Lou, by the way. Plain Lou will do fine."

The three of us had lunch together. The dining room held fewer men than women, most of the latter Jewish and some, to judge by the care with which they dressed, still on the prowl. We had a table to ourselves. The two men seemed to hit it off. Saying nothing about their careers — I hadn't clued my father in to his neighbor's identity — they talked about the old West Side, where both grew up. They had gone to different high schools, Lou to Marshall and my father to Crane Tech. Then Lou went on to the University of Wisconsin, while my father, already married, skipped college and went right to work after the war. The fork in Lou's hand clattered noisily against the plate as he stabbed at his food, an omelet and salad. My father lost the words "mutual funds" and "economy."

When we were alone again, I explained to my father that Lou Holmberg, in his day, had been a great athlete, one of a small number of Jews who had risen to the top in a sport then dominated by Gentile country-club culture. Always on the *qui vive* for anti-Semitism, my father seemed more impressed by his new neighbor's ability to survive in an alien world than by his athletic prowess.

"Seems like a nice man."

"I think so too, Dad," I said. "Maybe the two of you will become friends. When you go down to meals, it might not be a bad thing to knock on his door, see if he wants to join you."

"I don't want to be pushing myself on him."

"I don't think you would be, Dad. Who knows? Maybe he could use a friend, too."

My father put his hand on my cheek and jaw. "You're a good son, you know that . . ."

"Aaron," I filled in, for the first time.

"How come you never told me that Lou here was a big-time tennis champion?" my father asked me at lunch a few weeks later.

"I must have forgotten, Dad. Sorry." I had long ceased reminding him of things I had told him earlier; it seemed too painful for him, and pointless. Nor did we speak much any longer about the past, which was becoming more and more of a blur in his mind.

When I called to report on my father's deterioration, Dr. Spiegelman responded that things seemed to be going faster than he would have predicted. "These little jiggeroos are very odd," he added. "One person loses the power to recall common nouns, another the plot of his life. Causality is no longer discernible to a third. Sheer torture, let me tell you. And we know zilch about what causes it."

"So what's your prognosis?"

"Best I can make out, your father will eventually lose all

memory for language. How soon, I still can't say with any certainty."

"There's no way to slow this down?"

"I wish there were."

"So in the end my father will languish, who knows for how
long, with no words?"

"I'm afraid so."

"And there's nothing to be done."

"One thing," he said with a drop in his voice. "Pray for a
quick death."

My father and Lou Holmberg started to spend lots of time together. When I came to visit, which I now did at least three
times a week, including Saturdays for lunch, I'd usually find him
sitting in Lou's apartment, the television turned to the news or
some PBS program on wildlife. They had begun to eat breakfast together, prepared by my dad in his apartment, and in the
dining room they always sat at the same table.

Lou's wife had died a year before my mother. He had an
adopted daughter, who now lived on Long Island, but there had
been a falling-out of some kind, and she and Lou were scarcely
in touch. No photographs of grandchildren were to be found in
his apartment; if Lou had friends, I never saw any of them visiting at Highland Hills. But then, my father had been friendless,
too, though while my mother was alive it never seemed a deprivation: he had his work and he had my mother, who was his
best friend, and he had my wife and me and our two sons. Now
these two men in their eighties had become close. "We're like
an old married couple," Lou said one evening as my father
handed him a dish of ice cream.

"More like two old guys in some kind of . . ."

"Jewish joke," Lou filled in.

"Jewish joke," my father repeated. Years ago he would have

proceeded to tell several gags with opening lines like, "So these two old Jews were sitting on a bench on Collins Avenue in Miami Beach." But not tonight, or ever again.

For Father's Day, my wife and I took them both to dinner at Gabriel's in Highwood. My wife, who plays tennis, had read up on Lou Holmberg's career. "Did you ever think of turning professional?" she asked him.

"The serious money wasn't there when I was playing. Jack Kramer made all that possible, but it came too late for me."

"So you just stopped?"

"Pretty much," Lou said. "I didn't want to become one of those guys who're always hanging around, picking up a few hundred dollars here or there. Frank Parker — don't get me wrong, a nice guy, Frankie — did that sort of thing."

"No regrets?" my wife asked.

"Absolutely none. I felt about tennis the way Churchill did about alcohol. He said he got the best out of it before it got the best out of him. Something like that."

My father and Lou ordered filet mignon, and when the waiter set down their plates my father leaned over and began to cut his friend's steak. Looking at my wife, Lou said, "He does the work my hands can't, and I fill in some of the words he's lost. I'd say we're one hell of a doubles team."

My father smiled and gently patted his friend on the back. Did he want to add something but fail to find the words? At home, my wife said it was all she could do to keep from crying. I felt like my father: I couldn't find the words.

"So what're we going to do?" Lou asked me one Saturday, at the end of lunch, when my father had gone back up to get his checkbook.

"I wish I knew," I said.

"He's scared stiff, you know."

"He told you that?"

"He didn't have to tell me. I can sense it. Wouldn't you be if you knew you'd be living for who knows how many more years completely inaccessible to human contact? He did tell me that he's not sleeping well. That's one sign."

Just then my father returned to write out a check for $100 to my son Richard, in his last year at Colgate. He could remember things like his grandson's birthday but not the most ordinary words. Talk about jiggeroos!

Over the next four weeks, things grew rapidly worse. My father could hardly get through a sentence without losing two or three words. His awareness of his situation was evident in his face, even in his posture; for the first time in his life, he began to slump. Until now, he had been a man who seemed to know no depression, a believer in positive thinking — pull up your socks, soldier on, that sort of thing. Of course he had had his sadnesses, as when my mother died, but sadness is very different from depression.

"Your dad's really down in the dumps," Lou Holmberg told me over the phone. "He knows exactly what's happening. He described it to me as like being buried alive, though he couldn't come up with the word 'buried.'"

"I never thought I'd say such a thing," I said, "but the damn shame is that he is otherwise in such good health."

When I talked again with Dr. Spiegelman, who had reexamined my father, he said he thought it was time for him to be moved to the assisted-living floor.

"He's going to hate it."

"I know," he said, "but he's going to need a lot more attention."

"He has a good friend living next door," I said. "They're almost always together. My father's rarely alone."

"I don't think you fully understand," Spiegelman said. "Your father will soon go into something like a coma, except that he will be mobile. In effect, he'll be in a walking coma."

I put off giving my father the news, though I did tell Lou Holmberg.

"He's going to hate it," he said, using my very words.

"I know," I said. "It'll kill him."

"I only wish it would," Lou said. "He wants to die, your father does. You know that much, surely." He shot me a significant look and turned away.

Was I wrong to read in that look of his that it was my duty to find a way out — to save my father from years of living among the demented, in speechless incomprehension? This "way out" became the subject dominating all my thoughts. On the long drives from Winnetka to my office in the Loop and back, at breaks during the business day, at home at night, I tried to concentrate on a single problem: how to get my father off this earth before a darkness descended on him that to me, and evidently to him, seemed worse than death.

I was terrified even to let the idea enter my consciousness. This man who had helped bring me into the world, sheltered, fed, and protected me, always treated me fairly, showed me in the gentlest ways what it meant to live with honor — was it now incumbent upon me, for the most tender-hearted of reasons, to help him die? I had a nearly full bottle of sleeping pills, given to me after returning home from gallbladder surgery some three years ago. I had used only two of the thirty pills. What if I were to leave the remainder at my father's apartment in some conspicuous way? Might he make use of them? I would be conspiring in suicide, hardly an act to win moral approval. But I could not stop dwelling on what Lou Holmberg had said about my father's wishes, and I didn't know what else to do.

Just now, in any case, the question of the rightness and wrongness of things mattered less to me than my father's suffering. We were sitting in his living room, the three of us, eating cheesecake and watching a PBS show about lions on the Serengeti Plain. Very little was said. Lou's fork banged against his dish like a drum, and I found myself pulling for the antelopes and wildebeests that the lions had singled out for death. I was no longer certain how much my father was able to comprehend, let alone what pleasure he could take in the sight of a pride of lions gnawing at the bloody entrails of a once gracious animal.

At nine o'clock, Lou announced that he was off to bed. At the door he put a trembly hand in mine. I felt as if I were holding a small nervous animal. "Don't worry, Aaron," he said as I shook his hand, "it's going to be all right."

"Good night, Lou," I answered. "Sleep well."

"You too, kid."

My father had dozed off in his chair. I took the dishes into the kitchen, washed them, and then touched my father gently on the shoulder. He opened his eyes, smiled, grasped my arm. I walked him into his bedroom.

"Dad," I said, "are you worried?" I couldn't use the word "frightened," not with this old soldier. My father, even at the height of his salesmanly ebullience, was at his core a deeply reticent man, especially when it came to the important, the mysterious things in life.

In place of words he put both hands out, palms up, and shrugged, as if to say, What's the use?

"Is there anything you'd like me to do? I'll do anything you want."

In his eyes I thought I read both entreaty and forgiveness, but I can't be sure. He closed them and shook his head.

"Dad," I said, holding up the bottle I had stationed on his night table, "these are sleeping pills. In case you have trouble falling asleep, they'll do the job for you."

My father leaned over and embraced me. Against my face, his whiskery cheeks felt exactly as they had in the days when I would climb into his bed on a Sunday morning and he would read to me from what we used to call the funny papers.

Our arms around each other, I said, "I love you, Dad, very much."

"You too," I heard him whisper.

At eleven o'clock the next morning I received a call from Ernest Silverman, the director of Highland Hills, informing me that my father had died during the night.

"Of what?" I asked.

"So far as we know, of natural causes. He appears simply to have stopped breathing. He seems to have gone peaceably, which is a blessing."

No mention was made of pills. I told Silverman I would be in to settle my father's account. Apart from a few keepsakes, Highland Hills could have his furniture, some of which might be useful for future tenants. Silverman asked if I wanted Piser to handle the funeral arrangements.

When I got to the apartment I went directly to my father's bedroom, where I found the pills on the night table as I had left them. I counted them out: twenty-eight. For the second time that day, I felt relieved. I took the photos my father had kept of his grandchildren and of himself with my mother. His wallet, which contained $63, his Seiko watch with its black leather strap, and his electric razor I put in a plastic bag. The woman who let me in told me that, if I liked, she could arrange to donate his clothes to ORT, for which there would be a tax write-off. I thanked her, forbearing to mention that I was a tax lawyer.

I knocked at Lou Holmberg's door, but there was no answer. On my way out, a woman at the front desk handed me an envelope. Inside, printed in a large and very wobbly hand, was a one-sentence note:

> Aaron,
>> I told you not to worry.
>>> Lou

The funeral was a simple graveside ceremony. It was a cool day, but sunny. My wife and sons were there, and so was Lou Holmberg, whom we picked up in the limo on the way. The home had arranged for a rabbi, a young man with a dark beard, wearing Hush Puppies with his black suit. My father's body was lowered into a grave beside my mother's, and we each placed a shovelful of dirt on his coffin, except for Lou, who kept his hands in his pockets. During the proceedings, Mexican workmen in baseball caps leaned on shovels near a large yellow piece of earth-moving equipment.

My wife and I kept Lou with us on the way back, and our sons rode with the rabbi in his car. "I wish you had known my father earlier, Lou, when he was fully himself," I said a few minutes after we emerged from the cemetery and turned north on Harlem Avenue.

There was no answer. I glanced over at Lou, who had tears in his eyes. Removing a fluttering hand from his pocket, he dropped into my lap the second of the two keys to my father's now empty apartment. My wife shot me a look of accusation and horror. Not another word was said until the limo pulled up, nearly forty-five minutes later, before the entrance to Highland Hills.

My Little Marjie

WHEN MY BROTHER was born, my mother, phoning from her room at Michael Reese Hospital, asked what name I would like to give him. I was five years old. "Spencer," I said without hesitation, thinking of a skinny blond kid, a neighbor of ours on Sheridan Road, who must have been fourteen or fifteen at the time and had always gone out of his way to be kind to me. Spencer my little brother became, and that is the pretentious and slightly comical name he would have dragged through life had he not succumbed to crib death at the age of six months.

Such was the shock of this event that my mother waited a full six years before having her third child, my little sister. Again she consulted me. "Marge," I volunteered, after one of my mother's dearest friends, a tall and freckled and (though I wasn't aware of it) somewhat tragic figure.

Marge Lederer played cards with my mother: poker and kalooky and canasta. She never married but went around for nearly thirty-five years with a heavyset, gruff Irishman named Fred White, who, the story was, had been unable to obtain a divorce from his very Catholic wife. Marge worked as a book-keeper for a liquor store in the Loop and smoked Pall Malls, on which she would invariably leave a firm lipstick imprint. She used to say that I was going to be a heartbreaker when I grew up. Things turned out quite the reverse, but she won *my* heart with her sweetness and the tinge of sadness I sensed in this large and lonely woman. She died of a stroke in her fifties.

My baby sister and I connected immediately. She would reach up to grasp my finger as I hovered over her crib, while I, lightly touching her stomach and babbling her name, could almost unfailingly make her smile. If our mother could not calm her, I could sometimes do the job by taking her in my arms and patting her back. Although I was in every other respect a normal eleven-year-old boy — an athlete, a reader of comic books — I found myself spending an abnormal amount of time standing over her crib as she slept, handing her toys in her playpen, or, later, taking her for walks around the block in her stroller and playing with her on the grass in our small back yard. I can even remember leaning over my sister's crib at night and praying that no harm ever come to her.

Marjorie had our mother's good looks, her deep brown eyes and dark brown hair. There was a fineness about her face: high cheekbones, a small but not disappointing nose, good teeth, a winning smile. Her fingers were long, her hands well formed. Everything about her suggested intelligence. Before she was two, she had picked up on humor, knew what was expected of her, and was expert at manipulating others, not least me.

I wasn't sure what I wanted for my baby sister except, in a vague way, a grand life lived on a high plane. I know I worried about her becoming too popular. I wanted her to have in her social arsenal the power to charm, but never to waste it by using it indiscriminately. Perhaps even then I was afraid of losing her someday — though God knows there was little enough sign of that. On the contrary, as she grew older Marjorie came to think of me not only as her brother but as her adviser and protector. One of her first words was "Bruddy," short for brother, and Bruddy she called me ever after. "Bruddy" — I had only to hear the word to come running.

By the time Marjorie was in high school I was twenty-six, a graduate of the University of Chicago, my two years in the army over and done with. As I came of age I began to offer my little sister a fair amount of advice. A mild Francophile headed for a university career, I made sure she studied high school French, which she did with great efficiency, and in particular I put her on to the novels of Stendhal. I never told her why, but I was sure she would absorb their chief point — namely, that men, with their ambitions and romantic conceptions of themselves, are essentially clownish figures, never to be taken at their own self-valuation and predictably beastly in their use of women to bolster their always shaky egos.

At seventeen, Marjorie was tallish (five-seven or so), but she had never gone through anything like an awkward phase, and already it was clear she was going to be a knockout. She graduated ninth in a class of five hundred or so at Mather High and had her choice of colleges. I was against the University of Chicago; good as it was, the school seemed too dark and dreary for her. In the spring of her junior year I took a week off and drove her around to the eastern schools. Harvard, Yale, and Princeton were not yet coeducational. Vassar was too isolated; Bennington, despite the beautiful setting, too much the breeding ground of female neurosis. Between us we decided on Wellesley. The main point, I told her, was that she attend a college that the world reckoned excellent; although she would quickly discover otherwise, at least later in life she wouldn't wonder how things might have turned out if only she had gone to a supposedly good school. My father, less than eager to send his daughter so far away, succumbed to my argument that Boston represented a larger world than Chicago.

At Wellesley, whatever the reigning system of snobberies, she not only survived but flourished, graduating *summa cum laude* with a combined major in French literature and modern history. Her senior honors essay on Marcel Proust and the Dreyfus affair, a paper of some seventy pages, showed, I thought, an orderly, lucid, and well-stocked mind, especially for one so young. As a teacher by then on the Committee on Social Thought at the University of Chicago, I knew a thing or two about Proust myself, and I felt my baby sister had insinuated herself impressively into that little genius's richly textured and ultimately heroic mind.

So, apparently, did others. Her teachers in the French department at Wellesley urged her to attend graduate school, assuring her that a graduate fellowship at Harvard or Yale was a certainty.

"What do you think, Bruddy?" she phoned to ask me.

"Baby," I said, "I think you need a bigger playing field than any university can provide."

"I was hoping you'd say that."

"Great minds think alike, no?"

"Ours seem to."

Through a Wellesley connection, Marjie was offered, and took, a job at *Vogue,* in New York. It was 1969 and the magazine still wasn't hiring many Jewish girls, but for my sister they made an exception. Called an editorial assistant, she became in fact a woman of all work: proofreading, writing captions, turning out small gossip bits, occasionally going on photo shoots. She reported back to me on the wild comedy of life at the magazine under Diana Vreeland. "She's a genuine *monstre sacré,* Bruddy," she said. "Most of the time without the *sacré.*"

Marjie shared an apartment in the Village with a girl who had gone to Smith and who also worked at *Vogue*. The only men in Marjie's life, so far as I knew, were a third-year law student at Columbia named Jonathan Kahn and Richard Greenberg, an assistant professor of English at NYU. Once, on a trip to New York, I took Marjie to dinner and the latter met us for drinks afterward. He was clearly more taken with her than she with him. I thought him nice enough, but dull; not a serious contender.

I recognized that my solicitude for Marjie was above and beyond the ordinary. But then I thought of the two of us as above and beyond the ordinary in every way. I was intent on protecting her, even if I knew that I could do so only within strict limits. I was intent, too, on her happiness, even if the limits here were greater still. What I hoped — was this naïve? — was that at least I could steer her away from life's obvious mistakes and traps.

Not long after leaving school, I myself had begun keeping company with a dazzling woman named Sally Maddox, blond, green-eyed, bosomy, long-legged, the works. At first I thought myself privileged to be with so desirable a creature; later I started to feel edgy. Returning from the men's room in a restaurant or bar, I would discover guys had sent her notes or come up to the table to pitch her directly. Walking down the street, I would register the look in the eyes of the men we passed; even male dogs, I began to think, were stimulated by her. Unable to stand the pressure, I abandoned the field.

But a sister you don't abandon. Marjie was a Sally Maddox — for men of taste and sensibility. She had always been beautiful, but now, entering womanhood, she became sexy. A certain luscious ripeness about her caused men to stare as she walked past, then to do a double take, as if to say, Did I just see what I think I saw? The almost intimidating intelligence in her eyes, her natural refinement, would be enough, I felt sure, to put off most waiters, bartenders, and parking lot attendants, also most jocks and construction workers. But that still left a fairly full roster of potential predators.

In our conversations, Marjie and I always kept a balance between frankness and tact. We could be candid talking about other people, including our parents, or about money or politics. But in the realm of sex, diffidence remained the rule. Throughout her high school years there was generally some boy or other to take her to dances or to the movies, but no steady boyfriend. I assumed that my baby sister had gone off to college a virgin. At least it pleased me to think so — I speak here as a male of my generation, for whom sex, never a trivial act, was all the more desired for the prohibitions hedging it about and the dangers it entailed, including the dangers of pregnancy and, for a young woman, loss of reputation. I was on the old program, and in some ways still am.

What sort of man did I want for my sister? I had in mind a man of the world, settled in his vocation, certain in his integrity, strong and serious. I preferred someone perhaps ten or so years older than she, someone whose work opened the world at a wide angle — in high finance, say, or diplomacy, or international law. And I wanted someone for whom the problems of money were already well settled, who could give my talented baby sister the best chance to flourish at whatever it was that she eventually decided she wanted to do with her life.

What Marjie wanted to do was not yet decided. Opportunities opened before her, as they inevitably will for that small minority of women who are both strikingly beautiful and very smart. She was offered a job as a subeditor at *The New Yorker,* another in the antique furniture section at Sotheby's. She took the Sotheby's offer, which paid less but seemed to provide greater prospects. These included living in London, where the firm sent her for six months to learn the trade, putting her up in a small apartment on Marylebone near the Wallace Collection.

When I visited her there, I was amazed to see how cosmopolitan my baby sister had become. Taking me in hand, she made me feel very much the country mouse as she arranged tables for us at elegant restaurants set back in mews in parts of the city unknown to me. On one of these occasions we were joined by an attractive young guy named Paul Lester, a Balliol man who worked for the BBC. He had an upper-class accent and strong left-wing opinions and was clearly nuts about my sister. She seemed — appealingly, in my view — considerate but ultimately indifferent. If, as I believed, there was always an inequality in love, my sister was likely always to be the more loved party. The thought gave me pleasure.

Sotheby's sent Marjie on two-month tours of its Paris and Rome offices before returning her to New York. There she settled in again and soon became what I think of as a naturalized New Yorker. Although I was frustrated in my desire to have her near me, she did come back to Chicago at least twice a year: once for our father's birthday, which was on Christmas day, and once in the spring for Passover. And when I made my few trips each year to New York, we always saved at least one meal to be alone together, usually in her neighborhood on the Upper East Side where she would invariably know a quiet restaurant with splendid, no-nonsense food.

We always found things to talk about: books, movies, intellectual celebrities, our earnings, our expenses — everything but what, in another time, would have been called Marjie's love life.

Once, however, planning a one-day visit to New York on which my evening would be spoken for, I called to ask if she could set aside lunch, and she told me there was someone she wanted me to meet.

"His name is James Newbolt," she said.

At first I didn't recognize the name, but then I did, though barely. Newbolt was a sculptor, an abstract expressionist of the generation of the New York School. His work had been overshadowed by David Smith's, or so I learned when I asked a friend on the Committee on Social Thought who knew the intricacies of the New York art world. My friend told me, too, that the sculpture of James Newbolt could no longer be considered contemporary; it had slipped from the contemporary to the modern — which is to say, to the historical.

Newbolt turned out to be himself rather historical. We met for lunch at a small French restaurant. I had arrived first. Ten minutes later, I saw my lovely sister enter, accompanied by a tall, very thin man, bald, with steel-rimmed spectacles. When I say tall, I mean six-five or more; his slenderness made him seem even taller. A stiff leg gave him a pronounced limp. He had to be a man near seventy. Marjie was not yet thirty.

In the time I had had to do a bit of research, I had discovered that James Newbolt was a New Englander, sufficiently wellborn to be called a scion. He used to run with Jackson Pollock and Larry Rivers, was part of that hard-drinking crowd. Although I had never met any of the artists in this group, I had known the art critics Clement Greenberg and Harold Rosenberg, who were themselves fairly tough characters, intellectual bullies really. It was altogether a tough bunch, tough on one another and tough on the rest of the world. The thought of my sister falling among such tigers was not easy to contemplate.

Newbolt, who had been married three times, worked chiefly

in steel, and made vast, angular, abstract pieces carrying jazz-
song titles like *Stars Fell on Alabama* and *Softly, as in a Morning
Sunrise*. I gathered his critical reputation was now high and,
with David Smith dead, rising. In a brief comment, Clement
Greenberg had referred to Newbolt's "unvarying allegiance to
a chaste, immitigable, unforgiving modernism," four clearly ap-
probative words.

Marjie introduced us, and Newbolt shook my hand in a
loose, negligent way. His brown tweed suit was worn, he wore
a chambray work shirt and a black knit tie, the right temple of
his glasses was held together with Scotch tape, and one of his
lower front teeth was missing. His nails were gray, the skin
around them gritty — not so surprising, I suppose, in a man
working with heavy metal. The first two fingers on each hand
were orange from smoking: Camels, unfiltered, and lots of
them, to judge by his gravelly voice and the half pack or so he
sucked down at lunch. My mind involuntarily flicked on a quick
slide of those hands on my dear sister's body, causing an inward
shudder.

Newbolt wasn't much given to small talk; there wasn't much
give to him generally. He kept silent as I filled Marjie in on Chicago doings: marriages and divorces among our cousins, the
health of our father, who was recovering from the still relatively
new procedure of bypass surgery. Newbolt ordered a second
martini before we picked up our menus.

After we ordered, he turned to me. "Marjorie gave me some
of your stuff to read," he said. "It ain't much."

I wasn't expecting him to come on so strong so quickly.
"How so?" I managed.

"It doesn't do much to advance the argument."

"Sorry to hear that," I said, trying not to seem daunted. "Tell
me, what is the argument?"

"The argument is about the way people ought to live in a

time of heightened spiritual crisis. Nothing of yours I've read even touches on that."

"What do your sculptures have to do with it?"

"If you don't see it, then there's no point in my spelling it out for you," he said.

With that for starters, the rest of the meal went cold and sour before us. Poor Marjie, try though she might, could find no way to save it.

"Jim knew Edmund Wilson, Bruddy," she offered, knowing my admiration for the great literary critic. "He went to the same prep school, though of course much later. The Hill School, wasn't it, Jimmy?"

"Yeah," he said, "I met him a few times. A nonstop talker. A monologist. He always had to show you he knew more than you did about your own life's work. An arrogant bastard, for my money."

"Jim," she tried again, "tell Bruddy about Ravel. Bruddy loves everything about Ravel."

"An amazing little guy, really. Very small, very elegant, a dandy. As an artist, he claimed to have gotten more out of joy than out of suffering. I don't think it's true, but when he said it you tended to believe it."

"There's a remark of Ravel's that has always impressed me," I put in. "Someone once accused him of being artificial. He said that his accuser didn't seem to realize that some people — meaning himself, I assume — were naturally artificial." And here I couldn't resist a dig at this creep. "It also works if you turn it around: some people are artificially natural."

Newbolt ordered a third martini, the drinking of which sent him into a sullen silence. There followed oysters and a lobster salad, at both of which he picked while downing two German beers. While Marjie and I had dessert, he went for a Drambuie, double. Just as the check arrived he ducked into the men's room. I looked at my sister, who looked away as I took out my wallet.

The next evening, Marjie called me in Chicago. "I'm so sorry about lunch, Bruddy," she said. "You didn't see Jimmy at his best."

"I assume he can do better or he wouldn't still be alive. What's the matter with him, anyway?"

"I'm afraid," she said, "that he isn't very comfortable around Jews."

A long and awkward silence, which I was prepared to maintain for five minutes.

"I mean, Bruddy," she said at last, "he grew up in New England with shabby gentry, lots of pretensions, knowing no Jews at all. Then, when he came to New York, he felt the Jewish critics held him back. He still bears a grudge."

"But what about you, sweetie? You aren't exactly a Plantagenet."

"He makes an exception for me. He loves me."

"Why do you suppose that is? Maybe you help advance the argument."

"Bruddy," she said, "that isn't fair."

"What do you see in him? I don't get it."

"He's an artist, Bruddy, the real thing. And he seems to need me."

"Don't overrate art, Marjie," I said. "And especially don't overrate artists. It's all very well for the small number lucky enough to produce the real thing, but people who give their lives to artists usually come out with the short end of a very dirty stick."

It's not as if I didn't understand the special pleasure that comes from being singled out for the affection of an artist — being chosen by someone who himself seems chosen. But was this all there was to her infatuation for James Newbolt, who seemed a likely candidate for the most unappealing man I'd ever met? Was my sister telling me everything I needed to know?

Some women have convinced themselves that theirs is the magic that will transform every toad into a prince. My sister wasn't so foolish as that. Nor, in keeping company with a man nearly forty years older, was she seeking a father. She already had a good, sturdy, philistine father, the recognition of whose limitations never got in the way of her loving him.

But if I could not yet fathom what sort of fantasy was operating here, the question that interested me even more was how I could get her to cut away from this son of a bitch without pushing her further into his arms. In my twenties, I remember sitting toward the back of a Michigan Avenue bus on a steamy summer's day, coming in as an eavesdropper in the middle of a conversation between a mother and her adolescent daughter seated just ahead of me. I shall never forget the mother's strong Mitteleuropean accent as she said, "Sondra, lissen to me and you vill alvays treeumph" — or the sensation, upon hearing it, of a high heel being placed firmly on my Adam's apple.

But, since her adolescence, had I not been playing with Marjie exactly the part of Sondra's mother? Our parents, proud though they were of their daughter, also not so secretly thought that my ambitions for her were, as my father more than once put it, "hifalutin." My own two failed and fallow marriages did not give them much confidence in my judgment. They would have much preferred Marjie to stay in Chicago and marry what they called a professional man: a physician or dentist or CPA (although not a lawyer, a species against whom my father harbored a long-standing animus). It was from this fate that I had determined to set Marjie free. If only she would listen to me, follow my instructions on how to live her life, she would emerge triumphant. And so far, owing in large part to her own talent and good looks, she appeared to be well on her way — until now. I had set her free, all right: free, it had begun to appear, for James Newbolt.

Marjie and I talked at least twice a week, on Wednesday and Sunday nights, usually around ten. In our next conversation, I asked if it was all right to return to the Newbolt question.

"What precisely is the question, Bruddy?" I could feel a slight tensing in her voice.

"I guess it's why him? What do you see in him?"

"One of the things I love about you, Bruddy, is your relentlessness when it comes to motives. Does every act have to have a motive?"

"For people like us it does, baby sister. If we don't understand what people's motives are, we might as well be in the mail-order business."

"Is love an acceptable motive, Brud?"

"Is that really what we're talking about here? You feel love for James Newbolt? Or are you only swept away by his proclaimed love for you?"

"When you say his name, could you please try to restrain the industrial-strength contempt?" she said.

"Sorry, but you two aren't a conventional couple, as I'm sure you've noticed."

"I thought avoiding convention was one of your chief lessons to me, Bruddy."

"Sweetie, this guy is forty years older than you. I'm not saying anything about his drinking habits. But if you marry him and he lives long enough, you'll wipe the drool from his jaw, push his wheelchair down the boardwalk, change his diapers. That's a little beyond unconventional. Forgive me, but I think you're making a major mistake, a horrendous mistake."

"Sorry, Bruddy, but I happen to think otherwise. If you must know, I think Jimmy's a genius, and I take his love for me as a tribute."

"Genius?"

"Have you ever seen his work?"

"Only in photographs."

"Jim has a show right now at the Milwaukee Museum of Art. Before you say anything more, please run up there. Then maybe you'll know more about why I feel as I do about him."

I was prepared to despise everything that Newbolt had constructed, hoping to find a coarse and crappy life mirrored in his work. But once in the museum's sculpture garden — many of his pieces were too large to be shown indoors — I found myself deeply moved by a few of these cold but impressively suggestive works, awed by the monumentality of others, and swept away by the cumulative effect. I must have stood for at least fifteen minutes admiring a Giacometti-like figure titled *Our Davey,* which despite its abstraction uncannily caught the effeminate arrogance of the elegant little *David* by Donatello that I had seen years ago in Florence.

Who would have thought that the miserable James Newbolt had the power to charm? Maybe he really was a genius, I thought, reminding myself that one must never underestimate the secret powers of the artist — powers often capable of touching many lives other than his own.

"He's a considerable talent," I conceded to Marjie over the phone that evening, in what I hoped was a measured tone of voice. "No doubt about it. The real thing, just as you said. But then, why should I doubt your word in such matters?"

"Oh, Bruddy, I knew your judgment would win out over your feelings."

"Actually, they coexist. He's a serious artist whom I don't want connected in any way with my sister."

"Then you haven't changed your mind?"

"No, baby, I haven't. Forgive me, but I can't."

"You trust my eye but not my heart."

"Marjie, he's not for you."

"Who is, Bruddy? Who is for me?"

"Not James Newbolt — that much I know."

"Jimmy says you think the only one good enough for me is you, Bruddy. He says your feelings for me border on the incestuous."

"I'm not surprised to hear it. That whole generation is awash in cheap Freudianism. Tell him I said there's nothing wrong with incest, so long as you keep it in the family."

There was a short but significant pause — a beat, I think they call it in movie scripts.

"Bruddy," my sister said, "Jimmy and I were married in Maine on Friday."

"No, Marjie," I heard myself cry out. "Please God, no!"

"Bruddy," she said, "I want your blessing."

"I can't give it," I said. "I would like to, but I can't."

"I'll always love you," she said, "you know that."

"I know it," I said, "but this isn't the end I had in mind for you, warming the bones of this old boozer."

"Bruddy, he's my husband. Be careful."

"Don't you see you're writing the wrong ending to a brilliant life?"

"But, Bruddy," she said, strangely calm, "it's *my* life. It's my ending to write, not yours."

I didn't answer.

"Bruddy," she said, "I still want your blessing."

"Marjorie," I said, "forgive me but I can't — not now, not ever."

"Are you certain?"

"Of nothing more in my whole life."

I heard a gentle click on the other end.

This was the only argument my sister and I ever had. My parents never met Marjie's husband. As long as our parents were alive, she continued to visit Chicago, but now only once a year, on Passover; I always found an excuse to be out of town. My mother ceased talking about her in my presence. What, if anything, she and Marjie said about her marriage I never discovered. When my father asked me what Newbolt was like, I said that I had met him only once and hadn't gotten a very clear sense of him. Our parents pressed neither of us on the reason for our falling out, though once, my father asked me to make things up with Marjorie. "It's not your place to sit *shiva* for her," he said. "She's your sister. Call her and make up." But I never did.

Our parents died without grandchildren. As the years passed, whole days would go by without my thinking of Marjie; sometimes a whole week. I began to consider myself alone in the world, detached from family altogether. Then one day, more than two decades later, I returned after lunch to my office at the university to find a pink-slip message: "Call your brother-in-law." I was taken aback, not least by the thought that I had ever had a brother-in-law. The phone number on the message was somewhere in Maine.

"I've got bad news for you," Newbolt said.

You are bad news personified, I thought to myself.

"Your sister died last night, of bone cancer. It started as breast cancer."

"Dear God," I managed to blurt out. "Did she suffer much?"

"It wasn't easy," he said. "She's being cremated tomorrow."

"Did she mention me at any time?" I asked finally.

"Afraid not," he said. "She left no will. She wanted her ashes spread around her garden here."

"Thank you for calling," I said, and hung up, forgetting to ask him to send me something of my sister's, a piece of clothing, a photograph, a bit of costume jewelry, something to hold in my hand. She would have been fifty-two.

James Newbolt, so far as I know smoking and boozing at the same clip, died two years later, making it to ninety-one. His death was noted in a half-page obituary in the *New York Times,* with a picture of him in his studio and another of *Our Davey.* The *Times* mentioned his having been married four times, but no names of wives were given. An oversight, I guess.

Postcards

HEFFERMAN stood in line at the post office, between an East Indian man with two large parcels wrapped in thick twine and an older black man wearing a White Sox cap and giving off an aroma of menthol lozenges. The line was long. He must have been in it for nearly ten minutes, and he regretted not having brought anything to read. By now, coming here on the first of every month, he was fairly familiar with the rhythm of the place. It was always a mistake to arrive near five o'clock, which he had done today, or at eight-thirty when it opened. Hefferman generally showed up at three, not long after the Board of Trade closed, on his walk from LaSalle Street to his apartment at 880 Lake Shore Drive. His order was always the same: two packets of stamps (for paying bills) and twenty plain, stamped postcards.

Hefferman had begun sending out anonymous cards nearly a year ago. Anonymous isn't quite accurate. He signed them with false names — usually, but not always, Jewish names. His second postcard had gone to a literary critic named Louis Binstock, who had been given a prize by the American Academy of Arts and Letters. It was a two-liner:

> Dear Binstock,
> Congratulations on your award. A life of ass-kissing has not been lived in vain.

Hefferman signed the card Larry Goodman, with a Chicago return address. He tended to favor soft first names: Larry, Ronald, Teddy, Sheldon. The return addresses, like the names, he also made up.

Hefferman had a soft name himself. "Seymour Hefferman, the last Seymour in captivity," he would sometimes say when introducing himself. Something else he used to say, whenever anyone asked him where he'd gone to college, was "I was formerly very smart." Then he would explain that he had skipped two full years of elementary school and gone off to the University of Chicago at fifteen. It was in fourth grade at the Kilmer School that his teacher, a fleshy pink lady named Mrs. Murphy, had summoned his mother to tell her that her son's IQ had tested at 153.

"What's that mean?" Seymour remembered his mother asking.

"It means Seymour's a near genius," said Mrs. Murphy in a voice shimmering with significance.

"So if he's such a genius," his mother said, "how come his room's a pigsty?"

Hefferman never forgot that. Nor did he forget the number 153, which in later years he wished he had never heard.

The University of Chicago overstimulated Hefferman. In his second year there, at sixteen, he decided he wanted to be a poet. He never made it, or even came close. But he had caught the art bug, which for him meant that, next to being a writer, nothing else in life ever seemed worth taking seriously.

The young Hefferman produced a vast amount of verse between his eighteenth and twenty-fourth years, an amount made all the more impressive by the fact that he never had a subject. He wrote sonnets, sestinas, villanelles (a killer, the villanelle), free verse, and verse practically bound, gagged, and chained in Italian and French forms, all expressing one thing: the yearning to be a poet. He went under the name S. I. Hefferman — Ira was his middle name. Even back then he knew that, could he write with the divine touch of William Butler Yeats or Gerard Manley Hopkins, no one would ever read a poet named Seymour Hefferman. He submitted his poems to magazines that had more potential contributors than actual subscribers. Months would go by without a word, and when it finally came it was, inevitably, no.

Two years in the army, a year in law school at Northwestern, a stint as an architecture student at the Illinois Institute of Technology — and then Hefferman got a master's degree in English at Roosevelt University and took a few useless courses in education to qualify for a high school teaching certificate. That fizzled, too; teaching was not for him. He thought of moving to New York or California, but when his father became ill with cancer of the liver, he felt he couldn't leave his mother. For the four sad years of his father's dying he tried to sell real estate, consoling himself with the thought that Wallace Stevens had peddled insurance, though he knew Stevens wasn't a salesman but an attorney for one of the large Hartford firms. "A poet always cheats his boss" was the Russian proverb that Hefferman muttered to himself when knocking off early at an open house in Skokie or Morton Grove. But the problem was that, nearing thirty, he had begun to cease to think of himself a poet. He wasn't really anything.

With the money his father left him, Hefferman bought a seat on the commodities exchange. There he met all sorts of hustlers, whose unrelenting aggressiveness first impressed and then mildly depressed him. Still, he had studied the futures market with some care before buying his seat and discovered a way of making a decent living — $75,000 or so a year, not bad for a guy still single — if he hedged his bets and restrained himself from taking the plunge on wheat or soybeans or something else about which, like everyone else on LaSalle Street, he knew not a thing but its paper value at the end of the day. His earnings allowed him to spend a month each year traveling in Europe and to buy a one-bedroom apartment in a stern glass-and-steel Mies van der Rohe building on the Outer Drive facing the lake.

Living in his detached way, Hefferman had little social life: no close friends, no lengthy relationships with women. In his thirties and forties he went out with a number of divorcees; now, in his late fifties, graying and a bit paunchy, he was up to young widows. Somehow he couldn't quite take women seriously — the art bug again — and he wasn't altogether sorry to sense a diminishment in his once insistent appetites in this department.

The last time he'd brought a woman to dinner at his mother's apartment, he told his mother afterward that he wasn't much interested in her. "Don't be so choosy, Seymour," his mother replied. "You're no great beauty, you know." Ah, thought Hefferman, it's just as Freud said: a man confident of his mother's love is truly a conqueror.

Although having long since ceased to write any verse, Hefferman retained his interest in it. He was by now a forty-odd-year subscriber to *Poetry* magazine, and he also took the *New York Review of Books, The New Yorker, Hudson Review, Times Literary Supplement,* the *London Review of Books,* the *New Criterion,* and five or six other magazines. Through these, and occasional dips into the Internet, he kept up on current academic disputes, the culture wars, the announcements of genius grants, the whole goofy literary and intellectual life of his time, in which he himself took no part whatsoever. He had long ago decided that it wasn't such a great time.

As for the postcards, the very first one he sent wasn't to a poet or novelist or critic but to a guy at the commodities exchange named Marvin Feldstein. One day, in the men's room for members, Hefferman had noticed this Feldstein taking great care with his outrageous comb-over hairdo: carefully placing the lengthy, oily strands from below his right ear all the way over leftwise to cover his wide bald head, patting them into place with a sweeping motion of the hand before extracting a can of hair spray from his attaché case and firing away. It was pathetic, or might have been had Feldstein not been one of the most aggressive guys out on the floor, where he acted as if he were under the boards at a pro basketball game. Hefferman thought about it and thought about it and then one day sent him an unsigned postcard.

> Dear Marvin,
>   A word about your hairdo: that word is Preposterous. You may not be aware that this same hairdo is the cause of much mirth among your colleagues down on the floor. Whatever else you do, please do not abandon it; it brings too much gaiety to the grimness of our daily grind.

Within a week, Feldstein showed up properly bald and, if not less aggressive, then just a touch, or so Hefferman thought, less confident.

With this small victory he turned his attention to culture, and, starting with the poison-pen note to the critic Binstock, he was off and running. He had begun to think a great deal less of

Ravinia ever since it had been taken over by a small German conductor who wore a white tunic and hopped about on the podium. He decided to send him a postcard.

> Dear Maestro,
>
> How regrettable that as a conductor you turn out to be what a French writer on music called "one of those good dancers"! Your antics, like a great jackanapes, enormously increase your general grotesqueness. A mistake, I think, in every way. Stick to the music, kid, and while you're at it, my advice is to knock off the tunics.
>
> Sincerely,
Ronald Landesman

A famous poet, who a decade earlier had announced the onset of cancer, had filled the intervening years with all sorts of poems and essays about his approaching death. Meanwhile, though, the creep stayed alive; even his wife had died before him. At this rate, so would Hefferman. A postcard was in order.

> Dear Cancer Victim,
>
> Don't you owe your readers — not to speak of many editors — your life? It would be one thing if your imminent demise had been announced by someone else, but since you yourself promised it, don't you feel you ought to make good? Do consider pegging out before too much longer.
>
> Sincerely,
Sandy Cohn

When a now elderly and formidably boring teacher of his from the University of Chicago wrote a book about playing the viola in amateur string quartets, Hefferman, warming to his task as the Zorro of culture, seated himself before his laptop:

> My dear *dottore,*
>
> My idea of hell is you playing your viola while simulta-

neously lecturing on any aspect whatsoever of English literature. The thought of you scratching away for nearly
fifty years on your oversize fiddle makes me pity your
wife. Be merciful and give her surcease.

Sincerely,
Anson Ginsberg

Once fully into the swing, Hefferman found himself writing three or four or five postcards a week. Such was the quality of the culture that there was never any shortage of recipients. When an elderly novelist produced, not for the first
time, a book excoriating his previous wife, Hefferman saddled
up:

> Yo, Bluebeard,
> Time — no? — to stop using literature as a means of
> paying off old resentments, imagined wounds, petty in-
> justices way too deeply felt. Time, too, to stop insisting on
> the largeness of your soul. Now that your prostate must
> be almost as imposing as your ego, why not ease back into
> the gentle solipsism of old age?
>
> None of the best,
Myron Hausman

To a critic who wrote a self-serving article in the Sunday
New York Times in defense of the blacklisted Hollywood screen-
writers, Hefferman shot off another missive:

> Dear sir,
> It must be lonely for you, taking the courageous posi-
> tions you do. Lonely, that is, what with the red hordes to
> your left, the black hundreds to your right, and only one
> good man — that would be you, Jughead — in the middle.
>
> Hang in there,
Lenny Pomeranz

Another critic, a terrific operator, wrote regularly about the Jews, availing himself of a "we" that Hefferman disliked above all pronouns in contemporary writing. When a piece by this critic appeared in the *New Republic*, giving the Israelis all sorts of moral advice strewn with quotations from Kierkegaard, Nietzsche, and Walter Benjamin, Hefferman booted up again:

> Josephus,
>   What'll it take for you to quit writing about the Jews? I think I could get you a million bucks from prominent Americans who feel the same way I do. If you'll throw in a promise never to mention the Holocaust again — vas you dere, Charlie? — I'm sure the ante would rise still higher.
>
>   Shalom,
>   Lee Schwartz

All in all, thought Hefferman, not a bad week's work. The week that followed likewise began looking promising, with a scorching card to a novelist who, starting out as a chronicler of the miseries of contemporary Jewish life, had gone on to produce a pornographic bestseller, much cut-rate Kafka, and considerable diddling with the melding of autobiography and fiction. Ah, thought Hefferman, reading a typically approving review in the *Times* of the novelist's most recent production — the guy had lately adopted the mode of high moral dudgeon — time to put on mask and black shirt and ride out:

> Dear Moral Leader,
>   As a simple American, Midwest version, may I be permitted to apologize to you on behalf of all our countrymen for having let you down? Hard, I realize, to rise to your standard of moral equipoise as the self-acknowl-

edged legislator of mankind. But does the world really need a pornographic Polonius? Don't believe it does.

As ever,
Sherwin Skulnik

In the same issue of the *New York Times Book Review,* Hefferman also read an interview with a woman, a short story writer associated with feminist causes, in which she expressed her worries about turning fifty and facing the prospect of growing old alone. Hefferman cleared his screen for action:

Dear Ms. R,
I read with great empathy the interview in today's *NYTBR.* I wonder if it has occurred to you that you and your feminist pals have done everything possible to make yourselves disagreeable and unattractive — and *now* you worry about being alone. Isn't this a bit like the young man who murdered his parents and then threw himself on the mercy of the court as an orphan? Think upon it, sweetie.

Fondly,
Stu Jabowitz

Later that evening, hours after he'd mailed the card, Hefferman had a terrible, creepy feeling that, having put the card in with a stack of bills he was paying, he may have affixed to it a label bearing his real name and address. He spent a difficult night trying to remember what *exactly* he had done, and in the morning rose from his bed absolutely sure. What a screwup!, he thought. Gigantic!

He'd had an exceptionally good week in the market — made, for him, a small killing in beets. But that couldn't take his mind off the telltale label. He stopped sending out postcards. Returning each evening to his apartment, he ran through the day's mail with nervous fingers. Whenever the phone rang, his heart leapt with dread. A week went by, then another, and then a full month. She must, he assumed, have treated the card as the work of a crank and tossed it away with a sneer. Relieved, he turned again to his solitary pleasure. He began by shooting off a note to a man who at a youthful age had been named president of a small college in New York State and later turned up as a conductor — apparently a damned poor one — of an orchestra for which he had been able to raise funds.

> Dear Leonardo,
>   I address you as Leonardo because you are truly a Renaissance man. The only problem is that, with your third-rate college, your hopeless conducting, your many fatuous statements about education and the state of the world, you, kiddo, give the Renaissance a bad name. Do consider taking an early pension and retiring to a St. Helena of your own choosing, where we shall hear no more of your passionately expressed banalities.
>
>   Cordially,
>   Lyle Futterman

A model of the form, if he did say so himself: first drawing in this monstrous egotist with what appeared to be a compliment, then letting the air out before finishing with a flourish of stylish invective. Was he on to a new genre here — the brief blast, the vivid vituperation? A shame, Hefferman thought, that he hadn't kept a copy of everything he'd sent. There must be more than a hundred by now, almost enough to make a short book, a dirty little dormer window on the age.

Then one day, after a negligible session at the Board of Trade, Hefferman returned to his apartment, went through his mail — catalogues and bills — checked his e-mail, and listened to his voice mail. There were two messages. One was from his mother: "Hello, stranger. Haven't heard from you in four days. Call when you get a chance." Then a new voice, a woman's, came on, cultivated and very chill. "Mr. Hefferman, I recently returned from London to a most unpleasant postcard signed by a man named Jabowitz. I have received more than my share of hate mail, but your ugly little message was something special, distinguished by what I would call a disinterested malice, or perhaps dementia is the more precise word. I shall be in Chicago on the weekend of May 30 to 31, and I plan to call on you. I am very eager to learn what sort of lunatic would do so deliberately cruel a thing."

The caller did not give her name, but then she didn't have to.

Hefferman sat there trembling. He felt like a child, caught out at some mischievous and unexplainable act. He remembered sitting thus nearly fifty years ago on a bench outside the principal's office after he had kicked open a wooden locker in seventh grade because he couldn't get his combination lock to work, knowing there was going to be hell to pay yet hoping somehow to escape deep humiliation.

Outside the screaming commodities exchange, Hefferman led a quiet life. He had no taste for direct confrontation. What would he do when she called? He thought nervously of changing his phone number, of moving, of leaving the city for a few months. He thought, yearningly, of the federal witness-protection program. He imagined himself living in a motel outside Tucson, opening the front door cautiously for the morning paper, driving a gray Chevy, wearing plaid pants and solid-color golf shirts. He would call himself Jack Jacobs, or Jim Edwards, maybe Bob Simmons — nothing like his habitual aliases. He had to shake his head at his own nuttiness.

"*Du calme,*" he said to himself, "*du calme.*" The words, from

Conrad's *Heart of Darkness*, were the advice given to Marlow by a physician in Belgium for learning how to survive in the Congo. Hefferman often invoked them as a mantra on the floor of the exchange when things were going wild and he felt like taking the plunge on soybeans or corn. *"Du calme, du calme."* He wished he had kept a copy of the offending postcard. By now he could remember only the pleasure he'd taken in its composition, a pleasure now thoroughly blown away.

He went to Borders to gaze upon the photograph of Ms. Andrea Rubin on the dust jacket of her latest book. Unsmiling, she seemed every bit the more than mildly depressed moralist she had seemed in her interview. Slender, with a high forehead, she also looked to be tall. Hefferman himself was five-nine if he stood up straight. He hoped she wasn't taller; if a confrontation there must be, he didn't want her looking down on him.

Keep your perspective, kid, Hefferman told himself. You weren't *wrong* to send those postcards. Someone needs to tell these jerks how pretentious they are. And so, taking his courage in hand, he sat down and wrote back to her, suggesting that when she is in Chicago they might meet at a coffee shop in Hefferman's neighborhood. The place was tucked away in the lobby of a hotel, and the tables were set close: not much room to cause a scene, he thought.

At his computer, Hefferman composed his letter:

> Ms. Andrea Rubin
> c/o Farrar, Straus & Giroux
> 19 Union Square West
> New York, N.Y. 10003
>
> Dear Ms. Rubin,
>   Yes, I am the man who sent you that postcard. I did it for a reason. Enough is enough, and enough has already

arrived. No one wants to hear any more about the loneliness of the modern writer. You and your friends have
made Akim Tamiroffs of us all — we don't, that is, any
longer provoke. If you would like to talk about this further, I'll be waiting for you in the coffee shop in the
Knickerbocker Hotel, on Walton off Michigan Avenue, at
noon on Saturday, May 30. I'll recognize you from your
unsmiling book-jacket photograph. I'll be wearing a yellow sweater. Can't say I look forward to it all that much,
but I'll be there.

Hefferman signed the letter with his real name, sealed it, and
quickly walked it down to the mailbox before he could change
his mind. Pushing the letter down the chute, he spoke another
of his mantras, this one Harry Truman's words to his weeping
White House staff after announcing he would not seek reelec-
tion. "Calm down," Truman said, "and stay on the job."

At 11:45, he took a seat at a table for two near the window. As a
precaution — in case he got cold feet — he had on a dark blue
sweater instead of a yellow one. The blue also made him look
less paunchy. He ordered a cup of coffee. By 12:15, she had not
yet shown up. Hefferman decided to give her another five minutes before cutting out.

And then he saw her turn off Walton Street and pass through
the hotel's revolving door. *Du calme*, Seymour, *du calme*. She
wasn't tall but short, small-boned, petite. She was wearing a tan
jacket over a soft white blouse and dark pleated trousers that
made her legs seem long. Her dark hair, streaked silvery gray,
was pulled back, showing her forehead to good effect.

From his table Hefferman watched as she searched the
room. The young Chinese hostess asked if she would like a table. Taking three deep breaths — calm down, Seymour, and
stay on the job — he walked up to the front of the restaurant.

"Seymour Hefferman," he said, not offering a hand to shake. "I've got a table near the window."

"I was looking for a yellow sweater," she said with some irritation when they were both seated.

"When I went to put it on, I discovered it had a coffee stain," Hefferman said. "Sorry."

The young waiter was upon them, passing out menus, asking if they wanted anything to drink. She ordered iced tea; Hefferman already had his coffee.

"So," she began with a nicely controlled smile, "when did you first discover you were a maniac?"

"What's that supposed to mean?"

"What would you call a person who sends insulting postcards that he doesn't sign with his own name? Is this your notion of sane behavior? Do you do it often?"

"Now that you ask — fairly often, yes," Hefferman said. "Every opportunity I can find."

"Oh, really," she said. "Say a little more, please."

"What're you, a therapist?"

"Sounds to me as if you could use one."

"Nothing crazy about it," Hefferman said. "I've taken it as my duty to tell people in the culture business when they are out of line — usually way out of line. I figure they can stand a little shot of truth now and then. Where else are they going to get it? From editors, publishers, agents, critics? I don't think so."

"Really?" she said, an eyebrow going up.

The waiter arrived with her iced tea and took their orders: a caesar salad for her, for him a hamburger, medium rare, with a slice of onion, grilled.

"Yes," Hefferman continued. "After nearly forty years of observation, I happen to believe that most people who get involved with the arts lose their grip on reality, so it's not entirely a bad thing for them to know that someone in the world out there is watching them. Not Big but Little Brother, maybe."

"You have some examples, perhaps?" she said, lifting the tall glass with her slender fingers. No ring on her left hand, Hefferman noted.

"How about you? You publish a book. I assume your publisher arranges an interview to help promote it. In the midst of this interview, you begin to rattle on about your personal anxieties or about the painfulness of the writer's life. I mean, what makes you think anyone but you — and possibly your widowed aunt — could conceivably care?"

"Has it never occurred to you that writers represent something larger than themselves? That they often have feelings in advance of other people?"

"Chief among them is the feeling of selfish egotism, I'd say. I wouldn't want any of my children to marry a writer."

"Oh, you have children?"

"As it happens, I don't."

"Then I'd say your worries are over. Have you at least been married?"

"Nope."

"I gather you're not somebody who has taken many chances. I'm beginning to see why you get such pleasure out of writing those anonymous cards. You're desperately in need of a hobby."

The food arrived. Hefferman's hamburger was rarer than he liked and the onion wasn't grilled. He thought about sending it back, but this wasn't a good time to make a fuss.

"You're not married yourself, I take it," he said.

"Not at present." She ate her salad in the European manner, fork in left hand, knife in right; did it rather well, actually. "My ex-husband, who is a poet, Stephen Ludlow by name, left me for one of his students five years ago. I have two children, daughters, twelve and ten, Emily and Sarah."

Hefferman quickly pictured this all-female household: a crowded apartment on the West Side of Manhattan, mother scuffling to make a go of things, keeping up standards, supplying little touches of elegance on a limited budget, chasing after some bearded *shtunk* for child support. He felt a flash of pity.

"Not much of a poet, Stephen Ludlow," said Hefferman, who kept a vast catalogue of writers in his head. Ludlow belonged to the school of what he thought of as the falsely sensitives, tough guys, all soft inside. He recalled poems about childhood basketball games at the local playground, about a sister lost when she was six years old, then a series of dull sonnets about engagements with the paintings of the French impressionists — the usual crap.

"An even worse husband, let me assure you. But he did give me two charming daughters."

"Emily and Sarah are solid names. I'm glad you didn't name them after lamps, Tiffany and Brittany or some such madness. But what're you doing in Chicago?"

"There's a conference on teaching creative writing, which is what I do at Bard."

"A conference on teaching creative writing. Sounds to me like not dying but going to hell anyway."

"You have a lot of opinions."

"I do."

"All of them strong?"

"I have strong opinions weakly held," Hefferman said. "Do you know Chicago?"

"Not really."

"If you're free tomorrow, I can show it to you — that is, if you don't mind the company of a maniac." As soon as the offer was out of his mouth, Hefferman wondered why he'd made it. But it was too late now.

"I live in New York, I see maniacs all the time. Sure, why not. My flight home's not until Monday morning. But I won't be free till four o'clock or so. Better make it five."

"I'll pick you up at . . . where?"

"I'm at the Hilton."

"I'll meet you in front of the Hilton at five."

Driving down Michigan Boulevard, Hefferman wondered what he was up to. After their lunch he had gone to Borders and bought a copy of *The Estranged Cello,* her collection of short stories, which he began reading that night and finished in the morning. Now he pulled his Audi ahead of the cab line and spotted her standing at the Hilton's large front entrance. She was wearing tan pants, a blue-striped blouse, a red sweater crossed over her shoulders. He honked, stopped, got out of the car to open the door for her.

"For a madman," she said, "you have nice manners."

"For a woman whose ideas are calculated to scare off men, you dress well. I thought I'd show you the University of Chicago, where I went to school as a kid, then maybe dinner in Chinatown afterward. Sound O.K.?"

"Fine," she said. "But what should we call each other?"

"Why don't I call you Pro, short for professor, also for professional complainer."

"Excellent. And why don't I call you Manny, short for maniac."

"I can live with that," Hefferman said.

The Outer Drive was crowded with Sunday traffic. He did the tour-director bit, pointing out the Field Museum, the Shedd Aquarium, the Adler Planetarium, Soldier Field, off in the distance to the west the wretched public-housing project called the Robert Taylor Homes.

"Named after the actor?" she asked.

"More likely after some 280-pound alderman from the thirties," Hefferman answered.

Passing the lugubrious Museum of Science and Industry, they got to Hyde Park and he found a parking space on Woodlawn across from the Robie House. She studied the sleek Frank Lloyd Wright building with great intensity.

"It looks like an aircraft carrier," she said. "It deserves a better setting. Water nearby, maybe."

They walked up Fifty-eighth Street, past the Oriental Institute, the tennis courts, and into the main university quadrangle, Hefferman naming the significant buildings as they passed. The place looked beautiful on this late spring afternoon, the lawns manicured, lots of flowers. Few students were about. A *pock-pock* sound came from an older man and woman rallying tennis balls. The gray gothic buildings seemed solid, substantial, not as menacing as they loomed in memory.

"You're seeing the place at its best," Hefferman said. "In winter, it can feel very heavy, hide-the-razor-blades heavy, if you know what I mean."

"I can imagine," she said. "It must have seemed pretty daunting to you when you were a student."

Hefferman explained that he was fifteen when he began. "All the teachers seemed to have Teutonic accents — Hitler's gift to American higher education. Graduate-school and professional-school students dominated. Undergraduates were strictly a minority in every sense. Yet somehow the spirit of the place got through to me even as a kid, coming out of a home where nobody read anything heavier than *Life* magazine."

"What did you get out of it?" she asked.

"The idea that the life of the mind was the only life, and that everything else was trivial, without point. You had to be an artist or a scientist or maybe a statesman — or, at a second remove, a teacher of artists, scientists, or statesmen. Otherwise you were worthless, a cipher."

"So how come you never became any of those things?"

"I thought for a while about being a poet. I even gave it a fairly good shot, but then I realized that it wasn't in me. I didn't have it." Hefferman looked away as he said this.

They walked around the quadrangle. He took her into the Reynolds Club, the school's modest student union. He showed her where the handball court used to be in which they first split the atom.

"What I find hard to imagine," she said, "is the fifteen-year-old Manny in this setting. Very weird."

"When I think back on it, I guess it was, Pro, but what can I tell you?"

"You can tell me how soon we're going to eat. I'm starved."

In Chinatown, Hefferman took her to the Emperor's Choice, where he knew the menu and where the owner's wife, a heavy-set woman, greeted him from behind the small bar where she sat watching television. During dinner he questioned her about what it was like raising two girls without a father in Manhattan. He'd guessed correctly about her not having much money. At the end of the meal, after the check and the fortune cookies, she asked if he had ever read any of her stories.

"I spent last night and this morning with your most recent collection."

After a brief but embarrassed silence that was supposed to be filled by his praise of her work, she asked, "What did you think of them?"

Hefferman hesitated, then resolved to risk the truth. One of the things he prided himself on was never disguising his opinions about art.

"Very well written," he said, "elegant, even. But women's stories, if you know what I mean."

"No," she said, stiffening. "What do you mean?"

"All sensitivity and sensibility. Everything tending toward the small, oblique insight. Epiphanies, I believe you call them in the business. Expertly done, no question about that. But I prefer stories in which someone has to make a decision, if you know what I mean. A big decision, something crucial."

Her lips grew thin. "Odd that your taste runs to stories of that kind," she said. "Since you yourself seem to have made so few big decisions in your life."

Hefferman was about to pantomime the gesture of pulling an arrow out of his chest but stopped himself. Being truthful had probably been a mistake. It usually was. He took two twenties out of his wallet, dropped them on the table, and got up. She did, too.

"Have nice night," the owner's wife said as they left the restaurant.

The drive back, ten minutes down State Street, took place in utter silence. Pulling up in front of the Hilton, Hefferman once again got out to open her door but she beat him to it. Standing on the curb, she put out her hand.

"Thank you," she said coldly, "it's been an instructive evening."

"Look," Hefferman said, "I'm sorry if I was out of line. Will you forgive me? Please?"

"Don't worry about it," she said, and turned into the hotel.

Back at his apartment, which he had straightened up earlier, thinking that if things worked out, he might bring Ms. Rubin home, might even get lucky (some joke that seemed now), Hefferman switched on the television and sat in his reading chair, hoping to catch a game. The Sox were playing at Oakland, but after ten minutes or so he found it couldn't keep his interest. He got up. Looking out the large windows of his apartment on the twenty-sixth floor to the dark immensity of Lake Michigan below, he suddenly knew, as he had never quite known until this moment, that he would live out his days alone.

Jesus, Hefferman thought, what am I having here, a goddamn epiphany? His IQ of 153, his impressive education, his case of the art bug — could it be that all this was what put him, as Andrea Rubin so rightly saw, outside the realm of big decisions? Was the best he could hope for in life represented by these small, slanting insights, most of which arrived too late to do him any good?

Well, if little epiphanies were to be his lot, so be it. In the meantime, he thought, let me continue to send out a few of my own. That very morning, in the *New York Times*, a poet, a renowned shyster operating out of the University of Houston, had published a suck-up review of a book by a powerful female literary critic known for making and breaking reputations. The critic's initials were H. V., and the poets she praised were known in the trade as HV-positive. Hefferman sat himself before his computer and — Rosinante, to the road again — booted up:

> Mr. Deep Integrity,
> Noted your review in this A.M.'s *NYTBR*, which reveals you to be much more than the simple two-faced boy most of your readers have taken you for till now. Hope you've laid in a good supply of lip balm. Without it, friend, you'll be out of business.
>
> Most sincerely,
> Les Blumenthal

Tapping in the date — May 31 — Hefferman made a mental note to stop at the post office tomorrow for another twenty postcards.

Uncle Jack

LAST THURSDAY, heading out from the Loop to my apartment in Hyde Park, I was listening to a golden-oldies station. They were playing tapes of famous radio programs, and one of them was from the old *Art Linkletter Show*. Linkletter is asking a little boy what he wants for Christmas, and the kid says he wants a new bed. Linkletter asks why. The kid says because he usually sleeps in the same bed with his mother, but now he has to sleep on the couch because his uncle is staying over with her, only, you see, he isn't really his uncle. Roaring laughter. "Kids," the ever unctuous Linkletter signs off, "say the darnedest things."

I winced. Although I didn't grow up sharing a bed with my mother, I too had one of those uncles who wasn't really my uncle. Only *my* uncle, as I would learn, was one of the most powerful men in America. Not many people knew about him, but the small handful who did used to refer to him as Mr. Fix-It. The "it," as I was to discover when I grew older, covered a lot of territory.

My uncle could get the unions off your back, or get you a

sweetheart contract, or get you a million-dollar loan out of union pension funds at an attractive interest rate, at a time when a million dollars was a million dollars and not the salary of a utility infielder. He could get zoning ordinances changed, or set in motion the gerrymandering of congressional districts. He could persuade all sorts of people in politics, show business, and sports not to be stubborn about deals and contracts. I heard it said — whispered, actually — that, should it be required, he was the man to see if you needed to have a business partner, or a wife or husband, removed in a quiet and completely efficient manner. Jack Rafter was my uncle's name.

I have no memory of my father. He went off to war in 1942, when I was two years old, and died when I was five, shot down while copiloting a B-17 over Dresden in early 1945. A photograph of him in uniform, wearing his officer's hat in a fifty-mission crush, used to sit on the small mantel of our apartment on Pine Grove, off Addison. He is handsome and in the photograph looks very serious, though my mother told me that one of the things that originally attracted her was his sense of humor. Asked what he did for a living, he might answer, with a convincingly straight face, embalmer or safecracker or lion tamer. He was, in fact, an electrical engineer.

When I was a boy I used to fantasize that my father would return home happily recovered. He would take me to baseball games, teach me about electricity, instruct me in life's tricky spots, show me the ropes. I'm not sure which is worse, losing someone you've known and loved or losing someone you've never known at all. But I sorely missed not having a father, and even now, in my early sixties, I sometimes think I'm still not over it.

My father left little in the way of savings or insurance. His parents, who were immigrants, were in no position to offer my mother much help. Her own father had died in his forties, and her mother, my grandmother, lived with a brother in San Francisco. Soon after getting her sad telegram from the War Department, my mother went to work at Rafter's, a high-line women's clothing shop on North Michigan Avenue.

Twenty-four years old, a redhead with a natural sense of style in clothes — a "knockout" was how other men often described her — my mother quickly caught on. Lou Rafter and his wife, Estelle, who were childless, took to her straight off, and soon included us in holiday parties at their large apartment on Lake Shore Drive near Temple Sholom. It was at one of these parties that my mother first met Lou Rafter's brother Jack. He lived on the "coast," as people in Chicago used to say, and he was a lawyer, but the kind of law he did was unclear. He was twelve years older than she.

"Jack walked into every room confident that he was the most important person there," my mother told me much later. "And the fact is, Billy, he was. Did I ever tell you that President Kennedy's father used to send him a case of Piper-Heidsieck every year at Christmas?"

I never learned how Jack Rafter had swept my mother away, but it's not hard to imagine. A man who was said to own four points of the Riviera Hotel in Vegas, large tracts of real estate in Boca Raton, and the land in San Diego on which the San Diego Padres built their stadium, a man who in a pinch could persuade Jimmy Hoffa to call off the dogs — such a man could not have had much trouble convincing a war widow in her twenties, alone in the world with a young son, that he would watch out for her for the rest of her life. Which, after his fashion, and to give Uncle Jack his due, he did.

The problem was that when he met my mother, Jack Rafter was already married. He lived in Beverly Hills, and he wasn't the type to divorce or to abandon children, if only because divorce was much too sloppy for a man who instilled, maintained, and flourished on order. But evidently he did need a regular lady friend in Chicago, which he visited at least once a month. He was a man working deals sixteen hours a day, his mind churning away full time — manipulating, maneuvering, figuring angles — and although he could have had a different woman every night, he must have wanted company and stability of a different kind: the kind a woman as attractive and sensible as my young mother could supply.

In the early years, when their affair first began, I was shipped out to my mother's older sister, my Aunt Florence, and her husband, Julius, who lived on Sheridan Road with Lake Michigan as their backyard. This was no hardship, especially since I liked their two sons, my cousins Eddy and Sherwin, who flanked me by a year on either side. I must have been eight years old when my cousin Eddy told me my mother had a boyfriend. Until that moment, I knew nothing about it. He said it was practically his mother and father's only topic of conversation.

When I confronted my mother, she said it was true she had a friend; she never used the word "boyfriend." Things were complicated, she said, and she would try to explain them to me, though not all at once. Her friend was the younger brother of Uncle Lou and Aunt Estelle (as I had long ago begun calling the Rafters) and lived in Los Angeles, but she saw him when he came to Chicago.

"Are you going to marry him?" I asked. In those days, I was still hoping to acquire a father.

"I don't think so, Billy."

"Then what's the point, Mom?"

"The point is that he's very nice and wants to help us."

"How?"

"You'll see," my mother said. "Mr. Rafter is a very important man."

"What does he do?"

"He's a lawyer," my mother said, "but his real work is to smooth the way for people who need special favors."

I have never forgotten my mother's formulation of Jack Rafter's life's work. As pure description, I still cannot better it. Nor can I forget my mild surprise, the first time I entered the large office he kept in Chicago, to find not a single law book in the place. So far as I know, he never appeared in court or handled a legal document.

I was nine by the time I first met him. The ordinariness of his appearance threw me. He was compact, five foot nine or so, trim, not more than 140 pounds. Over the nearly forty years I would know him, his weight never changed. His shoes were always shined to a high brilliance, his nails were manicured, and his black hair, lightly pomaded and parted on the left, had that kemptness that comes from getting a haircut every week. He exuded an expensive smell, good leather mixed with lemon. All his shirts had French cuffs, and once I noticed the U.S. presidential seal on his links. Years later I read a novel by Henry James in which the main male character was described as not overly concerned with clothes but careful to own no vulgar things; I thought at once of Uncle Jack.

"Billy," my mother said the day she introduced me, "this is my friend Mr. Rafter. He would like it if you called him Uncle Jack."

"I'd like it a lot, Billy," he said, smiling and putting a steadying hand on my shoulder. "I don't have any nephews or nieces, and I'd like to think of you as my only nephew."

He said that he'd heard I was a sports fan and wondered if I'd go with him to a game. The day must have been a Sunday, in early or mid-September, because I still remember the choices: "We can go to Wrigley Field and watch Bob Waterfield and the Los Angeles Rams play the Bears, or we can go to Comiskey

Park and watch Bob Feller pitch against the White Sox. Up to you, Billy."

I chose the Bears. We were driven there, only a few blocks away, in a dark blue Buick Roadmaster by a large black man named Greenwood. At the stadium Uncle Jack had seats on the forty-yard line, in a box five or six rows off the field.

"I want you to meet someone," he said once we were seated. He took my hand and we walked to the rail, where he called out, "Bob, Bobby, over here."

A tall, deeply tanned man in a gold-and-blue uniform trotted over. "Jack," he said, "how goes it?"

"It goes well, Bobby," he said, shaking the man's hand. "Bob Waterfield, I want you to meet my nephew, Billy Siskind. Billy, this is the great Bob Waterfield, All-American quarterback of the Los Angeles Rams." I put out my hand, which was lost in his.

"Great to meet you, kid," Waterfield said, then signaled to the Rams bench where someone threw him a football. "Have a pen on you, Jack?" he asked. My new uncle took out a black Parker 51 with a gold cap. The ball was signed "To my friend Billy, best wishes, Bob Waterfield."

I still own that football — a Duke, the laces rising in high relief off its richly pebbled, deep brown leather — and the inscription and signature are still visible. Not long afterward, I learned that Bob Waterfield was married to Jane Russell, the actress whose low neckline in *The Outlaw* caused a great stir in the 1940s. Uncle Jack, as he used to put it, "represented" her. I may have been only nine years old, but I recognized that this new uncle of mine was no ordinary man.

Soon my mother and I had moved into a three-bedroom apartment on the ninth floor at 3300 North Lake Shore Drive, with a swell view of Belmont Harbor from the French windows in our enormous living room. One bedroom was my mother's, one mine, and one was reserved for Uncle Jack. His contained a single bed, a desk, a phone with his private number, and a tall mahogany dresser. In the closet he kept two suits, both of lawyerly dark gray, a beautiful maroon silk robe and pajamas from Sulka, along with slippers and an extra pair of shoes in trees. The desk drawers were locked, and I was instructed by my mother never to answer Uncle Jack's phone, which usually rang only when he was in town.

Around the same time, my mother acquired a sky-blue Chrysler convertible with real wood paneling, and I was transferred out of LeMoyne, the public school where I had gone since kindergarten, and put in Francis Parker, a private school. My mother kept her job at Rafter's on Michigan Avenue.

Jack Rafter always went first class, and as long as my mother was his special friend, so did we. But they seldom went out together in public. My mother was an indifferent cook, so when Uncle Jack stayed over, we either ordered in or ate at small and inconspicuous neighborhood restaurants. A couple of times he had his driver take us out to an Italian restaurant in Melrose Park called Slicker Sam's, where he was treated with almost regal regard and not allowed to pay his check. We never traveled as a family, but when my mother and I went anywhere, he always saw to it that we had the best accommodations. He even arranged, through John Balaban, who ran the Balaban & Katz movie chain in Chicago, a free pass admitting two to all the chain's theaters. It had my name on it and made me a great figure among my classmates.

At what point I became aware of my mother's real relationship with Uncle Jack I cannot say for sure. They were always discreet around me. At the age of eleven, when I was sent off to a summer camp in Eagle River, Wisconsin, I learned the facts of life. No boy, I suppose, wishes to apply these facts to his own mother, and so long as there is a father on the premises he needn't really do so. But my mother's irregular connection with Jack Rafter put such matters squarely in the forefront of my consciousness. One of the few words absent from the otherwise copious sex lexicon I picked up at Camp Ojibwa was "mistress," which of course is what my mother was.

One day Uncle Jack gave her a full-length mink coat, which in her excited pleasure she modeled for us the minute she took it out of the box. I shall never forget the sound and the sight of its hem swishing and sweeping just above the floor, my mother's thick auburn hair doing something of the same almost six feet above. At that instant I had no trouble understanding why a man like Jack Rafter would go to such trouble to be with a woman like her. Perhaps that was also why I was less than shocked when, a year or two later, my mother first told me he had a wife and two daughters in Los Angeles whose lives he did not want to disrupt. One girl was fifteen, the other my age. "Very vulnerable ages for girls," my mother said.

So far as I knew, Uncle Jack did everything he could to spare my mother the awkwardness of her position. In all their years together, I never heard them quarrel. Each accepted the limitations imposed by the relationship. When I had my bar mitzvah, Uncle Jack came to the small but elegant party at the Drake Hotel that he no doubt paid for, but he didn't sit at the head or family table. On all holidays, Jewish or otherwise, his family in Los Angeles, it was understood, had first call on him. He took my mother to New York on a couple of occasions when I was growing up, but I never went along.

In high school I finally came into a more precise knowledge of Uncle Jack's position in the world. As best as I could piece together the story of his career, not long after graduating from Loyola Law School, Jack Rafter went to work for some of the Mafia-controlled unions in Chicago, the movie projectionists' union prominent among them. From there he had spread out in a three-pronged attack — you have to imagine here a Movietone News map of the Allied fronts during World War II — in which his reach extended from the Mafia and the unions to the entertainment industry itself. When the three overlapped, as when the "boys" took over Las Vegas, or when strikes were threatened in Hollywood, Uncle Jack was in a commanding position.

In the 1950s, people in Chicago talked about crime the way other people talked about sports. Everyone was an expert on the subject. Bugsy, Greasy Thumb, Big Tuna — in Chicago these were names that resonated like the Babe, Joltin' Joe, the Splendid Splinter. People used to wonder why Jack Rafter was never called up before the Kefauver committee investigating organized crime — his name was mentioned on a number of occasions during the televised hearings. Another unanswered question was how, playing with the rough crowd he did, and at such a high-stakes game, he managed to avoid being killed.

Uncle Jack didn't travel with bodyguards, and as far as I know carried no gun. The closest I ever came to hearing him brag was when, staying in our apartment once for a full week, recovering from a bad case of flu, he told me that he had to get back on his feet soon. "I owe it to people, some of them fairly important, who get nervous if I show up with even a light cold. One of the secrets of life, Billy, is to arrange things so that even to your bitterest enemies you're much more valuable alive than dead." This, too, though its meaning was unclear to me then, has stuck with me forever.

Although he was always attentive to my mother, and stood as a model for how a gentleman ought to behave with a lady, Uncle Jack chose not to take the place of the father I had never known. With what I now regard as a species of high tact, he kept a restrained distance, somehow making it plain that, though we had no true blood ties, he would be there if I ever really needed him. He would occasionally take me along to a big sporting event — a heavyweight title fight, a crucial pro football game — but my allowance in high school came from my mother and so did all my disciplining and advice. I never mentioned Jack Rafter to any of my school friends, and those I brought home, if they hadn't heard otherwise, must have assumed that our money came from my mother's family.

Meanwhile, I was flourishing at Francis Parker, which I attended all the way through senior year. Everyone there was very bright, and so, I discovered, was I. I ran track, specializing in the 440, and I found and fell in love with mathematics.

One night toward the end of my junior year, Uncle Jack handed me a blank slip of paper and asked me to write down the names of the five colleges I most wanted to attend. I handed it back with the obvious names — Harvard, Yale, Princeton, Stanford, Chicago — and saw him tuck it into the pocket of his suit jacket. The following spring I received letters of acceptance from all five colleges.

It was a week or so later that Uncle Jack took me to the Cubs opener against the Cardinals. We sat in a box on the third-base line two rows behind the Cubs dugout. The day was cool, still in the low fifties. He was wearing a black coat with a chesterfield collar and a white silk scarf. His hair was turning silver at the temples.

"Your mother is very proud of you," he said. "Getting into every school you applied for is no small thing, especially with the Jewish quotas that some of them have. Where are you thinking of going?"

"I was thinking Harvard," I said.

"I want to ask you a favor," he said. "I want you to go to the University of Chicago. Naturally I'll pick up the tab."

"Why Chicago?"

"Because it's close to home, and I don't want you to be too far from your mother. She needs you."

"She told you that?"

"She didn't have to, I can sense it. In the end, you know, you're all she's got."

"What about you?" I said. As soon as the words were out of my mouth, I felt I was sailing into dangerous waters. But when he'd asked me his favor, a line had been crossed.

"Your mother is very dear to me. But for reasons I think you know about, Billy, I can't be with her all the time. I'm not asking you to be with her forever, but for now I think it best you be nearby."

"Can I think about it?"

"Of course," he said. "Take all the time you need. But remember, I'd consider this a very big favor."

"Now can I ask you a question?" I said.

"Sure," he said, "anything you like."

"You didn't by any chance have anything to do with my college acceptances, did you?"

"Not a thing. If you'd needed me to intervene, I would have been glad to help. But the fact is you didn't. You have my word on it."

"Have you ever done anything like that?"

"I'll tell you a story," he said. "A fellow in town here, a man in the appliance-parts business in Glenview named Meisels, called me one day to tell me that his son was on the waiting list at Northwestern Law School, and that he'd be grateful for anything I could do to get him accepted. I told him I'd look into it."

He paused to light a cigarette out of a red-and-gold box. "I didn't feel there was any rush about it, and anyway, I had more pressing business to attend to. Three weeks later, the son was notified that a place had been found for him, and that same week the man sent me a check for twenty-five thousand dollars."

"Did you keep it?" I asked.

"Of course. I didn't really have a choice. To return it would have been damaging to my reputation as a man of influence," he said, smiling almost imperceptibly. "How about a hot dog?"

I lived at home for my first two years at Chicago, but for the second two my mother insisted that I take an apartment on campus. I sometimes thought with regret about Harvard, but in my senior year all such thoughts disappeared when I encountered a brilliant teacher, a slender and warm-hearted Argentinean named Alberto Calderon, whose mathematical specialty was singular integrals. Taking me under his wing, Professor Calderon arranged a graduate fellowship, and I eventually went on to do my doctorate under him.

Uncle Jack was unable to attend my graduation. But a week later, I received a letter on his office letterhead:

> Dear Billy,
>
> Congratulations on your undergraduate accomplishments, which have made your mother rightfully proud.
>
> Four years ago, when I asked you to stay in Chicago for your education, I told you that I would consider this a significant favor, and I am a man who repays such favors. I would like you to know that my repayment is a small trust I have set up for you. It will provide you roughly $1,500 a month. This sum is not enough money, I hope, to smother your ambition or set you on the path to ruin, but will be something of a cushion and a comfort during your years of graduate study. The trust begins with the enclosed check. It is to run for five years, after which I feel confident you will no longer need it.

I see I have neglected to add that your achievements have made me very proud also.

Sincerely,
Jack Rafter

The year was 1961, and it is perhaps a sign of Jack Rafter's personal wealth that he was unaware that the $18,000 annual income from this trust, peanuts to him, was four times a college instructor's salary of $4,500. The money, coming in more than handy, gave me independence, the means to travel every summer to Europe for long holidays, and that greatest of all freedoms: not having to think about money at all.

But by then Uncle Jack was staying in our apartment less and less frequently. How my mother felt about this was not known to me. Maybe she was relieved. Maybe she felt she was losing her grip. Here was this beautiful woman, Jack Rafter's girlfriend, approaching her mid-forties, getting a little old for the job and perhaps beginning to feel it. I wonder if she worried about his looking for — or having already found — another woman, a younger version of herself, tucked away in Manhattan or even in Chicago.

One night not long before I finished graduate school, I brought in Chinese food, and my mother and I shared not one but two bottles of white wine. As we worked our way through the second bottle, I found the courage to bring up *the* subject.

"Mother," I asked, "was Uncle Jack a mistake?"

"Whatever do you mean?"

"I mean your friendship with him made it impossible for you to find another husband."

"Uncle Jack and I made a bargain, and he's kept it to the letter. I knew at the outset what I could expect from him and what I couldn't. I have no complaints, Billy, I want you to know that."

"Do you love him, Mother?"

"I've loved only two men in my life, your father and you. But I have the greatest regard for Jack. He's made it possible for us to live as we do. We were alone in the world before he came along."

"Did you do it for me?"

"If I said yes I'd be a heroine, wouldn't I? The truth is I did it only partly for you. I did it for myself, too. Jack isn't exactly charmless, you know. And his power in the world has its attractions, even if I share in it in only a very small way."

"If it were possible, would you prefer to be married to him?"

"I hope this doesn't shock you, Billy, but I don't think I would ever care to have been married to Jack Rafter." And here she paused. "He cheats on his wife, you know," she said, finishing the little bit of wine left in her glass.

Just then the phone rang. My Aunt Florence, a famous gabber, kept my mother on the line for half an hour as I cleared the table and washed the dishes. We never returned to the subject.

The blessed Professor Calderon arranged a job for me in the university's math department, and six years later I got tenure. In the same year I married another mathematician, which turned out to be a mistake: it lasted three years, with no children and no great recriminations afterward. It was shortly after my divorce that my mother began to get dizzy spells.

At first she thought it might be diabetes, which ran in her family, but when that proved negative she underwent the full buffet of tests, and cancer of the liver was discovered. It had metastasized from the pancreas, and the prognosis was not good. With chemotherapy, she was told, she could live two, maybe two and a half years. She had not yet turned sixty.

When Uncle Jack found out, he insisted she go to Mayo for a second opinion. We went, more to accommodate him than for reassurance. With Jack Rafter as our sponsor, the red carpet was set out, but in the end the verdict and the sentence were the same: liver cancer, two to three years to live if treated chemically.

Uncle Jack told me not to worry about expenses. Anything my mother wanted, she was to have. The problem was that there was nothing she really wanted but to be well again. He called nearly every night, asking how she felt, giving her what I took to be little pep talks that did absolutely no good. Not even the great fixer could fix this one.

Then one afternoon, when I had come to take her shopping for groceries, she called out from the kitchen: "Billy, come back here, please. There's something I want to show you."

She was seated at the counter. She had been losing weight, and the chemo had caused her skin and hair to lose their luster. I was grateful she hadn't yet lost her hair altogether. In her beautiful eyes was that slightly terrorized look of people with terminal cancer.

She pushed a copy of the *Sun-Times* across the counter, turned to the page with Kup's column. "Look at the last item but one," she said.

In bold type I read Jack Rafter's name. The item read: "Influential West Coast attorney Jack Rafter in town for reopening of Mr. Kelly's."

When I looked up, my mother said, "He called, as usual, but he never told me he was in Chicago."

"What does it mean?"

"It means your Uncle Jack doesn't like losers," she said, seeming oddly unmoved.

I was in my mother's apartment the next night when he called, heard her respond to his questions about her health, heard her ask about his own. She gave no hint that she knew he'd been in town.

Of course she was aware that she was dying. One Tuesday

morning, after helping her into the front seat of my Volvo to take her to chemo, I reminded her to put on her seat belt. She shot me a look suggesting I had made a joke in extremely dubious taste. On the short ride to the hospital, a barely perceptible groaning sound was mixed with her regular breathing. We seemed, my mother and I, to have run out of things to talk about.

"It won't be long now," she said after she had grown so weak she had to be hospitalized. And it wasn't. I sat by her bedside at Weiss Hospital, held her ringless fingers in my hand, listened to the low moaning that accompanied her breathing. My beautiful mother, I thought, I will not remember you in this terrible condition. I will remember you in your natural elegance, and I will always remember that you were the one person in this life I could count on.

She died on a Saturday night, which meant that Jack Rafter probably wouldn't get word till Monday: I didn't have his home number, and anyway, it wouldn't be right to call him there. Instead, I left a message on his office answering machine.

He called back Monday morning at ten, Chicago time.

"Billy, I can't tell you how sorry I am. It's a great loss" — he paused — "for both of us." There was something slightly perfunctory about his voice, as if he had already filed my mother away in a folder and placed the folder in an out box.

The funeral service and burial were scheduled for the next day. He said he hoped I would understand that he couldn't attend. "Lots of complications involved."

"I understand," I said.

"If you need help with any of the bills, please send them to me."

"No help needed," I said.

"Maybe we can meet in a couple of weeks. There are a few

items in my desk at your mother's apartment that I need to clean out."

When he stepped off the elevator, Uncle Jack seemed smaller than I'd remembered him — age, perhaps, although the years didn't detract from his usual understated stylishness. He was wearing a dark gray hat — men of his generation didn't go out without a hat — and one of his perfectly fitting black suits, with a lush, solid silver-hued necktie. He was carrying a plain black leather briefcase. At seventy-three or so, he was still very much in the game.

We shook hands. Looking down, I noted that he continued to have his nails manicured. "You holding up O.K.?" he asked.

"I'm O.K.," I said. "How about you?"

"Being in this apartment shakes me up a little," he said. "Your mother's death marks a major subtraction in my life."

I wondered. Jack Rafter was a man who never said anything that he hadn't carefully weighed, calculating its effects, side effects, and possible aftereffects ten years down the road.

"Sorry to burden you with this," he said after emerging from his old bedroom, "but I've left a couple of suits and some shoes in the closet. No hurry, but when you get a chance, you could maybe send them to me at my L.A. office. Bill me for the cost."

"I'll do it in a day or so," I said. I tried to imagine him leaving this apartment carrying his shoes and with his clothes over his arm, but I couldn't. Other people carried things for Jack Rafter.

"Well, kid, what can I say? Life goes on. Let's be grateful for your mother's existence."

"Look," I found myself saying, "there's something I have to know before you leave. What did my mother mean to you?"

"She was a charming and beautiful woman," he said, "and I cared very deeply for her."

"Do you have another woman in Chicago lined up to take her place?"

"A little out of line, don't you think, Billy?"

"Maybe it is, but who drew the damn lines in the first place?" My anger surprised even me.

"Your mother and I had a deal, and we both lived up to it."

"Strange kind of deal," I said.

"Your mother knew everything it entailed, down to the fine print. She never complained. Which is apparently more than can be said for you, though you also benefited considerably from our little arrangement."

"Little for you, maybe," I said. "For my mother it was her whole life."

"What exactly do you want, Billy?"

"I want you to tell me that my mother wasn't your whore."

"I never thought of her that way, I assure you."

"Then how did you think of her?"

"I've already told you — as a charming and beautiful woman who meant a great deal to me."

"'A great deal' sounds right, but then you're the world's premier maker of great deals, isn't that so, Uncle Jack."

"If taking a few shots at me will make you feel better, please, be my guest."

"Was my mother ever anything more to you than a convenience, a place to hang your goddamn Sulka robe?"

"If I said yes, would you believe me, Billy? Forgive me if I doubt it. I wonder if something else isn't at work here."

"Like what?"

"Like resentment. Some of us have tried to shape the world to accommodate our desires. You either dominate life or you're dominated by it. Don't know if that information comes with a Ph.D. at the University of Chicago."

He glanced at his watch. "My driver is waiting," he said. "I'd better get a move on."

"We probably won't see each other again," I said.

"Probably not." He put out his hand. "Good luck, Billy."

"You too," I said, deciding, what the hell, to shake his hand.

I walked him out to the elevator. As he got in and the door began to close, I glimpsed him standing there alone, ever so briefly, smiling, for some reason, to himself. The son of a bitch, I thought, he's probably working out a deal with God, with a small but decisive advantage to himself.

Joseph Epstein is the author of, among other works, the best-selling *Snobbery: The American Version*. Born and educated in Chicago, Epstein has been a lecturer in English and writing at Northwestern University since 1974. From 1975 to 1997 he was the editor of *The American Scholar*. His work has appeared in *The New Yorker*, the *Atlantic Monthly*, *Harper's Magazine*, *Commentary*, and other magazines. He is currently working on a book about friendship in the contemporary world.

Also by Joseph Epstein

SNOBBERY

THE AMERICAN VERSION

Selected as a Best Book of the Year by
the *New York Times*, the *Los Angeles Times*,
and the *Chicago Tribune*

CLEVER, INCISIVE, and immensely entertaining, the *New York Times* bestseller *Snobbery* explores the shallows and depths of status and taste — with enviable results. In these essays, Joseph Epstein skewers all manner of elitism in contemporary America. He offers his arch observations of the new footholds of snobbery: food, fashion, high-achieving children, schools, politics, being with-it, and much more.

ISBN 0-618-34073-4